Com
Alcohol,
Trauma and
Games

Becky Bexley
the Child Genius
4

Diana Holbourn

Fun and Discussion at University, and Becky
Helps Some People Overcome Problems
Including Post-Traumatic Stress Disorder

Windy
Seaside
Publishing

Cover design, book design and formatting by Gareth Southwell (art.garethsouthwell.com)

First digital edition October 2023

ISBN (paperback): 978-1-7391809-9-7
ISBN (ebook): 978-1-7391809-8-0

First published 2023 by Windy Seaside Publishing

Contents

Chapter 1

Becky Has Fun With Friends, Especially Her Friend Sharon

I t seemed strange to a lot of people that Becky Bexley went to university when she was just ten. She was a child genius; but still they thought it was remarkable, unsurprisingly. But since Becky had got used to being thought of as strange by then, having gone to school and done her A levels abnormally young, she didn't much mind it when people thought of her as weird, such as when students and tutors on the psychology course and the media studies course she was taking commented about how unusual it was that a ten-year-old would be doing such things, and wondered if she was really up to it. She was optimistic, and thought she'd just prove to them that she could cope with the work and fit in. It helped that she developed some good friendships with some other students, which kept her feeling quite cheerful most of the time.

After her first few months there, she was mostly unscathed, and had developed several especially close friendships with students she often met up with in the evenings, and sometimes earlier in the day.

The weather was horrible during her first winter at university, as could be expected. In February there was snow, and then gales and pouring rain.

Still, it didn't stop her and her friends meeting up and having fun.

One afternoon, Becky said to one of her best friends, Sharon, "Hey imagine if one day you heard the rain outside, but instead of coming down as normal, it was coming down in a rhythm. Imagine if a load of raindrops came down at exactly the same time, and then a second later a load more did that, and then a second later a load more did the same, and they kept on doing that, so it sounded as if the rain was marching down!"

Sharon grinned. Then she said, "Or imagine if you were out on a cold winter's night and suddenly you saw the sun come out, and it was shining really brightly. Do you think you'd be really pleased and think it was fantastic that it was warming you up and cheering the place up, or do you think you'd start worrying you were going mad, or that something spooky was happening?"

Becky thought about it and said, "I don't know. Maybe I'd be really glad when it happened, and only start worrying about it later. What do you think you'd do?"

Sharon said, "I think I'd love it!

"Hey imagine if a newsreader was about to read the news on the radio, and he was sitting by an open window, and suddenly there was a huge gust of wind and the news blew out the window, and when it was time for him to read the news he said, 'Sorry, but there isn't any news today. It's all just blown away.'"

Becky giggled.

Sharon grinned and said, "Hey I wonder what we'd have to do to get on the news ourselves!"

Becky said, "Something really dramatic, probably. Maybe you'd get on it if you learned to inhale raindrops and then squirt them out of your nose so far they'd land on a person's head 100 metres away or something."

Sharon chuckled and said, "I don't think I'll try that one!"

One evening, Sharon grinned and said to Becky, "Imagine if a boss kept sending his employees emails with typos in them, and he never got any more careful about reading them before he sent them to check they were OK, because no one dared tell him there was anything wrong with them. Imagine if he was always using sayings, but they often said different things from what they were supposed to, because he kept getting letters in some of the words wrong.

"So imagine if one day he said, 'I will have no sleeping in the office! If you're feeling under the feather, you should probably stop burning the midnight boil!' And imagine if another day, he said, 'I bought a new computer for my office. It cost an arm and a peg, but I think it's the best thing since sliced lead!' Or imagine if he said, 'It's the best thing since liced bread!'"

Becky said, "That would be funny! And imagine if he said, 'We need to improve the way we plan our business strategy around here! Don't put all your legs in one basket from now on! And don't bother me with worries over problems that might never happen! If they do, we'll cross that fridge when we come to it!'"

They both laughed. Then Sharon said, "I heard about a funny misprint in a newspaper. It said there was a villa in Italy that was at risk of being demolished, and it had 17-stone dwarfs surrounding it. The paper later printed an apology, saying a hyphen was put in between the words 17 and stone by an editor when it shouldn't have been, and what it really meant was that there were 17 statues of dwarfs made of stone outside the villa. It said the people at the paper didn't really have any idea how much they weighed."

Becky grinned and said, "Imagine if there was a misprint in a paper that made it say, 'The government are going to put a wax on sugar soon!' People would think, 'Oh yuck! What do they want to do that for!'"

Sharon giggled and said, "Yeah, or imagine if the misprint said, 'The government are going to increase wax in the autumn.'"

Becky chuckled and replied, "Yeah, people would wonder just how they were intending to do that, wouldn't they, and what kind of wax they were going to try to increase, and where they were going to put it, and why!"

They both laughed. Sharon said, "Yeah! Or just imagine if there was a misprint in a headline that made it say, 'A government minister was given a barking fine yesterday!' People would think, 'I didn't know it was illegal to bark; and what was a government minister doing barking anyway?'"

Becky grinned and said, "Imagine if a weather forecast had misprints in it, so instead of rain it said pain. So it said things like, 'There will be outbreaks of torrential pain this afternoon.' People would wonder what on earth they were in for!"

Sharon smiled and said, "Yeah, and imagine if it said funny instead of sunny, so it said, 'Today there will be funny spells and the risk of pain this evening.'"

Becky giggled and said, "Or imagine if it said flowers when it meant showers, so it said, 'Today there will be funny intervals and scattered flowers.'"

Sharon laughed and said, "That would be the strangest weather we'd ever had! Imagine if someone was going to a wedding when they read that. They might think, 'Oh how lovely! The weather's going to scatter flowers around the place so we don't have to bring confetti! That's good really; we can save it for the next wedding.'"

Becky said, "Actually, I remember I did find a typo in a weather forecast once, on the BBC website. It meant to say there would be some heavy bursts of rain, but it said heavy busts of rain! Then it said there would be mist in the evening, and I thought it would be a laugh if there were more typos and it said, 'This evening there will be whist' instead.

"Imagine if there were typos all over a BBC weather forecast, so the hourly forecasts kept saying there were going to be things like 'light pain' and 'light drain showers', and 'bunny intervals'."

Sharon chuckled and said, "Or imagine if the opposite happened and there were typos all over an article about new painkilling drugs, and it said things like, 'A drug company has invented a new rainkilling drug', and, 'Doctors are hopeful that this new drug will be more effective at reducing rain than some other drugs, which patients have told them haven't reduced the rain they feel very effectively'."

Becky grinned and said, "Or imagine if there was a misprint in a paper that made it say, 'A survey was done to find out people's favourite breakfasts. It turns out that most people in the country like to eat hot buttered post best.'"

Sharon giggled and replied, "Oh yuck!"

Then Becky said, "Imagine if a DJ sent an email to lots of people advertising a radio show he was doing that night, and he meant to say, 'I'll be playing lots of sad songs tonight', but

5

he accidentally said 'lots of bad songs'. He might spell check the email, but it wouldn't pick it up. He might wonder why he got lots of replies saying, 'I don't think I'll bother listening to that then!'

"He might think it must mean loads of people really don't like sad songs, and never play any again."

Sharon chuckled.

They carried on chatting and laughing for a while.

One evening when they met up, Becky said, "It's nearly Valentine's Day. Are you going to send anyone a card?"

Sharon replied, "No. I'm not really interested in boyfriends yet."

She joked, "Maybe I'm a late developer, so I'll start fancying a relationship when I'm about thirty, marry at about forty, get broody for a baby when I'm about fifty, and be able to have one because it'll turn out that everything about me's developing late, including ageing. Then maybe my hair will start going grey when I'm about ninety, I'll have to go into a nursing home when I'm about a hundred and fifty, and I'll die when I'm about two hundred."

Becky chuckled and said, "You'll be lucky!"

Sharon said enthusiastically, "Yeah! Mind you, maybe we could make a Valentine's card to give someone just for a laugh. I've been thinking that would be fun actually. We could cut it out of a cardboard box, maybe part of an old teabag or cereal box or something. Let's think about what we could write inside it. Maybe things like,

" 'I love you because your hair is made of straw; your fingers are like mini carrots, and the hairs on your chest are like long grass. You look a lot like a beautiful nature scene I saw on a postcard once.' "

6

Becky giggled and said, "Yeah! And you could say, 'One thing that attracted me to you is that I saw a scan of your brain once and it looked just like a big block of marzipan. I love Marzipan!' "

Sharon said with a grin, "We'd better not give it to someone who's easily offended!

"Maybe another thing we could say is, 'You have a gorgeous nose; it looks just like a tennis ball!' "

Becky giggled and said, "And how about, 'I love the fact that your arms are long sticks of celery; I'd love to eat them all up, but since that would mean you wouldn't have any arms left, I know that wouldn't be fair.' "

Sharon replied, 'Yeah! And we could say, 'I love the fact that your chin is a potato and your feet are Cornish pasties. I love the fact that your back is like a filing cabinet, full of drawers people can store paper and pens and paper clips and things in, and your stomach is like a beach ball we can take out and play with.' "

Becky said, "Maybe on the front of the card we could write in big letters, 'I love you because . . .', and the person who gets it might think it's serious, and open it and find all that."

Sharon grinned. She said, "Yeah, let's do that! And maybe another thing we could say in the card is, 'Your head is a coconut and your legs are giant fish fingers.' "

They did make the card. They got someone to push it under the door of the room of one of the students on their course called Keith, who they were quite friendly with, but who wasn't in the group of friends they went around with. They thought it was a laugh because they sat near him in lectures that day, and he asked them and others if they had a clue who could have sent him this weird Valentine's card, showing it to them.

They didn't admit to it, but made unhelpful suggestions for fun like, "Maybe it was one of the lecturers. Have you noticed you've had a better grade than you expected for anything? If you have, maybe one of them's in love with you . . . although if everyone's got better grades than they expected, maybe it means they love us all!"

They couldn't keep straight faces when they said things like that, but Keith thought that was just because the card was amusing and they were laughing at what they were saying. To their knowledge, he never found out who'd really sent it. But perhaps he often enjoyed puzzling over it.

Chapter 2

Becky's Stand-Up Comedy Sessions

On some evenings, local up-and-coming bands, and occasionally more famous ones, did concerts at the university. Other performers sometimes did shows too. They were popular among the students, and it didn't cost them much to go to see them.

A local comedian was invited to do a show one evening. A couple of Becky's friends planned to go. They'd never heard him before and didn't know what kind of jokes he told. But they were beginning to feel a little bit down, since the weather had turned colder and the sunshine had deserted the place, and they fancied a laugh. So they hoped he'd be good.

Becky asked her mum if she could go to the show. Her mum wasn't sure it was a good idea, since she wondered if the jokes would be appropriate for a child as young as Becky. But she was reassured when Becky told her about her friends who were going. They were friends her mum liked and respected, and she assumed they wouldn't want to go to see anything particularly indecent. So she gave Becky permission to go, and said she'd collect her and bring her home afterwards.

Then Becky asked her friends if she could tag along with them. They weren't sure it was wise, since they wondered if the jokes might be inappropriate for someone of Becky's age. But Becky told them her mum had given her permission to go, and given her the money to pay for it, and her friends liked her mum and felt sure she wouldn't let Becky go to any show where the jokes were going to be too risqué or nasty for someone of Becky's age, so they said they were happy for her to go with them.

They all happily went to the show together and sat down about a quarter of an hour before it was due to start. They'd gone that early to try to make sure they could get seats near enough to the front to get a good view.

The comedian was on stage making sure the microphone worked and making a few other last-minute preparations. When he saw Becky, he felt a bit worried, since some of his jokes were about things he didn't think it was appropriate for someone of her age to hear. He assumed she must be the daughter of a mature student, who perhaps hadn't been able to find a babysitter. He didn't want to be awkward, but he thought he'd have to go and say something. He went and spoke to a couple of university staff members, saying there was a little girl in the audience and he didn't think it would be appropriate for her to hear some of his jokes, and would feel uncomfortable telling them in front of her. He gave them a couple of examples of the jokes he wanted to tell, and they agreed it wouldn't be a good idea for a child to hear them.

One of them went into the audience and told Becky that the jokes were meant for an adult audience, and asked her nicely to leave.

She got a bit upset. "That's not fair!" she shouted indignantly. Then she asked just what she was supposed to do if she left, since her mum wasn't going to come and take her home till the show finished.

One of her friends kindly suggested they could go out and stay with her till then, and the university staff member offered to phone her mum up and ask her to come early. But Becky protested again, saying she didn't understand why she shouldn't be allowed to stay.

Then, she said in anger, "I bet I could do a better job than that comedian anyway! Tell you what: I'll get up and do the show for him!"

Becky wasn't Really sure she could do a good job of being a comedian, especially not having planned what to say, but in her anger, she thought she'd rather give it a try than be made to leave.

The university staff member and the comedian had a bit of a talk about the dilemma. A lot of the comedian's jokes would be OK for someone of Becky's age to hear; there was perhaps about ten or fifteen minutes' worth that he thought wouldn't be. It was decided that Becky could go on stage and do a comedy sketch if she thought she could, and while it was going on, the comedian would think through his comedy routine and look through his script, and decide what jokes to take out.

He went off to do that, and the university staff member told Becky she could go up on stage. She suddenly felt nervous, but decided she'd give it a go.

The university staff member announced to the audience that she was going to do a roughly ten-minute comedy sketch while the comedian was finishing his preparations. She had a quick think, and came up with a few ideas. She went up to the front and said:

"Hello. I've been asked to take over from the comedian you were expecting to see for a while, because it seems he got a bit self-conscious about some of his jokes, and wondered if they would be OK, so he's just checking. So I'll try and entertain you in the meantime.

"I was on the way to the dentist the other day, but then I changed my mind . . . That's right – I took my old mind out and put in a new one. Now I've got the mind of a train driver. Does anyone fancy coming to the station with me and having a ride in a train I take over?"

Several students giggled. Then Becky said, "I could drive you all down to the seaside. Then I could change my mind again to the mind of a ferry driver, and take you all over to France."

She saw lots of grins from the audience, and her confidence grew. She continued:

"Imagine if you could swap minds with another person. Imagine if heads had lids, and you could unclip some clips and open them, and take your brains out and swap them with someone else's. So one good thing would be that if you couldn't drive and they could, and you wanted to go somewhere by car, you wouldn't have to go to all the trouble of learning to drive; you could just swap minds with them for the time it took to go there and back again, and once you'd put their mind in, you'd know how to drive. So as long as someone let you borrow their car and their mind, you could use them yourself.

"Mind you, I suppose it might be a bit awkward, since when you had their mind in, you might start thinking you were them. So you might have been going to drive to the house of a friend of yours, but as soon as you had their mind in, you might forget your friend even existed, since all the memories of being their friend would be in your own mind, not in the mind you were borrowing, so you might decide to drive to, say, a bingo hall instead, since the mind's real owner might like bingo, whereas you might not normally think much of it at all. Then when you put your own mind back in, you might be sorry you missed out on seeing your friend."

Several of the students watching seemed interested in what Becky was saying and were smiling, so she was encouraged, and carried on:

"Perhaps heads would have combination locks on them, and people would just know what the number was to unlock their own heads so they could open the lids from an early age. There would have to be some kind of security system in people, since otherwise, some people would try to steal other people's minds, for instance if they weren't very bright and wanted better minds.

"But imagine if it was still possible to steal minds. A chemistry student worried about not passing his exams might somehow be able to sneak into his chemistry professor's room while he was asleep and carefully open his head and take out his brains and swap them with his own. Then he might suddenly become really good at chemistry and pass his exams with no problems, as long as he still somehow remembered he needed to take his exams, while the chemistry professor might wake up the next morning, and instead of working on chemistry all day as usual, he might decide to lounge around in bed till late in the morning, and then get up and play a game on his computer before getting around to getting dressed, and then grudgingly decide to do a bit of work for a while, and then afterwards go to the bar for hours.

"Or imagine if the parts of the brain were split neatly into compartments, with each one wrapped in a membrane, with them all being clipped together, and it was possible to just unclip and take out one compartment that did a particular thing, leaving the rest of the brain in place. So some of someone's memories might be taken out in their sleep and replaced with someone else's memories. Maybe students would sneak into the room of a physics lecturer while he was asleep one night and replace a couple of the compartments in his brain with ones belonging to a sociology lecturer, so he'd wake up and know he had to go and do a lecture in the physics department, but go there and give the students there a sociology lecture. I wonder what they'd think!

"It might even be possible for surgeons to give people brain transplants to cure illnesses. Actually it wouldn't even take a surgeon; your mum could do it. Or your little brother. If people could sign up to a register of people who were willing to donate their brains if they died while they were still in good working order, someone who got, say, Alzheimer's disease, might have their brain removed and replaced with the brain of a keen young skydiver who'd just had an instantly fatal accident.

"But just imagine what might happen! Their memories of who they used to be wouldn't be there any more, and they'd have memories of skydiving instead. A frail 85 year-old man might say, 'I must get out for another skydive soon!' His son might say, 'Dad! You're 85 years old!' His dad might refuse to believe him because he'd think he was a young person, and he'd wonder who this person was who was calling him Dad anyway, and think he lived somewhere else.

"Maybe after a few early bad mistakes, it would be realised that it was important to only replace the bit of the brain where the short-term memories were, and a few other bits that were broken, leaving the long-term memories in place so people still remembered who they were.

"Imagine if it wasn't just brains that ordinary people could take out when they wanted. I heard that a Roman general started a speech to some top Romans by saying, 'Friends, Romans, countrymen, lend me your ears.' Imagine if ears were attached like suction toys that you wet a bit and then push down on things and they stick to them, so they could be pulled off and stuck on other things or people. So imagine if when he said that, the people listening to him thought he literally meant he wanted their ears for a while, and they all pulled them off and stuck them on him. He probably really just meant he wanted them to listen to him, but the result of what he said would be the exact opposite of what he wanted – they wouldn't be able to hear him at all once they'd pulled their ears off and all stuck them on him. He might end up with dozens of ears all over him.

"And imagine if it wasn't just bodies that worked differently, but some of the gadgets we use. So imagine if not only humans perked up and felt more energetic after drinking strong coffee, but if you spilled some on a watch or clock, instead of breaking, it would speed up. So you might arrive early for an appointment, and when they told you you were early, you might say, 'Oh sorry, my watch must be fast because I accidentally spilled strong coffee on it earlier.'

"And I've heard that chemicals in some foods like Turkey can make people feel sleepy. So imagine if watches would start going slow if people dropped a bit of food like that on them, so people might turn up late for appointments, or late for exams! Some people might be so worried about dropping the kinds of food on their watches that made them slow down that they might not wear them at all before important appointments and exams in case that happened, but then end up missing them altogether because they had no idea what the time was!

"And just imagine if in the future, space travel's common, and they have space roads and spacecars and spacetrains and things. Imagine if lots of them had been invented, and one day a huge space lorry was on the way to space when it dropped a massive cargo of caffeine that hurtled down onto the earth, and it made the earth start spinning faster!"

The comedian finished rearranging his script and started listening to Becky. He began to worry that what she was saying might be more entertaining than what He'd planned to say, and that the students might be disappointed if he stopped her and then they didn't like his jokes as much. There wasn't much laughter in the place, but the audience did look as if they were enjoying themselves. But he thought he'd better go on stage, since after all, he'd been paid to do the performance, and it wouldn't look good if he decided not to do any of it after that.

So he went up to Becky and whispered that he was ready to do his show. Becky was running out of ideas for things to say, so she didn't mind.

Before she left, the students clapped and cheered her enthusiastically. She went off stage feeling very happy.

A few days later, her picture was on the front page of the student newspaper, with the story about what had happened. She was pleased, and her friends praised her and joked about her having taken over part of the comedian's show.

Some of the students who'd enjoyed listening to her asked the university staff if she could be invited back to do another comedy act. The people who booked performers to come to the university asked Becky if she'd like to do one for half an hour one day before another comedian did a show. She was excited at the thought, and said she would. So they arranged a day and publicised it.

Quite a few students turned up to hear her do her comedy sketch.

She'd had a good think about what to say, and discovered she had a talent for making up funny stories. She'd thought she might have one before, because of her experience helping the children at her old school make up humorous little stories about things they'd supposedly done, to play an April Fools' trick on a teacher who'd asked them to write about lots of interesting things they really had done for their homework – way more than some of them could think of, which had made them unhappy with the task, and pleased when Becky had offered to help them make up funny stories and see if the teacher believed them.

But she discovered she was good at making up longer stories too.

When she went up on stage, she said, "I'm going to tell you about some of the people at my old school. There were some weird people there!

"There was one boy who was convinced he was really clever and good-looking, and he thought there was something wrong with anyone who didn't think he was, and he would insult anyone who said he wasn't as great as he thought he was. He had such a big head, he found it hard to get in the classroom door. His head touched both edges as he walked in, and it made creaking noises as he made efforts to pull it through. Then it grew even bigger, and he couldn't get in at all. They had to take the door frame out.

"But then it grew some more and he couldn't get in the doorway. The teachers made us all go and have our lessons outside from then on so he could join in. They bought plastic schoolbooks for everyone for when it rained, and we couldn't use anything that wasn't waterproof. We didn't enjoy that, but no one was allowed to say anything against it. If anyone did, the teachers called them politically incorrect scumbags, and things like that.

"But then the boy's head grew even bigger, and he didn't have the strength to hold it up any more, so he started crawling along everywhere he went, with it dragging on the ground. When he stayed still, some people thought his head was like a convenient stool, and sat on it. He thought that was proof of how attractive he was, and his head grew even more. In the end it was too heavy for him to have the strength to drag it around, so he started walking on all fours with it perched on a wheelbarrow. But then one day that broke. His head hit the ground really hard and broke off his body.

"We would have sent it to scientists to investigate why it was the way it was, but it would have cost hundreds of pounds to send through the post. So we told them that if they wanted it, they could come and get it. At first they were interested, but when we told them what the boy had been like, they weren't sure there would be enough of a brain in his head to make it worth studying. So we hired a van in the end, and sent his head to a museum of curiosities.

"Another weird person in my class was a girl who literally had a chest of drawers – she really did have drawers in her chest! She had drawer handles where other girls had breasts.

At first some of the other kids made fun of her for having what seemed to be weird-looking breasts, but they stopped when she showed them what they really were. She could open the drawers and put things in them. She kept pencils in them, and paper, and all kinds of other things. At first when she took her top off to open one, the teacher shouted at her, saying she was being obscene. But then she offered to store the teacher's handbag in there for safekeeping while the lessons were going on, and the teacher was pleased and said she'd like that, and from then on she didn't mind the girl taking her top off to get things out of the drawers or put stuff in.

"There were other strange people in my class too. There was one boy who seemed to have a bottom made of straw. He had a layer of skin over it, but he said it had been discovered that there was straw underneath. Whenever he sat down, it made a rustling sound. At first the teachers told him off for making a noise, and some wouldn't believe he had a bottom made of straw; but when he told them they could come and look if they liked, since the skin over it was becoming trans-parent, none of them did, and let him get away with rustling around from then on.

"And there was one girl who was really really fat, and she had a belly button that was about two feet wide! I know you don't believe me, but it's true! She's as real as the man in the moon, and the fact that the earth is flat! It was scary! Even though she was really fat, she was really strong, and she could lift people up with no effort. She used to threaten to push anyone who annoyed her into her belly button, and keep on pushing till they disappeared into her stomach.

"She actually did that to one boy once. We never saw him again. She just picked him up and pushed him in! After that, every so often we'd hear someone shouting, 'Help!' and a noise that sounded as if someone was banging on her stomach from the inside. Sometimes we'd hear other voices, so she must have pushed other people through her belly button into her stomach too, maybe members of her family.

"After we heard voices that shouted for help from inside her, we sometimes heard other voices from there that said things like, "Oh shut up! I don't know what you're complaining about! Things aren't that bad! Look on the bright side! We certainly get enough food down here! Alright, it's food that's already been eaten once, but it still tastes nice. And we can breathe whenever she swallows air. She benefits because she doesn't embarrass herself by burping it back up anywhere near as often as she used to before we started breathing it in, and we benefit because we can breathe it. And we don't have to work for a living; we can just sit here all day and enjoy each other's company. We'll never be lonely as long as we all live. So be quiet and just count your blessings!'

"That reassured everyone in the school that the boy in our class who she'd pushed into her belly button must be alright really, so no one ever tried to help him escape. But no one dared say a bad word about the girl after that, because they were scared they would end up in her stomach too.

"Another strange thing about my old school was that one of the teachers had a wooden leg, and a wooden eye. I'm sure doctors don't usually replace damaged eyes with wooden ones. I thought they used glass ones. But this teacher had a wooden leg that was actually attached with elastic to her wooden eye. Every time she sat down, she'd take her wooden eye out, and give the elastic a bit of a pull, and her leg would come off, and she'd put it on the floor beside her. If a student played up in the lesson, she'd pick up her eye, and tell them that if they didn't behave, she'd keep an eye on them for the rest of the lesson. If they carried on misbehaving, she'd fling her eye at them, and then pull it back with the elastic, and keep doing that for the rest of the lesson, or aim it at their desk and just leave it there when it landed there. It seems the elastic was long enough that it wouldn't just ping it back when she threw it there.

"Sometimes the misbehaving pupil would run out of the room, scared of having a spooky eye on their desk.

"The headmaster wasn't any better. He had this weird speech defect. I don't know why he was chosen to be headmaster, but maybe it was because he made the people responsible for deciding who would be headmaster laugh, and they thought he'd make them laugh in boring meetings where they had to go and have discussions with whatever headmaster they chose.

"When he said certain words – I don't know why he did this – but it seems he just had to say certain other words every time he said them. Whenever he said the word children, he'd always say sweating afterwards. When he said teachers, he'd always say head lice just before it. When he said work, it seems he always had to say the word boring right before it. When he said the word school, he'd always say the word pit right afterwards. When he said the word pleasure, he'd always say stinking just before it. When he said learn, he'd always say slog just before it. When he said record, he'd always say pathetic first. When he said country, he'd say insect right before it. And he said other things like that.

"So sometimes in assembly, he'd say things like, 'We pride ourselves on having a school pit where children sweating can come to slog learn in a happy environment. We have every confidence that our head lice teachers will make slog learning a stinking pleasure. We know the boring work we do at this school pit will lead children sweating to have a bright future. One day they will be grateful for all the boring work the head lice teachers made them do here. We have an excellent pathetic record of achievement! We believe it's one of the best in the insect country!'

"I don't know why he was like that! But he was always saying things like that.

"And one of the teachers said funny things accidentally too. I don't know why. He used to say insulting things to any children he didn't think were trying to work hard enough or were misbehaving; but when he got a bit angry, he'd start saying 'I' when he meant 'you', and 'my' when he meant 'your', and things like that. He never realised he was doing it, and wouldn't believe anyone who told him. So he would shout things like, 'What have I been doing when I was supposed to be concentrating on the lesson, boy? I clearly haven't been paying attention at all! If I don't buck my ideas up, I'm going to fail all my exams! And what am I doing talking in that silly whining voice, and winding bits of my hair around my fingers! If I carry on like that, I'll end up in a mental institution! I need help boy! Get help!'

"Anyway, that's enough about the people at my school. They couldn't help the way they were! . . . Now let me tell you about some of the other people I've met!

"My mum's a nurse, and some of the patients she has to help are weird! Or at least, weird things happened to them. There was one man who had a rose bush growing out of his nose. It was so big it hung down over his whole body, and it took him all his strength to hold his head up. He said it had started growing in his nose when he sniffed a rose on a bush so enthusiastically for hours on end one afternoon that he got rose seeds up his nose, and the powerful upward suction of his sniffing had eventually drawn earth out of the ground and it had hurtled into his nose along with them. He had to walk around naked, because his clothes wouldn't fit over the rose bush.

"He'd been taken to hospital after the police had arrested him for walking around naked in public and he'd told them he couldn't help the way he was, and explained that the rose bush had started growing in his nose by accident. The doctors had to do an operation on his nose to take the rose bush out.

"And then there was another man who had a desk stuck to the top of his head. He said it had happened when he spilled a drink on his desk and had put his head down to take a good look and to lap it up, and the top of his head had rested on the desk for a while, and some of the drink dried and went sticky while he was lapping up a puddle of drink that was still liquid, and his head had stuck to the desk. It wouldn't come off, so he'd turned the desk upside-down and had just gone around with it on the top of his head from then on. But he said it was difficult to get through doorways with it, so he'd decided it would be better to go to hospital and get it removed.

"The surgeon removing it had to take all his equipment outside and do the operation in the hospital car park, because there was a problem getting the desk through the door of the operating theatre.

"Mind you, weirder things go on on telly, don't they! I was watching EastEnders the other day – you know, the episode where aliens came down in a spaceship and sucked up all the residents in a massive hoover-like thing and hurled them right up into space, and then flew to another country and snatched up some people who speak a completely different language and dumped them in Albert Square – or whatever it's called – it's about the only time I've ever watched that programme.

"But in their language, lots of English words mean different things. So you think they're saying one thing, when really they're saying something completely different. I mean, one of the new EastEnders characters said something that sounded like, 'I hate you! You betrayed me, and that was downright cruel. I hope you rot in a barrel of festering old socks!' And almost everyone watching it was convinced that was what they meant, when I happen to know that what they really meant was, 'My family have just been on a holiday to the sun, and we really enjoyed ourselves! The sea was so warm, and we only had to call on the American air force to deploy a missile against a nasty jellyfish that might have attacked us otherwise once!'

"Anyway, enough about television programmes. Real life's more . . . well, real, so it's more worth talking about. So I'll tell you more about that.

"One of my tutors told me his wife's a sea monster. She decided to try to live on land so she could be with him. But she found it was a bit difficult, so they filled their bedroom full of salt water, and turned it into a pool where she feels happier. He's learned to sleep floating on top of it all night. He used to come to work with soggy soaking clothes on, till he came up with the idea of keeping his wardrobe and chests of drawers in another part of the house so they can stay dry.

"The thing is, every time they open the bedroom door, water gushes out, and that's bad for their carpets, so they've learned to go outside and climb up the drainpipe and then climb in the window whenever they want to go in the bedroom.

24

He doesn't mind. Even in winter, he says he thinks the exercise is good for him, so he can put up with the cold.

"He says one reason it's worth staying with his wife is that she often goes shopping and gets out of the shop without paying, since the store detectives are too scared to run after a sea monster and ask her if she paid for what she's got, even though they don't mind chasing hardened criminals.

"Mind you, I've been telling you about other people who are weird, but I can hardly talk! There are weird things about my own family! For one thing, my mum was born with bright orange hairs on her chest. No one knows why. The doctors in the hospital thought the hairs might make her stand out in a way that got her made fun of and that wouldn't be fair, so they painted the rest of her bright orange so the hairs wouldn't stand out so much."

Becky talked on for some time, and the students laughed and smiled. When she finished her comedy sketch, they gave her a great round of applause.

Chapter 3

Some of the Students Discuss the Effects of Alcohol, Including Some Experiences They've Had While Drunk

The Students Reminisce About Amusing Incidents at University

One warm day in late spring, Becky and some of her fellow psychology students were sitting around together in the local park. They started reminiscing about the time they'd spent at university up till then.

One of them, Matthew, said, "Hey, do you remember when there was a big thunderstorm in the middle of a lecture, and the tutor said, 'Sometimes an angry client will come to therapy and say . . .' and just at that very second, there was a big thunderclap, and the tutor said, 'Actually I think it would take an angry god to say that!'?"

The others giggled.

Then one of the group, Colin, said, "Hey Tom, do you remember when you got so drunk that your legs gave way and you just sat on the ground in the middle of campus and said you didn't feel like moving, and then it started snowing, and someone said that if you stayed there much longer, he was going to cover you in snow and tell everyone you were a snowman he'd made, and you said, 'They'll find it hard to believe you when I move and talk', and he said, 'I'll just tell them we know how to make moving talking snowmen in the engineering department nowadays'?"

The students laughed again. They joked around and reminisced for a while longer. Then things got more serious for a while.

The Students Talk About One Possible Benefit of Alcohol

One of the group, Heather, said, "I never knew alcohol could do this before, but oddly enough, I've noticed that when I have an alcoholic drink or two when I'm trying to get down to writing my essays, my mind seems to be sharper than normal, and ideas come to me more easily, and I feel contented to just sit for hours working through stuff I normally find a bit tedious, when if I don't drink alcohol, I can keep getting restless and distracted because I want something more stimulating to do.

"A bit of alcohol makes me feel more motivated to get down to writing essays in the first place as well, so I can get on with them more easily and do a better job of them than I would have done without it. It just gives me more of a no-nonsense attitude somehow, so I just want to get down to them instead of procrastinating by going to Facebook or a forum, or going to a humour site or something because I feel like doing something I like better than working, or that's less effort or a bit more stimulating than working.

"I don't really understand why that would happen, but I had a think about why it might, and I wonder if the thing about ideas coming more easily and it being easier to get on and write stuff after an alcoholic drink or two might sometimes be partly because alcohol reduces inhibitions, so when people have had a drink, they might be more likely to just come out and say or write down exactly what they think, without feeling as if they ought to keep it to themselves out of politeness, or out of doubts that it's the right thing to say; or they might be less dithery and more decisive, because they're not so preoccupied with feelings that make them think they can't be bothered to do a thing, so they just get on and do it; so they can come across as being more quick-witted or intelligent than they would sober, because they let their thoughts and instincts about what would be a good thing to do or say flow more freely. A drink can stop me personally feeling so apathetic about getting on with things anyway.

"Actually, part of it might be that alcohol's a mild sedative, so that's how it might soothe my feelings of boredom and rest-lessness and grumpiness at having to get down to doing things I'm not keen on doing, so it makes it easier to settle down to them and feel content to slog through them."

Becky grinned and teased, "You're not suggesting you say impolite things in your essays, are you? And you make 'quick-witted' jokes in them? What do the tutors say?"

Heather replied, "No, I don't do that! I was talking about people in general, doing things in all kinds of situations. Still, it's probably best that I don't drink more than I do while I'm working, or who knows what might happen!

"Actually, I think I have had a bit too much to drink once or twice while I was writing essays, and I've noticed that drinking too much makes me so happy-go-lucky I don't care if I do a good job of them or not, so then I end up doing things like not bothering to put stuff in them that I should, and not checking what I've written after I've finished to make sure it's OK.

"I'm sure people have got to be a bit careful with alcohol, because of that warning about how the more we drink, the more our judgments will be impaired, so the more likely we will be to start talking rubbish without realising it's rubbish. Who knows what drunken students might sometimes have put in their essays!

"But still, I'm getting into the habit of always drinking alcohol before writing essays now because of the effects it has on me, like making me more content to get down to doing things I'm not that keen on doing."

Another one of the group, Mya, said, "You'd better watch that a bit. You don't want it to become too much of a habit, especially because people's bodies build up a tolerance for alcohol so it takes more to get the same effect over time, so people can end up drinking more and more, and that can get worse and worse for their health. I've never found essays that irksome to do. Are you sure you're on the right course? You might enjoy something else better."

Heather replied, "It's not that I don't like the subject. It's just that I'd often prefer to be doing something I find entertaining, or learning about interesting things I've never heard about before, or doing interactive things like discussing things with people, than doing something that takes effort and feels a bit boring. So I can dither around and procrastinate before I get down to work, and again if I get a bit bored during it so I feel as if I need a break. A bit of alcohol's just useful for me, because of the help it gives me with disciplining myself to just get on with things, and the way it stops me getting the restless feelings I often have when I try to do coursework without it. If I found a healthier alternative that had the same effects on me, I'd happily switch to that.

"Other things can work to some extent. The other day I didn't have any alcohol in my room, but I did have a big packet of crisps, so I nibbled on those all the way through writing part of an essay instead, and it helped. Actually, sunshine helps too. I do find it easier to slog through stuff if I've got sun shining on my face. It partly depends on how boring I'm finding what I'm doing though.

"I've noticed it helps if something gives me a good laugh or some other good fun before I start as well, so I'm in better spirits when I do. I think that makes it easier for me to tolerate doing more humdrum stuff than I normally can before I get bored. And it helps to have music on in the background that suits my mood or that perks me up a bit.

"I suppose I might drink alcohol more often than I need to, because I just assume I'll need it when I could do without it really. Not long ago I didn't have any in my room again, and decided to try to write part of an essay without it. I got a bit of a craving for it while I was working on a bit that seemed especially tedious, and wished I had some to hand so I could make the feeling go away; but I didn't go out and get any, and several minutes later I got on to a bit of the essay that was less boring, and the craving went away and didn't come back. I realised I would have had some when I didn't really need any if I'd had some in stock. I do find I often get more done when I drink a bit of alcohol though, because it stops me feeling frustrated about having to concentrate on work I'm not keen on doing, and helps me feel content to settle to it so I can just focus on it and get more done."

Colin said, "Aren't there a few types of herbal tea that are supposed to calm people down a bit? I don't know how well they work, or how healthy they are, but it might be worth looking into them as a substitute for booze. Or I wonder if wearing yourself out with exercise before you start working might make you feel less restless."

Heather laughed and said, "If I wore myself out, maybe I'd just flop around and sleep instead of getting into the kind of decisive no-nonsense mood that would help me just get on with work without dithering over it. I suppose I could try a bit of exercise and see if it helps though. I'll be surprised if it helps as much as alcohol, but I suppose you never know."

One of the others, Debbie, said, "I sometimes use alcohol the same way you do, Heather, to help me stop dithering around and just get on with work when I don't feel like it.

"I wonder if the effects alcohol has on a person partly depend on their personality though. Some people don't need to have had a drink to be decisive! I dread to think how decisive they'd get if they had some, and it had the same effect on them as it does on us! . . . Well, I'm thinking about one person in particular, and I presume she hasn't been drinking most of the time when I meet her, which is often early in the morning! A bit *less* decisiveness might be nice where she's concerned!

"Well, I don't get the problem here, because she isn't here; but at home, she'll waltz into my room sometimes and say irritably, 'Isn't it messy in here! You never change! Look at this empty envelope! It's obviously rubbish! Why do you never throw anything away?' And in the bin it goes! Afterwards I think, 'Well it might have been rubbish; but what if I was keeping it because I wanted to use it for something, like for a bit of scrap paper to write a few notes on, or to put things like pencils or sweets in to keep them together, which you might actually like me to do, because it would be a bit neater than having them lying around all over the floor or my desk, or over the ceiling or the walls . . . no, they wouldn't really be there; but you wouldn't approve of them lying around anywhere! It would have been nice if you'd at least asked me before throwing things away!' "

Becky said, "I'd want to banish a person from my house if they did that to me! . . . Come to think of it, my mum's done that kind of thing a few times. I don't suppose it would go down too well if I tried to banish her from my house, especially since it's actually hers!"

Debbie grinned and said, "No! It's actually a relative of mine who does that to me, and somehow I don't think trying to banish her from the house would go down well with the rest of my family!"

They giggled.

Then Matthew said, "About that thing about alcohol making people a bit more decisive and quick-thinking though – well, people who it's possible to make more like that anyway – I think I remember reading that one reason the first drink might make people a bit more keen-minded or sharp-witted is that the body can release adrenaline when people first start drinking, which increases alertness levels. They often don't stay more alert though, because once people start drinking, they can often feel as if they want more and more, in the same way that you can eat a bit of chocolate and then have an urge to have some more; and the more people drink, the more their judgments will be impaired, so the more likely they will be to do silly things. But they might not realise that the things they're doing are silly. They might think they're not far off just normal, I'm not sure."

Heather Said, "I think one problem is that you can drink a bit, and then you want to keep the effect it's having on you going and make sure it doesn't wear off, so you drink some more; but instead of just keeping the effect of the first couple of drinks going, it makes the alcohol have a different effect on you than it did at first, because there's more in your system than there was at first; and the effect's one you could really do without. Like instead of helping you continue to feel contented to get down to work, it makes you more likely to do it in a slapdash way; or if you're out, instead of giving you the courage to introduce yourself to new people, and helping you relax and feel comfortable chatting to them, like the first couple of drinks might have done, it makes you say silly things without realising they're daft! That kind of thing's happened to me anyway.

"Maybe it's best to wait till the alcohol doesn't seem to be doing anything any more before having more, although it's tempting to have more, especially if you're offered it, or if you're trying to work and you don't want to start feeling discontented again before you have another drink, so you have one when the first signs of restlessness come on, but then you still end up with more drink in your system than you had after the first one or two. It would be nice to be able to get the effect of the first couple of drinks all day without it wearing off at all."

Becky grinned and said, "You know, maybe you'd better read your old essays, Heather and Debbie, just to see if there's any rubbish in there that the tutors were too polite to comment on."

Debbie said, "I don't think there is in mine. I never drink all that much when I'm working on them. Well, not normally. There was a day when I came back from an evening out where I'd had a fair bit to drink and worked on one for a while, and when my tutor was commenting on it, he told me I'd missed a word or several out in a sentence, and said in a fun way that he didn't know how much I'd been drinking when I wrote it. It said something like, 'A therapist can frequently in a situation like that.' Frequently what? I can't remember what it was supposed to say now. Perhaps I should have proof-read it before I gave it to him."

The students laughed.

The Students Talk About the Undesirable Effects of Alcohol

Then one of them, Bonnie, said, "I think alcohol must have different effects on people depending on what mood they're in when they start drinking, and who they're with, and maybe other things too.

"The other day I was feeling a bit grumpy, and I decided to have a couple of pints of cider while I was alone in my room, because I wanted to go out a bit later and I thought it would make me feel more sociable and put me in a better mood when

I did, so I'd enjoy myself more. But it didn't! I felt pretty much as grumpy when I'd finished it as I had when I started! I might have been better off waiting till I was with my friends before drinking, since whatever alcohol I had then would have been helped along by a friendly atmosphere. I realised that afterwards.

"And when I was drinking the cider on my own, I was thinking it would be best to guzzle down quite a bit as quickly as I could, so the effects would kick in more quickly, so I'd start feeling better right then. So much for that idea! I'm wondering if actually, the atmosphere you're in has quite a bit to do with how you feel, so drinking more slowly and doing other things to make you happier at the same time would be more effective at bringing on the effect you want the booze to have than drinking more quickly but not enjoying yourself while you're doing it, at least if you're using it to put yourself in the mood to relax and socialise."

Matthew said, "I've heard about a few people who used to drink alcohol to help them relax, doing things like pouring themselves a drink or two every day as a treat when they got in from work. but they developed a bit of a drink problem, so they started thinking they'd better give it up, and they managed it, and discovered that they could relax just as easily if they poured themselves non-alcoholic drinks at those times. They realised that what must have been helping them relax before was not the alcohol, but the ritual of pouring a nice drink and then sitting down to enjoy it, and then repeating the process if they felt like it. It was like a wind-down routine, and they found it could be just as satisfying when they treated themselves to an alcohol-free drink they enjoyed."

One of the group, Suzy, said, "I wonder if most people get into drinking alcohol just because it's the norm, and because they've come to expect it to make them feel good, so they assume drinking is just the natural thing to do when they go out, and that they'll be missing out if they don't do it. Maybe some of us could experiment with going out and not drinking alcohol, just to see how the amount of fun we have compares to the amount we used to have when we got drunk.

"Not that getting drunk is always fun. There was one time when I went to a party, and I was feeling a bit upset about something that had been going on when I started drinking, and it's actually embarrassing looking back, because the booze didn't make me more cheerful, but instead, when I was quite drunk, I started crying stupid amounts, when I'd never have even shed a tear about what was bothering me if I'd been sober! So I thought alcohol must often just make any mood you're in to begin with more intense."

Mya said, "I remember hearing something on the radio about this man who did an experiment, drinking pints and pints, and getting a friend of his to observe him and tell him afterwards how it changed his behaviour at every stage of getting drunk. I think he started off happy, but then he went through a phase of just wanting to cry for no good reason.

"I read that there are well-known stages people often go through when they drink: First of all they can feel happier and more carefree and confident and daring, and get more talkative, when alcohol begins to dull the part of the brain responsible for self-control and careful thinking. So people can start acting on impulse more. So they can enjoy getting into the party spirit more easily. But if they drink a bit more, they can sometimes start doing things they end up regretting, like having a fling with a total stranger they wouldn't even like if they met them when they were sober. I suppose it must partly depend on what kind of personalities and values people have though, because if a person would normally be morally opposed to having a fling with a stranger, I wouldn't have thought they'd suddenly decide it was alright if they'd been drinking. I don't know all that much about it though.

"Anyway, according to what I read, if people drink a bit more, it starts interfering with the part of their brain that controls emotions, so it can't do such a good job of it. So someone who was depressed to begin with can start crying for no good reason, maybe thinking everything they were a bit upset about before is way more of a big deal than it really is, or feeling like letting their stress out, and maybe pouring their heart out to random strangers. And some people can start overreacting to things. Like if someone says something they don't like, or even just if they have a thought about something they feel annoyed about, or if they misinterpret something as annoying when it wasn't intended to be, they can get way more annoyed about it than is sensible."

One of the students, Charlotte, smiled and said, "I think a lot of people do that when they're sober!"

Mya said, "Probably. But it seems people are even more likely to do it when they're drunk . . . Maybe the people who do it a lot when they're sober get hyperannoyed instead of just ordinarily annoyed when they've been drinking!"

Becky remarked for fun, "I wonder if there's anyone who'd get really annoyed with someone who called them an idiot while they were drunk, and feel insulted and hit them for it, but if they thought to themselves, 'I'm an idiot!', they'd get annoyed and hit themselves."

The students grinned.

Mya said, "I suppose you never know.

"Anyway, talking about the stages of drinking again, I read that when people drink some more after drinking enough to make them more likely to overreact to things, another part of their brain begins to shut down a bit, and they can start slurring their words and finding it harder to do things that require movements that are a bit intricate, like doing up buttons or clasps on necklaces and things.

"And if you drink more than that, then although you might not realise it, your vision starts being affected, and it gets harder to judge how far away things are and how fast they're moving, and to spot things out to the sides of you. That must be one reason why it's dangerous to drink and drive. I thought it must just be because people's reaction times get slower, and they might not feel the need to concentrate on the road as much as they normally do, and their movements can get less precise so they maybe can't handle the steering wheel as well, and things like that; but it seems it's because they can't see what's going on so well too. After all, if you aren't so good at telling how far away from you things are and how fast they're going, and you don't spot so many things, that's going to make driving risky!

"And I read that if someone's had a lot to drink, when they go to bed and wake up in the morning, they can actually still have too much alcohol in their system to drive safely! And I heard that alcohol stops people sleeping so deeply, even though it helps people get to sleep more quickly in the first place, so sleep deprivation can affect people's driving the next morning too, because they've been deprived of good-quality sleep, and they'll often wake up earlier than they would have done if they'd gone to bed sober.

"And That reminds me of a thing on telly where they said that when people are sleep-deprived, even if they haven't had any alcohol at all, their driving can actually be worse than the driving of someone who's had a couple of drinks."

Becky quipped, "I expect that's especially if they fall asleep at the wheel!"

Mya said, "Well, there is that. I actually heard that driving in the wee small hours of the morning's the most dangerous time to drive, because a higher percentage of people than normal will be sleep-deprived and at risk of falling asleep at the wheel then, or not driving so well; and the second most dangerous time of day to drive is in the early hours of the afternoon, because it's normal for people to feel more sleepy at that time of day.

"I mean, obviously it's not so dangerous to drive then that you're at a massively higher risk of having an accident, or you'd see more of them, or there would be laws forbidding driving then or something. Well, maybe anyway. But I mean, you can tell the risk can't be all that big when you see all the masses of cars going by without anything bad happening year after year. But there is a bit more of a risk. I can't remember what the estimated increase in the risk is; actually, I don't think I ever heard anyone say what it is. I think I just heard that there is an increase in the risk.

"But the statistic about how there are more accidents when people are most likely to be a bit sleepy just brings home the fact that people ought to not take the risk of driving if they feel a bit sleepy, if they can avoid it, in case they're a risk to themselves or others."

One of the group, Dave, half-jokingly said, "This is a bit depressing! Oh well, maybe I've just discovered there's an advantage to finding it hard to get up in the morning. I'm less likely to be out on the roads in the very early hours of the morning when people are more likely to die in accidents! Mind you, I suppose I might have to start getting up early when I get a job. Hopefully not all that early though!

"Hey, do you think an employer would let me off getting up early if I said I was so dedicated to working for them that I needed to get up later so I'd be coming in a good clear six hours or so after the time when I'd be at more risk of being killed on the roads and not being able to work for them any more?"

Matthew chuckled and said good-naturedly, "Don't be daft! They'd tell you to just come in by train, or to stop being so paranoid!"

The students giggled.

Then Mya said, "Anyway, what I read about getting drunk was that after the stage where people start not being able to see so well, if they drink some more, the part of the brain that controls balance starts to shut down till the alcohol wears off, so they can start falling over.

"If they have more to drink after that, it shuts down some more, and they can find it hard to get up if they've fallen over, and even go unconscious. If they do, it's best if they're lying on their stomach, because they can be sick, and if they're lying on their back, they can choke on it, and that might kill them.

"If they've had enough to drink to go past that stage, the part of the brain that controls breathing and blood circulation can shut down, so they'll die. That's if they don't vomit lots of the alcohol out."

Tom said, "I'm not sure how high the risk of dying can really be, because it's quite common to hear about people passing out drunk, but it's far less common to hear about people dying of alcohol poisoning because they partied too hard . . . Mind you, I suppose there might be a bit more of that if there were no hospitals, so people couldn't get treated for getting ill with alcohol poisoning when they were really drunk."

Debbie quipped, "If there were no hospitals, so no one could go there to be treated for anything, more people might actually *want* to drink themselves to death!"

The students smiled.

Tom said, "Yeah, we're lucky to have them really."

Some Humour Breaks Out

Charlotte said, "Hey, just imagine if there was an office party where the boss decided to be really generous and provide loads of booze, and everyone except him got really really drunk, and they all ended up dead, and at the end of the evening, the boss started getting worried about what to do with all the dead bodies all over his floor, and how he was going to cope after his entire workforce had all died in one go!"

They laughed, and Bonnie said, "Wow, that would be a scandal, wouldn't it! Imagine what it would say on the news! And imagine if he got taken to court for murder, and he had to try to explain how he really hadn't been trying to poison everyone, but he'd just been trying to be nice. Wow, wouldn't that be embarrassing for him . . . and even worse for his business, of course!"

They giggled again, and Dave said, "Don't people start feeling hungry sometimes when they've been drinking? That could be dangerous, because they might decide to cook things, and then pass out, and wake up with the house on fire or something. But I was just thinking that one way the boss could avoid having the scandal discovered and being taken to court and things is if he got really hungry when he saw all the dead bodies, and decided to eat them all ... Mind you, it would be an effort, wouldn't it, one person trying to eat a whole load of other people ... unless the boss was massively massively fat, maybe. But it would probably still be an impossible effort, trying to cram a whole load of dead workers down your throat. The effort would probably kill you!

"Imagine if in the morning, someone came in and found just one dead body on the floor, the boss's, but his stomach had swollen up to such massive proportions it spread right across the room! ... Well, I'm sure that couldn't really be possible. But imagine if it was, and his stomach had swelled up so much it was blocking the door from opening. Maybe no one would ever be able to get in the room again, and forever afterwards, while the building was still standing, there would be this mystery room, and it would go into a mysterious legend that said a load of people were partying one night, and then no one ever came out of there again.

"Maybe years after it happened, a daredevil would find a way to get in, and find just a skeleton in the room. If the boss had been drunk enough himself to eat all the people, and somehow managed to get all their clothes and their bones down him as well, the daredevil might not find any evidence that anyone else had been in the room, just a load of empty drink bottles and glasses, so they'd think this one person must have gone on a massive, massive alcohol binge and drunk themselves to death!"

Colin grinned and said, "Hey imagine if when we're doing our final exams at the end of our course, a topic about the effects of drinking comes up, and we all let our minds wander and start thinking about this stuff. Imagine if we all somehow decided it was a good idea to write stories about a worst case scenario where bosses could eat all their workers at an office party, instead of just writing what we're supposed to write! Imagine what the person marking our exams would think! I don't suppose we'd get any marks for it! Then we might all end up thinking it was a pity examiners didn't give marks for creative writing in psychology exams!"

They laughed again.

One Student Tells the Rest AboutReasons Why the Same Amount of Alcohol can Get People More Drunk at Some Times Than at Others

Suzy said with a grin, "It would be worse if for some reason we all decided to write about the most embarrassing things we've ever done when we were drunk in our exams! . . . Or maybe I should say, decided to write in our exams about the most embarrassing things we've done when we were drunk. doing drunken embarrassing things in our exams would be even worse!

"Actually, seriously though, I've been embarrassed a few times because I thought I'd worked out the amount I could drink that would get me just a bit tipsy but not actually drunk, but then sometimes I drank that amount, or maybe just a little bit more but not all that much, and I must have started saying a few silly things or something, because the next day, a couple of people laughed at me and said, 'You were drunk last night!' But I hadn't intended to get drunk. But then at other times,

44

I've had the same amount to drink, but it didn't seem to have any effect on me at all, so I started thinking, 'There isn't much point in drinking this stuff!'

"But then I started wondering if it's possible that people can get more drunk sometimes than they do at other times, even though they're just drinking the same amount. I know people can build up a tolerance for alcohol, so the same amount of booze doesn't affect them as much as it used to; but I wondered if there are other reasons why alcohol can affect people in different ways at different times. I started wondering that after someone on an Internet forum said people can get drunk by accident, because certain things can make alcohol make people drunker than they intended to get. They didn't say what things. So I decided to look it up on the Internet.

"I found out that there are quite a few things that can make booze have a more powerful effect than it was expected to have, or a less powerful effect, and also a more powerful effect on some people than it does on others:

"One is how much you've eaten before you start drinking. Actually, I knew before I read the information that alcohol doesn't have such a powerful effect on people who've eaten a lot before they start drinking it. But maybe food makes more of a difference than I thought: It seems that when people have eaten a fair bit before they start drinking, it means the alcohol stays in the stomach for longer than it would otherwise, mixed in with all the food, and that means the enzymes in the stomach have longer to break it down into separate parts along with the food that's being digested than they would otherwise, so the alcohol doesn't have as much effect as it would if it got through the stomach and went into the blood-stream more quickly.

"Another thing is that if people are a bit dehydrated to start with, they might get drunk more quickly than they normally do, since water in the body dilutes alcohol, so if there's less water there, the alcohol will get less diluted. So if someone's got an infection that means their body gets rid of more fluid than usual, like diarrhoea, or maybe even a cold if they're blowing their nose a lot, or else if they've just been exercising hard and they got really sweaty, or for some other reasons, the alcohol in their blood will be a bit less diluted than it would be otherwise, so it'll have more effect on them."

Becky quipped with a smile, "Of course, having an infection might stop people getting as drunk as usual instead, for instance if they're coughing all over their friends in the pub and some of them tell them to go home and stop spreading their germs, and they obey."

Suzy said, "There is that. Anyway, it seems there are other things that can make a difference to how drunk people get too: I read that muscles contain more water than fat does, and alcohol that gets into the muscles in the body will be diluted by that; but if someone hasn't been exercising for a while, their muscles will likely have got smaller so they won't hold so much of the alcohol, so more of it will go into the bloodstream where it'll have more effect; so people who haven't been exercising for a while might get drunker on the same amount of alcohol than they used to when they were exercising more often and they had bigger muscles.

"And since water dilutes alcohol, alcohol gets less effective when people water drinks down before they drink them to try to make them taste less disgusting! . . . Well, I personally think a lot of neat alcoholic drinks taste disgusting anyway.

I'm presuming a lot of other people do too, otherwise why would anyone water them down?

". . . I don't know how much difference any of this stuff really makes. I suppose it might be worth looking into more.

"But I also read that if a person's recently lost quite a bit of weight, they can get drunk on the amount of alcohol that just made them tipsy before, because their body's smaller, so there won't be as much of it to dilute the alcohol. That's also a reason why women can get drunker than men on the same amount of alcohol – because women are smaller on average, so there isn't as much of their bodies to dilute the alcohol, and not as much water in their bodies; and also women's bodies are made in a way that means they just naturally tend to have more fat on them than men's do, and less muscle – maybe because they're meant to be nice soft places for babies to be cuddled on – and fat doesn't absorb alcohol well, so more of it gets into women's bloodstreams where it can have an affect than gets into men's bloodstreams, it seems.

"I even read that eating low-fat foods before drinking can mean people can get drunker on the same amount of alcohol than they would if they'd eaten high-fat foods instead, because the fattier foods are, the longer they can take to get digested and leave the stomach, so the alcohol will be mixing with them and being digested itself for longer before it goes into the bloodstream."

Charlotte said, "I think another reason people can get less or more drunk than they expected to is if what they're drinking has less or more alcohol in it than they expected. The other day I discovered that a supermarket has information on their web-site about the number of units in a drink I was thinking of buying, but it says there are one or two more in it than the website

47

of the drink's makers says it has. So if you're calculating how much to drink by the number of units in each drink you have, you can get it wrong."

Mya chuckled and said, "Wow, you must have been dedicated to buying that drink if you checked as thoroughly as that!"

Charlotte replied, "Not that much. I was just curious."

Suzy said, "Anyway, another thing is that it seems that older people's bodies can't break down alcohol as efficiently as young people's can, for some reason, so older people might find themselves getting more drunk than they used to on the same amount of alcohol.

"And it seems that sleep deprivation can have an affect too, even after just one night of it, since when people are a bit sleep-deprived, the brain doesn't work so fast, so the effects of alcohol can be made worse by that, with people getting even more dull-witted than they would normally be when they're drunk.

"And I read that a similar thing can happen when people drink alcohol while they're taking medications that make them feel a bit drowsy.

"And some medications can intensify the effects of alcohol – not just prescription ones, but some over-the-counter ones too. I took an aspirin once, hoping it would get rid of a period pain I had. I didn't have anything better to hand at the time. It was an old aspirin I found in my parents' first-aid box. It didn't work; but I went to a party later on, and I did drink quite a bit, but it got me drunker than I expected; and the next morning, I remembered doing a couple of daft little things the night before, and thought, 'Why did I get drunk enough to behave like an idiot at the end of the evening?' So I thought the aspirin might have made the alcohol have more of an effect than I expected, since I got more drunk than I expected to on the amount of alcohol I had . . . Or I suppose I could have been just over-estimating my tolerance for drink, although I thought I'd drunk as much as that before without getting that bad.

"Genes can make a difference too, it seems, since some people's genes give them more stomach enzymes to break down alcohol than other people have, so they can do it more quickly. And I read that women often have fewer of those, so that's another reason why women can get drunker than men do by drinking the same amount of alcohol, since more gets into the bloodstream before it's been digested.

"And drinking faster can get people more drunk than if they drink the same amount of alcohol but more slowly, because the body can only get alcohol out of the system at a certain speed, so drinking faster than it can process it means the alcohol will likely have more effects before it's got rid of than it would if a person's drinking so slowly that the body can break down all the alcohol before it has much effect.

"And I read that just as watering down alcohol will make it have less effect, since it'll mean it's more diluted so it doesn't have such a fast impact, because the body's got more oppor-tunity to break some of it down before it all gets into the bloodstream, mixing it with sugary drinks will mean it gets absorbed more slowly too, since it seems it spends longer in the stomach while the sugar's being broken down than it would otherwise, so more of the alcohol gets digested before it gets to the bloodstream.

". . . Mind you, drinking it with more water or something sugary can at least make it taste tolerable enough to get it down you! I decided to try drinking something I wouldn't normally drink anywhere near neat with a fair bit less water than I'd normally put in it not long ago, to see if it had more effect on me than usual, and it was disgusting! I'm not going to do that again! I think the possibility of it having less effect on me if I dilute it with more water will be a price worth paying from now on! I'd give up drinking altogether if all alcoholic drinks tasted that yucky and it was somehow impossible to dilute them!

"But then, the yucky drink didn't seem to have any more effect on me than it did when I drank it before with more water in it.

". . . I'm not trying to suggest ways people can get drunker faster here by talking about what might make people more drunk, by the way, just in case anyone's wondering. I just think the information I found about it just shows that it isn't always a person's fault if they get drunk, so it's not always fair for people to look down on other people for doing silly things when they've had a few, because they sometimes might have assumed they would be able to drink as much as they've drunk before without getting any more drunk than they did before.

"Mind you, I've heard that some people do horrible things when they're drunk, like attacking people, that they actually plan to do before they start drinking, and they get drunk so afterwards they can use the excuse that they did them because they were drunk."

Becky said, "That's horrible!"

The Students Talk About Embarrassing Things Done While Drunk

Then Heather said, "A couple of months ago I got drunk accidentally! I just wanted a bit of alcohol because I was hoping it would perk me up a bit, because I was in that mood again where I was feeling as if I couldn't be bothered to do anything much, work-wise, and I was hoping it would change that, because I thought I'd better do some coursework. Like I said before, sometimes a bit of alcohol puts me in the mood to just get on with things and stop dithering around not feeling like getting down to them. I had a big cupful of wine, from a bottle of cheap wine I'd bought not long before. I don't normally drink wine, but I thought I'd try it.

"It didn't seem to do anything for me. So I decided to have a bit more. I'd had a beer or two before that which was supposed to be a bit stronger than the average beer, but it didn't seem to do anything for me either. That's why I decided to have the wine. Maybe the alcohol was just taking longer than I expected to work though, because it did have an effect after a while!

"But before it did, since the wine didn't seem to be having any more effect than the beer had, I just assumed it wasn't going to do anything much for me either. I started wondering if I was just a hardened drinker who needed more than a lot of people would. After a couple of minutes when the second lot of wine didn't seem to have made me feel any different, I decided to have another lot. I ended up finishing the bottle!

"But not long afterwards, I realised it had been a bad idea! I tried to send a couple of emails to people, and my hands wouldn't type as fast as I wanted them to, and I couldn't think as clearly as normal about what I wanted to say. I think I might have gone from being stone cold sober, straight past the phase where I might have felt a bit perked up, to being more like some kind of stupefied zombie.

"I'd been meaning to go and see someone who lives in the next corridor to me and ask her if she wanted some perfume someone had given me for Christmas but that I wasn't that keen on. She wears perfume a lot, so I thought she might like it.

"But I hadn't really felt like going to speak to her for a while before then, because she'd lent me a book some time before that, and I'd kept it for longer than I should have done, and I wondered if she might have a go at me for it, so I felt just a little bit nervous about going to speak to her. I thought giving her the perfume might be like a kind of peace offering in compensation for her not getting her book back for a while.

"I'd been thinking of drinking a bit before going to give her book back, because I thought it would stop me feeling a bit nervous about doing it. So I thought that since I'd drunk a bit already, it would be a good time to go and give it back, and then I could achieve two things by drinking that day – getting down to coursework, and feeling OK about going to give the book back. But I think I drank more than I would do to just help me get down to working partly because of that.

"I started feeling sorry for her for not getting her book back for ages instead of feeling a bit nervous when I'd had a bit to drink. So I decided it would be a good time to go.

"But it turned out she wasn't annoyed with me after all. She was friendly. But now she probably just thinks I'm an idiot, because I probably said some daft things that I couldn't remember the next day! Well, there is one thing I can vaguely remember. When she opened her door to me, someone else was walking past, and they said something to her, and I answered, as if I somehow thought they were talking to me. They told me they were talking to her. You know it's like the part of the brain that thinks sensibly begins to shut down when you're drunk? I think mine must have shut down a bit. So I might have sounded like a nutter, for all I know! And they both probably didn't realise I was drunk; so now they probably think I'm always like that! And when I started speaking to the girl whose book I'd borrowed, I realised I was slurring my words a bit, and I tried to speak properly. I don't know how well I succeeded.

"Mind you, afterwards, I wondered if she might have been a bit drunk herself, because when I offered her the perfume, she said, 'Has that got mustard in it?' I was a bit surprised. Why would anyone expect perfume to have mustard in it? Well, I think that's what she said anyway. I suppose it could have been something else, and my drunken brain just interpreted it to mean that. Or maybe she thought it looked like a bottle of sauce or something similar at a glance instead of perfume.

"I didn't stay there that long, because she was watching some television programme she was interested in. Probably just as well!

"When I got back, I tried to read something for my course, that I'd thought I'd be better off reading after drinking some alcohol, because it seemed really tedious when I tried to do it sober. I'd been intending to make notes on it, but somehow that never happened. And the next morning, I'd almost completely forgotten what it said, so I had to read it all again!

"And when I got up in the morning, I realised I couldn't find my door key! I couldn't remember what I'd done with it! I did find it in the end though. At least I didn't go out without it and shut the door so I was locked out! I must at least have had enough brain power left not to do that, somehow!

"I woke up in the early morning and couldn't get back to sleep for ages. I've heard that can often happen to people after they've had some alcohol the night before; I think it's something to do with the effects it has on the system; it can help people get to sleep more quickly, but then they're more likely to wake up in the early hours of the morning, I think because of the efforts the body's making to process the alcohol, or slight withdrawal symptoms from it or something, so they end up not getting as much sleep as they need.

"But I managed to go back to sleep in the end. I had a horrible vivid dream though, where I woke up and looked at my alarm clock and it was really late, which made me think, 'Oh no!' And then I got up, still just in my dream, and discovered I'd broken something on my desk that I must have accidentally knocked off the night before when I was drunk, but I couldn't remember doing it. I examined it and wondered what to do about it. Then I woke up for real, and I was relieved when I realised it had just been a dream! But I wondered if I'd broken something for real and not consciously remembered doing it because I'd got too drunk to consciously remember things, but part of my brain had brought it up in a dream. So I was a bit worried about that. But I checked around my room, and nothing seemed broken, and I hadn't knocked anything off my desk after all; so I was glad about that!

"But I thought, 'Note to self: In future, wait five or ten minutes after drinking alcohol before deciding whether it's had an effect or not! It might just be taking a few minutes to kick in!' I'm hoping I'll have the sense to do that from now on!

"And it occurred to me the other day that instead of drinking in the first place to make me feel a bit braver, it might work if I just wait a while till I'm naturally in a less cowardly mood! It might happen, you never know! I got the idea after I felt like drinking a little bit again one day to give me the courage to do some other petty little thing I should really have the guts to do without needing any alcohol, but I didn't have any booze in my room, so I put off doing it, but then a few days later I felt a bit more courageous and felt like doing it when I hadn't been drinking at all! It would be nice not to be such a wimp really!

"But maybe I'll try and think of non-alcoholic ways of stopping myself feeling a bit nervous about going to speak to people, and also getting through boring coursework, and perking myself up a bit when I don't feel as if I can be bothered to do much. I'm hoping I'll think of something in the end!

"I'm still embarrassed to think about what I might have said to that girl when I gave her her book back and that perfume! I think when I meet her next, I might start worrying about it and feeling a bit embarrassed again!"

Bonnie said, "Don't worry too much. Things could have been worse. I read that someone on an Internet forum started a thread asking for advice, saying she was at college, and she'd got drunk not long before, and in her drunken state she decided it was a great idea to email a tutor she had a crush on and tell him all about it. Then the next morning she remembered she'd done it and got really embarrassed! She asked the people on the forum what they thought she ought to do about it. I don't know what she did in the end.

"Anyway, I've heard of people doing worse things than that when they've been drunk. At least you didn't go to give that girl's book back and throw up in her room or something! Just imagine it! You go to give her some perfume, and you say, 'I thought you might like this!' Then you throw up on the floor, and she says, 'Some gift! Thanks! I'll need that perfume you've got now to try to cover up the horrible smell you've just made, when I've cleaned up the mess! . . . No actually, I'd like you to do that! . . . Oh no, actually, maybe you'd better not, in case you make more mess by being sick again! You'd better just get out of here quick!'"

Heather and the other students laughed.

Then Suzy said, "A while ago, I found a thread on an Internet forum where people were all talking about embarrassing things they'd done when they were drunk, and one said she'd trained to be a paramedic, and when she and the rest of her class finished, they had a party to celebrate, and she got really drunk; and she was walking home when she saw there had been a car accident, and there were policemen around the place; and she went up to one of them, wobbling drunk, full of good intentions, and said, 'Is there anything I can do to help? I'm a paramedic.' I think the policeman just ignored her. She realised why the next day!"

They all chuckled.

Then Tom said, "I made a joke when I was drunk once that I regretted making afterwards. Well, it was a pretty harmless little joke really, but I think it annoyed one of my Facebook friends.

"For some reason, a status update from her husband popped up on my newsfeed. I'd never had any contact with him before. Actually, I'd never even heard his name. I didn't know he was her husband. I just thought that since he had the same surname as her, he was maybe a relative of hers.

"He said, 'I need a haircut, so I'm going under the shears tomorrow.'

"I replied, 'Is your hair made of grass then?'

"I'd only ever heard of grass shears before, so I thought what he said sounded amusing. I used to use those things when I was little to cut a bit of grass in my parents' garden ... Not to vandalise it, you understand, but just because my mum told me to.

"I wouldn't have asked that question about grass if I'd been sober, at least not to a random stranger. I might have said it to someone I knew, if I was confident they'd just take it as a joke. But I suppose if a random stranger says something like that to you out of the blue in reply to something you say on Facebook, you're not going to know whether they mean it as a joke, or whether they're mocking you, for reasons best known to themselves, and whether they might carry on."

Charlotte said, "I went out with some friends in the Easter holidays, and I like to have a maximum limit for drinking nowadays – not that I always stick to it – because I don't like to get drunk. That's ever since I did one night and ended up snogging a pest I didn't like, who I'd only met that night in a student bar, who started pestering me to go out with him. When he wouldn't go away for ages, I eventually decided it might be fun to kiss him a bit, even though I didn't like him, which I wouldn't have done if I'd been sober, so we did go out, literally – not far outside the door.

"I don't think I did a good job of kissing him though, because he walked away not long after we started, calling me a rude name, although I suppose that could have been because I was leaning up against him, not realising his back was being pushed into some railings, and there was a prickly bush just behind them. I suppose that might have hurt. What a pity! Oh well, serves him right for pestering me. We were both drunk, so I suppose we just didn't think to choose a sensible spot . . . Well, I was the one who chose it, but that was only because I wanted it to be somewhere near the door, so people who came out would be able to see us, because I didn't want to go somewhere private with him in case he got aggressive or insisted we do more than I wanted to do with him.

At least I still had the sense to think of that, although somehow I wasn't bothered about being seen kissing someone I hardly knew!

"Anyway, when I went out with some friends that time in the Easter holidays I mentioned, I ended up drinking more than I'd intended to, because we were out for a couple of hours longer than usual, and a couple of people offered to get me drinks after I'd had the amount I'd normally have, and I didn't think it would do any harm to have them; and then someone had this bottle of whisky, and let us all have a couple of mouth-fuls. It was funny actually – I thought it would taste too strong for me, so I asked if she'd mind if I had it with blackcurrant. She said, 'No! It was really expensive! That would be a waste!' So I decided to drink it neat. But it would actually have tasted a lot nicer with blackcurrant; it tasted like some kind of ointment, like Savlon or TCP! . . . Not that I've ever tasted that, but it tasted the way I can imagine it tasting. Someone else said they thought it smelled like that, and I said, 'It smells like the kind of thing you'd put on wasp stings!'

"Anyway, I gulped it down pretty much in one go, because I didn't like the taste and thought I'd get it over with. The person who'd offered it said, 'Wow, I can't even do that and I've been drinking it for years!' She thought it must mean I was a hardened drinker!

"Soon after that, I went to phone my parents somewhere quiet, just to reassure them that I was intending to come home soon, because they like me to do that; and it was weird, because for some reason, my dad's voice sounded like one of the men in my group of friends! I thought, 'This is so weird! Is this the effect the drink's had on me?' Alcohol's never had that effect on me before. I suppose it could have been just a strange effect caused by a dodgy phone signal. Anyway, I didn't want to speak to him for long because I thought it was weird!

"Then I went back and spoke to a couple of other people for a while. I'd wanted a break from my friends for a bit, because they'd got too rowdy for me. So I sat down with some other people I'd met before but didn't know that well. One of them was telling this sad story, that started years earlier when he first started working at the place, and I remember sitting there listening, caring about what he was saying. But it was strange, because a couple of minutes after he'd finished, I realised I couldn't remember what he'd said! I hadn't thought I was drunk at all, because I wasn't being rowdy or saying silly things or anything like that; I was just sitting there quietly . . . Well, I might have behaved like a bit of a twit a little while later when I was having a conversation with someone else, but not just then. I didn't feel drunk when I was just sitting listening to the others. And I didn't drink any more that night.

"But when I realised I'd forgotten this man's story, I thought, 'Could the part of my brain that retains information be beginning to shut down because of the drink or something?' It was odd, because I could remember a conversation I'd heard about twenty minutes before that really well, and I hadn't drunk anything after that! Maybe I was a bit sleepy; or maybe more alcohol had got into my bloodstream by then. I don't know. But it sounded to me as if I was slurring my words a bit too! . . . Not that it takes all that much to make me do that, probably!

"Anyway, after a while, this man said something about having worked in the place for forty years, and I was surprised, because I hadn't even realised the place had existed for that long! I just looked really surprised; and he said, 'Catch up!'

He must have said he'd worked there for decades before but I'd forgotten, and he must have thought I couldn't have been listening to him properly.

"I thought him telling me to catch up like that was funny, and it sparked off some thoughts that were amusing me; so I was just sitting there for a while with this grin on my face. But the next morning I thought about it, and it occurred to me that I shouldn't really have been doing that, since he'd just told this sad story, even though I couldn't remember what it was! I thought that maybe if I'd been sober, I'd have had the sense not to have been doing that. So I wondered whether it would have been better not to have drunk so much after all."

Colin said, "I was out drinking with a group of friends once when we were sitting on a river bank. I got up and slipped on some mud and fell in! It was just an accident, that could probably have just as easily happened if I'd been sober. I was alright; but a few weeks later, one of the others told me that one of the group, Brian, had been having a laugh about it since then, telling other people I'd done it when I was drunk, as if that was the reason it happened. Someone who hadn't been there even told me Brian called him over specially to tell him the story and have a laugh with him about it.

"It just shows you how you can get a bad reputation even if you don't deserve it! Mind you, Brian really had been accused of being a heavy drinker before then, after he started drinking the leftover drink in other people's glasses one night when he was drunk.

"But I started wondering if it was worth drinking when I was out with people after that! After all, thinking about it, I probably mostly just do it because everyone else is and I think it'll make things more fun, but I'm not sure it does really."

"At least not when you fall in a river!" quipped Becky with a grin.

Suzy said, "It probably isn't worth drinking on a river bank anyway, even though the place might feel nice and atmospheric or something, considering that some people are more likely to take silly risks when they're drunk, like going swimming in a river even if it's fast-flowing and there are rocks they could get injured on; or they could be more careless, like walking on bits of ground that they would have realised weren't stable if they'd been sober – I'm not saying that's what happened to you, Colin; but I think some people can do that kind of thing.

"I went on a canal trip in the Easter holidays with a group from university, and a couple of the lads had been drinking in a pub, and they somehow forgot to turn left to go down the towpath towards the boat when they got to the canal on the way back, and walked right into it! Splash! . . . Actually, we all thought that was funny! . . . Well, I'm not sure if they did, but the rest of us did."

Debbie said, "A couple of months ago, I was doing some really boring work, and I decided to drink some alcohol to help me manage to stick to focusing on it, since like I said, I've discovered alcohol helps me tolerate boring things without getting restless and distracted, just like it does for Heather, although I do wish I could find a healthier way of doing that, like she does.

"But anyway, it worked for hours. But I think I must have got a bit carried away and had a bit too much to drink. I didn't feel drunk. But I started feeling a bit sick. So I thought it might be a good idea to get up and go to the bathroom and lean over the loo in case my body wanted to throw up some sick in it. But when I got up, I started wobbling around, and realised I must be drunk. I wobbled towards the door, but just before I got there, I think I must have clipped my foot on something, and I overbalanced and fell over onto my back.

"I didn't bother getting up, because I felt comfortable there, and I thought it would be nice to stay there for a while. That's not the kind of thing I'd normally think; you know, I don't make a habit of lying down in the middle of my room and just staying there contemplating life or anything. It must have been the influence of the drink. I suppose it's lucky I didn't hit anything on the way down.

"I didn't think I'd hurt myself at all when I fell over; but the next day I noticed I had a bit of a lump on the back of my head where there isn't supposed to be one, and I went on a rowing machine in the gym, and my bum hurt a bit when I sat down on it. It didn't hurt when I sat on soft chairs. But it made me think I might have given my bum quite a clonk when I fell on it, as well as my head, without realising I'd done it at the time! I think people are often less sensitive to pain when they're drunk.

"But anyway, after a while of just lying on my back feeling comfortable after I'd fallen over, I think I went to sleep for a while. When I woke up, I didn't feel sick any more, and I got up without wobbling around, so maybe some of the effects of the drink had worn off by then.

"But I realised I was lucky I didn't vomit while I was asleep, because since I was lying on my back, I could even have choked on it and died, since it would have got caught in my throat instead of pouring out of my mouth, like it might have done if I'd been sick if I was lying on my stomach. I read that being drunk slows down the gag reflex as well, so vomit can get further into the lungs before a person gets the urge to cough or vomit it out, so they're more likely to seriously choke on it. I don't know how much I was really at risk; but I woke up the next day feeling glad I was still alive."

Dave said, half-joking, "Do you have to tell us so much detail about being sick? That's too much information! Ugh! How am I going to be able to eat my lunch now? . . . I know, I'll eat yours instead."

They all grinned.

A Student Tells the Others About the Long-Term Effects of Alcohol on the Body

Then Mya said, "I think it's worth hearing about this kind of thing, since it's worth remembering we ought to be a bit careful. I've read some things about the effects of alcohol on the body. They're not nice. It's pretty disappointing really! Most of the things that make people feel better seem to be bad for you!

"But I read that alcohol can have serious effects on quite a lot of body parts. One's the liver. Everyone's probably heard that. But I read some things I never knew before. Alcohol can damage the liver over time, but a person will likely never know about it till the damage gets pretty severe, because the liver's good at managing to do its job even when it's damaged a bit. I read that every time a person drinks alcohol, some of the liver cells die. But it's good at making new ones till the damage gets so severe it just can't do it any more.

"I read that drinking a lot of alcohol, even just for a few days, can bring on a build-up of unhealthy fats in the liver.

It can be a sign that harm's being done; but if there's no more drinking for a couple of weeks, the liver will get back to normal. But that means it's best for people to have a lot of breaks between the days when they drink alcohol, to give the liver time to make new cells and recover.

"But if a person carries on drinking a lot for some time, they can get worse liver problems, that can even become life-threatening if they do it for years.

"The worst is liver cirrhosis, where the liver gets pretty scarred, and the scarring can't be reversed. A person might still not get any noticeable symptoms for a while, so they might not realise they've got a life-threatening condition. But if they've got it and they give up drinking before it's too late, it at least won't get bad enough to kill them. If they leave it too long though, they can get liver failure and die.

"People who carry on drinking when they've got it have a more than 50 % chance of dying within five years.

"And alcoholic liver disease can increase people's risk of getting internal bleeding, and problems caused by toxins getting into the brain because they're not being filtered out of the system by the liver, because it isn't working efficiently any more; and they're also at risk of liver cancer, and kidney failure, and increased rates of infection, because the liver can't help protect them well any more.

"And I read that drinking alcohol quite a bit can increase people's risk of other cancers as well, including cancer of the mouth, the lips, the tongue, the throat, the stomach, the pancreas, breast cancer, and bowel cancer!"

Bonnie said, "Wow, I didn't even know some of those cancers existed! Imagine getting cancer of the tongue! What would doctors do, cut your tongue out or something? Yikes!"

Mya replied, "I don't know. But I read that drinking and smoking in combination increases the risk of that one a lot more than just drinking or smoking on its own, maybe because alcohol can enable harmful chemicals in tobacco to get inside the cells of the mouth and throat where they can do more damage and impair the body's ability to repair them.

"And alcohol can damage people's DNA, partly because while the alcohol's being digested by the body, it produces a toxic chemical, before that's broken down further into a more harmless one and flushed out of the system. But it's thought that the toxic chemical can cause problems with DNA while it's around that can increase people's risk of cancer.

"And I read that alcohol can cause the stomach to produce more acid than normal; and over time, if people drink a lot, that can cause the stomach lining to become inflamed, which can even make it bleed, and contribute to the development of stomach ulcers, and cause toxins to leak into the bloodstream. Some symptoms of that condition can be stomach pain and diarrhoea. Mind you, those things can be symptoms of lots of different things, so doctors would have to look for other signs of damage to the stomach lining if it was suspected.

"Another problem is that alcoholism can cause malnutrition, partly because people who are often drunk are less likely to feel like bothering to make healthy meals for themselves, and partly because alcohol can stop the stomach absorbing some vitamins and minerals so effectively, such as the mineral zinc, which everyone needs, partly because it helps the immune system function well and helps the body heal wounds. And alcohol can also make it harder for the body to absorb protein.

"I read that another thing zinc deficiency can do is to make it more likely that a person will get symptoms of irritability and depression. And I read that alcohol can stop the body absorbing B vitamins so effectively as well, and one of their functions is to help the brain make the feel-good chemicals dopamine and serotonin that can boost the mood. So regularly drinking a lot could make people feel more depressed or anxious over time, even if they feel better while they're actually drunk.

"And over the long term, I think there are other reasons why drinking a lot can increase people's risk of suffering depression and anxiety, or make them worse if they've already got them. I think it disrupts people's brain chemistry a bit. I read that some people with depression and anxiety who've been used to drinking a fair bit can actually start feeling better after a few days or weeks when they cut down on alcohol."

Bonnie said, "That's interesting. So some people might drink to try to stop themselves feeling anxious or depressed, when it's drinking as much as they do that's causing their mental health problems, or at least making them worse, without them realising!"

Matthew said, "Maybe lots of people think they need alcohol more than they really do. There was a thread on a forum recently where people were telling each other about their attempts to stop drinking or reduce the amount they drank, and a few of them said they'd been to family gatherings not long before, and they used to drink quite a lot when they got together with the family, but they hadn't had any alcohol the last time they were there, and they were surprised to discover they had just as much fun, or more fun, than they'd had before when they used to drink.

"Then again, one or two of the others said being around drunk family members was no fun at all while they were sober, because they just seemed silly, while they would have been just as silly themselves if they'd been drunk, so they'd have fitted in, not realising how they were coming across to anyone sober there."

Mya said, "It's nice to know at least some of them still enjoyed themselves. Maybe I'll start experimenting with staying sober when I go out in the evenings at some point. Not that I drink that much. I don't want to get into drinking any more than I do after reading about all the health effects drinking too much can have.

"I think too much alcohol can lead to depletion of some other vitamins and minerals besides the ones I mentioned, and that can contribute to mood problems like depression too. I read that reducing alcohol can help some people's recovery from things like that, when it's been one of the causes, alongside eating things that are high in the nutrients that can help restore the body's supply of the vitamins and minerals that can help improve the mood, like fruits and vegetables, and also eggs and dairy products like cheese.

"Another thing I read though is that alcohol somehow reduces the ability of the pancreas to produce digestive enzymes that help the body break down fats and carbohydrates so they can send any nutrients in them to places in the body where they'll do some good. I'm a bit vague on the details of that though, and can't remember if that was exactly what I read.

"But I think another reason why people lose some decent vitamins and minerals when they drink a lot is because alcohol makes people want to wee more, so they can wee out some vitamins and minerals the body might have otherwise used to do healthy things. I think I remember that that was what something I read was saying anyway. It might be worth investigating.

And people who drink a lot can vomit a lot as well, which gets rid of some nutrients that could otherwise help the body stay healthy . . . besides getting rid of some half-digested alcohol and half-digested food, of course."

Tom quipped, "Blimey this is a gloomy conversation! You're not being paid by the Salvation Army to tell us all this stuff to put us off drinking, are you?"

Mya joked, "No, but there's an idea! Perhaps I could offer to work for them, going round bars clanging a bell of doom and yelling about how alcohol's going to harm anyone drinking it."

Becky grinned and quipped, "You might have to get used to putting up with streams of insults coming your way!"

One of the Group Tells the Others About Some Humorous Conversations They Had on an Internet Forum

Then Charlotte said, "I used to post on this forum where there was this man who used to like insulting people, but his insults weren't very creative. He just used to call people sacks of vomit, and things like that. I'll call him Troglodyte for the purposes of this story, just for fun. If someone said something he thought was daft, he used to just swear at them or tell them he thought they were stupid. The threads were often quite playful though.

"One day he responded to something someone said by just saying, 'Dimwit'. I thought it would be fun to tease him for that, so I pretended to have misread what he'd said as gin dip, and said to him for a laugh,

68

" 'Why did you just randomly say gin dip? What is one of those anyway? Is it something you dip in gin, like chips that you use the way my brother used to sometimes use them, dipping them in his Coke at school? One day a boy went past him and saw him doing that, and grabbed one of his chips and dipped it in his Coke and then tasted it, and then walked off shouting, "That's disgusting!" But maybe you're one of the people who likes that kind of thing?

" 'Do you keep a supply of old cold chips around, so you don't have to go to the bother and time of cooking any whenever you suddenly decide you need a glass of gin with a "gin dip", so you can just take the days-old or weeks-old chips out from the back of the fridge and dip them in it right then? Don't they ever go mouldy, or do you still use them when they do, as if you think eating mouldy chips makes the experience even more special and exotic?'

"Troglodyte replied to me by saying, 'Always and incessantly insane.'

"I replied to him by joking, 'And as if to demonstrate that you are, you perform the stereotypical "first sign of madness", talking about yourself... Oh no, it's talking *to* yourself that's the first sign, isn't it. Talking about yourself, no matter how unflatteringly you do it, no matter if you're saying, "Hey look at me, I'm insane", isn't classified as a sign of madness, is it. Oh well, I suppose you can get away with it then.'

"I used to make fun of Troglodyte in other ways too, just playfully. Like there was one time when he was having an insult match with another man who called himself Vengeful Parrot on the forum, who really didn't like him and was saying abusive things, and I said to Vengeful Parrot, 'There's no need to be nasty to Troglodyte... Do something cunning instead. I've got an idea:

" 'Draw up a document known as The Insult Code. It'll be a list of words you substitute for his insults. Whenever he says something insulting to you, quote what he said when you reply to him, except you substitute one of the words in the Insult Code for the insult in the quote, so it just sounds funny. So, for instance, the word for vomit in your code could be lemonade. So if he calls you a sack of vomit, you quote his post back to him, only this time, his post seems to call you a sack of lemonade. Then you reply by saying something like, "What a funny thing to say! Why did you just call me a sack of lemonade?"

" 'If you do that kind of thing every time he says something insulting to you, he'll soon run out of insults he thinks will have some impact and wonder what to do. He might become bewildered and confused.'

"Not long before that, Vengeful Parrot had written a funny story, and the end of it was about someone killing Troglodyte . . . That bit wasn't so funny. I said, 'That was a great story. But did Troglodyte really need to be killed? Wasn't there a less harmful fate he could have suffered? Perhaps he could just be put in a caveman museum, with a notice above the big case he's being displayed in saying, "You might think what he says sounds like foul language; but this is how they used to communicate in the Stone Age, when language was just developing. It's just ordinary ancient language, and the words mean different things than what they mean nowadays. He really means things like, "I'm going to carve a tool from this stone", and, "Let me show you how to light a fire with these bits of flint".'

"And there was one time when Troglodyte insulted me, and I joked, 'How can I let myself be spoken to like that by a talking walking bale of hay! Oh yes, I remember the time when an extremely highly-qualified medical professional told us on here that after very careful examination and a myriad of tests, he'd concluded that that's what you are, among other things!

" 'Oh yes! I remember it well! He gave it as his most professional opinion that you've got frogs' legs for brains, weeds for hair, a chicken leg for a tongue, a carrot for a nose, an orange for a chin, paper plates for ears, a beer barrel for a neck, bamboo canes for arms, wet fish for hands, runner beans for fingers, table legs for legs, bricks for feet, stick insects for toes, tomato ketchup for blood, and twigs for bones!

" 'Then I remember he did some further examination in one of the best medical laboratories in the country, and he said he'd discovered you've also got potato skin instead of human skin, cherries for eyes, clothes pegs for teeth, a bale of hay for a torso, blocks of marzipan for cheeks, chips of flint for fingernails, eggshells for toenails, and dandelion leaves for a beard. You strange old thing!' "

The Students Talk More About the Harmful Effects Alcohol Has on the Body

Mya smiled and joked, "Maybe if we were all made of stuff like that, we could drink as much alcohol as we wanted to without it badly affecting us . . . Well, that's if it was actually somehow possible for people who were made of stuff like that to drink, or even to be alive! I wonder what effect alcohol would have on animated beings who had bales of hay for torsos and frogs' legs for brains."

Becky said, "They'd probably get very soggy stomachs, for one thing, with all that moisture clogging up the hay."

Then she became serious and asked, "Do you know any more about the effects of alcohol on real bodies?"

Mya said, "Yes. I read that it can cause brain damage over time. It can even cause a kind of dementia, if people keep drinking a lot of it, although it's often reversible if people with it stop drinking. That kind of dementia's partly caused by alcohol decreasing the body's ability to absorb and store and handle a vitamin that's important for brain function, vitamin B1.

"But also, I read that drinking a lot kills nerve cells in the brain, and it can shrink brain tissue. And people who drink a lot can also be more likely to fall and hit their heads, and get into fights that can cause them head injuries, which increases their risk of going on to get dementia too.

"Alcohol can increase people's risk of getting the kinds of dementia that aren't reversible, as well as causing some unlucky people who drink a lot over time to get that reversible kind.

"And drinking a lot of alcohol can increase people's risk of getting high blood pressure and having strokes as well.

"And if all that wasn't bad enough, alcohol's pretty high in calories!"

Debbie said, "I discovered that, after I drank quite a bit of Cinzano for a week to help me tolerate doing boring work – which a few of us seem to be using alcohol for, for some reason. A certain person on our course once told me she's even had a drink before a boring class sometimes, to dull her senses a bit, because she thought its tutor made it a mind-numbing waste of time that didn't teach anything worthwhile, and she was getting stressed at the thought of having to put up with any more doses of it . . . I'm not sure why she didn't just skip going to it a lot.

"Anyway, I'm glad most of our classes aren't like that!

"I know it sounds a bit extreme to drink to make a tedious class or boring essay writing feel easier to settle down to. I hope some of us aren't going to be rampant alcoholics by the time we're thirty! Mind you, I think I remember hearing somewhere that the people most likely to get addicted to alcohol are people who get a real buzz from it. I don't get a high from it; it just helps me feel less restless … and turns me into a twerp if I drink too much, I suppose. I wonder if some people get a lot more pleasure out of drinking it than others do, and whether the effect it has on people's minds depends to some extent on their genetic makeup or personalities.

"I don't know about all the reasons why people become alcoholics. I think one reason is if they get into the habit of drowning their sorrows or trying to dull other strong emotions with booze, either because they're in stressful or sad circumstances, or they've got some kind of mental illness, or because of the way they've got into the habit of dealing with routine annoyances and stresses by brooding on them a lot till they work themselves up more and more with anger or distress about them, till they can't stand feeling the way they do any more and feel the need to drink to relax and numb their feelings.

"Anyway though, I was going to talk about Cinzano, wasn't I."

She joked, "If I was on an Internet forum and started a thread about my Cinzano experience, and then I replied to myself with a post about alcoholics and drinking before boring classes, maybe a strict moderator would scold me for being off-topic, even though it was my own thread."

Then she continued, "Anyway, at the end of the week when I'd had all the Cinzano I said I drank, I began to feel a bit flabby! I wondered why. But then I looked on the Internet, and discovered Cinzano's really high in calories, probably partly because it seems to be sugary enough to make it taste a fair bit nicer than a lot of other alcoholic drinks. Well it does to me anyway.

"But then I got curious about the amount of calories in other alcohol, and I found out that all alcohol contains a lot of calories! I think it's something to do with alcohol being fermented from sugars, some of which are just there in the fruits that are used to produce some alcohol, or else it's fermented from starch in other foods, which is broken down into sugars and also contains a lot of calories. I read that a gram of alcohol contains almost as many calories as a gram of fat, and there are about eight grams of pure alcohol in a unit of booze. And bear in mind that most cans of beer are about two and a half units, which must mean that a lot of them contain the same amount of calories you'd get in about twenty grams of fat, just in their alcohol content, and that's besides all their other ingredients. Yikes!"

Becky said in an attempt to be reassuring, "A gram's very light though."

Debbie replied, "True. But I read that just three pints of good-strength beer can contain nearly half the number of calories it's recommended that people take in in one day! A lot of beers have about 240 calories per can, although it varies quite a bit; lower alcohol beers often contain fewer. But I read that lots of kinds of beer have around the same number of calories per can as a normal-sized Mars Bar . . . I wonder if it would be less unhealthy to eat a Mars Bar than it is to drink a can of beer.

"Some alcoholic drinks are a mixture of alcohol and other fattening things, especially if they're mixed with something that's high in sugar, that'll probably make them taste a whole lot nicer, but it'll mean they'll be more fattening."

Charlotte asked for fun, "Do you think you'd like beer better if it had Mars bars mixed in with it?"

Debbie grinned and said, "I doubt it! I wouldn't like to try that! Would you?"

Charlotte chuckled and replied, "No. It would probably be more like some kind of gel than a drink."

Then Debbie said, "Anyway, I learned that if you were to drink a whole bottle of Cinzano in one day, and nothing else – which obviously isn't recommended, because you'd probably end up pretty drunk – you'd be taking in well over the maximum number of calories a person's supposed to have in a day! I think I drank about half a bottle over the course of a day on most days during the week when I drank a lot of it, mixed with soft drinks, which would have had calories of their own; so it's probably no wonder I ended up feeling a bit flabby! Over the course of a week, I must have taken in the equivalent of well over three days' worth of extra calories! Something like that."

Dave playfully teased, "Flab monster!"

The Conversation Becomes Humorous Again

Becky was drinking a little carton of fruit juice. Just then, she accidentally dripped a bit on her clothes. She said, "Oh that's annoying! I've just spilled a bit of my drink, and it's gone on my clothes!

"Wouldn't it be good if clothes had special sensors in them that could tell if things were spilled on them, and they'd shoot them straight off again before they had a chance to stain them!"

Tom grinned and said, "You'd have to be careful. They'd shoot them straight into your eye if you had your face too close!"

Becky replied with a smile, "That's true. Maybe that idea needs a bit of work!"

Suzy said, "I actually watched a telly programme once about how there are plans to invent glass that can repel dirt somehow. I think there might be some kinds of chemicals in it that somehow react with daylight to stop the dirt getting stuck on it, and then rain washes it off more easily or something. I can't quite remember now, but it'll be good if it turns out to work well."

Bonnie grinned and said, "That sounds great! And wouldn't it be good if everything in our homes could be made to be self-cleaning! . . . Well, maybe not everything could be. I mean, I don't suppose it'll ever be possible for anyone to invent cups and plates and things that organise themselves into a team where one puts the plug in the sink, puts washing-up liquid in it and turns the taps on and puts lots of water in it, and then they all fly into the sink and wash themselves up. Wouldn't it be good if they could do that!"

Charlotte joked, "Yes, and imagine if things got even more sophisticated than that, and it became possible for us to have self-cleaning body insides, where waste products could be sorted from nutrients in there, and the waste products could be flushed out of the system . . . Oh hang on, we've got body parts that do that already, haven't we, like the digestive system and the liver and the kidneys. Silly me! . . . It's a pity they can be damaged by alcohol."

The Students Talk About
Toxins Affecting Developing Babies

Then Bonnie said, "My older sister had a baby not long ago, and she gave up drinking altogether for her whole pregnancy . . . Well I mean drinking alcohol, obviously. Giving up drinking altogether would have meant she didn't survive very long. I wonder if it would be possible to persuade some people that giving up drinking everything for a whole pregnancy was good for you. I mean, some people get hooked into believing really weird things, don't they. Hopefully if anyone ever did get persuaded to believe that, they'd give up the belief pretty soon!

"But giving up drinking alcohol for the whole of that time sounds pretty impressive, although it seems like a bit of a sacrifice."

Suzy said, "I know. It might be worth it though. I've read that unborn babies in the womb can be affected badly if the mum smokes or drinks alcohol, and some of the effects can last all their lives. I was reading something not long ago that said there are quite a lot of health problems children can develop if their mums drink or smoke, or even over-eat when they're pregnant with them, because harmful chemicals get passed into the babies' bloodstreams, and their livers aren't developed enough to break them down and get rid of them as easily as adults' livers can.

"It said there was a study that was done at a university that found that the children of women who even just had about one alcoholic drink a week were about three times more likely than the children of mothers who didn't drink while they were pregnant to be diagnosed with behavioural problems like aggression and more difficulty paying attention and remembering things, and diminished ability to think things through properly before doing them, so they could do more things that could be harmful as a result of not thinking through the possible consequences very well; and it said that women who even just had an average of one or two drinks a day had a higher risk of having kids with various learning difficulties and lower IQ's, as well as behavioural problems like ADHD.

"I don't know how high the risk really is, like how many children out of a hundred are thought to be affected, compared to the number of children of non-drinkers. Maybe it's not all that many. We can hope. And I don't know whether other things made a difference too that the study didn't take account of, such as if the women who drank the most were also the ones who were most likely to parent their children badly at times in their first few years, and that made part of the difference in their IQ levels and ADHD-type symptoms, but the study didn't investigate the effect of parenting styles on the kids.

"But what I read said the children of heavy drinkers can be at risk for all the problems I mentioned like ADHD, plus heart defects and hearing problems, as well as other conditions.

"There must be lots of different causes of those kinds of things, so it wouldn't be fair to just assume a mum must have been on the booze if you meet a child of hers and they've got a condition like that. But still, it's worth knowing that drinking can be a risk factor.

"One article I read quoted a doctor as saying it was very worrying that a lot of mothers had 'binged' on drink, by drinking six or more units of alcohol in a single session at least once during their pregnancies. I thought, 'What? You call that a binge? It's less than two good-strength pints of beer!' It sounds a bit worrying, how careful people really ought to be!

"And I read that smoking during pregnancy, especially all through the pregnancy, can put babies at risk of being born prematurely so they haven't had enough time to develop as well as they should have in the womb, so that makes them more likely to have health problems. And they can even be a bit more likely to have birth defects, like missing or deformed limbs. And a couple of articles I read said mums who smoke are more likely to have miscarriages, or their babies can be at a higher risk of dying from things like cot death.

"And one article I found said there was a study that discovered that babies of smokers can actually have what seem like withdrawal symptoms from nicotine, such as getting more stressed, and crying more and being more difficult to comfort than the average baby. And if the mums or the dads carry on smoking, the babies can get breathing problems and be more likely to have ear infections. The article even said they're quite a bit more likely to be hospitalised in their first year with pneumonia than babies of non-smokers!

"And I read that some scientists are doing studies that seem to be finding that smoking during pregnancy might cause problems for the children for years to come, because it could change how certain genes in them function in some way. I'm not sure how. And I don't know how big the risks of those kinds of things happening really are or how much smoking increases the risks. But I wouldn't want to start smoking, even if I knew it just increased the risks a bit.

"I think it's a good thing that there are at least organisations that can help people give up smoking and drinking if they're finding it hard to do it themselves!

"Maybe there ought to be organisations that help people give up junk food habits as well! I don't know, but I heard on a science programme on telly that if pregnant women eat a lot of junk food instead of nourishing things, their babies can be born less healthy than the babies of women who ate healthier food, and it might even affect their immune systems, and do other things as serious as that, because they won't have had enough nutrients in the womb to enable some of their bodily functions to develop as well as they should have. And it said they can have more tantrums and be harder to soothe than babies whose mums ate a higher percentage of healthy food when they were pregnant.

"Again though, I don't know how big the effects are, or how much higher the risk of those things happening is, or how confident the scientists were in those findings."

Debbie said, "Having a child sounds like a heck of a responsibility, doesn't it, when you have to start being careful about what you do right from when you're first pregnant, or ideally even before that, and even little things like drinking what you think is just a reasonable amount could make a difference to your baby's long-term health! Yikes!

"And you might have to go on making sacrifices for your children all your life! I know someone who's nearly seventy years old, and she's still babysitting for her grandchildren a lot because her own children want to work and do other things. She loves her grandchildren, and does like looking after them, but she'd prefer it if she had more time for herself, and she feels a bit used by her kids sometimes, and sometimes feels really tired after a long day of looking after her grandchildren. She'd like to do things for her own enjoyment that she hasn't got time for. But her kids rely on her a lot. It seems a shame really, as if her life isn't really all her own. And she might not have all that many years left to do things she'd enjoy doing.

"But it just shows how much of your life you can have to give to children if you have them. There might be lots of grandparents who babysit their grandchildren a lot. So it seems that women can start making sacrifices for their children right from when they first get pregnant with them, and they might still be making sacrifices for them over fifty years later, you know, like letting them have some of their money when they start running out, babysitting for them a lot, and who knows what else! Maybe if people could only ever get pregnant by choice, and everyone thought of having kids as meaning they'd have to make about half a century of sacrifice, no one would ever want them, and the human race would have died out long ago!

"But I've read that health professionals recommend that women don't drink alcohol even if they just think they might get pregnant, since it's especially likely to cause damage to a developing baby in the very early stages of pregnancy."

Charlotte said, "It really does sound like a sacrifice, giving up drinking altogether during pregnancy, when there might be days when you feel a bit down, and you just feel sure that having a couple of drinks would cheer you up, or if it's someone's birthday or something, and everyone around you's drinking and you feel left out, because you think you'd enjoy yourself more if you had something to drink, and at other times like that."

Bonnie said thoughtfully, "Well it might be hard to stay off alcohol completely, and obviously anyone who finds it really difficult should probably get help from an organisation that can give them professional advice and support like the health service.

"But if it's just a bit of a pain to stay off the booze, but nothing all that serious, there are probably things people can often do to substitute for it. Like if someone's feeling a bit down, maybe sometimes a big hot nourishing meal would cheer them up, or a bit of exercise – well, I'm not sure that would help me, but with some people it might – or a chat with a friend, or finding something funny to laugh at, or getting absorbed in something they enjoy, or where they're feeling an emotional connection with someone who's going through problems of their own, so they can sympathise with each other and feel as if they're kind of companions in going through things that are bothering them. Or they could do things that stimulate their brain power in a nice way, so they start to feel as if they're doing something enjoyable, or they at least get distracted from feeling fed up, like if they learn something interesting, or go to a forum and debate something they're keen to talk about, or do whatever else would perk them up."

Becky and Another Student Tell Stories About People in Boring Jobs Who Found Ways to Motivate Themselves to Get Down to Work or to Make Work More Fun

Becky smiled and said, "That's if they're not at work, presumably – although drinking alcohol at work wouldn't be a good idea either, of course! I wonder what would help people who are working.

"I wonder if some of Bonnie's ideas might work for you, Heather and Debbie, so you end up in a better mood to just get on with doing your essays . . . I suppose doing things you enjoy first could have the opposite effect though, and you could get so engrossed in them that you just don't get around to working.

"I've heard of one thing you could try: I think sometimes it helps to decide on a specific length of time you're going to work for, say an hour, and decide that after that, you're going to get up and reward yourself for sticking at it for that long by having a cake or something. And you split the day up into chunks of time like that, working for say an hour, and then getting up to reward yourself with something, unless you've got so absorbed in what you're doing you don't feel like stopping.

"That means that when you get down to work, you won't be put off by feeling as if you're going to have to be slogging non-stop all day, but you'll have your cake or some other reward to look forward to every hour, and you'll know it won't be all that long till you can have a short break from work and eat it, so you'll probably feel more cheerful, because you'll be looking forward to it; so that might make it easier to work.

"Actually, we could all try that. It might help us get motivated to slog through revision for weeks before our exams, now they're coming up ... Mind you, I suppose we'd better not eat a cake every single hour of every day for weeks, till the exams are over and we can have a break from work, or imagine how fat we'll all be by the end of it! Maybe we ought to try and think of other things we can reward ourselves with sometimes."

The others chuckled.

Then Becky said, "I've read about people who had really boring jobs, who managed to find ways of making them more bearable. Maybe we could think about whether there's anything about their stories that could spark off ideas we can use to help us make our work more interesting.

"There was a man who worked in a factory and thought his job was really boring, because he was just doing the same thing over and over again. But he didn't feel like leaving because he was worried he wouldn't get another job. One day he had an idea and had a chat to the man working next to him, and they decided to have races to see which one could work the fastest. They both found they enjoyed their jobs more after that, probably partly because the competition gave them an adrenaline boost so they felt more lively. It must have been a job where going faster wouldn't have put them at risk of getting more careless and making mistakes.

"Then the foreman was impressed with the speed and accuracy of the man who'd had the idea for the competition, and gave him a better job. Over the next few decades, he got promoted to higher and higher positions, till he was actually president of the company!

"I don't suppose such dramatic success stories as that happen very often, but even just making work more fun must make it worth making the effort of trying things out.

"And there was one woman who had a really tedious job in an office, just filling in forms with figures and statistics all day, who decided to make it less mind-numbing and try to get a bit of an adrenaline boost to cheer herself up, by having a competition with herself to see if she could get more forms filled in in the morning or the afternoon. Not my idea of fun, but still! She'd count the number she'd done each morning and try to beat that number in the afternoon. Then the next day she'd try to beat the number she'd done the day before. And so on. Soon she was filling in the most forms out of everyone in her department. And she found she was leaving work in a better mood than she had before every day, and that gave her more energy to enjoy her spare time more.

"And I read about another man who got really successful after having a boring job. Mind you, he ended up doing something I wouldn't fancy, but it seems he really enjoyed it!

"At first, when he was a boy, he had a boring job in a school, washing up and scrubbing worktops, and dishing out ice cream to other boys. I don't know why he was working there when he was just a boy. But anyway, he thought it was boring and felt left out when he saw other boys playing outside in the sunshine. He'd love to have been out there with them. But then he decided to make the job more interesting by studying ice cream, learning what ingredients went into it and how it was made, and what made some ice creams have a better quality than others. He was studying chemistry, and decided to find out all about the chemistry of ice cream. That made him more interested in his chemistry course so he did better in it. He Got so interested in the subject that he even decided to go to college and study food chemistry.

"Later in life, he was finding it difficult to get a job, so he started a laboratory in the basement of his house, hoping he could hire himself out to do jobs there. Not long afterwards, a new law was passed that decreed that the bacteria in milk needed to be counted, maybe to make sure they weren't at dangerous levels. He thought it was just the job for him! So he advertised his services, and soon he was counting bacteria for all the milk companies in his town. He was getting so much work he had to hire two assistants!

"There can't be many people who end up counting bacteria for a living! Well, there can't be many people who want to!

But the story just shows that you can be better off if you try to think of ways of making things you're doing more interesting, if you can, although it's probably a lot easier to make some things more interesting than others!"

Bonnie said, "That reminds me of something I read. Nothing to do with bacteria this time. There was a man who didn't mind his work, but it was summertime, and he really wished he could be out sailing and hiking and having picnics with his girlfriend, who was a teacher so she was off for the summer. He would sit at work thinking about it, and that made him feel more miserable, so he felt even less like being there. As soon as he got to work, he would think, 'I don't want to be here!' and he'd think thoughts like that all day, getting more and more miserable the more he thought them.

"That meant he just couldn't concentrate on his work, so he got behind, and he got more and more annoyed about having to be at work, till at the end of each day, he went home feeling miserable, dreading having to go back, so he wasn't in the mood to enjoy his spare time. And he felt guilty about not getting much done.

"He realised something needed to change, but he couldn't think of anything that worked. At first, he tried telling himself, 'You're being an idiot! You're stuck here, so you've just got to put up with it! Just get on and do some work!' But he found that dispiriting, so it didn't help him to get down to work at all!

"Then someone asked him what he'd say to a younger person having the same problems as him. He said he'd tell them they'd start feeling better if they got down to work. The person trying to help him asked whether he thought it would help him if he often said that to himself, and how he thought it would help him if he actually did get down to work.

"The man said he'd get more done, so he'd leave at the end of the day in a better mood, not feeling guilty about not having done much, so he'd enjoy his free time more.

"He decided to write the phrase, 'You'll start feeling better if you get down to work' on a piece of paper, and stick it on his desk in a place where only he would see it. Then he often read it to remind himself.

"It took him three weeks to stop having all the thoughts about how he was unhappy being at work and would prefer to be out in the sun, but when he did, he felt a lot better, and was spending a lot more of his time working, so he wasn't leaving work feeling guilty and unhappy any more."

Debbie said, "Actually, I've noticed that if I'm studying or writing an essay about something that's quite interesting really, once I'm absorbed in it I can sometimes find myself enjoying it; but I often can't predict when that'll happen, so it can take ages for me to get down to doing it if I feel as if I can't be bothered. I can just mooch around sometimes feeling discontented, or distract myself with something else for some time. Maybe if I keep trying to persuade myself I'll likely feel better once I've got down to it, it'll be easier, although I can imagine it being hard to convince myself sometimes. It might be worth a try though. It'll be healthier than using alcohol to undither myself anyway, I suppose. I call alcohol my undithering juice. But it would be nice if I found another way of motivating myself to just get on with things."

—

The Students Discuss Things That Can Hinder and Help People Reduce Their Alcohol Consumption

Mya said, "I heard something on the radio not long ago that said that for people with more serious drink problems who are beginning to contemplate giving up the booze, one thing that can sometimes help them decide to, and help them stick to their decision, is motivational counselling, partly because it can give people hope that their lives can improve if they give alcohol up. It's all about encouraging people to think of different ways their lives could get better if they did, and then helping them plan ways they can improve it if and when they do.

"And one thing I've heard can help people who've recently made the decision to go sober is trying to make a new set of friends, people who socialise without drinking much and don't normally talk about alcohol. That'll make it easier for them to stick to their decision to give up the booze than they'll find it if they're often in the pub with the other alcoholics or heavy drinkers they might have spent time with before, because if they still spend time with those, they'll be reminded of booze all the time, and they'll likely often be tempted to indulge in it, because they'll see people around them doing that all the time. So kicking the habit will be a lot harder. It's similar for drug addicts.

"I can see the logic in often spending spare time with people who don't even talk about alcohol; I mean, even if you're with people who are talking about how they really need to get sober, it's going to keep putting alcohol on your mind, isn't it, and just the thought of it might start you wishing you had some.

"I'm not saying it's unhealthy to be in a support group of people all trying to give up the booze. That could be encouraging for people who feel comforted to know they're not alone with their problems, and that there's help and understanding on offer. It's just that they might do best if they're not exposed to excessive conversation about alcohol, since that might just stir up a longing in them for it.

"I mean, you can see how that could happen, can't you, because it would happen with other things too:

"For instance, imagine if you were going shopping, and most of the time when you went, you'd feel a twinge of grumpiness when you went past the chocolate bars, because you'd always feel tempted to buy one or two, but you knew you'd better not, because everyone needs to keep their weight under control. Well imagine if you decided that to try and stop yourself being tempted, every time you went past the chocolate bars from then on, you were going to say to yourself, 'I mustn't have a chocolate bar! I need to stop my temptations to have a chocolate bar! I need to stop thinking about chocolate bars!' Well you might discover that your craving for them suddenly intensified massively, because instead of feeling that twinge of craving and grumpiness and then forgetting about it as you moved on, it would be on your mind for longer, and the more you insisted to yourself that you couldn't have one, the more you'd be reminding yourself of how much you wanted one. So the more you'd be sparking off a longing for one in yourself.

"Try it . . . if you don't mind risking getting addicted to chocolate.

"Mind you, it's probably different if you just think, 'Right, I've got to stop thinking about chocolate', and then go off and get involved in something else, so soon you just automatically start thinking about something different, so you haven't got chocolate on your mind any more.

". . . I wonder if it's possible to get chocolate withdrawal symptoms if you eat chocolate every day for a while and then stop. Probably – well, minor psychological ones anyway. I remember hearing that chocolate's actually got a substance in it that boosts a feel-good chemical in the brain a bit. I think some other foods have too. I think cheese might. I'm sure I've had cheese withdrawal symptoms once or twice before, feeling a bit down till I've had cheese again . . . Obviously I'm not saying that would be serious, like alcohol withdrawal symptoms. Imagine it, having to go to Cheeseaholics Anonymous to help you come off the cheese, or having to go to hospital or the doctor to get medication to help you withdraw from your cheese addiction!"

The others chuckled.

Then Heather said, "The other day I ran out of chocolate; and the next morning, a couple of things made me feel a bit depressed and as if I couldn't be bothered to get on with anything, and I thought chocolate would cheer me up a bit. I started craving it a bit. Then I thought, 'I think I must be having chocolate withdrawal symptoms. I really need to get some more!'

"Then I wondered if I might be a bit addicted to it, and I thought for fun that maybe there ought to be an organisation called Chocoholics Anonymous. Not that I can imagine many people wanting to go to it, unless it was a fun one where their twelve-step programme was all done in the course of a day and went something like:

"Step one: Buy yourself a good-sized chocolate bar. Step two: Open it. Step three: Eat a bit. Step four: Eat a bit more.

Step five: Eat a bit more, why not! Step six: Eat another bit! Step seven: You've probably nearly finished it by now, so you may as well go on and eat the rest! Step eight: Buy some more. Step nine: Eat a chunk or two. Step ten: Eat some more, why not! Step eleven: Eat a bit more! Step twelve: Go on, eat the rest, why not!

"Actually, I'd like it if it was an a hundred step programme, and all the steps just repeated themselves like that!"

Matthew sniggered and said, "If you went on that programme and did all that in one go, you'd probably make yourself really sick, and every time you thought of chocolate after that, the memory of feeling really sick would flash into your mind and put you right off the idea of eating it, so you'd never feel like eating it again! . . . I suppose that would be one way of curing a chocolate addiction!"

They all giggled.

Then Mya said, "That doesn't work with alcoholics who get hangovers, or drink so much they vomit. Mind you, maybe that's because the good feelings some people get from alcohol last a lot longer than the odd bit of vomiting, and people don't get hangovers while they're getting drunk; people wake up with them the next morning, so maybe they're not connected so much in the mind with doing the actual drinking.

"Actually, I heard a psychotherapist give a lecture where he said the reason people can start longing for a drink when they hear someone talk about having a nice drink in the pub or they go past a pub can be because immediate memories come into their brains of times when they enjoyed themselves with friends in pubs, and they want that feeling again. It's the feeling of enjoying themselves with friends they want, but it can make them crave alcohol, because they usually drink alcohol when they're doing that, so they associate drinking with having a good time.

"They're far more likely to quickly remember things like that than the hangovers they had, because the part of the brain that immediately brings memories to mind won't instantly associate those with drinking, because they'll have happened the next day, not while they were actually drinking.

"I once heard someone else say she'd heard that when people have an alcoholic drink and then want more when they weren't that bothered about having one before they started drinking, it's not really a personal desire for more, but the chemicals in the alcohol creating a craving for more. She said knowing that helped her give up drinking when she decided she'd been drinking too much every day and she was unhappy about it. I've read the stories of a few recovering alcoholics who said they didn't have a craving to drink till after their first one, but then they did, so they would drink more and more, and end up drunk.

"The woman who said she'd found it helpful to know it wasn't her personal desires fancying alcohol after her first glass but the chemicals in the alcohol influencing her said another thing that had helped her give up was not putting herself under the pressure of telling herself she was giving up for good, but just telling herself she was giving up for as long as she decided to. That meant she didn't get thoughts about how she wouldn't be able to have alcohol ever again that might have made her anxious and brought on cravings for it as a reaction to feeling as if she'd be missing out, but she could feel calm about the idea, knowing that whether she drank or not was up to her. But she actually got to prefer her lifestyle without the drink."

92

Bonnie said, "That's interesting. I've heard something similar, that one thing that can help people who've been heavy drinkers and alcoholics who've started to go sober to resist cravings for alcohol so as to try to prevent themselves relapsing is if when the urge for booze comes on, rather than coping with the anxiety of telling themselves they've forbidden themselves to drink, they tell themselves they'll decide whether to allow themselves to have a drink if they've still got the cravings after fifteen minutes. Chances are the cravings will have died down by then, especially if they've become absorbed in something in the meantime so their minds are taken off them; but if the cravings haven't gone, they can decide again at the end of the fifteen minutes whether they really need a drink, or whether they'll try waiting another fifteen minutes to see if the cravings go down to tolerable levels or disappear in that time.

"Then after that fifteen minutes, if the cravings are still strong, they can make another decision about whether they can cope with waiting a bit longer for them to die down, or whether they really need a drink. And it can go on and on like that. But the cravings will likely fade over that time."

Matthew said, "I can see how that could work. It'll be nice if it helps some people resist the temptation to relapse. I'm not sure it would work for people who are just starting out trying to give up alcohol though, since people with serious alcohol problems often need medical treatment as well as psychological techniques to help them give it up, because suddenly giving up after drinking heavily every day for some time can cause physical withdrawal symptoms that can even be life-threatening.

"I've heard stories from people who managed to give up alcohol after their doctors gave them medication to help them.

One said his doctor gave him a week's worth of tranquillisers to stop him getting dangerous physical withdrawal symptoms, and he had a high dose for the first few days and slept through most of it, and then tapered them off over the next few days till he could cope without them. I'm not sure how the tranquillisers prevented the withdrawal symptoms coming on."

Debbie said, "I heard someone say he was put on a medication that stopped him craving alcohol, so reducing the amount he drank over time and then giving it up altogether wasn't a problem for him."

Suzy said, "I remember reading that about half of all alcoholics who try to come off the booze will have withdrawal symptoms. I think that's the statistic anyway; and I think I remember reading that some scientists think it happens because something in alcohol substitutes for a chemical the brain produces, so it stops producing it when people drink all the time, or there would be too much of it, and it still doesn't produce it for a while when they stop, maybe because the part of the brain that regulates its chemical balance is still expecting it to come from alcohol. But the body needs the chemical, so that causes problems. So it helps if people go on a kind of medication while they're withdrawing that substitutes for the chemical; and then the medication can be gradually reduced, so the brain gets used to producing it itself again over time.

"I don't know how heavily a person has to drink and for how long before the brain stops producing that chemical or reduces the amount it produces, or whether it varies from person to person, depending on their genetic makeup or something."

One Student Tells the Others About Motivational Interviewing, Designed to Persuade Addicts to Give Up What They're Addicted to

Mya said, "I'll tell you a bit about motivational counselling. I meant to say something about it before, but I must have got sidetracked. I remember reading that it's used to increase a person's motivation to give up the booze, or drugs, or gambling, since a lot of heavy drinkers or drug addicts or gamblers won't want to give what they're addicted to up, even if they know it's ruining their health, or causing problems with their relationships or family, or they're going short of money because of it. They'll enjoy the sensations the thing they're addicted to causes too much, or they'll be worried they'll get horrible withdrawal symptoms if they come off it if it's a substance, and they might have other reasons too.

"I think someone who's doing motivational counselling with them will reassure them about ways they can kick their habit without having too many nasty symptoms, and encourage them to come up with ideas about the things they think they could gain by giving it up, in the hope that when they think and talk about that kind of thing more and more, they'll decide it would be worth giving it up after all, and that they've actually got more to gain by doing that than by staying addicted.

"Then the counsellor helps them plan just how they'll go about improving their lives over time if they do give it up.

"I read that if someone knows they really ought to give up the booze, or some other substance or activity they're addicted to, but they really don't feel like it, it can help them decide to if a motivational counsellor, or just anyone really, first shows them some understanding about how it must be hard to give it up, and then, instead of trying to persuade them to, by talking about the harm they're doing to themselves and maybe their families, which might just sound like a lecture that tells them things they already know but don't want to hear, so it might make them want to just stop listening, the counsellor or ordinary person suggests that the addict themselves thinks through in detail what the benefits are of carrying on taking what they're addicted to, versus the things that aren't so good about it.

"It'll often turn out that the addict's got a few reasons why they want to carry on taking what they're addicted to, such as because of the high it gives them, and the companionship of their addict friends when they're all taking the substance together, or how it can help them relax and become more chatty so they can have better conversations with people, or how it stops them feeling stressed.

"But according to what I read, addicts normally have a much longer list of reasons why it would be a good idea to give up what they're addicted to, and more serious ones, such as the bad effect it has on their families' attitudes to them when they do stupid or reckless or cruel things under the influence of it, how they're at risk of being sacked from their jobs, how they might be arrested for things they do under the influence, and maybe other things like that. And it'll be brought home to them after a while that their own reasons for thinking changing is a good idea are more important than their reasons for wanting to stay addicted, and that there are more of them. They might start to think about them a lot more often and a lot more deeply after discussing them.

"A motivational counsellor can ask them questions that inspire them to do that. They can be asked what they think the future will hold for them, both if they stay as they are, and if they give up what they're addicted to.

"Apparently, it's worth trying to persuade someone who's addicted to alcohol or drugs or gambling to get some motivational counselling even if they're opposed to giving up what they're addicted to, since it could change their minds.

"I read that it's common for therapists who try to counsel addicts when they aren't trained in the motivational technique to make the mistake of giving them all the reasons why it would be a good idea for them to change, and then to find themselves in an argument with them, because the addict will just reel off the reasons why they think they can't change. But it seems it's actually possible to get the addicts to be the ones who list all the reasons why they ought to change, and then to even start to think of change as a good thing, instead of an impossible one that they don't really want.

"A therapist can try to do that by asking them what their hopes and dreams and expectations for their future were when they were younger, and how well they've been living up to them so far, and also about how they think people ought to ideally live their lives, and how they would ideally like to be living themselves.

"Then the therapist can ask them what things they think they'll have to do to start living a life that's more in line with the kind of life they themselves think is a respectable life, the life they'd like to live if they could, that's more like the life they maybe used to imagine they'd be living when they got to be older. And the therapist ought to ask how they think what they're addicted to gets in the way of living the life they would ideally like to be living. Then the addict themselves will likely start talking about reasons why their lives would be better if they changed.

"All the while, the therapist needs to show them understanding, like when the addict talks about how hard it is to give up what they're addicted to.

"After the questions about what kind of life they'd ideally like to be living and all the ways their addiction stops them living it, they can be asked how likely they are to make the changes they know they'd have to make to be able to live more the way they'd ideally like to, and what they think stands in the way, as well as what or who there is around them that could help them make the changes.

"When they've answered, the counsellor might ask them a question like, 'On a scale of zero to ten, how important to you is it that you give up what you're addicted to?'

"If the addict gives a number higher than zero, the counsellor can ask them how come it's that number rather than a zero. Then the addict might start talking about the reasons why they know giving up the habit would be a good idea really, even though they're not keen, maybe even saying things they'd have been annoyed to hear from someone else trying to persuade them to give it up, because then they'd have felt as if they were being nagged or something.

"It's best that a counsellor doesn't ask them why the number they picked was less than ten or so low, because then they'll start talking about all the reasons why they're not keen on changing, and they'll maybe end up convincing themselves it would be a bad idea.

"The counsellor might feel tempted to give them more reasons why changing would be a good idea if they haven't come up with many; but like I said, it's best not to, because then the addict might start to feel as if they're being pushed into it, so they'll likely argue against what the counsellor's saying, telling them why changing would be harder than they seem to think, and why they'd prefer to stay the way they are. And the more they argue, the more they'll convince themselves that changing would be a bad idea or impossible.

"So it's best if they come up with the reasons why changing would be a good idea themselves, and if the counsellor tries to respect their opinions as far as they can, and tries to understand why they're the way they are, instead of trying to persuade them to change. The addict might respond quite differently from the way they might if they think they're just being ordered to change or something and it makes them feel defensive. They can feel encouraged instead if they feel as if their concerns are really being listened to, although some might make a lot of excuses that aren't really the concerns they're making them out to be.

"That doesn't mean the counsellor shouldn't suggest various possible benefits of giving up addictions and ask them for their opinions about them. The addict might never have thought about them before. But some of the benefits might occur to them themselves while they're thinking through the answers to the counsellor's questions.

"Some other questions a motivational counsellor or interviewer might ask are things like, 'Where would you like to be with your life five years from now?' 'What do you really want out of life?' and, 'If you do decide to kick the habit, how will you go about it?'

"If the addict's expecting the counsellor to argue with them to try to persuade them to give up what they're addicted to, even if they haven't, they might start insisting that it'll be really hard to give the addiction up. But if instead of arguing, the counsellor just paraphrases what they're saying back to them and asks questions, like saying, 'It seems from what you're saying that realistically, you're not going to be able to make a change in your life. What do you think about that?' then if they really do want to change deep down, they won't like the thought that there's no hope for them, and they might say that change isn't impossible, and start talking about how it might be done. But the person helping them needs to respect the fact that it will be difficult for them, and show understanding of what they personally want out of life, for the addict to have enough confidence in them to really want to work with them, so the technique's more likely to succeed.

"That's the gist of the technique anyway. I thought what I read was interesting."

The other students thought it was too.

Matthew said, "I think addicts can get discouraged sometimes if they try to give up what they're addicted to and fail; but I've heard that the more attempts they make to give it up, the more likely a lot of them are to succeed in the end, and they often manage to give it up for longer each time they try. And they can find their quality of life improves more and more over time when they do, for reasons such as that they can develop better relationships with their families and other people, they'll have more money, and they can achieve more in life."

The students were pleased to hear that.

They discussed things for a while longer, and then parted.

Chapter 4

Becky Has a Laugh in the Park
Talking With Friends

On one spring afternoon, when Becky and some of her friends were taking time off from doing their work to sit in a park chatting, enjoying the sunshine and the sight of ducks on a pond and the new flowers, one of them, Mandy, said,

"I found out something interesting today. I expect we all think of names like Gladys and Mabel as old people's names that must have been popular years ago but are well out of fashion now. But I was reading a book that said they only came in at around the beginning of the 20th century! It wasn't a book by someone who studies these things, so it's possible it might have been wrong; but it's interesting if it's true. I wonder where the names came from. They can't have been fashionable for long then."

One of the group, Luke, said, "Like the fashion for clothes. I read a funny Oscar Wilde quote recently that said, 'Fashion is a form of ugliness so unbearable that it has to be changed every six months.'"

Mandy replied with a grin, "Come on; I don't like those names; but I'm not sure they're ugly enough to deserve to have been replaced as soon as that."

Luke responded, "I didn't say they were."

Becky said, "I wonder where those names came from. Hey, imagine if the first letters of names had to change every year as a sign of how many years it was since the name was officially classified as being well-known in the country. So all the parents who wanted to call their baby girl Jane would have to call her Pane if she was born six years after it was classed as well-known. And a parent who would have liked to call their daughter Ruth would have to call her one that sounded like Tooth if she was born two years after the name was recognised as well-known. And every 27 years it would get back to the same letter."

Luke chuckled and said, "Yeah, so three years after the name Clare became popular, it would be Flare, and the year after that it would be Glare. And one year, the name Deborah would have turned into something that sounded like Zebra."

Mandy said, "What about some of the letters in between? In some years names would be hard to pronounce. Clare would be Dlare the year after it was Clare."

Becky replied, "I expect some people would give up trying to pronounce them and give kids nicknames instead of the names their parents gave them. They might call Dlares Snares and things."

Luke said, "Imagine how embarrassing it would be if you were a famous person with a funny name, like if you were called a name that sounded like Zebra because your parents would like to have called you Deborah but couldn't, because it was the year when the name Deborah had to start with a Z instead of a D!"

Becky said, "Or what if people got called ordinary names, but they had to change them every year and call themselves something that began with the next letter of the alphabet, as some kind of record of how old they were. Actually that would cause chaos, like if everyone had to get their driving licences updated every year so they would have their proper updated names on them, and they weren't allowed to drive till they had their new ones. And every year on Facebook, they'd have to update their names and tell everyone their new names. So for instance, Someone called Tony would have to tell all his friends he'd become Bony one year, and Fony another. And one year his name would be Pony."

Mandy said, "Just think, one year you'd have to call yourself Muke, Luke, and the next year Nuke!"

Luke laughed and said, "What a horrible system! I'm sure there would be lots of people trying to change the law that brought that system in!"

Becky replied, "I don't know. If people thought that was the way things had always been, they might just accept it and not even think of trying to change it."

Mandy said, "Maybe it would depend on how chaotic things got. Anyway, why would it have come into being in the first place? Mind you, I've been reading about stupid laws on the Internet, although it seems some of them might not be real. I read that a supposed law that says it's illegal to die in the houses of parliament was voted Britain's most ludicrous law, but it turned out it doesn't really exist! Maybe there's one a bit like it though, I'm not sure. Imagine a law being made by people who were convinced everyone could tell when they were going to die, and that they could be punished afterwards if they broke the law by dying where they shouldn't! Surely you'd have to believe those things to make a law like that? Some websites say the law's real though, along with claiming lots of other laws are real that other websites say are fake.

"I don't know why people said they thought the one about dying in the houses of parliament was the most ludicrous, instead of saying to the person who told them it existed, 'Come on, I know politicians can be a bit daft, but I can't imagine them enacting a law that silly! Why would they ever have done it?'

"Mind you, there are some laws that I think are definitely real that would sound daft if they were applied today, but they made sense in the old days. I've heard there was a law that said taxi cabs had to have a bag of hay in the back or they were breaking the law. It was only repealed in 1976. But I don't suppose anyone got prosecuted for not carrying hay after taxis all became motorised . . . or at least I hope they didn't! In the old days before that, taxis were horse-drawn, and the horses would need to be fed, so it might have been cruel not to keep hay handy for them."

Becky said, "Maybe the make-believe laws about names changing might have come in in the old days before people had birth certificates or could read and write, as a way to try to make sure people weren't underage when they went into a pub or something. I mean, what if someone called Mark went into a pub. When he was about 14 he'd be called Bark, and when he was about 16 he'd be Dark. So when they asked him his name, if he said Dark or Bark or Cark, they'd know he was underage."

The others laughed, and Luke said, "You might have your maths a bit wrong there, but never mind. Those bar-tenders would have had to be pretty good at maths themselves to work out if people were underage! But anyway, I bet they didn't have age limits for drinking in those days. I think most people left school before they were twelve, if they even went to school at all, and most people drank beer – even the kids, because the water was so horrid and dirty, and there weren't many other drinks around."

Mandy said, "Wow, they must have all gone around half-drunk! Maybe that's how they got through life when the standard of living was so much worse than it is today."

Becky said, "OK then, what if a tyrannical government with a sense of humour ruled, and thought they'd bring in some stupid laws just to inconvenience people, because they thought it would be a laugh? Maybe they'd bring in a law that said that it was illegal to do a fake Australian accent in a public place, and anyone caught doing one would have to confess what they'd done on the steps of the town hall at midday on a Saturday. Maybe that would be the punishment for lots of little crimes they invented, and Confession Time would become a public entertainment, and lots of people would go to listen, just as people used to go to watch hangings. Maybe writing a public sign with no apostrophe in a word that should really have one would be another offence punishable by being made to publicly confess the crime at a Confession Time.

"And imagine if they made it illegal to make a spelling mistake in a letter or email written on a Monday or Tuesday. It would be alright to make them the rest of the week, but on a Monday or Tuesday the person who made it could be punished by being made to go back to school for a day with kids who were in their first year of primary school, and the kids would be told by the teacher that the adult was there because they'd made spelling mistakes even after years of education.

"Or what if it was illegal to wear a woolly hat between say, the 10th of March and the 23rd of October, because the law decreed that the weather would be bound to be too warm for it between those dates, so it would be a perversion to wear one then; and anyone who was caught wearing a woolly hat between them would be made to kneel in front of a field of sheep for several minutes and apologise loudly for misusing the products of their good bodies, and they'd have to beg forgiveness from them?"

The others chuckled, and Mandy said, "Yikes, and we think our government's bad!"

Luke said, "Just imagine if another offence was vandalising the grass by sitting or lying on it, and the punishment was to count all the leaves on a tree with a policeman watching, and if you lost count, you'd have to go all the way back to the beginning and start again, and keep going back every time you lost count till you managed to count them all without any mistakes. Becky, you'd get done for vandalising the grass!"

Becky was lounging on the grass at the time. They all laughed.

It was a fun afternoon, one of many the friends had at university, especially in the first year, before they started spending more time on their work to try to make sure they passed their degrees.

Chapter 5

Becky's Friends Give Her an Entertaining Birthday Party

B ecky's best friends decided to throw a party for her birthday. They thought it would be fun to make it a funny story
party, where each one of them made up one or more
funny stories or told real ones to entertain her, and she could
tell ones herself if she wanted. They decided to all tell stories
about their schooldays.

On the Saturday just before Becky's birthday, they all sat
outside together in the warm sun, with lots of party food. They
ate it first, and then after a short time, they played around
with a football for a little while. Then they spent a couple of
hours telling the stories. Becky's mum came along to enjoy the
party too.

One of the friends, Jane, a student Becky had spent an entertaining afternoon with at Christmas playing funny party
games Jane's family had invented, started the story-telling.
She said:

"One of the most memorable things about my schooldays was that one day, the teachers all gave us a lecture about how we should all be more interested in science, and how bad it was not to be interested in it. every one of them joined in the lecture, and it had a surprising similarity to a song where people were singing solos in turn. They didn't sing; it was just that one would speak for exactly sixteen seconds, and then the next one would speak for exactly sixteen seconds, and then one would speak for exactly thirty-two seconds. Then the next one would speak for sixteen seconds again, and it would carry on like it had before, with the timings being the same as they were at first. They were speaking in a kind of rhythm, with exact timings, but managing to give us a good telling off at the same time. Being interested in music, I was somehow managing to calculate how long each one was speaking for instead of listening to a word they said. A girl called Jackie told me what they'd said afterwards.

"After they'd finished, Jackie thought, 'Right! They're insisting we all be more interested in science: I will do something scientific, and show them just how interested I can be!' So she decided to excavate the floor, to see if there were any ancient ruins or objects of interest underneath it. Considering how old that school was, not to mention how old all the teachers were, and even a few of the pupils, Jackie thought it was quite possible there might be some very ancient things underneath it indeed, like medieval false teeth that some of the teachers or the oldest pupils had dropped between the many cracks in the rotten old wooden floorboards or something. She thought she'd be in favour with both the science and the history teacher if she found some. At least, that's what she told them afterwards.

"So, apparently eager to please, she started pulling up all the floorboards in the school. We all thought it was a great new plan, so we all enthusiastically helped her, till all the floorboards in the entire school had been pulled up, apart from the ones in the staffroom, where all the staff were having a meeting at the time.

"One teacher came out of there while Jackie was pulling up all the floorboards in the corridor outside, because she wondered what the noise was, and she asked her what she was doing. Jackie stood up, turned towards her and shouted, 'How dare you come out of your meeting and interrupt me while I'm performing this very important feat of scientific excellence! This is a scandal, and if you carry on standing there instead of going back into your meeting, I will have you reported to the home secretary! Since floorboards are generally associated with homes, I presume he's the one responsible for them, so I'll have you reported to him.'

"The member of staff began to shake, and begged, 'No, please don't report me to the home secretary!' Then she scuttled quickly back into the staffroom and shut the door. Some of the staff were scared of Jackie because she was so frightening when she told them off like that, so none of them dared stand up to her when she did that. So they left her alone, and she finished pulling up all the floorboards in the school.

"There was a whole load of rubble under them all, and she pulled it all out by hand. There must have been tons – it went down for feet and feet and feet under the floor, and she pulled out the entire lot and threw it out the windows onto the lawns outside, till they were all like slag heaps.

"Then, she suddenly discovered a Roman soldier, complete with armour. She lifted all the rubble off him and discovered he was very well preserved, so well preserved in fact that he was still alive. He said, 'Oh, thank goodness someone's come to rescue me after all this time! You cannot know how horrible and boring it's been to just lie here for the past 2000 years! And I'm so hungry now! I don't even know if I can move, I haven't been able to move for so long because of all the rubble that was on me!'

"Jackie helped him out of the big hole in the floor and brushed him down, and then told him she'd give him a tour around the school if he wanted, and tell him all about what went on there, and about all the modern equipment people used. He said, 'I can't believe it's any better than the things we Romans invented! We were the most superior people on earth, we were!'

"It seems he'd somehow learned English from hearing everyone talk for so long while he was under the floor.

"Jackie wanted to make him feel at home, so she said she'd introduce him to the Latin teacher. He said, 'Are you seriously suggesting you think I need to be taught Latin? It was my mother tongue, you twit!'

"Jackie said, 'No, I just thought you might want to speak it with her. But never mind. If you're hungry, come and have dinner.'

"She took him into the dining room where dinner was ready. She sat him down at her table and got him a portion of food. He tried it, but then he said, 'Ugh! What's this rot? We had better food than this in the Roman army!'

"Jackie said, 'Sorry. It's the only thing there is. It's called Toad in the Bin. It's a bit like toad in the hole, but we reckon it must be covered in leftovers that should have been thrown away days ago. That's the kind of stuff they give us to eat round here.'

"Just then, a member of staff came over and shouted, 'Jackie! Who's that man you've got with you? You know you're not allowed to bring men into the school! Get him out of here immediately!'

"Well the Roman soldier was fed up. He said to the staff member, 'Oh, you didn't mind me lying in the school under the floor for 2000 years, not being able to eat anything that entire time! But as soon as I poke my head out and try to get something to eat, you can't stand me being here any more! What kind of a place is this? Not one I want to be anywhere near!'

"He got up and ran as best he could out the school, trying to avoid falling down one of the holes where the floorboards used to be and ending up back where he started. No one knows what happened to him after that. He just ran away and never came back.

"The staff made sure all the holes in the floor were filled in quickly and the floorboards were put back, just in case there were any more ancient men underneath who might come out; it was a girls' school, and we weren't allowed to bring men into it."

Becky's friend Shirley told a story next. She said:

"I had a girl in my class called Jackie too. It was a boarding school for naughty children, and after lights-out once a week, she used to put her radio on and we used to listen to comedy programmes on it. You won't have heard of them; you have to be as old as me to know about them. I'm 304. These comedy programmes were on the radio when I was little, in about 1695 or something. It was fairly early radio. Jackie had a radio in those days.

"Radios worked in a very different way in the olden days to the way they do now. Switching them on could take as long as ten minutes. People in those days would switch them on by lighting a fire and boiling a saucepan of cabbage on it, and the steam from the boiling cabbage water would rise up and turn a handle that would turn the radio on. It had to be steam from cabbage water; nothing else would work. I don't know why – something to do with ancient chemistry.

"So Jackie used to wander around the school grounds looking for wild cabbage, or sometimes she'd sneak into the cook's vegetable garden if she felt unsqueamish enough to leap over the pit of worms they had all around the garden to deter people like her from sneaking into it. She was a very good long-jumper in those days. Maybe she still is. Not many of us would have dared to try to leap over the worm pit, but she was good at it.

"So sometimes she used to get some cabbage, and then after lights-out in our dormitory, she would get a pile of old magazines and schoolbooks she particularly hated, put it in the middle of the room and set fire to it. It's lucky she was good at putting out fires so they never got out of hand. But when she'd lit them, she would put a saucepan of cabbage in water on the fire.

"When it boiled, the steam would rise up and turn the handle of a radio she'd cleverly fixed into the ceiling above it. Then the radio would turn on, and the comedy programmes would come on. We all used to gather round and listen. I can't remember much about them now, but they were good.

"That was one of the best things that happened in that mouldy old place they called a school."

Luke told a story next. He said:

"Funnily enough, I had a girl called Jackie in my class too who did some strange things. One day, she decided she was absolutely fed up of work. she hated it. Well we all did. But she hated it more than most people, and one day, she just came out and told all the teachers she hated their lessons and she wasn't going to do any work ever again.

"Well naturally they didn't like that, and each of them gave her a different punishment. The maths teacher, who was called Mrs Dragonbottom, honestly, made her climb up to the ceiling in all the rooms in the school and take down every cobweb that was on there, one by one, by hand. When she'd done that, the maths teacher thought it would be a good maths exercise for her to count each and every one of them. She hated the idea, but she did, because she was worried the maths teacher might make her pick up all the cockroaches from the bottom of the maths cupboard or something if she didn't.

"So she counted them, and there turned out to be forty-six thousand five hundred and thirty-four. The maths teacher was impressed with Jackie's feat of counting, and decided it would make a great maths exercise for everyone, so she made us all count them. She said that if we got different numbers to the one Jackie got, we would all have to count them again and again till we all ended up with the same number as her. That really is the kind of thing they made us do at my school. So we all made sure we had the same number as Jackie, even though it meant one girl who ended up thinking there were two more decided to eat them quickly before any teacher could find out. She hated them. But she managed it just in time before she was spotted.

"After all that, the teacher was satisfied that justice had been dispensed, and she let us go to our next lesson. We were only 4 and a half hours late. Somehow none of the teachers seemed to mind. I think they might have been spending the time they should have been teaching us looking in the window watching us all counting cobwebs, and having a laugh.

"Anyway, Jackie decided to make Mrs Dragonbottom a dress made entirely of cobwebs and give it to her for Christmas. She was the most skilful sewer in the entire school. She could take really delicate material and make some truly beautiful things. So she took all the cobwebs and made them into a really delicate-looking beautiful dress. She gave it to the maths teacher, without saying it was made of cobwebs, and the maths teacher loved it! I don't know if she realised it was made of cobwebs, but every day for a year, till it started falling to bits, she wore it to school.

"All the other women teachers, and some of the men, admired it and asked her where she'd got it. She said Jackie made it, so they all asked Jackie if she could make one for them too. Jackie didn't really like the idea of making lots more dresses made out of cobwebs, but she went around the school and collected millions more and made some, and the teachers she gave them to loved them too, and they all wore them every day for the next year till they started falling to bits too. Oddly enough, every single one of them started falling to bits exactly a year and a day after she'd given them to them. A funny coincidence."

One of the friends called Gary told the next story. He said:

"You'll never believe it, but we had an especially talented girl called Jackie at our school too.

"Well, she wasn't good at everything; but one thing she enjoyed at that place was PE and athletic things. One thing she was the best in the class at doing was balancing; from time to time the PE teacher made us all stand on a long beam – it was a piece of gym apparatus that was about five inches wide, so we had to stand with one foot in front of the other, and see how long we could balance there. I could never manage it for much longer than two seconds; but Jackie used to be able to balance for ages!

"One day she managed it for twenty-two and a half hours non-stop! The teacher congratulated her afterwards, and said she'd beaten the school record by twenty-one hours and twenty-seven and a half minutes. Jackie had set the previous record herself.

"Poor Jackie was tired after standing there for all that time! But she was proud of herself, and everyone else was in awe of her.

"The thing we didn't like was that the PE teacher made us stay there witnessing it for the whole time, and she wouldn't even let us go to sleep. That was what the teachers were like at our school. I don't know how the PE teacher managed to stay awake all that time herself, and it's amazing that Jackie did! But every time one of us dropped off to sleep, the PE teacher would wring a flannel full of cold water out over our heads, and then make us sing all six verses of the national anthem. She said she was sure we'd be awake by the end of that!

"It was funny though, because none of us knew the words to all six verses of the national anthem, so we all just made up things, like, 'God save our favourite beer, even though we don't get none here; God save our beer.' Each of us made up different words, and the ones of us who fell asleep more than once made up different words each time, because we couldn't remember what we'd sung before.

"Oddly enough though, the teacher didn't tell anyone off for singing the wrong words, which must either mean that she didn't know them herself, or that she thought what we were singing was funny so she didn't feel like telling us off, or that the words were being rewritten every five minutes or so, and we were all making remarkably accurate guesses as to what the new words were, and the teacher somehow had a secret hotline to Buckingham Palace or wherever else the new words were being made up, so she kept being updated as to what they were. That's what we assumed must be happening.

"It really was an amazing experience; for everyone to be guessing so accurately what the new words were must have meant we all had extremely good guessing powers, or that we were psychic; so it boosted our confidence no end, knowing we were so good at something, even though we couldn't understand how it was that when a few of us had to sing at the same time, because a few of us had fallen asleep at the same time, we were all singing different words, and yet we were all guessing what they were accurately at the same time.

"When Jackie couldn't manage to balance on the beam any more after nearly twenty-four hours, we all celebrated our newfound abilities, by dancing around and eating abnormal amounts of chocolate."

Mandy was the next to tell a story. She said:

"Funnily enough, I had a girl called Jackie in my class at school too. She invented a new religion once. In our religious studies classes, we learned a bit about different religions, mainly about their festivals, like the Hindu Festival of Light. One day, Jackie stood up in a religious studies class and said to the teacher, 'I've invented a new religion called Jackieism. I'll tell you all about it, and then you're going to have to teach everyone in the school about it. If you don't, I'm going to take you to the headmistress and accuse you of discrimination, because you teach about other religions, and it just won't be fair if you refuse to teach everyone about mine.'

"She gave the teacher a pile of information about her new religion, and the teacher agreed to teach the whole school about it. It took two lessons. It had rules like, 'Every Thursday, we must all be given our favourite meals for dinner', and, 'Every Friday, all the pupils in the school must be given a chocolate bar by the teachers before each lesson', and, 'Every third week on Friday afternoons, there must be no lessons, but instead we must have a party, with games and a party tea'.

"Every single pupil thought it would be wonderful to have the school turned into a Jackieist school after we heard about the rules, so we camped in the corridor outside the head-mistress's office for days, clamouring for it to be turned into one. But the headmistress refused. We threatened to take the case to the European Court of Human Rights, but she wouldn't change her mind. So eventually we gave up clamouring.

"Jackie scrapped the Jackieist religion after that; she said there was no point in having it if we weren't going to be allowed to practise it. So after we'd learned about it for two entire religious studies lessons, it didn't exist any more. It was a shame. It had been a great idea!"

Sharon told the next story, saying:

"Funnily enough, I had a girl called Jackie in my class at school too, who did things like all the rest of the Jackies you're describing; and I went to a boarding school for naughty children just like some of you.

"Me and Jackie and another girl, Debbie, decided to play a game one morning. Me and Debbie picked Jackie up; I held her legs and Debbie held her top half. We wanted to see how near the ceiling we could get her. Or something. I must have been feeling lazy that day, just like I do every day, because I leant on a washbasin that was right behind me for support. With a massive crash, it broke off the wall. Unfortunately, it pulled the bit of wall that was attached to it off too, and that pulled the bit of wall that was attached to it down, and that pulled the bit of wall that was attached to it down, and it carried on and on like a domino effect till the entire school fell down! It collapsed in a heap!

"Thankfully no one was hurt, because everybody hated the school so much they tried to keep out of it as much as possible, so even in the winter, most people would be outdoors. Thankfully me and Debbie and Jackie didn't get hurt either, because the water jets that came out of the pipes when the sink came off the wall were so powerful they flung all the bricks out of our way, so we were standing in the midst of all this rubble, with our way clear to fresh air, if only we could manage to climb up and clamber over it all. So we did that. It was quite an adventure really.

"Of course the headmistress wasn't happy with us. She decided we simply must have been involved in a scandalous conspiracy to knock the whole school down, and declared we needed to be punished. But first, they got some emergency builders in, and they managed to rebuild the entire school before nightfall that day! It really was amazing!

"The headmistress decided we were all going to be punished by not being allowed to wash for the entire term, in case we were just longing to break another sink off the wall, and the temptation would be too much for us if we were allowed to use one.

"She wrote letters to our parents explaining that we might look and smell as if we hadn't had a wash for weeks when we came home, but it was only because we'd knocked the school down with a sink, so we couldn't be allowed near one for the rest of the term in case we tried it again."

After a couple of hours of story-telling, Becky told a story last. She said:

"Funnily enough, we had an especially talented girl called Jackie at my school too. And it was a boarding school for naughty children just like Shirley's and Sharon's. We used to be allowed to keep rabbits at that school; they thought that since we were away from home, it would be nice if we could have a few creature comforts. I had one once that could run really fast, and kept trying to escape. When it did escape it was hard to catch it. It gnawed right through a rabbit hutch once and got out.

"One day, it got out and managed to get right out of the enclosure the rabbits were kept in. Jackie offered to run and catch it for me. She was a very fast runner in those days, maybe the best in our class. But the rabbit was very quick too. It was a Dutch rabbit, and I think it might have felt homesick, because it ran right across London, and didn't stop till it got to the coast, where it got in a queue for the ferry to Holland.

"All that time, Jackie had been right behind it, almost catching up with it but not quite. That might have had something to do with the fact that Jackie had more road sense, so she would always wait at roads for the traffic to stop before crossing, whereas the rabbit would often just chance its luck, probably believing it was so fast it could skilfully outmanoeuvre any car that came along.

"Anyway, when it queued up for the ferry, Jackie thought, 'Now's my chance!' But the rabbit must have looked round and seen her, because it quickly rushed to the front of the queue, and then, not even stopping to get a ticket, it dashed onto the ferry as soon as it could.

"Jackie knew she wouldn't be allowed on the ferry without a ticket, so she thought she'd better run after the ferry instead of getting on it. She knew that if she ran as fast as she could, she'd almost be able to keep up with it. So when it started moving, she dashed into the sea and started running. She ran so fast that she didn't sink, because there just wasn't time to do that, since each of her feet was only on the water for a split second every time she put it down. When the ferry got to Holland, she was still right behind it. She was relieved to have a rest when it stopped, although she knew she'd soon have to start running again.

"She saw the rabbit coming off the ferry. It must have believed it wasn't being followed any more, because it just lolloped around for a while enjoying the sights and sounds of home. But that meant Jackie could catch up with it, and she picked it up.

"She was getting a bit tired, but she didn't dare delay, because she knew that the longer she held the rabbit for, the more chance there was of it leaping out of her grasp and running away again. Besides, she wanted to get home before it was bedtime at our school, so she wouldn't be late and have to face the wrath of the fearsome house staff. She was already late for lessons, and knew she'd be told off by the teachers when she got back. So she started back across the sea immediately, running almost as fast as she had before. She knew she couldn't afford to have a break even for half a second, because then she'd start sinking. But she managed to make it right back across the sea safely.

"She didn't stop when she reached the land; she knew she was going to have to hurry if she wanted to make it back to school before the house staff missed her at bedtime; so she just kept on running, right across London and back to the school.

"She cheered as she put my rabbit back in its hutch. It wasn't very pleased to be back where it started, and for a while after that it growled whenever Jackie went near it. But it got over it in the end."

Becky's friends enjoyed listening to her story, along with everyone else's.

Soon after that, the party ended. Becky had had a lovely time. Her mum had enjoyed it too. But her mum had never heard anyone telling stories like the ones Becky and her friends told, apart from the odd one or two her sister Diana had made up. As they went home, Becky's mum grinned and said to her, "You've got strange friends!"

Becky smiled slightly and replied, "I thought you already knew that. Anyway, They're good fun to be with, so I don't care who thinks they're strange."

Her mum said reassuringly, "I was only joking."

The next day, the two of them went to Becky's mum's parents' house and had more party food. So Becky had a good weekend!

Chapter 6

Becky Helps a Girl With Post-Traumatic Stress Disorder

Since Becky had helped a teenage girl called Stephanie get over a dog phobia at the seaside a few years earlier, they'd kept in touch by email occasionally, mostly when it was Christmas or their birthdays. But one day in the middle of the summer holidays, Stephanie emailed Becky to say she had a new friend called Zoe who'd never got over something that had happened a few years earlier, when she'd been carrying her baby brother at the local station, and someone had rushed past and knocked her over, and she'd dropped her brother, and he'd had to go to hospital and have stitches in his head. She still had nightmares about it, and sometimes thought about how terrible it would have been if something worse had happened. Stephanie wondered if Becky could help her get over the memories.

Becky said she'd try to help. Stephanie suggested they all go out together one day. Her family liked Zoe, and after hearing about what Becky had done to help Stephanie, they thought that maybe she could help Zoe. They decided it would be nice to take them to the seaside for a day out. They thought that after they'd had some fun, Becky could talk with Zoe, hopefully in the sunshine, and then they could all have some food together.

Becky liked the idea. She fancied a day out at the beach, and she thought it would be nice to find out if some of the things she'd been learning in her psychology classes actually helped anyone.

The Day Begins With The Little Group Having Some Good Fun

They met up one Sunny morning at Stephanie's house, and Stephanie's dad drove them down to the beach.

On the way, her mum made them all laugh by telling them about Cockney rhyming slang. She said she and Stephanie's dad had both grown up in London, and she'd had grandparents who'd sometimes used a bit, and had taught them some. She said:

"I think I've forgotten most of what I got taught, but some things have stuck in my mind. In Cockney rhyming slang, a little phrase is used as a substitute for a word, and the last word of the phrase rhymes with the word; but then people often just use the first word of the phrase to mean the word, so it doesn't rhyme at all and doesn't seem to have anything to do with the word. Actually, an example you probably all know is that 'apples and pears' means stairs; so I suppose a mum might say to a child, 'Get up those apples and go to bed!'"

They grinned. Stephanie's mum continued, "I don't know if anyone's really sure why Cockney rhyming slang came into being. I think some people think it was made up by criminals or other groups of people in Victorian times, to keep what they were doing secret from people who heard them talking; but other people think it might just have been made up for fun. Anyway, I don't think it was long before lots of people started using it. Some of it goes back to Victorian times, but people have carried on making up phrases ever since, and they're still doing it today, not just in London either, but in every English-speaking country. At least, that's what I've heard. I think a lot of people must think it's fun to use.

"You can make some funny sentences with bits of slang. Another bit you've probably heard of is that 'plates of meat' is rhyming slang for feet. So someone might say, 'Thanks for offering to let me borrow your shoes, but I don't think my big plates will fit in them.'"

They laughed.

Then Stephanie's mum said, "And cabbage patch means scratch. So I suppose someone might say, 'I went to pick a load of gooseberries from that old prickly gooseberry bush we've got in our garden. It was nice, but I came back with a load of cabbages on my arms!'"

They giggled again.

Stephanie's mum then said, "And mince pies means eyes, and fireman's hose means nose."

Becky grinned and said, "I wonder if that means someone could say, 'My wife does look pretty; she's got beautiful blue mince pies that often look thoughtful. She'd look even nicer if she didn't have such a great big fireman's hose sticking out of the middle of her face!'"

They all laughed yet again.

Then Stephanie's mum said, "Baked bean means queen."

They grinned again, and Becky said, "Does that mean that on Christmas Day, some people say, 'Let's turn the telly on; it's time for the baked bean's speech'?"

(This was all taking place when Queen Elizabeth was still alive.)

Zoe was laughing along with the rest of them, and said, "Or I wonder if they'd say, 'Let's go and visit Buckingham Palace and see if we get to see the baked bean.'"

Then Stephanie's mum said, "Biscuits and cheese means knees; so maybe you could say to someone, 'Get down on your biscuits and pray!'

"And the word shirt is Uncle Bert. So you could say, 'I'm just off to iron my uncle.'"

"And the phrase used for legs is bacon and eggs, so you might say, 'Corr you walk fast! It must be because you've got really long bacons!' Or if you were trying to dress a child, I suppose you could say, 'Come on, put your bacon in your trousers.'

"And you've probably heard that the word phone is dog and bone; so maybe someone could say, 'I'll answer your question in a minute; I'm just going to answer the dog.'"

Stephanie said, "I suppose anyone could make up a bit of rhyming slang, couldn't they? So maybe if I decided that a good slang phrase for cheese could be bottle of fleas or something, and I told everyone what it was, maybe if enough people got to hear about it and started using it for fun, it would make it into Cockney rhyming slang dictionaries and things."

Becky smiled, but protested, "You wouldn't want to call cheese that! Cheese is nice! At least some of it. Maybe you could call that mouldy cheese something like that. I've never tried eating that; I don't know how anyone dares! But some people must like it, and they'd probably think I'm really fussy for not

126

daring to eat it. But maybe you could call ordinary cheese honey for bees or something."

Stephanie's mum said, "One slang phrase for money is bees and honey."

Zoe said, "So maybe someone could say, 'Let's take some bees out with us; it'll be good to have some in case we stop to buy ice creams.'"

There was more giggling.

Then Stephanie said, "I remember you telling me that whistle and flute means suit, Mum. Maybe that means a person could proudly say, 'I've just got a new job promotion. I'll be working with managers now. I'm going to buy a whistle for when I start there.'"

Becky grinned and quipped, "People might wonder whether that would be to whistle a happy tune or to try to keep the managers in order."

Stephanie's mum said, "I don't know if I've ever told you, Stephanie, but the slang for daughter is 'bricks and mortar'. So when you were smaller I could have told people, 'I'm just taking my bricks to school', or, 'I'm just going to collect my bricks from school.'"

Becky grinned and said to Stephanie, "You don't look much like a pile of bricks, but I expect they come in all shapes and sizes nowadays."

Stephanie laughed.

Her mum said, "And the slang for son is currant bun. So someone might say, 'My currant's nearly old enough to go to school now.'

"And the slang for street is field of wheat. So you might complain, 'I've walked down this whole field and I haven't seen a single bus stop!'"

Stephanie giggled and said, "Yeah, or maybe you might say, 'I wish there weren't so many cars whizzing along this field!'"

Her mum said, "A slang word for car is motor, and a rhyming slang phrase for that is haddock and bloater. They're both fish. So you might say, 'Let's go for a ride in the haddock!'"

They had fun talking about Cockney rhyming slang all the way down to the seaside.

When they got there, they all had fun swimming and playing in the sea, except Stephanie's dad, who decided to sunbathe and read a book and guard their things instead.

When the others had finished having fun in the sea, they sat down to sunbathe too. Becky and Zoe sat at a little distance from the others, so they could talk privately while the others chatted.

Zoe had been feeling nervous about talking to Becky when they'd started out that morning, but the things Stephanie's mum had said to make them laugh on the way down to the beach and the amusing conversation they'd had, and then their play in the sea, and the sunshine, had made her feel much more relaxed. She started feeling a bit nervous again as they sat down, but then Becky said, "Let's just sit back and enjoy the sunshine for a few minutes before we start talking."

They sat back and relaxed. Then Becky said with a smile, "Hey, how would you like a pet seagull?"

Zoe laughed and said, "I wouldn't, thanks!"

Becky said, "Imagine if there were really big seagulls, and you could go for rides on them! Would you want one then?"

Zoe giggled and said, "No way! It would be like going on a rollercoaster ride, wouldn't it! Imagine being on a seagull when it swooped down into the sea to catch a fish, and then zoomed back up to its nest again! You wouldn't need to go to a theme park for exciting rides, would you!"

They both laughed.

Zoe Tells Becky About Her Traumatic Experience

After a few moments, Becky asked, "So what did Stephanie tell you about me?"

Zoe said, "She told me you helped her get over a dog phobia when you were only about seven! I thought that was impressive! She said you might be able to help me with my nightmares and other things."

Becky said, "Well, I can't promise anything. I only know what I've read in psychology books and heard in lectures. But I've read a few books that give some information about ways of getting over the kinds of problems I've heard you're having; so I'll do my best to help. Tell me what happened the day of the accident that was so upsetting that you still have nightmares about it today."

Zoe said, "Well, it was a few years ago. Me and my family thought we were going to have a really nice day out. We were going to go up to London and go to some museums and see other things. We started out early in the morning because we wanted to spend hours and hours there. We were going to have a picnic in the park at lunchtime, and see if there were any tame squirrels that might want to eat out of our hands. My mum said she went to London when she was a teenager, and she was eating a jam tart when a squirrel came up to her, and she held out a bit, and it took it out of her hand. So I thought it would be cute if one did that to me.

"But we never got that far. My brother was still a baby, just beginning to get good at walking. When we got to the station, my mum told me to pick him up and carry him, because we were in a bit of a hurry, and also it was easier than trying to get him up and down all the steps in his buggy. So I carried him onto the platform.

"Our train came in and stopped. We spotted a carriage with some space in it, and we were heading for it, when a train door opened and a couple of young men jumped out the train and started running fast without carefully looking where they were going. One of them crashed into me and knocked me over. I dropped my baby brother with the shock, and because I was knocked off-balance and fell over, and he fell on the ground. He got quite a few bruises and hit his head hard.

"The men just ran off without taking any notice. We took my brother to hospital. It looked as if his head was bleeding badly, and it needed stitches. Then they kept him in for a few hours to make sure he didn't have any symptoms of concussion or anything. They said he seemed alright. Then we took him home, and he stayed in bed for the rest of the day.

"He was alright in the end, and there's nothing wrong with him now.

"But I keep having nightmares where I'm carrying him along a train platform, and then the young men jump out the train, and one bashes into me as he runs past, but instead of falling on the platform, my baby brother flies off it with the momentum and falls on the rails and gets electrocuted. Or I dream that his head injury was worse and he got brain damage, and never learned to talk, and couldn't go to an ordinary school, and the doctors said he'd be mentally handicapped for the rest of his life. I always wake up feeling upset after those nightmares. Then I get depressed for hours, thinking about how bad it would have been if one of those things had happened."

Becky Gives Zoe a Few Suggestions to Try to Help Her Stop Getting Nightmares

Becky said sympathetically, "That must be scary! But something some psychology books recommend people try when they're having nightmares is keeping a notebook by the bed, and when you've just woken up from a nightmare, start imagining happier ways it could have ended, and write them in the book. For example, you could maybe fantasise that when you drop your brother, some nice person with quick reflexes sees what happens and grabs him before he falls on the ground; or if you dream that he gets flung onto the railway, you could maybe fantasise that some kind-hearted person risks their life by climbing down and grabbing him quickly and putting him back on the platform, and he's alright.

"Or if you dream that he's ended up brain-damaged, you could maybe start fantasising that it gets better and better and better over time, and you're all really pleased when you see signs of improvement, till he's completely normal.

"Then if you write those things down in the notebook, it'll mean your brain pays more attention to them than it would have done if you'd just thought them, since you might forget them again soon if you only do that; so they might stay in your memory better, especially because you can read them whenever you want, to remind yourself of them.

"Or instead of writing, you could draw pictures, like a picture of your brother fallen off the platform but some nice person climbing down to get him, or him happily running around or playing with toys not long afterwards, proving he didn't get brain damage.

"If when you wake up from a nightmare you start fantasising much more about how things could have gone right or did go right than about what went wrong or how things could have been worse, you'll start feeling less upset about what happened, so chances are you'll have fewer and fewer nightmares about it."

Becky Tries to Persuade Zoe to Stop Blaming Herself for The Accident

Zoe said, "I like some of those ideas, and I'll try them. But I'm a bit worried that if I start fantasising that someone catches my baby brother, I'll start regretting that no one caught him for real before he fell on the ground, and get all depressed about it. I often get depressed now because I blame myself for what happened. I keep asking myself why I couldn't have got out of the way when I saw the boys coming! If I'd only sidestepped them, I could have saved my brother from being injured! When we were at the hospital, my mum asked me angrily why I hadn't got out of their way. Now I keep calling myself stupid for not getting out the way quick enough."

Becky asked, "What did you say to your mum when she asked you why you hadn't got out of the way?"

Zoe said, "I said they took me by surprise, and ran towards me so quickly I didn't have time to think about what to do, and I just assumed they were going to avoid me. I just didn't think they might not be looking where they were going properly."

Becky said, "Well that's it then. Why don't you tell yourself that now when you call yourself stupid for letting it happen? After all, your mum might have just said what she said because she was upset, but when she really thought about it, she might have realised it wasn't your fault."

Zoe responded, "Maybe I shouldn't blame myself. I just feel sure I could have done more if I'd had my wits about me."

Becky replied, "Think back to the way you were feeling just before they jumped out the train. Did you have any idea they were about to come racing towards you and bash you?"

"No," responded Zoe.

"Was there any way you could have predicted it?" asked Becky.

"No," said Zoe.

"And when they started running towards you, was there any way you could have known they weren't looking where they were going properly?" asked Becky.

"No," replied Zoe.

"And how many seconds would you say there were between the time they started running towards you and the time one hit you?" asked Becky.

"Not many at all," said Zoe.

"Enough for you to have thought through the risks and got out of the way just in case?" asked Becky.

"No," replied Zoe.

"So," said Becky, "You're blaming yourself for something you couldn't have predicted, something that took you by surprise so you weren't braced to react, and something that you didn't even have time to weigh up the risks of and react to after it started happening."

"I suppose I am," said Zoe thoughtfully.

Becky said, "Tell me: If a friend of yours was carrying a baby and the same thing happened to Them, would you say it was their fault? Would you say they should have known better and known to get out of the way?"

"Gosh no!" said Zoe.

"What would you say?" asked Becky. "How would you reassure them if they were blaming themselves?"

"I'd comfort them," said Zoe. "I'd tell them they couldn't have foreseen what was going to happen, and they couldn't have been expected to get out of the way when it happened so quickly. I'd say it wasn't even as if they had the experience to spot the risk immediately, because it's not as if that kind of thing happens a lot."

Becky said, "So if the same thing happened to a friend of yours, you'd say everything you could to reassure them that it wasn't their fault. Why do you hold yourself to a higher standard then? Why do you blame yourself when you wouldn't blame a friend? After all, all the reasons why a friend of yours couldn't stop it happening are true for you too."

Zoe became a bit tearful and said, "You've got a good point there."

Becky asked, "Are you going to keep on blaming yourself from now on then?"

Zoe said, "I suppose I shouldn't really."

Becky said, "Well whenever you catch yourself doing that from now on, remind yourself of all the reasons why you don't need to."

134

Zoe said she would.

Becky said, "Really, the person who should take the responsibility for what happened is the man who bashed into you without looking where he was going, not you. He probably didn't do it deliberately, but he should have known better."

Zoe agreed.

Then Becky said, "Even if you could have done some things better, instead of feeling upset with yourself because you didn't, think of it as a learning experience; hopefully such a thing will never happen again; but if anything like it does, you might have quicker reflexes, because you've learned from what happened before that you can't trust people to look where they're going. So whenever you start feeling depressed about what happened, think of the ways you're wiser now than you were before because of it; if you can think of anything positive that came out of it, it might not be so upsetting to think about."

Zoe said that sounded as if it could be a good idea.

There's a Break For Some Relaxation, and They Get to Have a Laugh

Then Stephanie's dad looked around, saw Zoe looking a bit tearful, and came over and said, in a tongue-in-cheek way, "What have you been doing to Zoe, Becky, you tormentor? Hey, would you two like me to buy you some ice creams, and then you can carry on your chat afterwards?"

They liked that idea. He went and bought them some.

They were thoughtful as they ate them. But they managed to relax a bit in the sunshine, and felt a bit more cheerful afterwards.

Stephanie's mum came up to them and asked if they were alright. They said yes.

Then Zoe said to her, "Hey, tell us more about Cockney rhyming slang."

Stephanie's mum said, "Alright. There's a Cockney rhyming alphabet too. Actually I think there are several versions. I think the first one was made up just for fun, in about the 1930s originally, although more have been made up since. You know how sometimes when little children are taught letters, their teacher might say things to them like, 'A for apple; B for bottle; C for coat . . . or coke; D for drink', and so on? The Cockney alphabet's kind of a fun version of that. Here are some of the letters:

"A for 'orses. That's really hay for horses, but dropping the Hs like Cockneys do. N for eggs – that's hen for eggs. Q for tickets – that's queue, as in wait in line. Sometimes it's Q for hours, or Q for almost everything! Then there's C for miles – that's see for miles, like you might do on top of a steep hill. And there's Y for girlfriend – that's wife or girlfriend."

They giggled.

Stephanie's mum said, "Tell you what: I'll test you, to see if you can guess some words: B for mutton."

Zoe said, "That must be beef or mutton."

"That's right," said Stephanie's mum. "T for chewin'?"

"Teeth are chewing?" asked Becky.

"Good one," said Stephanie's mum. "Or it could be teeth For chewing. What about "E for Adam?"

They thought for a few seconds, and then Zoe said, "Eve or Adam?"

Stephanie's mum smiled and said, "That's right! OK, what about G for police?"

136

They both looked a bit puzzled for a few seconds, and then Becky said, "Chief of police?"

Stephanie's mum said, "Very good! OK, what about M for 'sis?"

After a second or two, Zoe grinned and said, "Emphasis?"

"That's right," said Stephanie's mum.

Then Becky asked, "What's your favourite one?"

Stephanie's mum said, "I don't think I've got a favourite. Mind you, one I like is O for the garden wall – that means over the garden wall."

They chuckled.

Then Stephanie's mum said, "I'd better leave you to it now, I think, so you can discuss more of what you came here to talk about, if you like."

They said that was OK, and she walked away.

They giggled a bit more with each other, and then they became thoughtful again.

Becky and Zoe Discuss the Idea That Worthwhile Lessons Can be Learned From Bad Experiences

Zoe said, "That thing you said about thinking of things that happen as experiences you can learn from might help a bit. But I think it might still be possible to be taken by surprise by things that happen and not be prepared, so I make the same kinds of mistakes. Still, I might be wiser in some ways because of what happened; I'll think about it."

Becky replied, "Oh yes, I agree. I wasn't suggesting you'd be any more to blame than you were before if something similar happened again and you couldn't stop it."

Zoe said, "That's nice. I've tried to put things down to an experience I can learn from before, but I'm not sure it always works. This is just a minor example, but me and my family went on holiday not long ago for about five days, and we went in the sea, on the only day when it didn't rain and the sun was actually shining! The sea was colder than it is today. I think that was partly because the day before, it had rained all day, so there was no sun to warm it up all day, and loads of cold rain must have mixed with the water.

"I still had a swim in it though, and I wouldn't have minded it being so cold that much if I'd got warm soon after I came out. But it was quite windy, and that made the air cold. I'd brought a scruffy skirt, to make it easier to change my clothes without showing my private bits than it would have been if I'd been wearing trousers, because I could put some things on underneath it. But I realised I should have brought trousers too and put them on when I came out of the sea, because after I did, we sat around for ages, eating chips and just relaxing and things. But all that time, I was cold, till I thought of wrapping a towel right around my legs.

"I didn't enjoy myself much because of those things, and I felt a bit down about hardly enjoying the holiday up till then later, because I knew my parents had paid quite a bit for it. But that night, I tried to cheer myself up by thinking, 'Oh well, I'll know better for the rest of the holiday; I'll put what happened today down to experience, and next time we go to the beach, I'll take trousers to wear, and make sure I've got a jumper with me to warm myself up after I've been in the sea, and I'll take other trousers and a tracksuit top to wear in the sea over my swimming costume, because I bet they'll keep me warmer.' I felt better then. But the rest of the holiday it rained, or was all cloudy, so we never went in the sea or sat on the beach again!"

"That's a pity," said Becky sympathetically. "Still, I notice you've got trousers with you today, and a bag with some other clothes in, so it seems you at least remembered the lessons you learned for the future."

"That's true," said Zoe. "I just hope I don't forget the lessons again before the next time they'll come in useful! I didn't wear clothes over my swimming costume in the end today because it seemed such a nice hot day that I thought I might not need them, and I thought I could always come out the sea and get them if I did, but I didn't need them in the end, so that was nice."

"It was fun in the sea, wasn't it!" said Becky. "My auntie Diana said that when her and my mum were little, they used to play games in the sea where they threw seaweed at each other or draped it around each other's necks, or piled loads of it on a lilo and pushed it around, or one of them would get on the lilo and the other one would push it around, and things like that."

Zoe chuckled.

Then Becky said, "Once they went swimming and they stood on this little wall around a closed-off part where some boats were kept. They were having fun jumping off it, but then two boys, who might have been about ten years old, swam up to them. Then one of them started shouting for help. At first my mum thought they were just messing around, so she told my auntie Diana not to do anything. But the boy kept on shouting. So Diana decided she would after all and jumped in. She sat the boy on her hip and did this sidestroke thing back to the wall, and lifted him onto it. The other boy climbed up there too and they ran off."

Becky grinned as she said, "My auntie Diana had done a life-saving badge at school, but she said she bet the teacher who taught them the techniques they were supposed to use would have been shocked and horrified at how ungraceful she must have looked as she did the clumsy sidestroke to the wall – not the way she was taught to do things at all!"

Becky Gives Zoe Advice on How She Can Stop Having Panic Attacks

Zoe laughed. But then her expression turned sad, and Becky guessed that the story about the boys had made her think about her little brother having his accident. She thought it was probably about time they did what they'd come to do and got back to talking about the problems it had caused for Zoe.

She said to her, "Stephanie said something about you having nasty panic attacks where you feel really scared."

Zoe said, "That's right. They're horrible! They started not long after my brother's accident. The first one I had was by the train station. A couple of my friends had decided to go to London for the day, and asked me if I wanted to go with them. I thought it would be nice to spend the day with them, and it sounded as if they were going to do some things that could be fun. So I agreed to go. But I got nervous in case another bad thing happened. I got more and more worried while I was getting ready to go.

"I was going to meet my friends at the station. But while I was on my way, I started feeling ill. My heart started beating faster, and I started feeling dizzy. When I was nearly there, I started feeling so bad I just didn't feel as if I could go on. I was feeling as if I just couldn't get enough breath, as if I was desperate for more. And I was feeling really scared. And my heart beating so fast and the other things that were happening made me feel as if I was going to faint or die or something. I didn't know it was a panic attack at the time. I'd never heard of them. I only found out that that must have been what I had from a school counsellor later, when I went to see her after I'd had some at school.

"But when I had the one when I was on my way to the station, I needed to stop and sit down, because I was feeling all shaky and light-headed.

"I had to stay sitting down for a while, and then I started feeling a bit better, but I had to phone my friends and tell them I couldn't go with them, because I thought I might feel bad all day. They were worried about me, and wondered what was wrong with me. But I told them to go on their own and not to worry. They phoned me up later to see how I was, and I was alright by then.

"But it wasn't long after that that I had the first panic attack at school, when a history teacher started talking about trains being invented. It seems it instantly reminded my brain of what happened with my brother, and brought on some horrible feelings. I was feeling alright before, but they came on all of a sudden. I told the teacher I was feeling ill, and asked if I could go out. He said I didn't look well, so he let me go. I've had quite a few panic attacks since then.

"I felt a bit better after talking to the school counsellor. She advised me to try and breathe very slowly whenever I start feeling stressed, or when I can feel something happening in my system that feels like the beginnings of a panic attack, saying that would calm the symptoms down. I've been trying that, and if I can discipline myself to breathe *really* slowly, I think it does start to help a bit. But it would be nice if I could get rid of the panic attacks so they didn't even begin."

Becky said, "Yes, I expect you would prefer that! I'll tell you what I've learned on my psychology course about panic attacks:

"It might surprise you, and you might find it hard to believe, but as bad as panic attacks feel, the body has them for what the part of the brain that stirs up and regulates emotions thinks is a good reason . . . Well, it doesn't think much. Well, hardly at all really. It just starts to put the symptoms of panic in motion automatically if it feels as if it's detected a need for them. You might think that must mean there's something wrong with it. But really, it's just making a mistake when it sparks off panic attacks when there's no need to panic, and it can be trained by its owner not to do that. It just thinks there's an emergency sometimes when there isn't really one, because it automatically assumes there is one whenever its owner's anxiety levels get really bad, or else if something reminds it of a situation where they did, or of a place where something terrible happened, so it thinks there might be danger.

"As strange as it sounds, that's actually a protection mechanism. Or at least, it's supposed to be one. I know it won't feel a bit like one, especially when you even feel as if you might die because your heart's beating so fast and you're struggling for breath. But if you needed to fight or run away at that moment, you'd be breathing in more air without a problem, and your heart beating faster would actually help you. I'll tell you why in a minute. It's something to do with the heart beating fast because it's pumping more blood than usual around the system to give you more energy.

"But the thing is that if you know why the symptoms are coming on, you probably won't worry about what's happening so much, because you'll know they're not happening for a scary reason; and if you're not so worried, the panic attacks won't get so bad, because when you're scared about how bad they're going to get, and about what's actually happening to you, because you don't understand why you're getting the symptoms you are, or you worry and worry that it'll be really embarrassing if you have a panic attack in public, or about something like that, then that fear makes the panic attacks get a lot worse. Then you'll get worse symptoms, so you'll get even more scared of what's happening, and that'll make them even worse, and it can carry on like that till they're really bad.

"But if you can remind yourself as soon as you can, before the symptoms get so bad it's near-impossible to think straight, that you're getting some sensations and feelings your brain's just set in motion because the poor thing thinks you're in an emergency where you'll need more energy quickly when you're not really, you're more likely to be able to put up with them, and not get nearly so worried about them, so they won't be made worse by you worrying and getting more and more scared. I know it won't be easy, because panic comes on so quickly, but it'll be worth trying to have a go immediately you recognise the typical first signs of it, or even just if you notice your anxiety's building up, but you don't know if it's due to lead to panic. Then you might be able to head it off to try to make sure it doesn't get going.

"The reason the brain makes a snap decision to start the symptoms off, before you can even think about it, is because it's programmed to do that, because if you'd started feeling scared because you really were in an emergency, there might not be time to think; it might be a matter of either having to react really quickly to give yourself a good chance of survival, or risking being harmed – say if there was a fire at your school or something; you wouldn't have time to stand in a classroom where you were taught something you hate, and gloat about the school burning so you wouldn't get taught it for much longer, or anything like that! The fear would give you a strong urge to get out of there quickly; so there wouldn't be any chance of you staying there to watch and cheer till your life was in danger. That's the kind of thing fear's for."

Zoe chuckled as she said, "gloat and cheer! I don't hate my school that much!"

Becky grinned and said, "That's good. My mum told me there was a fire at her school when she was there, started deliberately, probably by a couple of pupils who hated the place. She wasn't there at the time, because it was in the middle of the night. But it burned down the part of the school where they did cookery classes. I think it was in the middle of the night anyway; not during a cookery lesson. Imagine the teacher being asked questions about that one if it had been! Imagine them being called to answer for their actions in front of a board of school governors, and one of the governors asking, 'Were the children actually following your instructions when the place caught fire? Just what food is meant to be cooked by setting the room alight in the process? It must be a speciality you've invented! Please never instruct the pupils to cook it again! Stick to the curriculum!' "

Zoe laughed.

Then Becky started talking about panic attacks again, saying, "You could compare the part of your brain that sets off emergency signals but sometimes does it when it shouldn't to a smoke alarm. When one of those goes off, it could be a genuine warning of danger. But if it's close to the kitchen, it might often go off when you've just burned the thin edge of a crust of toast a little bit but it's still perfectly edible, because it doesn't distinguish between a real emergency and a thing like that. So it'll sometimes be an embarrassment instead of a help, especially if the neighbours hear it.

"The part of the brain that sets all the feelings and instant reactions that people have when they have panic attacks in motion actually blocks the part of your brain that lets you think from functioning for a while when it does that; so don't be surprised if you can't really think straight when you start panicking.

"The reason it does that is because in an emergency, similar to what I said before, standing around thinking about what would be best to do for too long could mean you were in big trouble before you'd decided on anything; so instinct just takes over and gives people an urge to get away, or to fight off something or someone that's threatening them. But the emotional part of the brain that controls panic symptoms doesn't make a distinction between real emergencies and things it's become over-sensitive too but that aren't emergencies. Maybe that's because even taking time to make that distinction might take valuable seconds you should be using to spring into action in a real emergency.

"What the brain's really doing by setting off those scary bodily reactions that start off panic attacks is gearing your body up to take really quick action, at least if the action you need to take is fighting or running away! That would be kind of inappropriate in a history lesson or something though;

so you have to just put up with the symptoms there, so you'll just feel bad."

Zoe grinned despite herself and said, "Yeah, somehow I don't think the history teacher would appreciate it if he'd just started talking about some battle or other, and then a panic attack started off and I started fighting him! I'd have to use an excuse, like saying I thought he might enjoy it if we had a battle reenactment in the classroom."

They both laughed.

But then Zoe said, "I don't understand this thing about the symptoms being the body gearing people up to fight or run away though. I always feel like doing the exact opposite when I get panic attacks, because I get shaky and light-headed, and just feel ill."

Becky replied, "Yeah, that's partly because it would be inappropriate for you to act on the symptoms when you get them, so you just have to put up with them; and sitting putting up with them feels horrible. But you might feel quite differently if you actually did start running or fighting when they started coming on. I'll tell you what the body's really doing when they come on, as far as I know:

"When a person's really stressed, the brain causes adrenaline to be released into the system, and then quite a few things happen. One is that their heart starts beating faster; and the reason it does that is because when it does, blood will start pumping around the body faster; and the reason the brain thinks that needs to happen is because it'll cause nutrients to start to get to certain parts of the body more quickly to give them more energy. In fact, you might find this hard to believe, but the blood actually contains some oxygen; and that gives the body extra energy when the blood starts being pumped around the system faster.

"The oxygen isn't sent all over the body though when that happens. It's especially sent to the muscles in the arms and legs and to the brain, so the muscles will have the energy to fight better, and the brain will speed up its responses so it can make the body release more adrenaline into the system even more quickly, and things like that, which isn't actually what you want to happen if you're just sitting in a history lesson or something; but still.

"But at the same time, to make sure the brain and muscles have got as much oxygen as the part of the brain that sparks off emotions supposes they'll need, oxygen-containing blood is taken away from the parts of the body that the brain thinks can do without so much for a while, like the skin and the digestive system, because it thinks some of their activities can be put on hold for a bit, so some of the oxygen fuel that powers them can be sent to the muscles instead, that it thinks will need it more for a while. The way the body makes that happen is that the blood vessels in the arm and leg muscles and brain get bigger so more blood can flow into them, while the ones in the skin and the digestive system get smaller for a while, so they push blood out, so it can go to those muscles and the brain, to provide reinforcements of energy to them.

"The thing is that when the blood vessels in the skin get smaller and push some blood out so it can be redirected, it can actually show visibly, in the form of people becoming pale with fear, because part of what gives the face its colour is the blood flowing around under the skin, so if there's a bit less blood there, there'll be less colour."

Zoe said, "Well, I didn't know that! I didn't think I was going to be learning about that kind of detail when I came out this morning! . . . Hang on though: People don't get pale when their adrenaline surges in other situations where they need the extra energy their muscles are being given, do they, like when they're doing a work-out in the gym. Exercise doesn't make people go pale. But the adrenaline must still be making the body take blood away from the skin to send it to the big muscles, if that's what it normally does."

Becky replied, "True. When a person exercises, without being stressed at the same time, I think all the pressure on the body from the exercise will cause their heart to pump blood faster all around their body, although I'm making a bit of a guess here. I'm not sure exactly how it works. But maybe the release of adrenaline has to be accompanied by anxiety to make the body put the fight or flight response into operation, where some blood quickly flows away from the skin so more can go to the leg and arm muscles. Other hormones are released at times like that besides adrenaline, like cortisol, which is a stress hormone, so I expect that makes part of the difference.

"After all, when it isn't accompanied by anxiety, an adrenaline boost can be a pleasurable sensation that people want more of. There are even adrenaline junkies who like to do extreme things to get more of it.

"If a release of adrenaline is accompanied by excitement though, people can get butterflies in the stomach, and that's another sensation that can come on during a panic attack, although then it can sometimes feel more like stomach cramps. It's caused by blood being pushed out of the digestive system so it can flow into the muscles."

Zoe said, "That's interesting. It's nice to know what causes that kind of thing."

She grinned and said, "Mind you, I thought the things you were going to tell me would be more psychological. You're making it sound as if the body's just like a machine that can go wrong and needs fixing, as if what you need is a mechanic to mend it, not a psychologist, as if the technology of the future ought to make it possible to go into a special garage and order a repair to your brain or something."

Becky giggled and said, "Well, for people with really serious problems, brain surgeons can tinker around with their brains; I suppose they could be called brain mechanics. And maybe other doctors could be called body mechanics. It would be funny if hospitals started being called body garages, so someone might say, 'I've got to go to the body garage today because I've got an appointment with a body mechanic.' "

Zoe laughed.

Then Becky got serious again, saying, "I'm coming on to the psychological bits though. The thing is that when you know what all the sensations you get when you have panic attacks are caused by, they probably won't be nearly as scary as they were when you didn't understand why they were happening; and if you're not nearly as scared of them as you were before, then they probably won't get so bad, because it's being scared of what's happening that can make them get as bad as they do; the more scared people get, the worse they'll be.

"Another thing that happens when the adrenaline gets released into the system is that the tubes in the lungs that take in oxygen expand, so as to take in more of it, so the body can get more energy, since a bit gets into the bloodstream when people breathe, and the heart pumps it to the muscles. The lungs trying to take in more oxygen than normal is partly what causes the feeling of being desperate to take in more air that people having panic attacks can get; the lungs are trying to breathe more so more oxygen can be sent to where the brain thinks it's needed. People who are feeling anxious or panicky typically breathe faster than most people do, and that's one reason why.

"The problem is, though, that when people breathe too fast – and this might sound bizarre – it certainly did to me when I first heard it – but it's actually possible to breathe out too much carbon dioxide! I used to think carbon dioxide was a bad thing that needed to be avoided, and that people might breathe it out, but they certainly wouldn't want to breathe any more in again than they had to breathe in with it being in the air around us. Well, obviously if people breathe in too much over time, they'll get poisoned and die. And actually, I found out that breathing in too much carbon dioxide can cause a biological reaction in the body that spurs off a panic attack, especially in some people who've inherited a hyper-sensitivity to it. It's because when you get a big dose of carbon dioxide, and you're breathing a lot more of it in than oxygen, your body senses that you're suffocating, and it can automatically set off a panic response so you do something about it.

"I even heard there was a woman who had some kind of genetic defect that gave her a brain disease that made the part of her brain that regulates emotions waste away, so she couldn't feel fear. You might think it would be really nice not to have to feel that; but it would mean you wouldn't recognise danger easily, because your brain wouldn't give you that jolt of emotion that made you want to get away or combat whatever the problem was.

"This woman once walked through a park in a rough neighbourhood late at night, and saw a man who seemed to be playing with something. She wondered what it was. He called her over, and she was curious about what he was doing, so she went over to him. Only then did she discover it was a knife he was fiddling with, and he held it to her throat. She managed to get away though. She heard a church choir singing in the distance, and it gave her the inspiration to confidently say, 'If you're going to kill me, you'll have to go through my God's angels first.' It seems that put him off the idea.

"She might not have had that experience at all if she'd felt some fear though, because she wouldn't have walked through that park in the middle of the night, or if she absolutely had to, for some reason, she probably wouldn't have gone over to the man when he called her over, curious to find out what he was doing, but she would probably have ignored him and walked briskly to the other side, pretending she hadn't heard him and hoping she'd be OK.

"Scientists wanted to study the woman to see if they could find anything at all that would make her feel fear. So they did experiments on her to try to find something that would scare her. For a long time, nothing did. But they eventually gave her a huge dose of carbon dioxide, and she had this massive panic attack! It turns out that the brain pathways that trigger off fear when part of the brain senses a possible threat coming from outside the body are a bit different from the ones that trigger it off when the threat's coming from inside the body, for instance when there's way way more carbon dioxide than oxygen in the system all of a sudden so the person's suffocating.

"But surprisingly, I learned that there actually needs to be a certain amount of carbon dioxide in the body – not much, but just enough so that there's some kind of balance. Carbon dioxide actually does some important things in the body: I learned that it helps to cause the blood cells that store oxygen to release it, so the tissues in the muscles and other parts of the body can make use of it for energy. So if you lose too much carbon dioxide, your heart will beat faster to try to pump more of it around the body so it can help to release the oxygen. So that's one more reason why it can beat faster during a panic attack. But the heart beating a fair bit faster than normal can be worrying for people who don't know what's causing it, so their panic symptoms can get worse.

"At least, that's how I understand it, although it's possible I'm misremembering a few things I was told, so if you're in doubt about anything I say, look up information from websites you know have got a good reputation.

"But I heard that when people breathe fast during a panic attack, they can breathe out too much carbon dioxide, and then the tubes in their lungs get narrower, to try to stop them losing any more. But that makes it harder to breathe. That's another reason why people having panic attacks can feel as if they're gasping for breath, not being able to get enough, as if they're suffocating or choking. And when the tubes in the lungs get narrower, the brain and heart won't be getting as much oxygen as they need, and then people can even get a sensation of chest tightness or pain, and heart palpitations, where they can get the impression that their heart's beating so powerfully it's going crazy. What it's really doing is trying to compensate for the fact that there's not as much oxygen in the blood it's pumping around the body as the brain thinks there should be, by pumping faster, to pump more around that way.

"You wouldn't lose too much carbon dioxide and start to feel as if you might flake out because of it in a real emergency, because if you were running or doing another really energetic thing, you'd be automatically breathing in a lot more deeply so you'd be taking in a lot more air. People with anxiety problems often automatically breathe shallow breaths but very fast ones from day to day, that get even faster when they're panicking, so that's what causes the temporary carbon dioxide deficiency.

"But not having enough carbon dioxide is what can make you feel faint and dizzy; and people can even get weird visual effects. It must be a horrible sensation, and no wonder it's scary! But getting scared will make the brain make a panic attack worse, because it's like fear piled onto fear. Any increase in fear will make part of the brain think you must be in an even more dangerous situation than it thought, where you'll need to run even faster or fight harder than it thought you'd have to; so it'll increase the fear symptoms, because it thinks that's what's needed to make you react faster so it can protect you. But naturally, that just scares people even more when they don't understand what their panic symptoms are happening for.

"Breathing out too much carbon dioxide can give people other symptoms too, like feeling disorientated, and getting tingling sensations or cramps in places like their hands and feet, and then feeling muscle weakness. So I think that would have been why you got symptoms a bit like some of those.

"It might sound strange, but some psychologists actually recommend that people having panic attacks breathe into a paper bag to relieve the symptoms that are being caused by breathing out too much carbon dioxide – the thinking being that if you start breathing in the air you've just breathed out into the bag, you'll be breathing in a lot of the carbon dioxide you just breathed out, so that'll help the body replenish its supplies again, so your symptoms will fade. I can't say I'd fancy the idea myself! Well, not in public anyway. People would wonder what on earth I was doing! And I suppose you'd have to be careful you didn't do it for too long, in case your panic was partly being caused by your brain being hyper-sensitive to too much carbon dioxide so it triggered off more panic because of that.

"They say it has to be a paper bag rather than a plastic one, because paper's porous, whereas plastic isn't, so there would be less chance of you suffocating if you got carried away somehow and breathed in it for ages and ages.

"But it's not as if it's necessary. If it sounds inconvenient, and possibly embarrassing if you're in public when a panic attack comes on, I don't think you really need to carry a paper bag with you around everywhere, because another thing that can calm down the symptoms and restore the balance of carbon dioxide to oxygen in your system is if you really really slow your breathing down, so you're breathing in very slowly and steadily and gently, and then breathing out even more slowly, so your body has a chance to absorb any carbon dioxide it needs before you breathe it all out. And breathing very slowly will help to calm down symptoms like your heart beating faster. So if you do that for a few minutes, your panic symptoms will hopefully fade away. It might be hard to breathe slowly when your instincts are giving you an urge to breathe fast. But if you can manage it, it might well help.

"It isn't necessary to do that breathing technique if you'd rather not, since other techniques can calm people down too, or even just waiting the panic out can, because the body just naturally calms down after a while, although just waiting till it does and having to patiently put up with the fear till it fades away isn't easy or pleasant for people, because it feels so horrible.

"One technique you could try is talking to or about the emotional part of your brain that's setting the symptoms off, as soon as you feel a twinge of panic coming on, before you're in too much of an emergency mode to be calm enough to do that, for instance saying, 'Come on brain, don't kick off again. There's no need for this. I'm not in danger. You're making an error, you poor old thing.'

"It might not be easy to catch the panic in time to do that before it gets really strong, because panic can come on very quickly; but whenever you can, you might even be able to stop a panic attack in its tracks, by reassuring the emotional part of your brain that there's no need for one.

"In fact, if you can predict that one might come on, for instance if one always does when you're in a certain situation, then whenever you're about to go into that situation, before you even get a twinge of panic, you can give the alarmist part of your brain a bit of a pep talk to try to keep it calm and sensible.

"Another technique you could try is describing to yourself the reasons for each panic symptom as they come on, as best you can, for instance thinking, 'There goes my heart beating faster! It must be trying harder than usual to pump oxygen to my big muscles to give them more energy.'

"If you make a list of the causes of all the symptoms today, and then often read it to remind yourself of what they are, it'll be much easier to bring them to mind when you first suspect that panic's coming on than it would be if you had to dredge up half-forgotten information from the back of your mind, when you might be quickly getting way too stressed to feel like doing it.

"Using a breathing technique's another option though. So I think your school counsellor gave you good advice when she recommended that you breathe really slowly when a panic attack comes on."

Zoe smiled and said, "Oh, that's one good thing about school at least then."

Becky grinned and said, "Yeah. I think it would be good if things like this were taught to everyone in actual lessons, in case they need it . . . I mean I think there should be special lessons where it's taught; I don't mean they should teach it in the kinds of lessons they have now, say in the middle of a geography lesson or something. Imagine that! Imagine the teacher saying things like, 'The highest mountain in the world is Mount Everest. It's a very difficult mountain to climb, and if the thought of climbing it makes you feel like having a panic attack, you don't have to be as scared of the symptoms as you might think you do, because they're only being caused by . . . this, that and the other.'"

Zoe grinned and said, "If a teacher taught us that anything was just being caused by 'this, that and the other', I don't think they'd be doing a good job of teaching the lesson!"

They laughed, and Becky said, "No! Imagine someone writing that that was the cause of something in an exam, thinking it must be the proper answer to the question, because that's what the teacher had taught them it was."

They giggled again.

But then Becky said, "Anyway, getting back to talking about panic attacks and controlling the breathing: I think some people find it very difficult to slow their breathing down when they're really feeling like breathing fast, like they will when they're having a panic attack; but if you're finding it difficult, there are techniques that might help you control the urge to breathe fast, so you can more easily discipline yourself to breathe slowly till the panic calms down, if you still want to try the breathing technique.

"One idea is that you could try to make sure you're breathing slowly enough by imagining you're doing something it would take several seconds to do each time you breathe, like imagining walking – not running – but just walking in quite a leisurely way, up a flight of, say twelve steps when you breathe in, and about fifteen when you breathe out.

"It'll be a lot easier to do that when you've just noticed the first signs of panic, rather than when it's in full swing though, since then you won't feel like doing anything calmly.

"But if you do manage to have a go at controlling your breathing, another idea is that maybe you could say something to yourself every time you breathe in and out that would take long enough to say that if you breathed in all the time while you were saying it, and then breathed out all the while during the time when you were saying it, it would make sure your breathing slowed down.

"So maybe when you breathe in, you could imagine you're a BBC newsreader, announcing on air for the whole country to hear, 'I've got a confession to make: For the past twenty years, we've been making up all the news we've broadcast.'"

Zoe giggled and said, "Gosh, imagine if they really did say that!"

Becky said, "Yeah! Wouldn't it cause a scandal! . . . Actually it was funny recently . . . Well, I shouldn't really have laughed, I don't suppose. But I turned the radio on in the afternoon one day, and the news came on; and the first thing they said was that a certain president of a far-away country had died. The first thought that came into my head was, 'Again? You told us he'd done that this morning!' Then I realised it must mean there wasn't much new news, so they were telling us the same news they'd told us hours before."

Zoe and Becky laughed. Zoe said, "That reminds me of something that I suppose you might call black humour that I heard on the radio once: I think it was a historical programme. People were talking about the Second World War. There was someone from a far-off country, telling us they were in a ballet dancing group in those days, as far as I can remember, and they said times were hard, and that one day, one of the group came in late. The teacher was annoyed with him. He apologised, saying his mother had just died. The teacher raised his voice and said sternly, 'Don't let it happen again!' He must have meant don't be late again; but it sounded as if he meant don't let your mum die again!"

Becky giggled.

Then she said, "That reminds me of an advert I heard on the radio once. I'd just smelled a nice smell that smelled like garlic bread, coming from a neighbour's house; and my mum had the radio on, and I heard part of an advert that must have been for a restaurant that said, 'Come and enjoy the best Italian cuisine, created by' . . . and I thought it was about to say, 'mixing garlic and olives' or something; but instead, it said, 'the best southern Italian chefs!'

"My first thought was, 'That's disgusting! I bet they wouldn't taste nice at all, you cannibals!' But then I realised they must mean the chefs made the food, not that they were actually in it!"

They laughed again.

Then Becky said, "Anyway, getting back to talking about breathing: When you breathe out during a panic attack, to make sure you only let your breath out slowly, while you're doing it, you could maybe imagine you're the same BBC newsreader as you did when you breathed in, saying, 'I know we ought to be sorry about making up the news all this time, but it's given us a good living and kept us employed, so we're not, and you ought to be pleased for us because it's kept us in work.' "

Zoe laughed and said, "Imagine if they really thought they could do that and get away with it!"

Becky grinned and replied, "Yeah! It would be funny! Another idea is that maybe every time you breathe in, you could imagine you were the prime minister, standing up in the House of Commons and announcing, 'Before I decide whether this policy's a good one, I'm going to have to see if my mum approves of it.' And when you breathe out, maybe you could imagine saying, 'I always have to consult with my mum about whether any new policies I think up are good ideas before I decide whether they're sensible ones for this government to have.'

"Anyway, try to time your breathing so the last bit of breath you breathe in or out always coincides with the last words you imagine saying."

"The last words I imagine saying?" said Zoe, grinning. "If I take too long to say those things, they just might be. Literally! My last words ever."

Becky laughed and said, "I think you'd have to take a very, very long time to say them for the effort of breathing out slowly while you were doing it to deprive you of so much breath it killed you!"

Zoe giggled again, and said she'd try Becky's suggestion, although it might be hard when she was in the grip of fear feelings and the horrible physical sensations panic caused.

Becky said, "Yeah, it might not be easy, especially if panic comes on quickly and you're really feeling like breathing fast, and you're not in the mood to say funny phrases or anything. It might be even harder if the panic comes on when you weren't expecting it, so it takes you by surprise, and you're off your guard, and it's making you feel as if there must really be something to panic about because it's making you scared. But with practice, it might get easier and easier. You could try it when you feel the very first stages of what might be panic, if there's time before it gets really bad, and see if you can concentrate on doing it then.

"Or you could even try it when you just feel a bit stressed, since anxious people often breathe too fast even when they're not panicking. If you can't do it, don't worry, because there are other ways of getting over panic, as I said. But see how you go."

Zoe said she would.

Becky said, "You could try writing funny phrases like that down, to help you remember them; and then you could say them in your mind while you're breathing in and out when you're just feeling normal, to get used to it, so it'll come more easily when you begin to have a panic attack. You could invent some of your own phrases for fun too, that are about the same length as the ones I've suggested, and write them down, and practise them sometimes.

"It'll be good to slow your breathing right down for a few moments anyway from time to time, maybe a few times a day, because sometimes you might breathe too fast without realising you're doing it, at times when you're not having a panic attack. If you deliberately slow your breathing down for a few minutes, it might stay slowed down for some time on its own after you stop, and that might help your stress levels go down a bit.

"Quick breathing will often not be fast enough to bring on any physical symptoms, but it can still be worth slowing it down. The thing is, breathing too quickly over time when you're stressed makes it more likely that you will have a panic attack, because it can cue the brain to gear the body up for fast energetic action, which makes it more likely that you'll start to feel a physical symptom or two, which you could interpret as an ominous sign of panic coming on. That might make your anxiety worse, or your stress might be increasing at the same time for some other reason, till it feels like anxiety that's high enough to bring on a panic attack. That could scare you, because panic's so horrible, but the fear brought on by that in itself will make it worse.

"I don't know how often fast breathing's likely to trigger off a panic attack. It probably varies a lot depending on how much of it people do, and how anxious they are at the time. There might not be that much need to worry about your breathing really. But still, maybe just when you've got spare moments sometimes, you could try the technique of breathing slowly, while you're imagining you're saying a funny phrase, both for practice so it's easier to bring to mind at the first sign of panic, and because it might calm down any anxiety you've got at the time.

"And whenever you start worrying that you might have a panic attack, because you're in a place where you've had one before, or something's happening that happened when you had one before, you could start breathing very slowly, and that might ward the symptoms off before they even start."

Zoe said she thought that might be a good idea. She asked Becky to repeat the phrases she'd suggested she imagine saying while she breathed slowly to calm down her panic symptoms, and wrote them down.

Then Becky said, "From what I've learned, doing exercise can help get the breathing back to normal, so you stop breathing too fast, or you start taking in more air than you were before, without you having to think about it. And it can help calm anxiety. In fact, if you can go for a good run or something when a panic attack starts, chances are the symptoms won't get any worse, because you'll be doing what panic attacks are designed to make you do – running away.

"I heard a therapist say that one day, a nurse came for therapy and told him she kept having panic attacks, and he told her it was the emotional part of her brain making a mistake and gearing her body up to run away or fight when it shouldn't. Then she started having a panic attack right then. Just outside, there was a big grassy bank. He suggested they both go and run up it, to prove to her that the panic was giving her the energy to run fast. She agreed, and they both raced each other to the top. She won. Afterwards, she felt good, and her panic had gone, while he felt out of breath!

"Maybe finding a way to do some really good regular exercise will keep your anxiety levels down a bit and your breathing more normal – that's if you breathe a bit too fast quite often, and that's part of what contributes to your panic attacks coming on, like it does with some people. Exercising can help work off the nervous energy that partly makes people more likely to breathe fast. So it could contribute to making it less likely that you'll get panic attacks in future.

"Hopefully, understanding what makes them come on will do that too, because then the panic symptoms won't scare you so much, so you won't start panicking more when they come on because they feel so horrid and you don't understand what's happening. So your fear of them won't make your panic attacks worse, like it might have done before. That's why I've been telling you about what causes what.

"Some people actually have panic attacks starting off when they exercise though. It's because the body does some of the same things to help people exercise that it does when people start having panic attacks, like making the heart beat faster so it can pump more blood around the body to try to give the muscles more energy; but because the symptoms feel so much like the beginnings of the symptoms of the panic attacks the people have had before, they get scared, so that makes the panic attacks begin to come on. Then they get more scared because they feel worse and dread another panic attack, so their body makes the symptoms worse because the emotional part of their brain thinks their fear means there must be danger; and the symptoms getting worse scares them more; and the cycle can quickly get worse and worse like that, till they have a full-blown panic attack.

"If instead of getting scared when you're exercising if you feel symptoms that are familiar because they're the ones you get at the start of a panic attack, you remind yourself that your body's just doing what bodies do during exercise to give people more energy, and if you try to relax and let any fear feelings you get at the same time just pass over you and then drift away, they're far more likely to disappear than they will be if you're sure they mean something's wrong so you just get more scared.

"I know that can be difficult for people to do, because the fear will often come on strongly all of a sudden, before people who have panic attacks even have time to think about it. But like I said, it might surprise you, but even the fear you feel when you have a panic attack serves a good purpose – or at least, a purpose that the emotional part of your brain that sets it off thinks is good: The purpose is to motivate you to take action quickly. It's too bad if you're just sitting in a lesson at school, or else innocently using an exercise bike at the gym, and it would be awkward to do something really energetic and active all of a sudden, like jumping up and starting to use a punchbag, pushing the person using it out the way first, which might result in a punch-up between the two of you.

"The brain's urgent reaction can be embarrassing if there's no need to do anything at all – the part of your brain that governs emotions wants you to anyway. It thinks it needs to do something dramatic to get your attention, because it thinks you're in an emergency and you need to run away or fight. So it gives you that really horrid fear sensation.

"The thing is that if it didn't give you any strong emotional signals ever, say if it was in the old days and big wild beasts roamed this country, and one day a great predatory giant tomato on legs started chasing after you ... well, OK, that would have been pretty unlikely, since I don't suppose any of those have ever existed; but just imagine if one chased after you, and you stayed fairly calm, and just thought, 'Oh my word! What could this be! I suppose I'd better be getting out of its way really in case it eats me!' or something, then it would probably have caught up with you and swallowed you whole before you could think another thing!

"Hey, imagine someone cooking a big tomato on legs with a head, thinking of enjoying it for breakfast, only to find a person inside that it had somehow swallowed, and that was the reason it had legs and a head!"

Zoe chuckled.

Then Becky said, "Seriously though, when the brain sends you a strong fear signal, it's its way of saying, 'Get a move on!', because it thinks you're in immediate danger, for some reason."

Zoe said, "That sounds daft. It's as if there's some kind of major design fault in the brain that makes the body behave as if it's in an emergency when it isn't at all!"

164

Becky said, "Well, I think the brain was programmed to help people cope with tougher living conditions than most people have to in this country – you know, like in the old days, when giant hairy tomatoes roamed around . . . Or whatever beasts actually did roam around eating people in those days.

"Anyway, even nowadays, some people will be living lives where they're likely to be in more emergency situations than a lot of other people will probably be in, and the brain's programmed so they'll react quickly, since even taking the time to think about whether the situation they're in really is an emergency situation or not could be the difference between life and death in extreme cases, such as if they're crossing a road and a car suddenly comes whizzing towards them, or like if you were walking down a dark alley, and you heard footsteps behind you, and wondered for some time whether it was likely just another harmless person or someone wanting to do you harm, and in that time, they caught up with you, while if the brain had triggered its emergency response and you started panicking and ran away, you might be saved, even if that did mean that sometimes, it really was just another harmless person behind you, who felt insulted because you ran away from them.

"It could even be that people who were a bit neurotic were more likely to survive in the old days than people who were more laid-back, who wouldn't have got so worried about what things like that might be. So neurotic people might have been the ones most likely to have lived to pass down their genes to future generations, which might be part of the reason why people's brains are the way they are today, although with some being more likely to set panic symptoms off than others.

"Having said that though, making quick decisions before you've even had time to think about it doesn't always mean you're more likely to survive, like if a person ran away, straight into a bog and sank in the mud or something. So I don't know how much of an effect getting scared quickly really had on survival."

Zoe said, "Actually, my mum gets easily stressed, so I wonder if my panic problems could have been partly to do with the genes I got passed down to me from her."

Becky replied, "Maybe. There could be other things going on though, if it's not just what happened to you and your brother that caused your panic problems. I've heard that there are a few physical conditions that cause symptoms like the ones that make people feel panicky. One is where there's a big drop in people's blood sugar sometimes, for some reason, and that causes the body to release adrenaline, because one thing adrenaline does is to cause the liver to turn a substance in the body into blood sugar that the body can use for energy, so the blood sugar levels will rise again. But at the same time as the adrenaline's doing that, it'll make the heart beat faster, and that can feel like the beginnings of a panic attack. So anyone who's scared it is one will get more scared, so they're more likely to have one.

"An overactive thyroid can cause symptoms a lot like anxiety too.

"And stress makes the body release a hormone called cortisol, which makes blood sugar levels really rise, which could be useful if extra energy's needed, but they can get way above what's healthy if the stress is really bad and goes on for a while. The thing is that exercise can lower levels of cortisol so it stops doing that. So regular exercise is especially good for people with anxiety problems. When levels of the stress hormone go down, people can feel quite a bit better.

"Anyway, maybe go to the doctor if nothing I say helps you, since it might be that medication could help, or that you need to be investigated for something else. But I don't think most of the illnesses that cause symptoms like the ones people can think are the start of panic attacks are that common."

Zoe smiled and said, "I hope they aren't. I wonder if eating regular chocolate would be a treatment for the one where blood sugar levels drop a lot though; maybe if people ate it often enough, it would replenish blood sugar supplies before the adrenaline kicked in, so they wouldn't get the symptoms that feel like the start of a panic attack. I don't suppose it would be healthy though! Imagine if chocolate was an official cure for panic attacks, and you could get it on prescription from doctors."

Becky grinned and said, "Wow, that would be good, wouldn't it – well, apart from the fact that going to the doctor's would make you unhealthily fat!

"There would probably be people pretending to have panic attacks though, just to get some chocolate on prescription. Or people might go to the doctor's and say, 'My panic symptoms are getting a bit better, but I really think it would do me good if you could increase the dose of chocolate you prescribe me, to make them go away altogether.'

"Imagine if a low dose of chocolate might be, say, one little chocolate bar a week, and then doses could go up and up, till the highest dose was, say, three great big bars a day! On prescription!"

Zoe laughed and said, "Wow! I think you definitely would need to do exercise then as a treatment, to lose weight!"

They grinned.

Then Becky said seriously, "Anyway, getting back to talking about your anxiety problem, your panic attacks might not be being caused by a physical condition; the problem might be all psychological. The emotional part of the brain can decide there's an emergency and set the symptoms of a panic attack off for a few reasons:

"One is if you're in a situation that has some kind of resemblance to one where you felt scared before. The brain will recognise it before you can even really think about it, and decide there must be some danger, because it knows you were scared there before, or in a place or situation that's related to it in some way, even if it's just that someone's got a jumper on that looks like a jumper someone near you was wearing when you had a panic attack before. So that might explain why you had a panic attack when you went to the station the first time after your brother's accident, and even why you had one in class when the topic of trains came up. The emotional part of your brain thinks it's doing its job and warning you that you're in a situation that's got a connection to one that was dangerous, thinking that might mean it's dangerous too.

"Brains can even set panic symptoms off if people are in situations a bit like ones they were in before that just *felt* dangerous but weren't really, such as if someone got scared because they suddenly saw a spider, but the spider was actually harmless.

"Another reason people's brains can start off giving them a panic attack is because they've been worrying and worrying so much, not necessarily about anything to do with something bad that happened, but just about anything, so they get more and more stressed, till the emotional part of their brain thinks something really major must be happening, so it sets off the panic symptoms. Or it can be because they worry and worry that they might have a panic attack somewhere where they had one before, thinking they really don't want that to happen because it was such an upsetting experience, and all the worry makes them more and more stressed, till again, part of their brain thinks something seriously bad must be going on, so it starts off a panic attack, the very thing they were worrying about having, because they really didn't want one.

"Then if they start worrying even more because they're scared it's going to be horrible, it'll get even worse, because of the worrying they're doing, that makes the emotional part of their brain think that whatever situation they're in must really be bad, so it sets off more symptoms. Also the worry itself will be making them feel worse.

"When someone has their first panic attack, even though it might just be brought on by stress that's been rising and rising till a little bit more stress tips the emotional part of the brain into setting off the kind of fear reactions they might have if they were in danger and needed to run away or fight to survive, the subconscious mind won't register that that's what's happening, because it instinctively associates panic feelings with danger, so it'll register the place the person's having the panic attack in as a dangerous place, without the thinking part of the brain realising it's doing it.

"But it means that the next time the person's in that place, or even just a similar place, such as if they're in a supermarket the first time it happens, perhaps getting more and more on edge before the panic strikes, because they're in a long queue and running out of time before they need to get back to work, and then a while later they go in a different shop with similarities to the supermarket, then unless they're a lot more relaxed than they were before, their brain might automatically set off alarm signals that feel like the beginnings of panic, because it mistakenly feels as if they're in a place of danger where they might need to fight or run away again.

"The person will likely have been so scared by the panic attack the first time that what feels like the start of another one will be just as scary. But their fear of the panic returning will add to the panic symptoms that are already there, so the panic will get worse. Then they'll likely get even more scared, worrying about why they're getting the horrible symptoms and whether they're going to get worse; but the increased fear will make the panic attack even worse. And so on.

"Then the subconscious part of the mind will assume that confirms that the shop they're in is a dangerous place, so the next time the person's in a shop like it, or even if they're just standing next to someone with a similar hairstyle to someone who was standing near them in the shop, or something else as minor as that, it might well set off more panic signals, and the same cycle of increasing panic will likely start again.

"That's how agoraphobia can begin. Some people get too afraid to even leave their homes in the end, because they're scared of having yet another panic attack in public, and they can't predict when one might be triggered off.

"But it's possible to reverse the process of having panic attacks in more and more places, if a person knows what's going on. The techniques I've been talking about will likely reassure the emotional part of your brain that things are OK and calm it down over time, so it becomes less and less reactive, less and less likely to misinterpret things that are really harmless as possible signs of danger that it needs to prepare you to quickly react to."

Zoe said, "I hope so. It's interesting to know what's really going on! I'll have to try and remember that."

170

Becky replied, "Write the techniques for dealing with panic down, along with a bit about the causes of it, and then maybe you can read the notes you've made sometimes to remind yourself, so the information will come to your mind more easily when you feel as if a panic attack might be about to start off.

"So, you know, there's the breathing technique, the technique of describing symptoms as you feel them come on so you're demystifying them, and a few more. One technique I can't remember if I mentioned is that if you can think to do it, you can imagine you're in control, with authority over the emotional side of your brain. So every time you feel a panic attack starting off from now on, as soon as you can, before it gets too strong for you to be able to think easily, you could firmly say to the emotional part of your brain something like, 'Alarmist part of my brain, no! This isn't an emergency, so you don't need to be giving me fear sensations, and you don't need to be making my body release adrenaline so it'll start giving me symptoms I don't want, like making my heart beat faster to pump oxygen to my muscles to give me more energy to run away or fight that I won't really need.'

"It'll be like the part of your brain that thinks things through before making decisions talking to the part of your brain that makes snap decisions when it decides there's an emergency.

"It might not be easy to do that, because panic comes on quickly, and when it does, people aren't in the mood to think of anything. But you could give it a go.

"Or maybe instead of talking to the emotional part of your brain firmly, you could talk to it sympathetically, trying to reassure it. You could maybe talk to it as if it's a friend who's really worrying about something, and say things like, 'Come on, there's no need to start a panic attack here.' "

Zoe smiled at the suggestion. She told Becky she thought it was a good idea, and said she'd try it.

Becky said, "Another thing you could try is reasoning with the emotional part of your brain, to convince it it's overreacting. For instance, if you're going past the station and it feels as if a panic attack might be about to come on, or even if you feel OK but just suspect one might soon, you could say to that part of your brain something like, 'Don't start a panic attack, will you. Come on, really, what evidence is there that something bad's going to happen to me this time? OK, something bad happened once. But it's not actually any more likely that something bad will happen to me than to anyone else; and think about how many people flood in and out of stations every day perfectly happily, without anything bad happening to them; I'd have to be very unlucky for bad things to keep happening to me. So there's no need to set off the panic symptoms.' That kind of thing might help calm you down sometimes.

"The thing is, your emotions might lead you to have thoughts that are tempting to brood on but that are in reality self-defeating, such as that stations are dangerous places. But giving them room to play on your mind will just increase your fears. So it's best to reassure yourself by reminding yourself of what you know really to be the truth, for instance that stations are normally safe.

"When you're feeling anxious, it might be hard for you to believe there isn't a good reason for it, because it's easy for people to presume they must be having the strong emotions they are because something's wrong or at risk of going wrong. It can be hard to believe there isn't really any significance in the emotions at times like that, because they give people a sense of urgency or risk that can feel very significant, so it can be difficult to shrug them off as the brain just making a mistake.

"But the more you let any thoughts that your emotions tempt you to think about how you're at risk take up room in your mind, the more you'll be stirring up the very anxiety that makes you think there must be something wrong. It can be a vicious cycle, with your anxiety getting worse the more you worry over them, and your worsening anxiety convincing you all the more that you're at risk, tempting you to think more of the thoughts.

"So it might be helpful for you to remind yourself that there's no reason for you to be scared really, and to think of yourself as being the boss of the emotional part of your brain, or the sensible one, so you can reassure it that it doesn't need to make you anxious or panicky."

Zoe said she could see the sense in the idea and she'd think about trying it. But then she said, "The thing is though, I know really that panicking is an overreaction to things. Actually, I feel stupid sometimes when I think about it; I feel as if I must be such a weakling, because a lot of people have had much worse things happen to them than I did, but I'm sure a lot of them don't have panic attacks and things like I do. You know, you hear about people who went through the world wars and things but still managed to carry on; if they were all having panic attacks like me, I wonder if the country could have even functioned properly! And yet here am I, panicking so much when things actually turned out alright for our family in the end!"

Becky looked sympathetic, and said, "Well, it's possible you could be genetically predisposed to suffering a worse reaction than some people do; but remember what I've been saying about what the emotional part of the brain does when it gets the impression it needs to warn you about danger in more and more places so it sets off fear signals more of the time. It isn't to do with some kind of weakness in you, just the emotional part of your brain making mistakes, which you yourself can train it not to do, with the more thoughtful side of your brain. It's just about the way brains work, not about some people being weaker than others. Some people's brains are more pre-disposed to triggering panic off than others, either because of their stress levels over time, or their genetic makeup, or because they developed more neurotic personalities than the average because of things that happened as they were growing up, or maybe other things. But there are always more complex things going on than just people being weak.

"A lot of people who went through the wars probably did have some kinds of mental health problems by the end of them. At least a lot of them would have had people around them who would have understood why they were having them and supported them. That must have made things at least a bit easier for them. I think people with mental health problems can often find support groups for people with problems like theirs a help today, partly because they can be reassured by knowing they're not alone with their problems, but that they can have the companionship of people who understand them and might be able to tell them about things that have helped them, which might encourage them to try them too. Maybe you could join a support group if your problems take a while to go away."

Zoe said she'd think about it.

Then Becky reminded her of the main things she'd said, and Zoe noted them down.

174

When she'd finished, Becky said, "You could see what works best to get rid of your panic whenever it begins to come on – reassuring your brain that it doesn't need to give you the symptoms, or breathing slowly, or both, or something else. Like I've said though, it'll be easier if you try whatever you try before the panic really gets a grip of you, since it'll be harder to concentrate once it does, although you still might be able to.

"Don't get discouraged and give up using a technique if it doesn't work immediately. It might work better with a bit of practice, or more gradually than you're expecting, or with a slight adjustment to it.

"Another one you could try, either when the panicky feelings start, before they get too strong for you to think, or if you keep having thoughts that worry you more and more, like about what might happen if a panic attack comes on while you're supposed to be doing something else, or about how you'll cope if another bad thing happens, or about anything else that worries you, is to tell your brain to stop, and then to deliberately distract yourself from your thoughts and feelings for a while by thinking about or doing something else, even if it's just counting the number of leaves on a plant, or the number of red cars going by or something. Or it could be trying to concentrate on looking at the scenery around you, or planning something you need to do, or trying to remember in detail something you did once, or tapping your foot on the ground and thinking about just what it's like to feel the sensation you feel when you do that, or whatever.

"But try to concentrate on whatever it is with all your attention, so you're not giving any attention to the panic symptoms. That way, you won't get absorbed in worrying about them, so they're more likely to fade away than get worse.

"Worry will automatically fade if you get engrossed in some kind of absorbing activity, because people can't worry and be giving their attention to something else at the same time. You don't have to try and force worry out of your mind by making efforts to get frantically busy. It'll start fading away naturally if you're focusing your attention on something you like or that's unrelated to it.

"You might not have to make deliberate efforts to calm your brain down for long; maybe you'll have fewer and fewer panic attacks the more you use the techniques. And maybe before long, you won't have to say funny phrases when you breathe or anything – supposing slow breathing does help you – because you'll just be familiar with the length of time it helps to breathe in and out for, so you'll do it automatically; and maybe soon, whenever you feel a panic symptom, you'll just automatically think something like, 'Oh there goes my daft old brain again, setting off panic symptoms by mistake', or you'll automatically know to distract yourself from the feelings or panicky thoughts so they don't go into that cycle of getting worse and worse the more you think about them. The more in control of them you feel, and the more under-standing you have of what's really going on in your body, the less panicky you'll feel about it, and then the panic attacks won't get so bad.

"In fact, after a while, or even pretty quickly, your brain might feel so reassured by you telling it there's no need to worry, or you realising what it's really doing, that it stops setting off panic attacks altogether."

Zoe started feeling more optimistic. She said she'd try doing what Becky advised.

Becky and Zoe Relax, and Have a Conversation That Makes Them Laugh

They decided to sit back and relax for a while.

But then Becky seemed to become a bit self-conscious. She frowned and said, "I think I'm getting too much belly flab! I really ought to put a dent in it!"

Zoe giggled and said, "Put a dent in it? Imagine how that would look! If it was vertically down the middle, you'd end up looking as if you had two bottoms, one at the back and one at the front."

They laughed. Becky said, "I just meant I think I need to lose a bit of weight. They do really nice food in the cafes at university! It's a pity it's fattening! . . . Actually, imagine if universities wanted to make more money, and realised the food in their cafes was so nice they could turn it into a tourist attraction, so they made adverts that said things like, 'Come to university for the day and enjoy our gorgeous food!' "

Zoe grinned and joked, "People might think it was a course to teach people how to enjoy eating food more. Or maybe they'd just go to that university for the day for fun, and all the real students would be annoyed because they wouldn't be able to get into the cafes because of the long queues of tourists outside, waiting to buy the food themselves!"

Becky grinned and said, "Maybe it would be the policy that they would have a course to help people enjoy the food at one end of the room, which mainly consisted of them just eating it, and then the tourists would go out of a door that was specially designated for them, and find themselves in a room where they were taught some good ways of losing weight after their feast, so they'd at least get a bit of education there."

Zoe chuckled.

Then Becky wiggled her toes in the sand, and said, "You know, we think of the desert as being all sandy, but actually, I heard that most of it hasn't got soft sand on it. Imagine if there was a campaign to put lots of sand on more of the Sahara desert, to make it more attractive, in the hope of enticing more tourists to go there, to help people who live there earn a good living."

Zoe smiled and said, "The desert would be a scary place to go on holiday! At least if you got lost there!"

Becky agreed. But then she grinned and said, "But imagine if the organisers were convinced they could make it sound attractive, and they planned to get more sand to the desert by recruiting people here to shovel as much sand as they could carry off a beach, and then travel with it to the desert and spread it out there, and then come back and get more, and then travel to the desert again and spread that out there. Imagine if their advert said that no one would be paid, but their reward would be that travelling all that way with as much sand as they could carry would help them lose weight, so they could think of it as a helpful weight loss programme. If you needed to lose weight, would you join up and work for them?"

Zoe laughed and said, "No way! I'm not that daft! Actually, I think I remember hearing that there are people actually selling Sahara Desert sand. I vaguely remember hearing that quite a bit was sold to Gibraltar, to make their beaches more sandy. Anyway, what would the beaches here be like if weight loss enthusiasts shovelled all the sand off them? What's underneath it?"

Becky wasn't sure. She said, "I suppose the sand here would need replacing. I wonder what they'd replace it with. Maybe sawdust and wood shavings and things – the kinds of things people put at the bottom of rabbit hutches and hamster cages to absorb moisture from their wees."

Zoe chuckled and said, "They'd be absorbing a whole lot of moisture when the tide came in!"

Becky grinned and said, "Or maybe the sand could be replaced with tons of tobacco! That would make tobacco companies happy! They'd stop minding it when people give up smoking, because they'd have another use for their tobacco."

Zoe laughed and said, "Somehow I don't think going to the seaside would have the same appeal if the beach was covered in tobacco instead of sand – well, apart from for smokers, who might nick some. Still, I suppose you never know. Imagine if people started saying things like, 'I do think it's nice to go down to the beach, have a sunbathe, and wiggle my toes in the tobacco, watching the kids happily making tobacco castles with their buckets and spades.'"

They both laughed.

Then Becky said, "A few minutes ago, I heard what I think must have been a seagull that sounded like a squeaky toy, for some reason. Imagine if cigarettes made noises like squeaky toys! Imagine if they'd always make a squeak on one note when a person breathed the smoke in, and then they'd squeak on another note when they breathed out. If there was a room full of smokers, wouldn't it make a racket! But I wonder if as many people would have started smoking if cigarettes had always made squeaky noises."

Zoe grinned and said, "I don't know. It wouldn't surprise me if some people still wanted to smoke. So imagine if the beach was covered in tobacco! Smokers would love it all being there! The beach might be a very noisy place if it was always full of smokers rolling their own cigarettes, and those ones made squeaky noises when they smoked them as well as shop-bought ones. And smokers would probably come to the beach at night and take bagfuls of tobacco home with them!"

Becky grinned and said, "They'd probably have to be brave to smoke it, when they knew people would have been trampling around on it all day!"

Zoe smiled and said, "Imagine if the tobacco on the beach started running low, and then a load of it got washed out by the tide! Imagine if the tide washed more and more of it out over time. Maybe lots of smokers would run into the sea and try to get it back. Imagine if the tide had often washed it out quite far by the time they realised it had done it. They might start swimming after it, trying to find it. Maybe some of them would end up swimming the Channel all the way to France in search of it if they couldn't find it."

Becky said, "Or maybe they'd employ divers to dive down and try to find it under the sea. Actually, maybe tobacco companies would employ the divers. Maybe sea-soaked tobacco would be advertised as a really attractive product, and become really popular, and tobacco companies would start replacing all the tobacco on the beaches when it washed away, so tourists and day-trippers at the seaside could feel the supposedly delightful sensation of tobacco under their bare feet and watch children building tobacco castles with their buckets and spades, and then the tobacco companies would pay divers to find all the tobacco that washed out to sea whenever a load of it did. Then they'd sell it to people as an exotic delicacy with the promise that it would bring to mind blissful thoughts of holidays in the sun, and the people who bought it would dry it out and smoke it."

180

Zoe giggled and said, "If they scooped it up from the bottom of the sea, imagine what else might be in it! There might be lots of little fish and other sea creatures!"

Becky laughed and said, "Well maybe people would get to like smoking fish. And maybe tobacco companies would advertise it as healthy. They might have adverts that said things like, 'Inhale nutritious omega-3 fatty acid and vitamin D while you're smoking our special fish tobacco!"

Zoe grinned and said, "Oh yuck! I still wouldn't fancy smoking fish, even if they do have a few healthy nutrients in them! And you don't know what else would be in the tobacco, do you, like little bits of biodegrading plastic from bags and things that had washed off the land onto the sea floor, and bits of rotting seaweed, and goodness knows what else!"

Becky replied, "That's true. Mind you, we don't know what they put in cigarettes anyway – all those unhealthy chemicals that are in them!"

Zoe became serious, and said thoughtfully, "That's a thought!"

Becky Advises Zoe On Ways to Stop Flashbacks, Where She Feels as If Her Traumatic Experience is Happening Again as Memories of it Intrude Into Her Mind

There was a bit of a pause in the conversation, and then Becky said tentatively, "I suppose we ought to get back to doing what we came here to do. Stephanie told me you get vivid flashbacks, where you suddenly get the impression that you're right back there on the train platform and what happened's happening all over again, and you end up feeling upset."

"Yes," replied Zoe. "They're horrible. Sometimes just hearing the sound of a train will set one off, or a television programme where there's a baby in hospital, because they remind me of what happened. Sometimes they start for no reason I can work out though; the other day there was something about kids at a school where they believed in teaching the kids traditional skills like cooking. Some kids were proudly showing off dresses and cuddly toys they'd sewn themselves. Suddenly I was having one of those flashback things. They make me feel as if I'm really back there in the station with my baby brother falling on the ground and screaming his head off, and his head bleeding.

"The other day there was a film on telly where some teenagers were walking in the woods, and a big dog came out from the trees, and they all got scared and ran away; and even that seemed to set one off!"

Becky thought for a few seconds, and then said, "I've heard that sometimes flashbacks can be set off if you have the same feelings you had when the bad thing that led to the flashbacks happened. Maybe you imagined how those teenagers must have been feeling when the dog came towards them, and it was like the way you were feeling when your brother got injured, and that's what reminded you of it. And maybe the thought of children sewing triggered off a memory in your brain about your brother needing stitches, and that was what set the other one off.

"Mind you, people can get better without knowing what sets them all off. I've read about a few techniques people can use to stop things like that in a couple of psychology books.

"One technique is to sit somewhere quiet where you won't be disturbed, not while you're having a flashback, but just at a time that's convenient for you, preferably when you're feeling relaxed, and then write down everything that happens in your flashbacks, and then read what you wrote, either to someone who cares, or read it out loud on your own and imagine you're reading it to a caring sympathetic friend who's saying comforting things to you while you're reading it, or whatever it would help you most to hear.

"When you've read it, rip the paper into shreds and fling it away in the most final kind of way you can think of, to symbolise that you've finished with those flashbacks.

"If you start getting different ones, try the same thing again – write down what happens in them from beginning to end, and then either read what you wrote to someone who cares, or read it out loud and imagine you're reading it to a caring friend who's concerned to hear about them and does their best to comfort you, or whoever you would find helpful to imagine listening.

"Something that can add to the success of that technique is if you take about an hour, maybe more, and draw three pictures to symbolise what's happened and the flashbacks or bad memories you've had that have intruded into your thoughts when you didn't want them to, and the improved state of mind you'll likely have in the future.

"You sit down with some coloured pencils or crayons, or whatever will help you make the images you draw more vivid. The first picture can be either a scene from what happened, such as you standing in the station looking upset, or something that symbolises what happened, like, say, an ugly dog trampling a bed of beautiful flowers, to symbolise your hopes and dreams of what that day would be like being trampled when some clumsy clot rampaged along the platform hurting people, or whatever feels real and has meaning for you, something you think can really represent your flashbacks. It could even just be something abstract.

"Then on another piece of paper, the psychologists recommend drawing something you'd prefer to be thinking about or feeling instead, or that symbolises the way you imagine things will be if they improve and you're not having flashbacks any more. Maybe for you, it could be something such as your brother reassuringly happy and running around or playing with toys or something, or him happily getting on a train while you contentedly watch, or whatever you like, that represents things moving on and getting better. Something that has real meaning for you.

"Then the idea is that you get a third bit of paper, and on that, you draw a picture that represents something you think up that you imagine is something that helped you get from having the nasty flashbacks to thinking the nicer things instead. For example, it could be you surrounded by caring people who are all saying encouraging things to you and hoping you get better. Or it could be another picture of your brother doing something happily, to symbolise that you felt more and more reassured about him being alright the more you saw him doing that. Something meaningful to you personally anyway.

"When you've done that, the idea is that you tear up the first picture, the one with the horrible images. That symbolises that the horrible thing's over and done with, or else that you're putting the flashbacks behind you. You can keep the other two pictures if you like, to remind yourself of how things have improved whenever you start to feel discouraged again."

Zoe said she thought Becky had some interesting ideas, and that she'd like to write them down before she forgot them all.

While she was doing that, Becky looked around to entertain herself.

When she did, she couldn't help but laugh when she saw a young man build an impressive-looking sandcastle, and call his little boy over to have a look. The boy ran over, but in his hurry, he kicked the sandcastle and it flopped into bits. His dad made a face, but then grinned and joked, "Right you, let's dig a big hole, and then we can bury you in it! Ha ha ha!"

The little boy said, "No! Let's dig a really really really big hole, and bury You in it!"

His dad said, "Ah, but if you bury me in the sand and I can't get out, who's going to drive you home? I'm the only one who can drive the car!"

The little boy said enthusiastically, "I'll drive the car home!"

His dad said with a grin, "I don't think you will, you cheeky monster! Come on, let's try building another sandcastle!"

Becky Gives Zoe Advice on Getting Rid of Upsetting Feelings

When Zoe had finished writing notes on what Becky had said to her, Becky said, "I'll remind you of what I said later by giving you a quick summary of it, in case there are some things you've forgotten already that you might want to write down if I can jog your memory about them . . . that's if I haven't forgotten them myself by then."

Zoe thought that was a good idea. Then she asked Becky if she had any other ideas to help her.

Becky said, "A few. Another thing that might help bad feelings about what happened go away, as well as helping to get rid of flashbacks, is if you write a letter, not to send, but just to get your feelings out of your system. You could imagine you're writing to the bloke who bashed into you at the station. You can tell him how angry you are with him for not looking where he was going and for not stopping after he must have known he'd knocked you over and made you drop a baby. You can write about how worried you were that it had caused something really bad to happen, and about all the anxiety you've had since. You can tell him he probably doesn't understand in the least how badly his behaviour affected your life, and that you're annoyed to think he might not even care, since it seems he ran off only thinking about himself.

"You could end by saying you hope he comes to understand the seriousness of what he did, and that he gets to be sorry.

"Or you can say whatever you like really. But end by explaining what kind of response you'd like from him to your letter, like telling him you hope he writes back and lets you know he's thought about it and now he's sorry.

"Then, either straight afterwards or the next day or in a few days or whenever you like, you could write another letter, pretending it's from the bloke to you. Actually the idea is that you write two of those, one straight after the other. They're to get feelings out of the system again, and maybe to help you start thinking of things in different ways, some of them less upsetting. Only do this if you think it'll help though.

"The idea is that the first letter makes believe he's really unsympathetic. You write in it all the things you can think of that you've been thinking when you've blamed yourself for what happened, and what other people have said to you that have upset you, and other things you've worried he might think, imagining he's saying them.

"But maybe – this probably wouldn't work for every kind of situation, like ones where the person writing the letters knows the person who hurt them well – but maybe you could imagine that when he says those things, he looks stupid. That's my idea, not the psychology book's. But maybe you could imagine he's at home, and he's in his kitchen with some dinner in front of him, but he's more interested in drinking than in eating his dinner; he's got a load of beer cans around him and he's swaying around on a stool. Maybe you could imagine he's got a poster on the wall that he's made himself, called, 'My favourite football hooligans' – you know, some people might have favourite football players or teams, but imagine this bloke has favourite football hooligans instead, and they all look like gorillas drinking beer.

"Maybe you could imagine he whips off his shirt and you can see primitive-looking tattoos all over his back, like one that says, 'The ideal macho man', and below it there's a picture of a big ugly dog sitting on a bar stool in a pub lapping up beer.

"Then maybe you could imagine he reads the letter you sent him, roars in anger, and says in a slurred drawly voice as if he's really drunk, 'Right! I'm going to tell you what I think of that! First though, I'll just make sure there are no policemen around! Oh no, there's one in the garden! Right, I'm going to deal with him!'

"Imagine he goes out, and he's mistaken a tree for a policeman! Imagine he thumps the tree hard, thinking he's whacking the policeman, but when his fist hurts, he yells out in pain and comes back into the house saying, 'Oh, if I'd known policemen's bodies are so hard, I'd never have hit him!'

"Then you could imagine he sits down to write back to you, and as he writes, he speaks what he's writing out loud, in the same slurred drawling drunken voice. You could write down the horrible things people have said to you and that you've thought yourself, imagining he's drunkenly bawling them, like, 'It's your fault, you stupid girl; you say I should have looked where I was going; well, you should have looked where me and the others were going too! If you'd held onto your brother tighter, you wouldn't have dropped him, you stupid bitch!' And things like that.

"Then imagine that when he's finished writing the letter, he passes out with the amount of drink he's drunk, his head falls forward, and his face goes splat, right into his dinner!

"Or you could imagine what you like really.

"Anyway, straight after you've written that letter, write another one pretending to be from him, but this time, imagine he's a nicer version of himself, and he's sorry about what he did, and he wants to tell you how bad he feels.

"So you could maybe imagine he says something like, 'I can understand you being angry with me. I know what happened was my fault. I should have been looking where I was going, and walking more slowly and carefully.

" 'I know I should have stopped to find out how you were and see if there was anything I could do to help when I accidentally knocked you over. It's not an excuse, but at the time, me and some friends had been on a stag do; we'd been drinking all night and were on the way home. I hadn't had any sleep and I was still drunk, and I knew we had to hurry to catch our next train. I just dashed out without thinking. It was stupid of me. I'm really sorry for being so thoughtless. I know I should have stopped when I hit you and you dropped the baby.

I feel really bad about making that happen now. I just rushed off at the time, but when we were on the next train, I started thinking about it, and I started feeling guilty, and worrying about you and the baby, worrying I'd caused something really serious to happen.

"'Since then, I've often worried about it. I felt guilty for ages. I'm glad your brother was alright after he got stitches in hospital.

"'I know I deserve all the things you said to me. But I really am sorry it happened.'

"Or again, you can say what you like, but imagine it's something nice and comforting.

"After you've written that letter, the idea is that you write one more. Not necessarily that day; it could be the next day or a few days later if you like. But the idea is that you make it a letter from you, imagining you're writing back to the man who's sorry about what he did. It could contain anything you thought of to say after you wrote the first letter, and also how you feel after reading that he's sorry about what he did and feels bad about it. Like maybe you might say you forgive him or whatever.

"The letters might help you get upsetting feelings out of your system and feel better than you did before. After all, for all you know, the man might really have thought about what he did and be sorry.

"The psychology book the letter writing idea comes from recommends people only spend about an hour on each letter. I think that's so people don't start thinking things over and over and brooding on what happened till they get more and more miserable and just end up feeling depressed.

"And if you get upset while you're writing them, you could stop and do something to help you calm down, and carry on when you feel better, or don't carry on if you think you'll just get upset again."

Zoe said she'd try the things Becky was telling her about.

Becky Gives Zoe More Advice to Help Her Stop Flashbacks

Then Becky said, "If you find you still get any flashbacks after that, or before you try it, then you could try one or two techniques I've read about for distracting yourself and reminding yourself you're in the present rather than back in the past.

"Here's one way of doing that: If you think you might have flashbacks when there are people you know with you, and you think they'd understand, you could tell them what to expect when you start having one, and that if they think that's happening, they could ask you questions to bring your thoughts back to the present, like asking you what their name is, what year it is, where you are, who's in the room with you, what your plans are for the day and so on. Tell them to keep asking you simple questions about where you are now and things like that till you respond. When you do, it'll mean you've been reminded where you really are, so you'll be coming out of the horrible flashback.

"Or a way you can distract Yourself and remind Yourself of where you really are is that if you recognise the signs that a flashback's just beginning to come on, before it gets too bad for it to be possible, you can immediately concentrate on what you can see around you, and count five things you can see, naming them in your mind. Then listen to what you can hear, and see if you can count and name five things. Then count and name five things you can feel or touch around you, either touching them, or noticing how they feel, like the sensation of your shoes on your feet, the sensation of you sitting on a chair, the texture of your clothes – anything within reach of you so you can touch it, including part of you that you can touch, such as your hair, or that you can feel touching something else, such as your back against a chair, and anything else like that.

"The idea is that if your mind isn't focused on your flashback, the flashback will stop, because you're concentrating instead on what's going on around you right then.

"If it still seems as if the flashback might come on or get stronger after you've finished noticing five things you can feel and touch, go back to counting what you can see again, counting four more things if you can; and then count four more things you can hear and then touch, and then three more if you have to, and then two and then one, till the flashback really does seem to have faded away.

"If you can't see that many things to count, or can't hear or touch that many, you could just count the same things more than once, or just move on to counting the next category of things. You might have to count some things several times, but that's OK.

"Hopefully the flashbacks will go away for good when you do the other things. But you'll at least have that technique if they're slower to disappear than you'd prefer, and to do before you try them.

"You can use the technique when you notice the first signs of a panic attack coming on too."

The girls sat thoughtfully for a while, not saying anything.

Stephanie's Family, Becky and Zoe Have Some Fun Again, First in the Sea, and Then Over Dinner

Stephanie had been looking around to see if they were still talking. Noticing a pause in the conversation, she came over and said with a smile, "Hey, Mum and me are going in the sea again. Do you want to come? Come on. You don't want to get too much of this therapy in one go, Zoe, even if it's good, or you'll get overloaded and forget everything!"

Zoe giggled. She fancied a break anyway, so she said to Becky, "Do you want to go in the sea again?"

Becky said she'd like that, so they ran down to it and went in.

When they came out of it, Stephanie's mum said to Zoe and Becky, "Stephanie and me are getting hungry. Are you? Let's have some food!"

Zoe and Becky liked the idea, so they went and sat down with the others. Stephanie's dad bought them some pies and chips.

While they were eating, Stephanie said, "A couple of kids went by not long ago, and I heard one of them say they saw a crab in the sea. It's a good thing none of us stepped on it! That might have been painful!"

Just then, a clock chimed in the distance. Suddenly Becky had an idea, connecting pain and bells chiming in her mind, and grinned as she said, "Imagine if whenever anyone felt any pain, if they moved, their body would play a little tinkly tune, and doctors would be able to tell what was wrong with them by what tune their body played. So someone might go to the doctor with pain in their wrist, and the doctor would say, 'Just move your arm a little', and when they did, it would go ding-a-ling-a-ling in a certain kind of way, and the doctor would say, 'Ah, you've got repetitive strain injury!'

"It would be good! Mind you, it would be a bit noisy if you were walking down the street and there were quite a few people who were in pain for one reason or another walking along near you! Or in a doctor's waiting room, imagine how discordant the clash of jingly tunes might sound when quite a few were going on at once!

"And imagine if some of the tunes the body played were inappropriately jolly, so someone might be walking down the street and trip over and bruise their leg, and suddenly their body might start playing a cheerful little tune that sounded as if it could be the melody to a song about being happy.

"And imagine if people's bodies played tunes when they had mental health problems too, so a psychologist might say to a client, 'Tell me about your past', and a load of painful memories might come into the client's mind, and suddenly a tune that sounded like a famous hymn might start blaring out, because that's what people's bodies always did when they thought of painful memories.

"And it would mean that if people went to a support group for people with their painful condition or mental health prob- lem, their bodies would all be playing the same tune. It could still sound discordant if they weren't playing it at the same time. But imagine if some of the tunes were ones it was pos- sible to play in rounds, the way you can get little songs people can sing in rounds. It might sometimes happen just by chance that someone would move and their body would start playing the tune bodies played when people who had the problem the people at the support group had, because moving a part of them was painful, and then just a few seconds later, someone else would move, and a few seconds after that someone else would move, and then someone else would, and their bodies would play the tune they played in a round.

"The others might say, 'That was really nice! Do it again!' "

Zoe and the others grinned. But Stephanie's mum said good-naturedly, "Becky, eat your food before it goes cold!"

They took their time eating their food in the sunshine. Then while they relaxed, Stephanie's dad entertained them by telling them a few funny stories from his childhood, like about the time when he watched a school bully jeer at a smaller boy, calling him a weakling and saying he could easily beat the living daylights out of him if he wanted, only to immediately slip over in the mud, fall flat on his face, and start crying about how he'd hurt himself, and how dirty his clothes had got, and how his mum was bound to tell him off when she had to wash them.

Everyone enjoyed hearing what he had to say. After a while though, he looked at the time and said, "It's getting a bit late! Zoe and Becky, would you like to go and spend some more time on that therapy stuff you're doing? You can take your time. It's just that in a couple of hours or so, I'm going to want us to start going back home."

Stephanie's mum said, "Come on, we don't have to get home all that early."

"I know. Well alright, three hours or so," said Stephanie's dad. "But I don't want us to get home too late. After all, what'll Becky's mum think of us if we drop her off when it's past her bedtime!"

He grinned.

"Hopefully the 'therapy stuff' won't take That long!" said Becky with a grin.

She and Zoe went back to where they'd been sitting before, while Stephanie went off to look at some amusements that were at the top of the beach, and her parents sunbathed and read books.

Becky Gives Zoe Advice on Stopping Herself Getting More and More Anxious With Worry

When they'd sat down, Zoe said to Becky, "Thank you for all the ideas you've given me. You know, this morning before we came out, I was really worried that something bad would happen. I always worry a lot before I go on a day out nowadays, or before me and my family go on holiday. I keep thinking there might be another nasty accident, and I worry and worry till by the time we go, I'm feeling really depressed, and not in the mood to enjoy myself at all. I'm glad Stephanie's mum made us all laugh on the way down here this morning. I was nervous about meeting you, and worried something bad would happen, but I felt much more cheerful by the time we got here."

Becky replied, "I'm glad you cheered up. You know, there are things you can do to stop yourself worrying so much. And if you do them and stop worrying, you probably won't have many more nightmares as well, which will be an added benefit. Nightmares often come on because a person's been worrying and worrying about things during the day."

"I can see how that would happen," said Zoe.

Becky asked, "How many days out in your life have gone badly wrong? Not just a bit wrong, but badly wrong?"

"Only the one where my baby brother got hurt, I think," said Zoe.

"And how many days out do you think you must have had in your life?" asked Becky.

Zoe thought about it, and said, "I don't know. Maybe I go on a few days out with the family or school every year. I suppose if I times that by the number of years I've been alive, maybe that makes about 50."

"What about if you include all the ones you've had while you've been away on holiday?" asked Becky.

Zoe said, "Um, well, I don't know; we've been on holiday for at least a week most years, sometimes two weeks. Maybe that would add up to, say, about twenty weeks altogether or something. So I suppose the number of days out during those times would be about, um, maybe about 140."

Becky said, "So if you add the roughly 50 days out to that that you've had when you haven't been away on holiday, that makes about 190?"

Zoe said yes.

Becky said, "So you've been on about 190 days out in your life, something nasty happened on one of them, and yet you convince yourself before every day out that something nasty might well happen on that one? When you look at it that way, the odds aren't very high, are they."

"That's a good point!" said Zoe. "Minor things have gone wrong on some of the holidays we've been on, like it raining most of the time and us not being able to do much, or some of us getting badly sunburned, or there was one a few years ago where the very day before it, I badly bruised my leg, and it hurt whenever I walked for a few days. But I still enjoyed myself for some of the time on most of those holidays; there's

196

only been one day out that was ruined and we had to come home.

"Mind you, the worst holiday where something went a bit wrong was a bit depressing, not because of anything that bad, but it seems my mum had started getting nostalgic for the days when she had her honeymoon, and she decided she'd like us all to go on holiday to the same place where she had it, thinking it would be nice to do the same things she did then.

"But halfway through, she got depressed, and said she thought she'd been stupid to think that things could ever be the same as they were back then, because now us kids were around, things were totally different; and she said she should have realised other things might be different too, such as the weather not being very nice; and she'd fondly remembered buying things like pasties and chips, but she'd bought them again and they weren't anywhere near as good as the ones she'd had before, so that was a disappointment; and she and my dad couldn't relax and be like a honeymoon couple, because the walls of the caravan we were in were so thin we'd all hear everything that went on; and the sea was colder so she didn't feel like swimming like she had before; and she'd expected to enjoy the same things she had then like fairground rides, but when she went on one, she found out it made her dizzy, so she thought she must be getting too old to enjoy the things she had before, and that thought was disheartening; and she complained about other things like that.

"I got depressed, because it sounded as if she was partly blaming me for things not being as good as they were before, and I felt a bit bad to think she might have had more fun if it wasn't for me and the others being around. I mean, before the holiday, my mum seemed to have this romantic idea that it would be nice to show us kids the places she'd been with Dad just after they were married. But maybe not having any really private time with him made her decide it had been a bad idea after all.

"Both me and my mum felt a bit miserable for a couple of days. But we still did a few things we enjoyed on the holiday."

Becky said, "It's a pity things didn't go better. Maybe you were getting more depressed than you needed to though; after all, there are only a couple of reasons in that list that had anything to do with you, and those weren't even your fault. But I wonder if maybe you worried over those and let the others drift to the back of your mind a bit for a while, so maybe it felt to you as if your mum was blaming you more than she really was, because it was as if you'd half-forgotten the other reasons she was disappointed with the holiday, so you only thought about the ones that had anything to do with you. I don't know. Mind you, if your mum was blaming you at all, it wasn't fair, because it can't have been your fault."

Zoe said, "You might be right about me partly feeling down because I was feeling as if I had some responsibility for the problems when I shouldn't have done, because it hadn't been my decision to do what we did. I did Try to think positively before the holiday though. Actually it was a bit daft, because I asked my mum a few weeks before it what we were going to do if it rained, and she said, 'Don't talk about it raining! Think positive!' So I did think positive; we didn't talk about what to do if it rained; we got there and it Did rain some of the time; and then we didn't have much of a clue about what to do, because we hadn't planned for what to do if it did!"

Becky couldn't resist a smile. She said, "Yes, some people's idea of positive thinking does seem a bit over-the-top! If you refuse to think about possible problems because you think that isn't being positive, you're not going to be able to work out how to solve them!"

Zoe smiled too then.

Becky, Zoe and Stephanie Have Some Relaxation and Fun Again

Then they decided to sit back and just enjoy a bit of sunshine for a while.

After a couple of minutes, Becky smiled and said for a laugh, "My grandma's got a cousin who's been on holiday to Cuba once or twice. I asked her what it was like and what she did there. She said the people were very friendly, and that one day she went to a jungle. I thought, 'I didn't know they had jungles in Cuba.'

"Maybe she meant it was a concrete jungle. Imagine an advert for a holiday saying people would get a tour around a jungle, but on the day it was supposed to happen, the tour guide led them around a run-down part of a town, with not a bit of greenery in sight, and when they complained that they'd thought he was going to show them around a jungle, he said, 'I am! This is a concrete jungle! Didn't the advert for the holiday tell you this is what it was going to be?' "

Zoe laughed and said, "I don't think the tourists would be very happy about that!"

Becky grinned and said, "Probably not. But just imagine if travel agents actually advertised tours around the most run-down areas of the countries of the world, and quite a few people actually wanted to go on them! Maybe they'd call it depression tourism."

Zoe Giggled and said, "Or depressing tourism!"

Stephanie walked down the beach while they were just sunbathing. She saw them smiling and relaxing, and came over to them, saying, "There are some boat swings at the top of the beach! I used to love going on boat swings! Are you two deep in thought, or would either of you like to go on one with me? I've got some change we could pay with."

Zoe said, "Actually I could do with a bit of a break on my own, to write down all my thoughts, and think about what Becky's been saying to me. You two go off and enjoy yourselves for a while!"

So they did.

The man in charge of the boat swings let them spend about twenty minutes having fun together on one.

While they were swinging, Becky grinned and asked Stephanie, "Have you ever been in the sea when you looked down at the seaweed and thought, 'Yum, that looks appetising!' and picked it up and ate it?"

Stephanie laughed and said, "Ugh no! I wouldn't do a thing like that!"

They both giggled. Then Becky asked, "How would you feel if seaweed mixed with ice cream was The fashionable must-have flavour of every summer, and if you didn't eat it, you just weren't considered cool?"

Stephanie chuckled and replied, "I can't believe enough people would like it that that could ever happen!"

Becky asked, "But what if somehow they did?"

Stephanie grinned and said, "Well, I've never been cool, so I wouldn't think it was worth pretending to be. But I suppose if

I was the kind of person who wanted to be, maybe I'd buy one sometimes . . . and then secretly go and give it to my mum to eat. That way, people would think I was buying it for myself."

Becky grinned and said, "Aww, just think! What if most people did that? There might be thousands and thousands of poor old mums loaded down with seaweed flavoured ice creams for days and days in the summer when their kids kept bringing them in after they'd bought them to look cool, and they might think they really ought to eat them whether they liked it or not, because they thought it would be a shame to waste them."

They both laughed. Then Becky asked, "How would you like to eat Christmas cake as part of a Christmas dinner – you know, if it was plonked on your plate along with carrots and turkey and stuffing and gravy and things?"

Stephanie laughed and said, "Ugh yuck! That would be horrible!"

Becky grinned and said, "Some people eat strange combinations of food though, don't they. My uncle Steven said his little boy was enjoying chips and ice cream the other day – and I mean both together! He himself used to enjoy chips dunked in coke. I think in some parts of the country, people eat mince pies with cheese. I myself have eaten cheese and honey sandwiches; they're nice."

Stephanie replied, "Oh yes, I've tried those. They are nice."

Becky said, "My auntie Diana had coffee mixed with tea once, to see what it would be like. She didn't like it.

"Hey I wonder what it would be like if coffee contained 300 times the amount of caffeine it does. I wonder if it would be banned as a dangerous substance, and gangsters would be selling coffee illegally on the streets. People would be put in prison for selling coffee. I wonder what it would do to you though if you had some. Maybe it would make you so hyperactive you'd get up and want to do all kinds of energetic things! Maybe if you were grown-up and owned a house and had a garden, you'd go out and do all kinds of nice things to it, like digging big holes in it and then lining them with concrete to make fish ponds. If you had a really big garden, you might end up filling it with fish ponds, making about 50 of them before the end of the day!

"And then you'd go to your neighbour's house and ask, 'Have you got any work in your garden that needs doing?' If they said no, you'd beg them for some! You'd say, 'But you must have work in your garden that needs doing! Surely you've got a tree that needs hauling down? Oh go on, let me haul your trees down! Please, let me haul your trees down!'

"And you might not go away till they let you! Or maybe you'd be happy enough if they said, 'No, I don't want you touching my trees, but how's this idea: I'll let you do some weight lifting with my washing machine. Actually on second thoughts, why not go home and use yours!' "

Stephanie giggled and said, "I can't imagine myself ever getting that energetic! And if caffeine really did have miracle properties like that, I bet body builders would have found out, and we'd have heard about them using loads already. Actually, it might even kill you if you have a massive overdose of it!"

Becky said, "Yeah, maybe."

When they'd finished having fun on the boat swing, they went back down the beach. Becky stopped to talk some more to Zoe, while Stephanie went for another short swim.

Becky Gives Zoe More Advice on Calming Herself to Prevent Anxiety Building and Ruining Her Day

Becky asked Zoe how she was feeling, and she said she was alright.

They got back to talking about attitudes to holidays and days out, and Becky said, "Anyway, it's a good thing only one thing has ever gone Seriously wrong on a day out you've been on. So in that case, before you go on one in the future, it might be helpful if every time you catch yourself worrying and feeling sure things have a good chance of going so badly wrong the day will be ruined, you say to yourself, 'Hold on!' or something like that. Then you can ask yourself some questions about whether the thoughts that are upsetting you are worth taking notice of. I mean, you could maybe ask yourself things like:

"'Are things really as bad as I'm thinking they are? Is there really a high probability that things are going to go horribly wrong, considering that when I worked out how often they did in the past, it was only on about one in 190 days out? That doesn't sound like a high probability at all. Wouldn't it be better to at least wait till I find out if things are going to go wrong instead of turning out a lot better than I think they will before thinking about things in a way that makes me all scared and depressed about them?

"'And even if things do go wrong, there will probably be people around who can help us; medical treatment's so much better than it was 100 years ago; and there might very well be things I can do myself to improve the situation. And there are things me and the rest of the family or friends can do to reduce the chances of things going wrong, or to stop them getting worse if they do, as far as it depends on us.'

"You could run through a list of everything you know you can do. Obviously you can't plan for everything that might go wrong, and everyone probably forgets to do things they know really that they ought to do from time to time; but there will at least be some sensible safety precautions you can take, such as bringing a first-aid kit, and your family driving at a sensible speed if you're going somewhere in the car. But don't think it's worth your mind getting absorbed in worries about things going wrong, since something's only gone seriously wrong a tiny minority of the time.

"And don't forget that when your brother had the accident, things turned out a lot less badly than you were worried they would in the end; so chances are, most other accidents might as well.

"Another thing you can think about to reassure yourself is that you know you've got some skills and resilience that could help you cope if things do go wrong. I mean, you might think you're coping badly with what happened before, with you having flashbacks and getting depressed and worried and things; but you could ask yourself, 'What have I done that's meant things haven't been worse than they have? I mean, I didn't let it ruin my life; I still kept getting decent grades in school; there were still days when I was happy; and at least what happened proves I'm a caring person, or I wouldn't have been upset at all; and I've spent quite a bit of time playing with my brother since, making sure he was alright, so I know he is.'

"Some people find it helpful to write down the stressful and depressing thoughts they find themselves often having, and then to write down reassuring answers to them. That way, they might remember the answers better, and whenever they catch themselves having the same old depressing and scary thoughts after that, they won't have to think up responses to them to reassure themselves all over again, since if they've read what they wrote down quite a few times, they'll be able to think of the answers automatically; and they can read them again to refresh their memories when they want to.

"So maybe you could write down responses to your thoughts that calm you down, and keep what you write down to read so as to soothe your worries whenever you find yourself getting a bit miserable. Instead of waiting till the next time you go on a day out and start feeling stressed and depressed and end up not feeling like going, you could sit down soon, think about all the horrible thoughts you normally have at times like that, and write down reassuring responses to them right there and then, or questions you could ask yourself about each one that you can think of calming answers to when it intrudes into your mind again.

"Questions you could ask about each bad thought you catch yourself having could be things like:

" 'Is this thought really realistic about the way things are? Could I be forgetting good things that have happened and just thinking about bad things so I end up thinking things are worse than they really are? Am I thinking things will probably go horribly wrong when I haven't got any evidence that they will?

" 'What's the worst thing I know for Definite will happen? Can I really be definite about anything bad happening at all?

" 'What things has this situation got going for it that mean that things are less likely to result in tragedy than they might do if it wasn't for those things?

" 'If the day out's much less likely to end badly than I'm thinking it will, what could I do to increase the chances that all of us actually enjoy it?'

"Thinking like that won't just help you have a better day, but it'll help you recover from your post-traumatic stress disorder altogether, because part of what causes people to get that is the way they think about what's happened after their bad experiences; it isn't just caused by the bad experiences themselves.

"On the other hand, if you write down a question you think you could ask yourself to challenge your negative thoughts, but then you realise it's sparking off more of them, because you get the urge to answer with things like, 'Yes, but what if this bad thing happens?' 'And what if that bad thing happens?' and so on, then you can cross out that question. Or if the whole technique just leads you to think like that instead of being able to think of calming answers to questions you ask, try something different instead.

"I don't suppose this could come easily for anyone it doesn't come naturally to, or for anyone to do it in every situation, but I've read that people who tend to just resign themselves to never knowing all the answers about why what happened to them happened if it isn't possible to find them out, and who just put it down to bad luck – being in the wrong place at the wrong time, or who think of what happened as being at least an experience people can learn from to try to reduce the risks of such things happening again, so they can at least find meaning in it, are less likely to develop post-traumatic stress disorder than people who often get absorbed in upsetting thoughts where they blame themselves for what happened, or ask themselves over and over again how such a thing could have been done to them or to people they care about, and what it must mean about how cruel human nature can be, and who get absorbed in upsetting thoughts about the unfairness of it all, and that kind of thing.

"I've also read that victims of deliberate cruelty are more likely to develop post-traumatic stress disorder than victims of natural disasters that can be just put down to random acts of nature.

"And camaraderie can help improve the mental health of people with post-traumatic stress disorder, if they join a group of people who've all been through similar things, so they know they can talk about what happened and the way they feel about it, and the way it's affected their mental health since, and they'll be completely understood, and not judged as weak or whatever. It can be comforting for people to know they're not alone with their problems.

"It might get a bit depressing after a while to hear about other people's problems though, so if you found a support group like that, it might be a good idea to sometimes ask yourself how much it was helping.

"But every time a person's alone and gets absorbed in upsetting thoughts about what happened, it's as if they're traumatising themselves all over again, so it'll take them longer to recover, and they might even start feeling worse than they did when the thing first happened.

"That's one reason why it might help if every time you start having upsetting thoughts about what happened to you, you've got prepared logical answers handy that you can talk back to those thoughts with to reassure yourself, since it'll help you start thinking of things in a down-to-earth way again, instead of what you might do otherwise, which is getting more and more absorbed in worries till you start imagining worse and worse possibilities about bad things that might happen, feeling as if they're more and more likely to happen the more you worry they will, till you're traumatised all over again, and part of your day's pretty much ruined, and you're more likely to have nightmares and so on.

"So like I said, unless disputing your worried thoughts is upsetting in itself, think about some of the depressing thoughts you often have, and work out how you can reason with them to stop them upsetting you so much you can't get on with life properly."

Zoe thought about what Becky had advised her to do, and wrote the ideas she'd passed on to her down.

Becky, Zoe and Stephanie Have a Bit of a Laugh Together

Becky had brought some sweets down to the beach with her. When Zoe finished writing, she offered her some, and Zoe accepted them and thanked her. They sat enjoying them together, and their mood began to turn more light-hearted for a while.

After they'd finished them, they sat for a little while just enjoying the sunshine.

Then Stephanie came out of the sea and came up to them, seeing they were relaxing. She asked them if they were OK and they said they were. Then she grinned and said to Zoe, "You know, when me and Becky were on the boat swing, she asked me if I'd ever pick seaweed up in the sea and just eat it! I saw some seaweed in the sea just now. I thought of picking it up and bringing it back to Becky and offering it to her, asking if she thought she'd like to eat it herself. Or maybe I could have draped it around her neck and asked her if she'd like to wear it as a necklace. Would you like that, Becky?"

Zoe and Becky giggled.

Becky joked, "No. But maybe you could have taken it home and eaten it instead of cabbage the next time you wanted something healthy."

Stephanie laughed and said, "Oh yuck! No thanks. I don't know how healthy it could be anyway when it's lived all its life in dirty seawater."

Becky grinned and asked for fun, "What about making other kinds of substitutions for things then? Have you ever substituted soap for soup, or soup for soap? Imagine if someone discovered they'd run out of soap, but they wanted to have a shower, and they thought, 'Oh well, I expect soup will do instead of soap; it sounds similar, so it'll probably have a similar effect.' And they went into the shower with a packet of soup, and spread it all over themselves mixed with water.

"What's the weirdest thing you've ever substituted for something else, say if you ran out of cheese one evening and you'd been intending to make a cheese sauce, so you thought, 'Oh well, maybe I'll put peas in it instead' or something, or you'd wanted to put a chicken's egg on your toast but you ran out, so you thought, 'Oh well, maybe I'll put a chicken's leg on it instead'? Or have you ever wanted to eat some blueberries but didn't have any, so you thought it might be nice to eat bluebottles instead?"

Stephanie laughed and said, "I don't think I'd ever do a thing like that!"

Becky continued teasing her in fun, saying, "What about this then: Have you ever used a word instead of the one you meant to use without realising, and wondered why the person you were speaking to didn't understand you? Imagine if you meant to say to someone, 'Let's have a game of chess', but instead you said, 'Let's have a game of chest'. And they said, 'What?' and you said, 'A game of chest! Come on, let's play chest!' Or what if you said cress instead, so you said to them, 'Let's get the cress board out and play a nice game of cress!'"

They laughed. Stephanie said, grinning, "You do come out with daft things, Becky!"

Then she looked at her parents and said, "Anyway, I'd better leave you to finish your therapy stuff now, just in case Dad decides it's time for us to go home soon."

She left to go and sit with her parents, and Zoe and Becky became serious again.

Becky Gives Zoe a Bit More Advice About Stopping Upsetting Thoughts Worrying Her

Becky said to Zoe, "You know, another thing you can do to stop yourself getting so many upsetting thoughts about what happened to you and your brother and about what might happen in future is to ask yourself what you'd say to a close friend who was making themselves upset thinking about all the things that might go wrong, and worrying that it might be best not to go out for the day. If you think you'd say comforting things to them, you could try saying the same things to yourself.

"If something does go badly on another outing, then when you think back over it, you could try reminding yourself that

210

it doesn't mean things will go badly on every one, and it doesn't mean everything in your life's going badly. A lot of things in your life might still be going well. And provided that what happened on the latest outing where something went wrong wasn't catastrophic, everyone might be getting over it soon. Can your brother even remember the time when you dropped him?"

The question surprised Zoe, and then her face lit up and she said, "Do you know, I've never thought about that! He was so little when it happened, maybe he can't! I've never heard him say a word about it since a few weeks after it happened, a few years ago, so maybe he soon forgot all about it. He's never been scared of stations or anything, so it seems it didn't have any kind of lasting effect on him. So maybe I've been far more upset and worried than I needed to be."

Becky said, "You might be right there. And maybe you're in the habit of being more pessimistic about things going wrong than you need to be. We've only been talking about the things that have gone wrong on days out today, but have you had days out that you've really enjoyed?"

Zoe said she had. She told Becky about a couple of them, and began to smile as she began to enjoy remembering them.

Becky and Zoe Have Fun Talking About Daft Ideas and a Wacky Story

Then Becky grinned and said, "My auntie Diana said there have been a few hot summer days where she wished that somehow in the middle of the night, part of this country turned round – so delicately that no one noticed till the morning;

but when they did, they realised that all the places that had been just south of London the day before were now right on the coast, so people like her could walk out of their houses and find beaches just outside where a road had been the day before, and they could just walk out of their houses, stroll down the beach and go for a swim in the sea."

Zoe said, "I suppose it might be nice to start living that near the sea. But actually, for most people waking up, it could be quite scary if they were somewhere they didn't expect! Imagine a family from just south of London going all the way down to the coast on holiday the day before, only to find themselves right back where they started the next day, without even having driven back!"

They both laughed.

Becky grinned and said, "Yeah, and wouldn't people who wanted to travel somewhere get confused when they realised all the places around them were the wrong way around!

"Mind you, how's this for a bad day out? Someone told me a friend of his got hassled on an Internet forum by this creepy bloke who kept asking her to go on a date with him. She didn't understand why he kept asking, since he didn't even live in the same country as her, or even in the same half of the world, so a date would have been a bit difficult! But he wouldn't stop asking, and talked as if he could just tell she was infatuated with him. Maybe he thought she was so infatuated, she'd happily pay for his air fare to come and see her!

"So she decided to make fun of him, and wrote a story where they did go on a date, but she made all kinds of mini disasters happen to him in the story to put him off asking her to go out with him again. It sounded funny! I can remember quite a bit of it. I think her forum username was Flowering

Hippopotamus, and his was Oyster Chomper . . . or maybe that was just the nickname the others there gave him.

"The story Flowering Hippopotamus wrote him said he agreed to go out with her for the whole day. They first went on a boat trip down the River Thames, but she told him to stand up to look at something in the distance she said looked interesting, and when he did, she pulled him round suddenly and stuck her foot out at the same time, so he tripped over it and fell in the water. People helped him out, but he was soaking wet. She apologised and said she'd only been trying to show him where to look. She bought him a cheap change of clothes in a nearby market, and ordered him to change in the park, saying no one would let him inside a building to change when he was dripping wet. So he did, but a policeman came by just then and arrested him for indecent exposure.

"He explained that he was only changing his clothes because he'd fallen in the river, and the policeman let him go. But lots of people had seen him, including passengers on another river boat, and there was an article about it in the paper the next day.

"Then they went to the Natural History Museum, and Flowering Hippopotamus deceived him into eating a precious plant specimen Charles Darwin had brought back from his travels, telling him it was a medicinal plant she'd bought for him on the market to warm him up and make him feel better after falling in the water.

"When he started eating it, she called for security, and he was arrested again. She whispered to him to tell the police he thought people were allowed to eat the plants in there, and he did, so they let him go, but there was an article about it in the paper the next day.

"Then they went to another museum, and she suggested he went into a particular room to look at some old treasures; but when he went to walk in there, she tripped him up again, and he bashed into some people as he stumbled around, and they thought he was trying to fight them, so they hit him back, and they ended up brawling. The police came, and she told him to run quickly. She told him she'd camouflage him so no witnesses could recognise him, and she spooned marmite all over his face and hair, telling him she was sure the police would think he couldn't possibly be involved in the fight then, since they'd think that surely no one clueless enough to get marmite all over their face and hair instead of in their mouth when they were trying to eat it would have the sense to even know how to get into a museum.

"They went to Trafalgar Square, and suddenly she got out a packet of bird seed and poured it on his head. It stuck there because of the marmite, and a flock of pigeons came down and dive-bombed his head, trying to peck all the bird seed off it. He ran round and round the place for an hour trying to shake them off, but he couldn't; they kept chasing him. Eventually she recommended they go to a nearby park where there were no pigeons. He agreed, but they all followed them.

"The pigeons didn't go back to where they came from, but stayed in the park, so there was an article in the paper the next day about how all the pigeons had deserted Trafalgar Square, and that someone had said he'd seen a man luring them some-where else by walking around with his head covered in bird seed.

"The way Flowering Hippopotamus said Oyster Chomper got rid of the pigeons in the end was by jumping in a lake in another park, and washing off the marmite and birdseed.

"Then he needed another change of clothes; but this time, he hid when he changed, so as not to be arrested again.

"Then they went to a restaurant for lunch; but when he wasn't looking, Flowering Hippopotamus poured a whole pot of pepper on his food. He didn't realise, and took a big mouthful, and then he jumped up, in a hurry to get some water to cool his mouth down. The pepper was making his eyes water so much he couldn't see that well. He banged into tables and people in his hurry to get somewhere where he could find water, bellowing in anger about how awful the food was; and they thought he was a madman trying to start a fight, so they chased him out of the restaurant, and the police were called again.

"They would have arrested him again, but Flowering Hippopotamus told them he was new to this country, and thought it was the custom here for people to put an entire pot of pepper on their dinners in restaurants, not realising it had a hot spicy flavour, so he thought he'd better put the whole lot on it, but then he discovered he couldn't tolerate his food that way; and he was only banging into people in his rush to get out to find some water to cool his mouth. So they let him go again. But there was an article in the papers the next day about someone putting an entire pot of pepper on his dinner in a restaurant the day before, and nearly starting a fight in his rush to find water to cool his mouth after eating a mouthful of pepper-covered food.

"Then a few more funny things happened, ending with Flowering Hippopotamus squelching a cream cake into Oyster Chomper's face, and him being so fed up of her that he ran away and jumped on a train to go home with big blobs of cream still all over his face. And then he realised he was on the wrong train, so he had to get on another one, still with blobs of cream all over his face, because it was a while before he remembered to wipe them off. And when he did, the only thing he had to wipe them on was his sleeves, because he'd run out of the cafe where he got the cream cake squashed in his face in such a hurry he'd forgotten to pick up his things, like the wet clothes from earlier he could have wiped his face on if he'd had those."

Zoe giggled. She said, "Yeah, I wouldn't fancy a day out where all those things happened to me!"

They laughed.

Becky Gives Zoe a Few More Suggestions About How to Avoid Stressing Herself Out

Then Becky said, "I suppose we'd better get back to talking seriously again before the others want to go home."

Zoe agreed.

Then Becky said, "Well, apart from doing things like the ones I suggested earlier about talking back to your upsetting thoughts that make you worry that something bad will happen before you go out for the day, you could do other things before outings that help you stay less stressed, like chatting to people who you know will lift your spirits, keeping yourself busy with something you like doing, watching something funny on telly or listening to some comedy on the radio, or a recording of a comedy programme you've got yourself, or anything like that that you think will be a good distraction from worrying thoughts and that'll help. If worrying thoughts don't come into your mind in the first place because your attention's absorbed in other things, it'll be better than if they do come into your mind and you have to calm them by reasoning with them, or distracting yourself when they've already made you anxious.

"Realistically, something's bound to go wrong some of the time; there isn't a person on earth who's never had anything go badly wrong in their lives; after all, if there was, they'd still be alive today, even if they lived a thousand years ago! That's unless you don't think of dying as necessarily a bad thing.

"None of us knows when we're going to die; but it's up to us to make the time we've got left – whether it's six months, six years, sixty years or anything in between or beyond that – count for something. Maybe you can set your mind to thinking about how you can try to improve your quality of life and make it as worthwhile as you can during however long you've got left. Some plans go wrong, but a lot don't; you can tell that by thinking about how much humanity's progressed since the stone age. If we were all doomed to fail, we'd still be in the stone age now, if the human race even still existed! So there's a fair chance you'll have a mostly decent life if you think about and plan how you can achieve it as best you can.

"A lot of plans have to be abandoned because of unforeseen bad or good circumstances that get in the way; but it's often possible to end up being able to make new ones, even if they're very different and not as good. But it's possible you'll end up doing something that makes you happy."

Becky Talks About How People Have Still Found Happiness and Fulfilment After Becoming Disabled in Accidents or Being Born Disabled

Becky continued, "The thing is that even if something really bad does happen, it might not be as catastrophic as you think it would be. For one thing – I know it's not a nice thing to think about – but even people who have bad accidents and become severely disabled can end up quite happy, although they'll probably be really upset at first for some time, and maybe in a lot of pain for a while.

"If that happened to you or me, we wouldn't be able to do a lot of the things we're used to doing any more, and there might be other things we could still find ways of doing but we might have to do them a lot more slowly than we used to and with a lot more difficulty, so we might get frustrated and stressed trying to do them. But there might still be parts of our lives that made us just as happy as we used to be, and we might even be able to find other people to do tasks for us that we never enjoyed doing anyway, like some of the house-work, while we're freer to do things we enjoy doing.

"I met someone once who'd had a nasty accident and ended up having to use a wheelchair because she'd become severely disabled, and I think she was depressed about it for some time afterwards, as you might expect. But she was helped to find things she could still do well. It was especially bad for her because she had a young family at the time who needed her.

"She told the people trying to support her that one of the things she'd really like to be able to do again was to cook for them. But it turned out that it wasn't really cooking she valued doing; it was that she felt as if cooking for the family would give her more self-worth, because she'd know she was doing something of value for them again, after becoming disabled had made her feel useless. I don't think she got to cook for them again in the end, but it turned out that she didn't mind, because she started doing other things that gave her the sense of self-worth she wanted. Someone else must have done the cooking for the family. I think one thing she might have started doing was painting, and got really good at it, so her pictures were admired, and that gave her self-worth again, but I might be confusing her with someone else there.

"But it's interesting how there can be more to something than there seems to be at first, like someone who says they want to cook again not thinking cooking's the important thing in reality, but it's really that they want a way to improve their feeling of usefulness.

"Someone did a little survey once where they asked people who'd been paralysed a few months earlier, and also lottery winners, to rate their happiness on a scale of one to five; and there wasn't as much difference between them as you might expect. I don't think they did much to find out about the reasons for that. Or if they did, I didn't hear about it.

"But people can get a lot of help to adapt to the new way of life they have to have. People who can't use their legs any more so they have to use wheelchairs can still do quite a lot of things they used to do, like working on a computer, and also driving, if they can get hold of a specially adapted car where they have hand controls to do what the pedals normally do – that's at least if they can still use their legs well enough to get out of their cars and into their wheelchairs, or if they've got people to help them do that. And they can cook themselves things if their kitchens are adapted so all the work surfaces and cupboards and other things they need are quite a bit lower down than normal so they can reach them. It might take quite a bit of work to make things suitable for them, but I think it can often be done.

"I'm not saying I think things could ever be easy for people with problems like that. And a lot of people might be upset about what happened to them for a long long time afterwards, and might never fully get over it. But there are at least things around that can make life easier for them than it would have been if no one had ever thought to invent or develop them.

"And just think: We're a lot better off living nowadays than we would have been living about 200 years ago, when there was a lot more disease around to harm or kill people, and when if people had accidents and became disabled, there just wasn't the professional support around that there is now to help people adapt and find gadgets and things to make life easier for them, and there wasn't the medical knowhow around that there is now to help people."

Zoe said, "That's true. Wouldn't it be good if all disabilities could be cured though!"

Becky said, "Yes. Maybe one day they will be. Hey imagine if there was a drug people could take and it would make the body start growing new arms and legs, and there old ones that didn't work any more would just drop off like milk teeth when the new ones started growing. But imagine if someone was accidentally given a really powerful overdose of the drug, and instead of just growing two new arms or two new legs, they grew about seventy! Or imagine if their arms and legs grew really long, so they ended up being about fifty feet long!

How do you think you'd feel if you had seventy arms or seventy legs, or your legs or arms were about fifty feet long?"

Zoe laughed and said, "I don't know! I don't think I'd like it. You'd look like some kind of monster! And just imagine going into a clothes shop and asking if they had anything to fit you!"

They both giggled.

Then Becky said, "Anyway, getting serious again: I read an inspirational story about a man who was seriously injured and had to spend a few months in some kind of convalescent or rehabilitation home, but after that he was well enough to start getting on with life again, and he started trying to help other people who'd been badly injured, mostly by being a counsellor, listening to their problems and trying to encourage them. He got a reputation as someone who could help people who were feeling especially angry and upset.

"One day, someone from one of the nursing homes he helped people in phoned him and asked if he'd try to help a man called Bill who'd just had both his legs amputated because he'd had severe blood clots in them. Why the doctors couldn't have just given him clot-busting medication instead of amputating his legs, I don't know. But anyway, he was really upset, and would hardly say a word to anyone, including his family. He felt as if his life may as well be over, especially because he'd been a keen runner, and had even run several marathons, and had enjoyed other sports. The thought of never being able to do them again made him feel hopeless about life.

"The counsellor just had a short conversation with him the first day he went to see him. Then he asked if he could come back the next day and bring a friend. Bill reluctantly agreed, but felt sure he wouldn't like the friend, if he was going to do anything like trying to cheer him up.

"The next day, the counsellor came back with his friend Tom, someone he'd met in a nursing home. Bill was sitting in a wheelchair looking even more bitter and depressed than he had the day before. He greeted Tom with a comment like, 'What do you want? Have you come to stare at a cripple or something?'

"Tom understood that Bill was just upset. He told him he'd like some help to write a newsletter about sport, and wondered if he could assist him in writing it. Bill looked frustrated and said grumpily, 'What's the matter, your hands broke or something?'

"Tom replied that actually he didn't have any hands at all. He got the counsellor to undo straps around his back, and then they could see that he had artificial arms attached to his shoulders. I don't know if they fell off when the straps were untied. Then the counsellor took off Tom's artificial legs. He'd actually been born without any limbs.

"The counsellor said Bill stared in disbelief. Then after a few minutes of silence, he Told Tom he felt really sorry for him, with an expression of awe on his face.

"Tom told him there was no need to feel sorry for him, since he didn't feel sorry for himself.

"Suddenly Bill started crying, and apologised for being rude before. Tom said he didn't need to worry about it.

"The counsellor said they spent about three hours together that afternoon. Bill did start helping Tom write the newsletter after that – Tom would dictate what he wanted to say, and Bill would write it down.

"Bill said he'd found Tom inspirational, not so much because he was still doing things even though he was disabled, but because despite his own major disability, he still had a positive attitude to life and was keen to help other people. It changed his attitude to his own disability, and he stopped feeling so bitter and depressed after that.

"Anyway, that just shows you it's not necessarily the end of the world if something nasty happens to you, or someone you know. I'm not suggesting it wouldn't make life very difficult and upsetting for a while; but there might be more ways round a lot of problems than you imagine.

"But actually, talking of feeling upset about having to give up doing sports, I'm sure it wouldn't bother me, personally, if I had to, because I've never been keen on sports; but I've heard there are ways a lot of disabled people can still do sports. I've heard there's even an aggressive game called wheelchair rugby, for people who've got serious problems using three or more of their limbs. Apparently it was first called murderball, because it's so aggressive; I don't know what happens – maybe men who are angry at becoming disabled try to knock other men who are angry at becoming disabled out of their wheelchairs to take their anger out on them while they try to whack a ball with something, before the men they're trying to knock out of their wheelchairs manage to knock them out of theirs, because they're angry about being disabled too and think it'll be good to take their anger out on Them. I don't know . . . Or maybe they just all think the game's fun. After all, I think a lot of men like that kind of stuff, don't they."

Zoe giggled.

Then Becky said, "Actually, my auntie Diana's in contact with someone who runs marathons, and does a lot of other running, even though she's blind. She links arms with volunteers, and they guide her round the courses. She goes in for a lot of park runs. She'll never win a competition with able-bodied people, because she can't run at top speed all the time, because since she can't see anything in front of her, her guide has to tell her what's there a lot so she doesn't bang into it or trip over it, like saying, 'Duck; there's an over-hanging branch', or, 'There's a tree root sticking up a few inches just ahead', or, 'There are several steps we need to go up here'. So they keep having to slow down so her guide will be able to tell her what's there in time for her to know before she gets there. But she still really enjoys it, for some reason, and lots of people volunteer to guide her, so there must be quite a lot of people who don't mind going slower themselves than they might do if they were on their own, so they can guide her, which is nice.

"There was an article about her in a running magazine, and one of the volunteers who guides her said that when they're running down an especially narrow bit of the track, like through a wood with trees on each side of the path, sometimes people run up behind them, and at first they're impatient, because they must wonder why a couple are running arm in arm, too slowly for their liking, blocking the narrow path so they can't get past. But when they hear all the things that are being said to let her know what's in the way, they realise it's someone guiding a blind person, and they end up admiring her and cheering her on, thinking she's inspirational.

"Her guides must be good, because I don't think she's ever been injured – or at least, if she has, I don't think it can have been very badly, considering the number of miles she runs a year, and it can't have happened often."

"Wow!" said Zoe. "She must be brave! I don't think I'd dare run fast if I couldn't see what was in front of me! I don't need someone else to make a mistake to hurt myself; I can manage it all by myself, just getting out of bed in the morning!"

They giggled.

Becky said, "Yeah, I feel the same way! But those things I've told you just show you that even when nasty things happen to people, provided they're still alive of course, once they're beginning to get over them, even if they've left them permanently damaged in some way, there might still be quite a lot of things they can do that make them think life is worthwhile, and that some parts of it can still be enjoyable, as long as they're not still in a lot of pain that isn't being helped by pain medication, for some reason, and as long as they've got the support they need.

"Just tell me if I upset you by saying what I'm about to say; I'm a tactless berk at the best of times – or so I've heard; it's just that I'm thinking that it's a good thing it didn't happen, but even if your little brother had hit his head so hard on the train platform he really had been brain damaged, then although it might have meant your family would have found it difficult to look after him for years, or God forbid, for life, so that wouldn't have been nice, they might still have got pleasure from being with him sometimes, and he might have still found that there were things in life he enjoyed, especially if he was taught to cope with his problems better than he could at first, if that was possible. There might even have been some things he was skilled at doing, and he might still have been affectionate, so he might still have been loveable, and have got something out of life.

"Hopefully the family would have got professional help and support from people who know how to look after people with brain damage too, so some of the pressure of coping would have been taken off them. So things might not have been as catastrophic as you've been thinking they could have been.

"I mean, there are people who get so severely disabled in accidents they end up with no quality of life, and their life becomes a burden to them or their families, so they end up feeling as if it would have been better if their lives hadn't been saved. But there are other people who are in that condition for a while, but then they recover to some extent.

"Anyway, there's no need to dwell on that kind of thing really, because thankfully your brother didn't get brain damage. And as we've talked about before, most of the time when you've been out, bad things haven't happened, have they; so for both those reasons – that bad things haven't happened that often, and that if one does, chances are it won't turn out as badly as you think it will, you don't need to worry before you go out as much as you think you do.

"Also, worrying doesn't achieve anything. It doesn't help people think up solutions to problems, especially if they don't even know if they'll have any problems! And it just gets people more and more worked up with anxiety; and the more anxious they get, the less they'll be in the kind of calm frame of mind they need to be in if they're going to be able to solve any problems. The stronger people's emotions are, the harder it is to think things through, because the emotion will temporarily block the logical part of the brain that can think about things carefully from working properly, because it gets so strong it crowds clear thinking out."

Becky and Zoe Have
a Bit of a Laugh Again

Zoe said, "I suppose you're right about worrying not doing any good. It's interesting how you know all this stuff at your age . . . I wonder what you'll be doing in fifty years' time!"

Becky said, "Oh I dunno." Then she grinned and said, "Maybe I'll be being carried around everywhere by my own private robot, even if I can still walk perfectly well – and chances are I will be able to. Maybe we'll all have a private carrier-robot each, so we won't even have to bother walking . . . apart from whenever we have to get off it to do all the exercise we'll need to do to make up for having not done the exercise we would have done if we weren't being carried everywhere."

They giggled.

Then Zoe grinned and asked Becky, "Would you trust a robot to cut your toenails?"

Becky said, "I don't know. Maybe it would depend on whether I'd heard about it doing a good job on other people's. Hey imagine if it somehow used bits of old toenail for fuel to power itself, so instead of cutting your toenails, it would nibble on them till they were shorter and a nice shape, and it would swallow down the bits it nibbled off, and they'd go into part of it that would process them and turn them into fuel."

Zoe chuckled and said, "That might be OK as long as it didn't nibble more and more of your toenail off the lower it was running on fuel, to power itself up properly again! You'd start worrying it was about to eat your toes! . . . Well, I would, anyway!"

Becky said, "imagine having a tank full of toenail fuel!"

They giggled. Then Zoe said seriously, "I've heard that scientists are beginning to develop technology to make fuel out of rubbish. Imagine how good it'll be if they manage to do that, with all the masses of tons of rubbish that just goes to waste now!"

Becky grinned and said, "Yeah, that'll be good! Imagine if they end up being able to power the national electricity supply on rubbish! Our computers and televisions and fridges and things will be powered by worn-out old shoe power, and rotten old banana skin power, and empty coke bottle power, and mouldy carrot power, and broken old radio power, and dirty tissue power, and used teabag power, and torn old sheet power, and things like that!"

They laughed.

Then they spotted some families packing up to go home, and it occurred to them that Stephanie's parents might want them to go home soon. So they decided to get back down to talking seriously again.

Becky Gives Zoe Advice on Getting to Sleep More Easily

Becky said, "Another bit of advice I can give you is that when you go to bed at night, if you find yourself thinking depressing or scary thoughts, again, don't just let your thoughts run and run till you get really depressed, but you can reply to them in your mind, reassuring yourself that things aren't as bad as your thoughts are making out they are.

"Or there are some relaxation techniques you could try, to calm yourself down and to help you get to sleep. One is imagining you're sitting in front of a blackboard – I know that doesn't sound relaxing; but you imagine there are lots of words on it, representing your scary and depressing thoughts. You keep blowing gently, or imagining you're blowing gently if you prefer, and as you do, you imagine that more and more of the words that represent your bad thoughts are disappearing from the blackboard, as if you're blowing them away.

"Or you could imagine you're lying under a tree in autumn, and your depressing thoughts are like dry leaves that have come off the trees, with more and more of them being blown away every time there's a gentle refreshing gust of wind.

"Or you could try to imagine you're lying in the sunshine, and that every time you breathe out, your worrying thoughts are coming out with your breath, and that it's somehow propelling them right up to the sky, and they're drifting away and disappearing. Or you could imagine they're turning into little clouds in the sky, that you blow some of away every time you breathe out, and that makes the sun shine brighter.

"Another relaxation technique you could try is closing your eyes and imagining you're somewhere you enjoy being, like on a beach. You can build up the image till it's as vivid as you can make it, perhaps by first imagining you can see five things, such as the sea, children playing, sandcastles, the sunshine, and people swimming or having a picnic. Then you can imagine hearing five things, which might be some of the same things plus a couple of others; and then you think about things you can imagine feeling, like the sand between your toes, a gentle breeze ruffling your hair and feeling cooling on your face, the warm sunshine on your skin, the sensation of your back against the back of a deckchair, and the warmth of a bag of freshly-bought chips and a pie on your lap, or whatever you like.

"It's a bit like the technique I told you about for distracting yourself from flashbacks, only done in slow motion so it's more restful and relaxing, and it's all in your imagination.

"If you can't think of five things to imagine seeing, you could count a few of the same things twice, or just think of fewer things, before you move on to imagining things you can hear and so on.

"And when you've thought of five things you can see, hear and feel, you can try to imagine more of each.

"If you end up in a better mood when you go to sleep, I think you'll be less likely to have nightmares. So that'll be another benefit of doing the relaxation techniques.

"Another thing that could put you in a better mood is if you start bringing to mind things that have gone well in your life, or that are going well at the moment, like some good things you've accomplished in life or during the day, something you've enjoyed, something you hope to achieve one day, like a university degree, some things you can feel grateful for having in your life or having had the opportunity to do, and things like that. If you fall asleep thinking pleasant thoughts, you're probably less likely to have nightmares than you will be if you go to sleep with worries on your mind.

"Thinking relaxing thoughts will help you get to sleep a fair bit more quickly than you would if your mind was being agitated by worries as well. Then you'll wake up the next morning feeling more refreshed than normal, so you'll be in a better mood to start the day.

"And the more you think about uplifting things in your life, the more you might get a self-esteem boost, so you get more self-confident; and then you'll be less likely to think thoughts where you put yourself down.

"And those relaxation techniques are also things you can do before you try writing those letters I suggested you write, where you imagine you're writing to the boy who knocked you over in the station, and receiving letters from him. You could also do one or two of them before you write down in detail what happens in your flashbacks before you read what you've written to someone who cares about you, or before you imagine reading it to a caring person. That's if you decide to do those things. The thing is that if you start using those techniques when you're relaxed, it might take longer for them to start upsetting you, and you might not get so upset by doing them as you would be if you were feeling anxious about it to begin with.

"But if you do get upset while you're doing those things, you could have a break and use those relaxation techniques to calm down, or do something else you know will calm you down. Don't wait till you feel really upset before you do that.

"You know, I think I've told you just about everything I can remember learning about this kind of subject now."

Those things were Becky's last bits of advice to Zoe, and when she'd finished talking, she sat back and relaxed. It was still sunny and warm, and children were still playing.

Zoe said she'd try the ideas Becky had given her. She thanked Becky for the talk, and said she'd think about all the advice she'd passed on.

Becky and Zoe Join Stephanie and Her Parents Again, and They Have a Laugh Before Going Home

Stephanie saw them relaxing, and came over and asked if they'd like to join the others. They did.

Stephanie's dad asked them how they'd been getting on, and Zoe said she'd found what Becky had said helpful, and that they'd just finished discussing it.

Then Stephanie's dad said, "I'm going to want us to start packing up to go home soon; but we can stay here a bit longer. We've been having a nice time all afternoon while you two have been talking. I've just been reading a book about criminals who made mistakes that made the crimes they wanted to commit go wrong. It's funny! One man was put on trial for armed robbery. He got fed up of his lawyer and sacked him, saying he'd defend himself from then on. Soon the woman who'd been serving at the counter of the shop he was alleged to have robbed got up and started telling the court what had happened. The robber flew into a rage, jumped up and bawled that she was a liar and that he should have blown her head off. Then he realised what he'd said and stammered, 'If I'd actually been there.' It was too late. The jury were convinced he was guilty by then and convicted him.

"And there was an unlucky criminal who'd just committed a robbery when the police started following his car. He tried to give them the slip by driving into a car park, but it turned out to be the car park of a high-security prison. He jumped out and tried to run on foot to find somewhere to hide instead, but ended up running into the lobby of the prison.

It seems he somehow thought it was a shopping mall. He was soon arrested."

They chuckled.

Then Stephanie's mum said, "I wasn't sure I was doing the right thing, but I thought you might like some light relief after all your talking, so I brought along a couple of funny stories I wrote when I was at school. I kept them all these years and fished them out the other day. There was one I wrote for an English class I didn't like. One day the teacher asked us to write about something interesting we'd done on our Christmas holidays. I think we were about thirteen at the time. Well I'd hardly enjoyed my holidays at all, and hadn't done anything interesting, so I thought I'd just make something up. The teacher really wasn't impressed! It's a shame really, because I thought it was good!"

She grinned as she said, "I'll read it to you. It says: "A man's flat roof blew off near the seaside near where an Aunt of mine lives on Christmas Day. The whole of it! And it was so windy, it blew right across the town. It blew over houses and shops, and landed right by the sea on the beach on its side, so it was kind of like a high wall. The council came and inspected it, and they decided it made a fantastic sea defence to protect the town when there are storms, so they won't let the man have it back now; and they're so impressed with it, they've decided to build a sea defence just like it right along the coast. They want to keep the original roof in place on the beach though, just in case they forget what it's like, so they're not sure any more what to model the new sea defence on while the rest of it's being built; and then they'll still want to keep the roof there, because it'll blend in so nicely with the rest of the sea defence.

"So the poor man hasn't got a roof at the moment. It's a shame it's been raining so hard ever since. He waded out in the rain and went around the town asking everyone he met if they could give him plastic sheets to cover his precious things in, and as many buckets as they could spare so he could collect the rainwater.

"He doesn't seem to mind though, surprisingly. It was reported on the news that he's one of these 'sickening eternal optimists', since he cheerfully explained that he was feeling positive about all the rain coming in, because he thought of it as a brilliant opportunity to collect a load of rainwater so he could put it on his plants in the summer when there'll probably be a hosepipe ban for a while. He said to everyone, 'Don't worry when the rain comes into your house! Think positive!' But he might not have thought so positively if he got back to find his things had been ruined.

"Anyway, the council are making good progress with building the new sea defences, modelled on his old roof. The only problem is, anyone who wants to swim in the sea in the summer is going to have to be quite adventurous, climbing over the roof-like structures to make it to the sea. Some people in wheelchairs have emailed the council asking them to make ramps so they can get over the structures in their chairs so they can go swimming in them too. I'm not sure how they're going to manage that, but they obviously know what they're talking about.

"The council said they wouldn't do it though, since the sea would be able to 'climb over the ramps and make it onto the land' – the council's words, not mine, you understand.

"Anyway, the people in wheelchairs aren't happy about that, so they've told the council they're taking them to court. The council have agreed to go, provided the court hearing takes place in the sea. I don't know what'll happen."

The others grinned when Stephanie's mum finished reading her old story, and Becky said, "What did your teacher say after reading that?"

Stephanie's mum said, "Well, she wasn't all that annoyed, but she gave me a low mark, telling me off, saying she could tell it couldn't have really happened and I was supposed to write about something real. I tried to convince her it really had happened, just for fun, but she wouldn't believe me! I didn't really mind though. Doing it was a laugh anyway."

They had a bit of a giggle.

Not long afterwards, they started packing up to go home.

Stephanie's dad stopped near a baker's shop not long after they'd started going back and got them some cakes. They enjoyed that.

Zoe and Becky swapped email addresses, and sometimes in the months after that, Becky would get nice emails from Zoe, saying she'd felt a lot better since their talk, and she wasn't getting nightmares and the horrible flashbacks and panic attacks any more. She would talk about how pleased she was when she went on another day out with her school or the family and found she could stop herself getting miserable before it.

Becky was glad.

Chapter 7

Becky Volunteers As a Teaching Assistant At Her Old School, and Helps a Little Boy With an Anxiety Problem That Makes him Too Timid to Speak

Near the end of her summer holidays that year, Becky did some voluntary work for a few weeks as a teaching assistant at her old primary school. Term started a few weeks before she was due to go back to university. She assisted with teaching in one of the infant classes, where the children were about five and six. She was only about five years older than them, but they didn't mind her teaching them.

Becky arrived early on her first day, and got chatting to some of the mums as they came in. Some of the children looked a bit upset to be there. Becky said hello to one of them, and he didn't say hello back. She asked him what his name was, and he didn't answer. She wondered why he didn't want to speak to her; but his mum told her he had an anxiety problem called selective mutism that made him scared to talk to anyone other than the family and their close friends. He was called Timothy.

Becky wondered how on earth he was going to cope with school if he wouldn't talk to anyone. His mum said he'd been in the reception class the year before, and had found it hard, especially because he'd felt more worried about talking the more the teacher had alternately ordered him to and tried to persuade him to.

Becky thought it would be nice to try to help him, and wondered how. Then she thought she just might have an idea.

When it was time for class to start, the teacher called the register. When she called Timothy's name, he didn't say anything. She said his name louder, but he still didn't answer. She wasn't sure what to do, so she just moved on to the next child's name. The year before, his teacher had started off thinking he might be just being naughty. So she'd told him off quite a bit, and that had made him more anxious. He'd recently been diagnosed with selective mutism, but the teachers didn't really know what to do about it.

Becky asked the teacher a bit later, "Can I take over doing the register for the next few days?"

The teacher said that was alright, and Becky asked her if she minded her doing things a bit differently. The teacher was doubtful, but said that as long as it wasn't too radical, it would be alright. She'd taught Becky herself several years before, and had been impressed by how clever she was.

They had fun catching up on all their news after school that day.

They met the headmistress, who'd also known Becky when she'd been at the school before. Becky and her had fun catching up on all their news too. Then Becky mentioned Timothy.

The headmistress said that at first when he'd come to school and didn't talk, they'd wondered if he was a late developer or had a hearing problem; but when they'd asked his mother, she said he didn't have a problem talking at home. They'd tried to coax him into talking after that, but he wouldn't, so sometimes they'd shouted at him, thinking he was just being naughty. But when he still wouldn't talk, often they'd just left him alone. They'd never heard of selective mutism before Timothy's mother had recently told them he'd been diagnosed with it.

Becky said she'd heard a bit about selective mutism, and she'd heard that people who'd had it but had eventually got over it had said it had made them feel like talking even less when people tried to pressure them into talking, since it made them more anxious; and then when those people got fed up and left them alone, they felt so relieved, it just made them feel as if staying quiet made them feel a lot better than talking would, so they felt as if talking was an even worse thing to do than they had before, because there was such a contrast between their feelings of relief at not being expected to do it and the times when they'd felt anxious because they'd felt pressured to do it.

Then when people got used to them not talking, they'd started worrying that if they did start talking, it would feel so weird because they weren't used to it that they wouldn't be sure they could keep it up, and then it would be all the worse if they didn't feel like it, because they'd be expected to talk then, so people would start criticising them for not doing it again, so it would be better not to start in the first place.

The headmistress said that had given her something to think about.

The next morning, Becky went up to Timothy before class began and said, "I'm going to call the register today. Since you're scared to talk, how would you like to do something else instead, like tapping your desk when I say your name? Nod your head if you like the idea and shake it if you don't."

Timothy shook his head slowly. Becky said, "What about making an animal noise, like barking like a dog?"

Timothy half smiled, but then shook his head again. Becky thought he probably didn't fancy being the odd one out. She said, "How about if everyone in the class pretends to be animals when their names are called out?"

Timothy chuckled at the idea, but didn't show whether he liked it or not.

Becky decided to try it.

Before the class started, she asked the teacher if she'd mind if they played games in class, where they could be split up into small groups, and each group could play an entertaining game. The teacher said Becky could organise things if she liked.

It turned out to be a noisy day! In fact it was a noisy week!

Becky stood up at the front and told the children that instead of saying 'Yes' when she did the register and called their names, they could do animal noises if they liked. She asked anyone who wanted to make an animal noise to put their hand up. A few hands went up. Becky asked their owners what animals they'd like to be. Other children started thinking the idea would be fun, and said they'd like to be animals too. Becky said she'd give them a few minutes to decide what animals they'd like to be for the week when she did the register in the mornings, and then she'd come round and ask each of them what their names were and what they wanted to be.

She let them think and chat among themselves for a minute or two, while she went and spoke to Timothy. She said to him, "How about you being a mouse? Then all you'd have to do is give a little squeak."

He looked unsure. she suggested he try it anyway, saying that then if he decided he didn't want to, or wanted to be something else, he could let her know afterwards.

Becky went around to all the children and found out what animals they'd decided to be. While she was asking, she was drawing a picture which she said was a class map, which was of desks in rows with animals on the chairs at them, with the children's names above the desks. She drew whichever animal a child said they wanted to be.

Jessica was the first child Becky spoke to, and she said she'd like to be a dog, so Becky drew a sketch of a dog sitting in her chair, and wrote her name above it. She did that with the other children too. She said it was to remind her who was which animal, and who was sitting at each desk. The picture did look funny. She stuck it on the wall at the front of the class. It made some of the children laugh.

Then Becky called the register. She called the first child's name, and a big meow was heard in reply. When she called the second child's name, a big neigh like a horse was heard.

Timothy felt nervous at first, not really liking the idea of squeaking when it was his turn. But as he heard kids snort like pigs, bark like dogs, bah like sheep, and do other things, he at first started smiling, and by the time it was his turn, he was laughing out loud. He didn't mind squeaking then.

At the end of the register, Becky said that for the rest of the week, it would be alright if the children wanted to get down on all fours and walk around their desks like animals as well as doing their noises. Later she told Timothy that if he wanted to, he could do a display of hiding under his desk like a mouse when it was his turn if he liked.

In the next few days, they started really getting into the spirit of things, till by the end of the week, children were barking like mad, panting and crawling on all fours around their desks like dogs, pretending to be chickens going after food, and ducks quacking and swimming around, and all kinds of things. The children all laughed at each other's acts. Timothy thought they were just as funny as the rest of the children did, and his laughter made his nerves disappear, and he happily played his part with the rest of them.

If any one of them got too enthusiastic about their animal noises, or did them for too long, Becky would order them to sit, in the same way she might tell a dog to. They all obeyed, like animals that had learned to understand commands.

During each morning, Becky organised a game too. She split the class into groups of four or five, and said each group could spend about half an hour playing a game where they pretended to be characters doing something or other. She gave them ideas for what they could do, such as pretending they were a family, or all firemen pretending to put out a fire, or in a shop, and one person could be the shopkeeper and the rest could be customers, or whatever they liked; but she left it up to them. She gave them a few minutes to decide what to play, and then wrote down all their choices.

She said She was going to play a game with one group. She'd chosen the people in her group: There was Timothy, two nice little girls called Kim and Caroline, and a boy called Peter.

Becky said to them, "Right: Let's play a game where Timothy's the baby, I'm the mummy, you're the daddy, Peter, and Kim and Caroline are Timothy's older sisters. Timothy has to cry quite a bit, and we all have to look after him. You don't need to talk at all, Timothy – actually we'd all get a shock if you did, because you're only supposed to be a few months old. So unless you want to see us jumping around, yelling in horror because we think a ghost must be talking and pretending to be you, you'd better not talk."

Becky said that with a grin.

Then she told Kim, Caroline and Peter to do the kind of things she was doing.

The game started, and she went up to Timothy and said, "Hello baby. You've had a nice long sleep. I'll get you your bottle now."

She went a few paces away and said, "I'm just making the bottle feed up; now I'm going to put it in the microwave to warm up. Right, I'll put it on for one minute."

She went back to Timothy and said one or two things, and then said, "Ah, I've just heard the microwave ding. That must be your bottle."

She pretended to look at a watch, and then leapt back and said in a horrified voice, "Oh no! I must have accidentally put that microwave on for an hour instead of a minute, and forgot about it! That bottle's been in there for a whole hour!"

She ran to where the pretend microwave was and opened it. She put her hand towards it, and then again leapt back, throwing up her hands and making an exaggeratedly horrified face, shouting, "Oh no! It's way too hot now! I can't touch that!"

She looked amusing, and the other children in the group, including Timothy, laughed out loud.

Then she said, "I know, I'll take the bottle out the microwave with oven gloves and put it in the fridge for five minutes. Then it might be just right, if all the milk hasn't turned into steam and escaped."

She pretended to put the bottle in the fridge, and then went and said a few things to Timothy again. Then she pretended to look at her watch, leapt back and threw up her hands again, and said in mock horror, "Oh no! I've accidentally left that bottle in the fridge for half an hour! It'll be cold now! I'd better put it in the microwave again!"

The other children laughed again. Then Becky said to Peter, "I know, Daddy, can You put the bottle in the microwave? You might know how to work it better than me."

Peter said he would, and pretended to. He came back to Becky and said, "Mummy, I think it would be nice to buy baby a teddy one day. What do you think?"

Becky had just begun to say it would be nice, when Peter pretended to look at his watch, and then leapt back and threw up his hands himself, shouting in a horrified voice, "Oh no! I've left the microwave on for an hour as well! Poor baby might never get his bottle! I'd better take it out and put it in the fridge quick!"

He pretended to do that. The baby thought it was about time he started crying, and yelled, "Waaaaaaaaaaaaaaaaaaaaaah!"

Becky and the other children rushed to Timothy's side and pretended to try and comfort him. Becky said, "I'm sorry I'm so bad at making up your bottle. I'll try and do it better next time."

Peter opened one of their schoolbooks to a page where there was a picture. It was quite a boring picture, but he pretended it was really pretty, and said to Timothy with a great show of enthusiasm, "Hey, look at the pretty picture! Isn't it lovely!"

Timothy burst out laughing.

Then Peter dropped the book on a desk as if he was startled, jumped up in mock horror and shouted, "Oh no! I've left that bottle in the fridge for a whole hour! It'll be freezing now! Oh no, I'll have to put it in the microwave again!"

The children laughed, and Becky said, "I know, let's ask Kim or Caroline to try; they might do it better than us."

First Kim and then Caroline pretended to have a go, but both of them pretended to make the same mistakes as the others had, jumping around in horror, shouting about how terrible it was that they'd put the bottle in the microwave and then the fridge for so much longer than they should have done.

All the children laughed. They were having a great time.

But soon the teacher told them their time was up.

The next day, they were split into the same groups for half an hour and played games again. This time Becky said, "I know: How about I be the baby today. Timothy can be the daddy, Caroline can be my mummy, and Kim and Peter can be my older brother and sister. What do you think?"

They agreed. Then Becky said, "Pretend I'm about six months older than Timothy was yesterday, so I'm just about beginning to learn to talk. But if I say anything properly, that's not really me talking; pretend it's just me thinking in baby language."

They agreed, and the game started. Caroline said to Becky, "Let me tuck you into your cot, baby." She pretended to tuck her in snugly, and said, "there you go. Look, here's your nice teddy!"

"Gaga!" Becky said, and smiled.

Caroline moved away several paces, and told Kim it was nearly her bedtime.

Becky sat up and started cackling. She said in a loud whisper to herself, "I can see Daddy in the doorway. I'm going to throw my teddy at him!"

She pretended to laugh with glee. Then she pretended to pick her teddy up and throw it, and said, "Weeeeeeeeeee-eeeeeeee!" She loudly laughed some more and said, "My teddy nearly hit Daddy on the head!"

Timothy rushed forward to Becky's side. Adrenaline was surging through him, and he'd forgotten all about being scared to talk. He felt at ease with the children in the group anyway because he'd been having fun with them. And the fact that he was playing another character, rather than self-consciously being himself, made it easier too. He was really getting into the game. He shouted at the top of his voice, "You naughty baby! You mustn't throw your teddies! Especially at other people!"

"Waaaaaaaaaaaaaaaaaaaaaaaaaaah!" yelled Becky.

Then Timothy said gently, "Sorry baby, but you mustn't throw your teddies. Alright, I'll pick it up and give it back to you. But don't throw it again!"

He pretended to pick the teddy up and give it back. Then he said, "Go to sleep now," and went and stood where he'd been standing before.

An evil grin came over Becky's face, and then she started cackling again. She said in a loud whisper, "I'm going to throw my teddy at Daddy again!"

She cackled some more, and then sat up and pretended to throw it, saying, "Weeeeeeeeeeeeeeee! Plonk!" Then she laughed and shouted, "My teddy nearly hit Daddy on the head again!"

Timothy rushed forward again and shouted at Becky, "I told you! You mustn't throw your teddies! Right! Because you've been so naughty, I'm not going to give it back to you this time. You'll only throw it at me again if I give it back to you."

Becky pretended to cry again. Timothy said gently, "Don't cry, baby. But you mustn't throw your teddies! I don't want to give you your teddy if you're only going to throw it at me again, do I! Daddies don't like having teddies thrown at them. Actually, no one does."

Becky started behaving as if she was loving all the attention her daddy was giving her, as if he was telling her how lovely she was, not telling her not to do something she wanted to do. She smiled, and said, "Gaga! Wawa! Baba!"

Kim came up to them and said enthusiastically, "Hey listen! The baby's trying to make words! Let's try and teach her to talk!"

She pretended to pick something up and said, "Look baby! Camera! Say camera!"

Timothy said, "I think that word's too complicated for the baby at the moment. Let's try and teach her short words at first. How about this?"

He leaned over towards Becky and said coaxingly, "Dada! Baby, say Dada!"

"Dada!" said Becky, and did a baby laugh.

Timothy and Kim praised the baby, saying enthusiastically, "Well done!" and, "Good baby!" Then they turned round and shouted excitedly, "Mum! Peter! Come here and listen to the baby! She's learning to talk! She just said Dada!"

Caroline and Peter ran forward and praised the baby as well.

Then Kim said, "I'll try teaching the baby a proper word now. Baby, say cot ... Cot ... Cot ... Cot."

"Dot!" said Becky.

"No, Cot!" said Kim coaxingly.

"Bot!" said Becky.

The other children all laughed. Kim said, "No, Cot!"

"Mot!" said Becky.

Timothy said, "No, Cot. Kuh-kuh-kuh-kuh-cot!"

"Cot!" said Becky.

The others praised her again. They put their arms around her and said things like, "Well done!" and, "You clever baby!"

Soon after that, the teacher said it was time to stop playing. Then she said each group could tell the others all about what game they'd been playing.

The children had fun telling each other what games they'd played. Timothy was happy to talk about it along with the others, laughing with them.

They laughed and chatted to each other about their games between lessons in the playground too. Timothy suddenly felt a lot more confident about talking. He made new friends while laughing and chatting about the game, and started happily joining in other games with them.

By the time Becky left the school to go back to university, there wasn't a trace of anxiety about him. He felt much more at ease with the others, and was as chatty as the rest.

Becky was pleased. But in the days before she went back to university, she felt a bit gloomy, thinking it would have been nice if she could have played a lot more games like the one they'd played when she was younger, just for fun, instead of having so much school and homework to do. Still, she'd had fun joking around with some of her university friends who were playful. When she went back, she had more fun with them.

Chapter 8

Becky and Her Friends Meet a Student Who Seems to Combine Litter Picking With Extreme Sports

One day, Becky and some of her friends met a student who told them things that shocked them a bit, about the number of tons of litter being dropped around the country, and where some of it ended up.

She was a litter-picking volunteer called Christine. She went on litter-picking days with other volunteers, where they cleared rubbish out of rivers and other places.

"One thing she did that made litter picking more exciting than normal was going out around the coasts near where she lived with a group of volunteers and helping to clear litter from hard-to-reach places. They would climb cliffs and scramble over rocks to gather it from places where the sea had swept it.

Sometimes they would swim out to sea to gather it, or go out in canoes and put litter they found in the sea in sacks, tie them to their canoes, and tow them back. Sometimes if they'd started climbing the cliffs above deep water and spotted litter in the sea, they would jump into the sea to get it, as long as they were absolutely certain it Was deep, without rocks sticking up, so they wouldn't be in any danger of hitting the bottom hard or hurting themselves on something.

Becky and her friends thought the extreme litter picking sounded like a fun thing to do; but Christine said they'd need quite a bit of training before they could do it safely, and she doubted Becky would be allowed to till she was a fair bit older, because it would be dangerous.

She told them some things that made them laugh. She said she'd once found a plastic false nose in a rock pool, and a half-used jar of coffee part-way up a cliff. They wondered how they could have got there!

Christine told Becky and her friends about other groups of litter pickers, one that would go scuba-diving to pull up litter from the seabed. They'd found all kinds of strange things down there, including a kitchen sink and a car!

She said she'd heard of people who'd found things like a packet of bacon on the beach, and even weirder things like half a canoe, and half a television, as well as a bath plug, a bird cage, some high heels- without the shoes, a toilet flush handle, a wedding gown and a whoopee cushion. She said that not long before, a wheelchair and a pair of crutches had been found by volunteers clearing litter from a canal! Some others had found a postman's trolley, and a safe full of locker keys and pound coins! She said,

"Besides those, it's surprising how many fridges and washing machines and microwaves get found in places like that.

Traffic cones have been fished out of canals, and even underwear."

Becky said, "That reminds me of something I heard about the weird things that get left behind on trains and buses and in hotel rooms sometimes. I heard about a woman who forgot her husband and left him in a hotel, and had been driving for half an hour when she remembered him and came back for him. And someone left a bucket of live crabs in a hotel. Someone even left some breast implants in one. Goodness knows how that happened! And someone left a pet python in one! Someone left a whole trunk of chocolate bars! I don't know how anyone could do that! And in just one year, over 75 thousand teddy bears were left in the rooms of just one hotel chain! People have even left artificial legs in hotels! How could someone walk out without their wooden leg? And someone managed to walk out without their Zimmer frame, completely forgetting to take it with them!

"And I heard that people have left artificial legs and breast implants and false teeth on underground trains too, as well as crutches and wheelchairs! And a judge's wig was left on a train."

The students found that amusing. Christine said, "Some of the things that get found on beaches weren't dropped there by litter bugs, but they've been washed out of cargo ships in storms. A few years ago, 28 thousand rubber ducks and other bath toys got washed out of a container ship going from Hong Kong to America, and since then, rubber ducks have been turning up on beaches all over the world. And thousands of bananas got washed up on a beach near Holland once. People eagerly rushed onto the beach to get some. There were so many they thought of donating lots to the local zoo for monkeys and other animals to eat."

Becky and her friends laughed.

But then Christine said that although it had a funny side, littering was really a serious problem. She told them some very sad facts about it. She said animals could often be injured and killed when they came across rubbish that had been thoughtlessly dropped. Becky and her friends just hadn't realised things were that bad, and were horrified. Christine said:

"So much litter gets dropped in this country, over 30 million tons of it has to be cleared up by local councils every year! Nearly a billion pounds gets spent on clearing it up. Every day, about 200 million cigarette butts get dropped alone! And apart from those, about a quarter of a million bits of rubbish get dropped every day! People would be knee-deep in it in some places if council workers didn't clear it up! They can clear up beaches and town centres and other areas one day, only for literally tons of rubbish to be dropped in them the next!

"All the money councils spend on clearing up litter could be spent on other things if people just didn't drop rubbish, but threw it in bins or took it home to throw away, so it didn't have to be cleared off the streets and beaches, and from other places. The money could go on providing better facilities for schools or hospitals, or for better care for old or disabled people or disadvantaged children, for instance. Or councils could reduce the amount of tax people have to pay them.

"It isn't just that. Animals can get hurt by litter left around. I've heard about animals like dogs that have reached their tongues out to lick the tops of drink cans on the ground because they liked the smell of them, and got their tongues caught in them. Birds can get their beaks trapped in them too. Sometimes they're not rescued and they can't get them out, and they die slow painful deaths.

"Some people drop glass bottles and they break, and animals can get their paws badly cut by them. Animals can wander onto roads attracted by the smell of food people have thrown out of their cars only half-eaten, and they can be run over.

"I've heard that around a million seabirds die every year around the world because of litter that gets washed or thrown into the sea or dropped on the beaches. A lot of fishing line and net ends up floating around the sea, and seals and dolphins and fish can get it caught around their necks and be strangled to death, and birds can get it caught around their legs or wings and can't fly off to get food. Fish hooks can get stuck in birds' throats. And birds can suffer lead poisoning if they swallow little lead weights that are used to weigh down fishing lines to make them stay under the water. Lots of those get left in the sea.

"And plastic bags and other plastic packaging can break down into little bits, and seabirds and other animals can often mistake it for food and eat it. At a glance it can look like jellyfish and creatures like that, so they pounce on it, and once they've swallowed it and realised it's not food, it's too late. And if that keeps happening, then because it doesn't get digested and doesn't contain any nutrients, but it might fill up their stomachs, they slowly starve to death for want of enough things to eat that are actually nourishing, because there isn't enough room in their stomachs for good food.

"Then if bigger animals eat animals with lots of little bits of plastic in their systems, they'll have the plastic in their systems too, and it might break down some more and release toxic chemicals; and if those animals are caught for food, humans might well eat them. Fish have been dissected that have been found to have loads of tiny bits of plastic in their stomachs.

"Even when people drop plastic bags and packaging in a town nowhere near the sea, it can get washed or blown into drains, and then it can flow down into rivers with the water in the drains, and then be swept out to sea.

"It isn't just soft plastic that seabirds and other animals accidentally eat, but bottle lids and other little things, even cigarette lighters. A whale was washed up dead on a beach, and it was found to have eaten a pair of pants, a golf ball, more than twenty plastic bags, and some surgical gloves.

"Even after animals are rescued, they can still die, because their injuries can be so bad that they just can't be saved.

"And chucking litter on the streets ends up being bad for humans too. A lot of half-eaten fast food gets thrown on the ground in some places, and then it attracts rats. More and more rats can end up living and breeding because there's such a lot of thrown-away fast food for them to survive on, till they're a problem for people in some areas. No one wants rats in their garden or finding a way into their house."

Becky and her friends were upset to hear what Christine said. Becky said, "I don't understand why people drop litter. No one in my family does. We always take a plastic bag out with us, and if we do something that ends up with us having rubbish, we put it in the bag, and wait till we find a bin to put it in, or take it home and throw it away in our own bins."

The others didn't understand why so many people drop litter either. One of Becky's friends, Clare, said, "You even see lots of litter near rubbish bins! It wouldn't take much at all for people to just walk a little way to a bin and throw things away properly, but some people won't even do that, for some reason!"

Becky and her friends thought it might be nice to be litter-clearing volunteers themselves, thinking it would be nice to protect any animals that might get hurt by rubbish if it wasn't cleared up.

But Christine said they'd really need a bit of training, even if they didn't do the extreme version of litter picking she did. She said there were quite a lot of guidelines she'd had to learn before she'd been allowed to take part in litter-picking days, even just around rivers and nearby fields. She and the other volunteers had been taught quite a few rules about what to be careful of, and different techniques for collecting litter. They'd been taught how to lift heavy things more safely, and they'd had to buy protective clothing and boots with ankle supports and rubber gloves, to prevent themselves getting scratched or cut or pricked by used needles, and to make it less likely they'd hurt themselves if they fell over. And she said they'd had to learn first aid, since some litter they found was quite hazardous. Sometimes they'd even found big cans of toxic chemicals, but they'd been instructed to leave those alone.

Becky and her friends decided not to join a group of litter-picking volunteers after all. But they thought it would be nice to do some things for the community, and decided it would be good to try raising money for charities. They looked on the Internet for ideas, and found lots. And they browsed it to find out information about charities so they could decide which ones were reputable enough to be worth supporting. They picked quite a few.

After that, they would quite often get involved in raising money for some charities. They loved it; they started getting together with lots of other people from the area who wanted to raise money, and would do sponsored events and other things. They'd enjoy meeting the others, since they were full of ideas for new things to do, and it felt good to be with people who were all achieving something worthwhile, and keen to do something positive, some of whom were full of plans and vitality.

Finding out about all the good so many people were doing was a nice contrast to turning on the news on the radio and hearing about the bad things going on; they'd never have guessed that so many nice worthwhile things were happening if they hadn't got involved with the others; it seemed to them that nice things like that were very rarely mentioned on the news, as if someone in authority had decreed that they just didn't matter, or that people were bound not to want to know about them.

Not that it wasn't depressing to hear about the causes the charities they volunteered for were helping with. But it was at least nice to know that things were being done to try to improve things.

Chapter 9

Becky and Her Friends Arrange a Charity Jokeathon, and Worried About Forgetting Jokes They Intend to Tell, Discuss Techniques for Improving the Memory

One day, Becky and her friends were chatting to a group of people from their local community after they'd taken part in an event to raise money for charity, when Becky herself came up with the idea of a charity event she and her friends could organise. She thought it would be fun to have a jokeathon, where all the people taking part would sit together in a park or some other open space, and they'd take it in turns to tell jokes. When they'd all told one, they'd take it in turns to tell another, and another and another, till they ran out of jokes, or till they'd told a certain number each.

Each participant could ask people they knew to sponsor them before the event, which could mean asking them to give them more money the more jokes they told, or to promise them some on the condition that they didn't forget any of the ones they were supposed to tell, or to just give them money anyway, for taking part. Also, people could come to watch the jokeathon, paying to hear them at the time.

Becky's friends liked the idea. They were on good terms with some of the people from the local community they'd met while they were taking part in charity events together, and the ones they were talking to liked the idea of the jokeathon. A few said they'd join in as well.

They set a date and managed to advertise the jokeathon in the student newspaper, and get a mention in the events section of the town's local paper, as well as putting information about it up on a noticeboard in their local library and in a community centre.

Quite a few people sponsored them, so they were optimistic they'd make quite a bit of money for the charity they'd chosen to donate to.

They each found several jokes on the Internet to tell.

Becky Has a Few Pre-Jokeathon Nerves, and Her Friend Sharon Decides to Try to Help

One evening, Becky was with her friends Luke, Sharon, Mandy and Gary, who were going to take part in the jokeathon with her, and she confided in them that she was feeling a bit nervous about participating in it, because she was wondering if her mind would get so full of the other people's jokes when she was having fun listening to them that she'd forget the ones she'd meant to tell.

Sharon said, "If I have a think about it, I might be able to help you come up with ideas for trying to make sure they stay in your mind . . . Actually, you could always write notes to remind yourself what they are, although I suppose some people might think that's cheating, since we've given them the impression we're going to do the jokeathon by memory.

"I've been reading about techniques for improving the ability to remember things by making them more memorable recently, for an essay I think I'm supposed to have done by now! It's a good thing it was only recently I learned about them, or I'd have probably forgotten them all by now. Mind you, I think I'm at least halfway to forgetting them anyway! I'll try and dredge up some of what I've written from my memory though, to see if anything still in it might help you.

"I'm about halfway through the essay I'm supposed to be writing now. I think part of the reason I haven't finished it yet is that I've had to wade through some dreary course books to get the information I need. Some of the techniques they were talking about are things I can't imagine anyone ever using, except if they want to go on stage in front of an audience and demonstrate how good their memory is.

"Mind you, some of the stuff was interesting and could be useful to some people, and I actually ended up having a bit of fun writing some of the essay!"

They were all curious to know why.

Sharon said, "Well, some of the techniques people can use to try to make things stick in their memories more involve doing things that can be fun. I'll tell you about some of what I wrote if you like . . . Well, at least the bits I can remember. Perhaps I'd be able to remember more if I'd actually tried some of these techniques. I didn't expect to need to though. Still, I think I can remember the best bits."

Sharon Gives a Few Tips on Revising For Exams

They were all interested in hearing more.

So Sharon said, "Actually, one thing that Wasn't fun, but which it's possible we'll all find useful one day, is to do with techniques to help us remember the things we try to stuff into our memories when we're trying to revise for exams. I'll tell you a bit about those, in case you find them handy to know about."

Becky was a little concerned and said, "You won't forget to tell me about ways of remembering jokes, will you? Or can the revision techniques be used for that, as if I can read the jokes before I go to refresh my memory about them and that'll be like revising them, and the jokeathon will be like a joke exam?"

Luke grinned and commented, "A joke exam? I wonder what one of those would be like! Imagine if you did what you thought was a university exam, and afterwards you were told, 'I know you won't like this, but actually that was just a joke exam. We tutors like playing practical jokes on students. Your real exam's tomorrow.'"

The others chuckled and grimaced.

Mandy said, "When I first heard the term 'mock exam', I wondered if it meant they were exams that were designed to make fun of us by showing up how bad we were at the subjects."

Sharon joked, "How do you know that's not what they really are?"

Mandy replied with a grin, "Well I hope they're not! Imagine a teacher one day saying to a class, 'You're going to have to do your mock exams soon. They're a good opportunity for us teachers to be able to look at your answers and mock you all for making all the mistakes you're bound to make! Don't worry, we'll tell you all where you went wrong, so you can improve before you have to do the real exams later in the year."

Sharon said, "That would be horrible! Anyway, don't worry, Becky; I'm planning to talk about ways of remembering jokes soon. I hadn't forgotten. I'll just say a bit about some other stuff first, like these tips for revising exams.

"One book I've been reading recommends that people stop revising every so often and refresh their memories of what they've just learned, and also that they go back and read the headings again when they've read a chapter or two of a textbook, to see if they can remember what's under each one, and so it'll refresh their memories about what's there, because, you know, things in textbooks aren't always that memorable."

Becky grinned and asked, "What, a textbook said that?"

Sharon grinned herself and said, "Well not quite all of it; I just thought up the bit about textbooks not always being that memorable a few seconds ago. I don't think I'll say it in my essay.

"Anyway, one nice thing one of the books said was that it's good to have breaks every so often, so we don't get so sick of concentrating on things that we decide we just can't be bothered any more, so we end up not learning as much as we would have done if we'd had the odd chocolate break or something . . . Actually, I can't imagine there can be many people who'd dare to decide they couldn't be bothered to study any more just before an exam, but still!

"But also, the book meant that it's a good idea to stop and think of what we've just revised for a while every now and then, since that'll help it go into our memories better than if we just read it over quickly and then move on straightaway to reading something else, hoping it'll get in there in the short time we're paying attention to it. It's hard for people to remember things they just think of for a very short time and then move on from to think about something else, because the things they were just thinking of don't really get a chance to get into the long-term memory properly first, since you have to think about things for a little while without being distracted for that to happen. That's one reason why it's easy to forget a lot of what you hear the first time you hear it – you don't think about it for long enough for it to be able to stick in the memory in the first place, because you soon get distracted when the person talking moves onto another topic, or whatever else happens."

Luke said, "It would help a lot, though, if exams weren't so close together! In my experience, there sometimes just isn't time in between some of them to stuff everything you'd like to stuff into your memory in there, and that'll be especially if you want to pause quite a bit to make sure you can still remember what you've just read! Oh well, maybe it's worth knowing you're supposed to do that anyway!"

Sharon Describes Techniques For Trying to Remember Phone Numbers, Computer Passwords and So On, And The Friends Begin to Have a Laugh

Sharon said, "Yeah, I agree that we could do with a bit more time between each exam to revise better.

"Anyway, another thing I wrote about was some techniques for remembering phone numbers. I don't know if any of you could do with knowing about any; but if I had to learn about them, I don't see why you shouldn't, so I'll tell you about them anyway."

She grinned as she said that. Then she continued more seriously,

"One of the techniques is splitting the number up in your mind in such a way that you can say it in some kind of rhythm, instead of as just one long string of numbers. That'll make it stick in the mind more. You know, like if a phone number was eleven digits long, you could imagine saying a few of the numbers, then pausing for half a second and then saying some more, and doing that for the entire number, maybe imagining a beat in the background to make it sound rhythmical. So you might say something like, 01 triple three, 419, 214 – you know, with the number split up into chunks like that. And you might be able to split it up in such a way that some of the chunks are especially easy to remember, for instance if they're things like 444, 1800, 1939 and so on.

"Another thing you could try is working out what letters of the alphabet the numbers correspond to, and making words from them – you know, like A is the first letter, so it could be 1, B is the second so it could be 2, C is the third so it could be 3, D is the fourth so it could be 4, and so on, up until J, which is the tenth, so that can be 0. Maybe it won't seem easy to think of phone numbers as being words made with those letters at first, to anyone who's not familiar with thinking about what letters correspond to what numbers; but since there are only ten that you'd ever use, it won't be that hard.

"You could at least use the technique with phone numbers that contain enough digits that correspond to vowels in them that it's possible to invent or find words in them. I mean, I suppose it would be hard with a phone number like 0203 444676 or something, because if you made letters from those numbers, they'd all be consonants, so whatever word you made up would be pretty unpronounceable! But there are quite a lot of phone numbers it would work with.

"You could make up practice words for fun – you know, like the number 297 would make the word 'big', because it would be made out of the second, then the ninth, then the seventh letter of the alphabet, which would be B, then I, and then G.

"You could make up all kinds of funny words like that. The number 2978514 would be 'bighead'. The number 214 would be 'bad'. The number 4514 would be 'dead'. The number 1-214-935-817 would be 'a bad ice hag' – whatever one of those would be! I don't think I'd ever like to meet one whatever it was!

"The number 255-3175 would be 'bee cage' – if there ever was such a thing! The number 71665-21475 would be 'gaffe badge'. I don't know what one of those would be, but I don't think I'd want one!

"They don't even have to be proper words or sets of words; they could just be nonsense words. You know, like the number 456294 would be 'defbid'. You know, it would still be memorable, even though it wouldn't make sense. So it still might be more memorable than just the number itself."

Gary grinned and said, "So as long as you could work out how to interpret it back into the number, you'd be alright . . . Well, maybe, apart from if you couldn't quite remember how your nonsense word was spelled, so, for instance, you assumed the word 'defbid' had an A in it, like the word 'deaf', so you put an extra 1 in the number. Who knows what would happen then! You might have been wanting to phone your auntie Sarah, and you might get through to the coal board . . . if there is still a coal board. You know, someone on the other end of the phone might say, 'Hello, you're through to the British coal board', and you might say, 'Oh stop joking! You must be my auntie Sarah's latest boyfriend! I've heard about you! She told me you've been complaining about your unusual foot odour. Did you manage to clear up the problem in the end?'

"You might deserve one of those 'gaffe badges' after that!"

They all giggled.

Luke asked, "So you actually put that stuff in your essay, Sharon?"

Sharon chuckled and said, "Well, not the kind of stuff Gary's just been saying! I did give a couple of the funny examples of words I mentioned though. You could picture the shape of the words you've thought up in your mind, to help you remember how they're spelled.

"And I said you could use a similar technique for trying to remember passwords you use on the Internet, and other things like that as well, although you could make words or nonsense words with just the letters, and keep numbers as numbers with those, to avoid confusion later if you've put both letters and numbers in them.

"Or you could try making a memorable sentence, with each letter or number being the beginning of each word – you know, so if you had a password that was dada96cc, you could make a sentence that included every one of those characters as the beginning of a word, like, 'Daniel and David ate 96 cream cakes'."

They all sniggered, and Gary said, "Yeah, and then you could have a password for another website that was dadwvvvs, which would stand for, 'Daniel and David were very very very sick!'"

They laughed.

Then Sharon said, "Yeah, maybe. There are other ways to remember phone numbers and things too though, like seeing if there are any quirks in them that make them more memorable, for instance if some of the digits make memorable dates from history, or years when members of the family were born, or if the last digits are the same as the first ones but in reverse, or if there are some double digits in a number, and things like that."

Mandy said, "It's all very well for you to tell us these things, but I think trying to use techniques like that might just complicate things sometimes. I remember when a cousin of mine moved house and changed her phone number, she told me what her new one was, and then she immediately went into this stream of ideas to help me supposedly remember it better, like saying, 'You can remember it easily because the first two digits are the date in the month when my mum was born, and you times it by three and divide by four, add twenty, divide it by two, add twenty-nine, and then take away seven, and then you'll have the next few digits.'

"Well OK, what she said probably wasn't quite that complicated; but at the end of it, I had several numbers swimming around my mind, and ever since then, it's been way harder for me to remember her number than it was to remember her old one, which I just remembered easily because I had the plain straightforward number in my head in a rhythm.

"You know, I think writing phone numbers down or putting them in your contacts in a mobile phone sounds far easier than using any of these memory techniques!"

Sharon replied, "There is that. And yeah, I can imagine it could be easy to defeat the object by making things too complicated to remember. I think one thing that definitely helps is to be able to get to think about a number for several seconds on its own when you're first told what it is, so it's more likely to go into your memory than it will be if you just think about it for a couple of seconds and then move on to thinking about something else, or immediately fill your mind with other numbers you hope will help you remember that one.

"Anyway, another thing the books I read were saying about memories is that sometimes you might think you've forgotten something, when it's really still in your memory, but it's as if it's stuffed under other things so it's hidden; but then a certain thing can come to mind, and it jogs your memory, and then it's as if those things step aside for a minute like a door opening, and the memory you want comes spilling out."

Becky grinned and joked, "Did a textbook really describe doors as stepping aside when they open, as if the person who wrote it believes they're alive? How very charming of doors to make way for us like that!"

Sharon smiled and replied, "No, that wasn't quite what the book said. OK, that was a clumsy way of putting it."

Becky continued to make fun of what Sharon had said, saying, "As for that thing about memories spilling out, that could be messy! You know when things spill, they can go all over the place! So are you suggesting that a memory that suddenly comes out might do something like that, so maybe you'll be trying to remember the name of your new tutor, and then something jogs your memory, and his name spills out all over the place, so it spreads all over other memories, so you might want to know the name of the last prime minister we had for a quiz or something, but all you can remember is the name of your new tutor, because it's obscuring the other stuff because it's spilled all over it, and you end up convinced that must be the name you're looking for, because it's come to your mind so powerfully, so you say it's that name?

"Or maybe one quiz question would ask what the name was of Britain's only female prime minister of the 20th century, and instead of saying Margaret Thatcher, the only name you might be able to think of would be Albert Spriggs, because that was your tutor's name. Or what if you only half remembered that, but you half remembered the right name. You might say the only female prime minister's name was Albert Thatcher."

Sharon giggled and said, "Come on, I didn't mean the spilling comment that literally, and you know it! It's a good thing the tutors don't make fun of what we say in our essays like you do! Imagine if you were a tutor here! People would be trying their best to explain things, and you'd write notes all over their essays, making jokes about what they said! Mind you, then you'd have students saying that if you found what they said that funny, you could at least have given them marks for amusement value!"

They all laughed.

Sharon Talks About Techniques Meant to Try to Overcome the Problems Absent-Mindedness Causes

Then Sharon said, "One thing I've been writing about in my essay is absent-mindedness. Actually, you should know a bit about this too, Becky and Luke, since you went to a lecture on it once as well as me . . . unless you're so absent-minded you forgot to listen. Gary and Mandy probably won't know what the tutor said though, since they're not on the psychology course, although I suppose you might have told them. If you did though, it's possible they still won't know, if they're so absent-minded they forgot to listen to you!"

The others giggled again.

Then Sharon explained to Gary and Mandy, "I've learned more about it than Becky and Luke have though, because I chose to do my latest essay about the memory, so I've read books about it, whereas they're doing their essays on other topics."

Then she said to everyone, "Anyway, one thing I've written about in my memory essay is how for anyone who sometimes forgets to lock their door when it gets dark, one thing they could try is hanging their door key around their neck on a bit of string, concealed under their clothes, so they'll always find it before they go to bed, and that'll probably jog their memory. Or they could have one or two pictures of keys where they often spend their evenings, so they'll often spot them, and that might jog their memory too. Or something like that.

"Or if they sometimes lock their door but then can't remember whether they've done it or not, one thing they could try is saying to themselves, 'I'm locking my door now' when they do it, just to make sure they're really noticing what they're doing, instead of just half-noticing it as they might normally, thinking about it for the second they're doing it, and then immediately moving on to thinking about something else. If they think about it for just that little bit longer than they used to each time they do it – the time it takes to say to themselves, 'I'm locking the door', it'll hopefully go into their memory better, especially because it'll mean they're concentrating their full attention on it, instead of doing it while their mind's mostly on other things, as they might normally.

"And they could do that with other things they often do but then can't remember if they've done them or not.

"Mind you, if there were lots of things like that, it would really slow a person down if instead of doing them and immediately moving on to something else, they thought they had to pause each time to say to themselves, 'I'm doing this now' . . . whatever it was. Maybe instead, if it's something they know they often forget they've just done, while they're doing it, they could say something like, 'Ping!' out loud, and they'll probably remember they did that better than they'll remember doing the routine thing they did, because it might amuse them or seem a bit daft or unusual, so it'll likely stick in their mind and help them remember they did the routine thing better."

Luke giggled and said, "Yeah, that'll be especially true if people like family members of theirs are listening, who think they're going a bit nuts, and ask them why on earth they just suddenly said, 'Ping!'"

Sharon said with a grin, "Yeah, there is that. I suppose the person will just have to explain to them what they're saying it for . . . and hope the family members don't order them to go and see a psychiatrist or something . . . although if the person who just said 'ping!' tells them they read about the technique

in a book that was actually written By someone like a psychiatrist, or that they were told about it by someone who got the
idea from reading one, they might decide it's best that they
Avoid mental health professionals in future instead!"

Gary remarked, "Of course, a more convenient solution to
the absent-minded person's problem might be for them to get
one of those family members to take on the responsibility of
locking the door instead of them!"

Sharon replied, "That's true!"

They all laughed again.

Then Sharon continued, "Anyway, another thing I wrote
about was how some people keep putting their keys down and
then forgetting where they put them. I know someone who
puts hers down in various places when she goes to church, and
then sometimes remembers she hasn't got them when she
goes to start her car to go home after the service, and has to go
in and search for them.

"When people are in their own home, they could do their
best to always make sure they put their keys in the same place
when they get in, so they'll only ever be in one place, so they'll
be easy to find every time.

"Another thing people who sometimes forget to lock their
doors at night could try is setting an alarm to go off when they
think it's an appropriate time to do that. So as long as they
remember what their alarm's going off for, they'll remember
to lock them. Or if it goes off and they're busy, they could set
it to go off in another few minutes, in case they decide they'll
lock the doors when they've finished what they're doing, but
then forget.

"They could set an alarm to remind them of when they've
got to go for appointments too, and things like that.

"And people could use that technique if they're cooking something too. I mean, they could set an alarm for when they think the food will be ready, and then if they find it isn't quite ready, they could set it to go off in a few minutes' time, so they don't just assume they'll remember to check on it and then go and get absorbed in something else and forget all about it. If they get something portable with an alarm on it, like a kitchen timer, or if they're wearing a watch with an alarm on it, they can carry it with them wherever they go around the house . . . or wear it, obviously, if it's their watch; and then they won't have to worry about not hearing an alarm if it goes off in the kitchen when they're in another room.

"Then if it's a timer they're using, they could take it back into the kitchen with them and put it near the cooker when it rings, so they'll spot it and hopefully be reminded they need to set it next time they put something on to cook, since forgetting to set it could obviously be quite unfortunate.

"Then again, if they're becoming that forgetful, it might be best if they give up cooking in the oven or on the hob altogether and use a microwave."

Mandy said, "The other day I wondered if it might be a good idea to have a going to bed alarm as well as one for getting up, since I sometimes don't realise how late it's getting, and end up going to bed at a stupid time that's way later than it should be! Mind you, I bet if the alarm went off while I was enjoying myself, I'd always reset it to go off a while later, but if I was doing coursework, maybe I'd always think, 'Oh, that's my bedtime alarm; I'd better stop now!' "

The others sniggered.

Then Mandy said, "Mind you, I suppose it's possible that you could set an alarm to remind you to do something, and then the alarm goes off, and you forget what it's going off for! . . . Hey I wonder if I could use that as an excuse: 'Sorry I'm late for your class again, tutor; it's the same old story I'm afraid; my alarm clock went off this morning, and I somehow just forgot what it was going off for, so I just turned it off and went back to sleep.'"

Luke grinned and said, "Somehow I don't think you'd get away with that one!"

Mandy replied, smirking, "No, I don't suppose I would."

Then Sharon said more seriously, "A couple of times, I tried making a cup of tea in a flask and putting it by my bed overnight so I could drink it when I woke up in the morning, because I thought that might give me more energy to haul myself out of bed. But something happened to the taste of it in the flask, for some reason, and I wasn't keen on it the next morning, because it ended up tasting the way I imagine liquid hay might taste. Maybe it was a bit stewed or something. So I stopped doing it.

". . . Actually I've just thought of another memory jogging technique: if someone keeps making cups of coffee, and they keep forgetting whether they've already put a sweetener in by the time they've put the coffee in, they could try to make it a routine of theirs to always put the coffee in before the sweetener, so they won't have time to forget whether they've put it in or not."

Gary Tells a Cautionary Tale About Hiding Things in Hard-to-Find Places, Only to Forget Where They Are

Gary said, "If people can even forget whether they've put sugar or a sweetener in their coffee within the time it takes them to put the coffee in, it sounds as if things can disappear from the memory really quickly! That's apart from all the things that can disappear from it over time!

"Actually, I've heard that people ought to be a bit careful about what they commit to memory, because it's so easy to forget things. I heard an unfortunate story about a man who for some reason kept a load of money in his cellar, in an old can. He thought it would be safe there, because he couldn't imagine any burglars looking there. At first, he used to go down there and enjoy looking at it. But he stopped after a while, and there came a time when he forgot it was even there.

"Then one day, he decided to have a clear-out and take a load of old cans that were cluttering up his cellar down to the local dump and throw them away. So he did. It was only afterwards that he remembered that one had a load of money in it!"

The others said things like, "Oh no!"

Sharon said, "Yes, I suppose that the more obscure something like a hiding place or a computer password is, the more likely you might be to forget it. I mean, it's best if things like that Are a bit obscure, obviously, so they're more likely to be secure; but maybe it's best not to try to rely on your memory any more than you have to. I mean, you could put most of your money in the bank, for one thing.

"Actually, I've said a few times during my memory essay that it might often be best not to bother with techniques to keep things in the memory, but just to write some things down."

Gary said sarcastically for a laugh, "I bet that'll go down well with the tutor who marks it! Sharon says, 'Don't bother trying to remember anything the course teaches us about how to remember things better; just do the sensible thing and write what you need to remember down instead!'"

They all giggled, and Sharon said, "Well I didn't say it quite like that! Anyway, the tutor will probably agree with me that it's best not to rely on your memory any more than you have to."

Sharon Talks About Ways People Who Often Forget the Names of People They Meet Can Try Not To, and Says More About Absent-Mindedness

Becky grinned and said, "I wonder what the tutor would say if you handed your supposed essay in, and all it turned out to say was, 'This subject has recently become pointless, as it's so easy to just write things down nowadays that there's no need to bother trying to remember them at all!'"

Sharon grinned and said, "I don't suppose I'd get many marks for that one!

"Mind you, I think it is still worth people learning ways of improving their memories. I read that one thing people often forget is people's names. It would seem a bit strange if whenever you met someone for the first time and they told you their name, you said, 'Hang on, don't talk for a minute; I'm going to take out a notebook and write that down before I forget it!' They'd think it was a bit creepy, wouldn't they!

They might think you were from a security service and you suspected them of a crime or something!"

They chuckled.

Then Mandy said, "The other day I asked someone their name, and they told me their surname as well as their first name. I thought it was weird, because it sounded as if they said their surname was 'Trolls'. I thought, 'That's a strange name!' But it turned out to be Charles really."

Luke said, "Imagine if their first name made it sound like an even more embarrassing name! Imagine if it was something like Cyril, and when they told you their name was Cyril Charles, you thought they said 'Several Trolls'. You'd think, 'You must have made that name up, because for some reason, you like to be thought of as not just one troll, but lots at once!'"

They laughed, and Mandy said, "Yeah, and just imagine if he was going to give a speech at an event you went to, because he was the mayor of a town, and he met you before he started. Imagine if you didn't know his name, and he came up to you and introduced himself by saying it was something that sounded to you just like 'Several Trolls'. Imagine if it was crowded and lots of people were talking, so you couldn't really hear him that well.

"You might think, 'Did you really just say, "I'm several trolls?" So you want me to call you a troll? In fact, you want me to call you more than one? You must be a nutter! You just never know who you're voting for when you vote for people like the next mayor, do you! I wonder if you'll come out with nutty things in your speech!'"

Becky grinned and said, "And just imagine if from then on, you called him what you thought he said his name was! He might think you were just being rude and making fun of him!"

Gary said, "And imagine if you introduced him to someone else, saying something like, 'This is our new mayor, Mr Troll!'"

They laughed.

Becky said, "I wonder if Prince Charles has ever said his name, and someone thought he was saying 'Trolls'!"

Mandy smirked and said, "Imagine him being introduced to a group of diplomats and businessmen as Prince Troll!"

Sharon said, "I suppose one way of getting someone to tell you their name again without having to admit you've forgotten it would be to deliberately call them something wrong, in the hope they'd correct you. You know, not necessarily anything that sounded rude, just the first thing that came into your mind."

Luke grinned and joked, "What, so if the first thing that came into a person's mind was ice cream, you'd recommend them saying, 'This is such an important business deal, Mr Ice Cream, that I think it would be great if it was accompanied by a charm offensive where my new acquaintance Prince Troll gets to speak at an event put on to celebrate it.'"

Sharon giggled and said, "That wasn't quite what I was thinking!"

Becky grinned and said, "That's just as well! What would the tutor say if you recommended people to do that in your essay!"

Sharon chuckled and said, "I don't know! Mind you, it could be worse! If I get really bored of it, I might recommend that if anyone can't remember a tutor's name, they could say, 'Hello Mr Peanut' when they walk through the door, in the hope he corrects them and tells them what his name really is.

"Mind you, I've moved on from the bit I was writing about remembering names now. I actually stuck to saying sensible stuff . . . Well, some of what I said was sensible anyway. One thing I got from the books I read for the essay was that the reason some people are bad at remembering other people's names might sometimes be that they're in the habit of not taking them in properly in the first place, because they're paying attention to other things at the time when they hear them, such as their thoughts about the kinds of subjects it might be good to bring up, other things that are being said at the time by the person giving their name, what they can see going on in the room, or something else. So names don't even have the chance to get into their memories properly in the first place.

"So the books recommend that one thing people could try if they know they forget people's names a lot is to repeat a person's name back to them when they've just told them what it is, and maybe say it a couple of times during the conversation, perhaps once when they say goodbye. That way, they'll be reminding themselves of what the name is, so they might be more likely to remember it the next time they meet the person.

"And if they meet a person later and realise they recognise their face but still can't remember their name, they could try thinking back to try and remember where they met them; and the more about that that they can recall, the more chance there might be that their memory gets jogged for their name.

"They could try using the same technique if they sometimes go into another room to get something, and then forget what they went in there for; if they try imagining themselves back where they started, doing what they were doing before they decided to go in the other room, or if they go back to what they were doing before they went in the room for real, and think about it, it might help them remember what they decided to go in there for.

278

"You can do a similar thing if you lose something; instead of frantically hunting around for it, it can help if you sit thinking about when you last had it, what you were doing with it then, and what you did next, and that kind of thing. It can jog your memory for where you put it.

"But another thing that people who go into another room and then forget what they went there for could try doing is to look around the room and see if anything they see gives them clues as to what they wanted to do. Actually, most people probably do that anyway.

"Or if they know it's common for them to forget what they went into another room for, then before they even go to do something in the other room, they could try picturing going in there and doing it in their minds, so it might stick in their memories more when they actually go there.

"Mind you, one problem with that is probably that a lot of the time, people don't forget what they're going into another room for. If it's impossible for you to predict when you're going to have a problem with it and when you're not, it'll be impossible to know when it's worth imagining going into the other room and doing something before you go, and when it'll just slow you down unnecessarily because you wouldn't have forgotten. Maybe it's only when forgetfulness becomes enough of a problem to be a real pain that people will think it's worth using techniques like that a lot . . . And then they might have the problem of forgetting to do them! Still, maybe some people can get better with practice, depending on what's causing their memory loss, and how bad it is.

"I think people can forget things like what they went into other rooms for more as they get older. It's partly because they think of something and go off to do it, but while they're going, they start thinking about other things, and their memories aren't as good at holding the information in their minds that was in there before they did that as they used to be.

"Mind you, I think when a person's memory gets worse, it isn't necessarily caused by something that can't be fixed; I read that certain medications can cause a person's memory to get worse, and also other things that can either be changed, or they don't mean something really serious is going wrong.

"Stress can really affect the memory. So sometimes, just doing your best to solve the problems in your life, or doing things to soothe yourself like relaxing and doing something you enjoy for a while, or doing exercise to work off nervous tension, could help you improve your memory for a while.

"I think things like that can even work temporarily for some people who've begun to lose their memory mostly because of things related to age.

"And also, I think regular exercise can sometimes even help to stop the memory getting so bad in the first place. Maybe that depends on what medical condition you get. But exercising gets the blood pumping faster, so the supply of blood to the brain speeds up, and blood contains a bit of oxygen, and the brain uses that as a nutrient, so the better a supply it gets, the better it can work . . . Well, within limits, I suppose. I mean, I don't suppose it's likely that a person could exercise so much and so intensely they die, but on their deathbed, they discover they can suddenly solve really complex mathematical equations when they were never any good at maths before or something."

The others chuckled, and Luke said, "Somehow I can't imagine anyone being willing to test that one out! There can't be many people in the world who'd be interested in doing maths on their deathbeds, or who'd think maths is more important than other things. Just imagine it! An enthusiastic mathematician's about to die, and some of his family come to see him, all upset, and they tell him they really want to say their last goodbyes, and he says, 'No, don't bother me now! I've just found this amazing equation in a textbook, and it says that very few people have ever solved it before! Imagine how wonderful it'll be if I manage to solve it before I go!'

"Mind you, it might be worse if there was a maths teacher who enjoyed marking homework so much, especially writing comments on the homework of the pupils who were no good at maths, telling them where they were going wrong, that he just couldn't bear to stop, even on his deathbed, so instead of saying goodbye to his family, he ordered that his pupils' latest homework be brought to him so he could mark it, saying, 'I just know some of my pupils will have got things wrong again, and I just must tell them how wrong they are!' "

The others giggled.

Then Sharon said seriously, "Actually, that reminds me of something else I wrote in my essay. I read that some people who go to their old school reunions decades after they were there can be embarrassed when they realise they can't re-member some of their old classmates' names, even if they can remember their faces. I read that one technique they can try is reading through a list of old pupils' names before they go, to jog their memories, and then it might be easier to put names to faces when they meet people. I expect that'll be especially true if they look at something where old photos of them are alongside their names.

"And another technique I read about that people can try to help them remember names, including the names of people they meet for the first time, is to think of words that sound like them soon after they hear them, that they imagine being associated with them in some way; so, if a person's called Lorraine, you could maybe think of her name as being like the words 'the rain', and then imagine her standing outside with a rain cloud just above her head raining on her, while all around her it's sunny, or something like that.

"Or if someone's called Joan, you could maybe imagine her chewing on a big bone, since the word bone rhymes with Joan. Or you could maybe imagine her having the bottom half of a skeleton and the top half of an ordinary person. Bony Joanie. So I suppose you'd end up thinking of her as some kind of monster!"

The others chuckled, and Gary said sarcastically, "I bet people would love you for that, if they ever found out what you were thinking about them!"

Sharon grinned and said, "Well hopefully they wouldn't, unless, I suppose, they wondered why you weren't paying attention to what they were saying, and you couldn't think of anything to say but to admit that it was because you were busy thinking up funny images with them in, like them chewing on bones and things, to try to remember their names by."

They laughed.

Sharon Talks About Ways of Remembering Such Things as Little Shopping Lists, and Several Jokes in a Row

Sharon said, "I suppose it's probably best if people try thinking the images up after the person's been and gone, really, if

282

nothing comes to mind immediately, and if they haven't already forgotten their name by then!

"And actually, even if they can't think of any images or other ways of remembering the name, the effort of trying will mean they've been thinking of it for much longer than they would have been otherwise, so just that might help them keep it in their memory.

"And that's not the only time when thinking up images can help people remember things. You could do it to try to remember all kinds of things. One thing you could try to think them up to remember is things on a little shopping list ... Well, that's if you can't be bothered to write it down, for some reason.

"Actually, there are a few different ways you could try to remember things on a list like that. One is grouping things in categories together in your mind, according to things you decide on; it could be what letter they start with, if there are, say, two things you want that start with one particular letter, and three that begin with another. You could think about that and try to remember it, so if you later forget something on your list, you can narrow down the search you do in your mind to things that begin with the letter you know it begins with – the one you know you should have another item beginning with, which will hopefully make it easier to remember.

"Or you could split the items on your list up into categories according to what kind of things they are, for instance cakes, meat and so on. Then you could try making up a rhythmical rhyme in your mind, like, 'Dairy three; meaty two; chocolate one.'

"Then if you repeat the rhyme in your mind till it's familiar, it'll probably come back to your memory more easily later. So if you're doing your shopping and you forget one thing, it'll be easier to remember because you can work out what category it's in – you know, whether it's meat or chocolate or whatever, and then you'll know it has to be a product in that particular category, rather than one thing on a much longer list of things that could be just about anything.

"Another way to try to remember things such as shopping lists, like I said before, is to use that technique where you make up images in your mind that represent the products you want to buy, or whatever else you've got on the list of whatever it is you're trying to remember.

"So, for example, imagine if you wanted to buy some mini pork pies, some cheese, some chicken fillets, some chocolate, some milk and some margarine, you could try and think up an image involving each one, and maybe turn them into a kind of story. So, say, you could imagine walking home from the shops with a big block of cheese on your head, trying your best to walk steadily enough that it didn't fall off; and you could imagine you had a pork pie on a chain around your neck, and you ended up sloshing through puddles of milk, for some reason, and then slipping on a layer of margarine that was mysteriously covering the ground. Then you shoved chocolate in your mouth for comfort, but you didn't feel comforted for long, because then you noticed a flock of chickens running after you, perhaps hoping to avenge the lives of the chickens you've bought the fillets from.

"If you run that daft image through your mind over and over again for a little while to get it fixed in your memory, imagining the scene in as much vivid detail as you can, you might remember it for a while afterwards, so it'll be easier to remember all the items of shopping you want to get that are in the image.

"The stranger the images are, the more they might stick in your mind.

"Actually, now I remember I mentioned trying to remember jokes in my essay. I didn't say much about it; just the odd paragraph or two."

"An odd paragraph? How odd?" asked Luke, grinning mischievously.

"Really really odd!" joked Sharon. "Well, alright, I'll tell you what I said, and you can judge for yourself."

"I was wondering when you were going to get around to that!" said Becky.

Sharon replied, "Sorry, I should have got round to it earlier really. I just thought the other stuff might be useful for people to know in case they know people who have little memory glitches they can pass the information on to, since I think it's quite common to have them, especially as people get older.

"I only suggested a couple of ideas in my essay, and I was just using jokes as an example of something you might want to remember to tell someone without using notes to remind yourself of what you want to say. I'm rubbish at remembering jokes myself, so it turns out that my essay might come in a little bit handier for me myself than I thought it would, now I'm going to be doing the jokeathon!

"One technique I read about and wrote about was that image thing again, where if you think of some kind of image that might jog your memory for a joke because it's related to some of it, or even just one of the main words in it, it might help the joke stick in your mind. So, for example, if you were thinking it might be nice to tell the joke, 'A Sunday school teacher asked her class why it's important to be quiet in church, and one said, "Because people are sleeping,"' you could perhaps invent an image that you hope will stick in your mind of someone walking into a church, only to find the entire congregation asleep and snoring, lounging around on the pews.

"Or you could think of keywords you could try to remember the joke by. So if you were trying to remember that particular joke, maybe you could try to remember the phrase, 'sleeping church' or something, which might be much easier to keep in mind than the entire joke, but when you think of it, it might refresh your memory for the whole joke . . . Well, with that particular joke, it's so short that you'd be less likely to forget the whole thing than you would if it was a longer one; but you could use the technique with longer jokes too.

"And I wrote that If you've got a whole list of jokes you'd like to tell, say because you want to be good company, and you're so rubbish at any other kind of conversation you think that if you've got enough jokes, it might prevent the person you're talking to from noticing that, with any luck . . . no, actually I didn't say that last bit in my essay, but if I learned a list of jokes myself, for any other reason than this jokeathon we're doing, it's just possible that that would be the reason . . ."

Gary interrupted, grinning, "Oh come on! You're not really rubbish at any other kind of conversation! After all, if you were, you wouldn't have been able to spend the last six hours telling us what you put in your essay!"

Sharon smiled and said, "Six hours? Cheek! Well OK, maybe I'm not as bad at conversation as all that.

"But anyway, what I said was that if you want to remember a list of jokes, you could try remembering a list of keywords, one word representing one joke, which will hopefully refresh your memory for the entire joke when you think of it. You could even turn the keywords into a sentence, since a sentence will be easier to remember than a list of random words that don't seem to have any connection with each other.

"So, for instance, if you wanted to tell a joke involving a giant, a joke that had something to do with a helicopter, a joke about a tourist, then one about a letter you got, and then one that had something to do with a church, you could try and connect the keywords you'd decided to use to jog your memory for the jokes by making up a sentence involving all of them, even if it was a really daft sentence! I mean, it could be something like, 'A giant helicopter landed on a church and ate my letter, which impressed a tourist.'

"You could repeat that sentence to yourself over and over again while you were getting ready to go out, and also while you weren't doing much else while you were out. Hopefully you wouldn't end up remembering the daft sentence but not the jokes it was supposed to help you bring to mind!"

They giggled.

Luke Tells the Others Something He Read About Someone Being Taught Ways of Remembering Things After His Brain Was Damaged

Then Luke said, "Actually, I've read a bit about this kind of thing, in a book that was mostly about something else. It was by a psychiatrist, I think, who said there was a man on a ward in a hospital he worked in who'd had a cycling accident, and he'd got brain-damaged because he hit his head hard and hadn't been wearing a helmet. He was really forgetful after that.

If he parked his car, he would forget where he'd parked it as soon as it was out of sight. He'd go to a shop but then forget why he'd gone there. He couldn't remember people's names minutes after he'd been told them, and if he made an appointment with someone, or someone gave him some important information, he'd soon forget it.

"He could remember things that had happened to him before his accident without a problem, and if he managed to think about something for long enough for it to be transferred from his short-term memory into his long-term memory, which I think tends to take several minutes, it would stay in his memory a lot better. But he couldn't remember a lot of things that had just happened. The psychiatrist who wrote the book was saying things that are similar to what you've been saying, Sharon.

"He said that at the hospital, they taught this man ways of remembering things and coping in other ways that helped him a lot. It turned out that his memory for pictures and shapes was quite a bit less damaged than his memory for words, so one thing he was taught was to think of pictures that would remind him of things that had just happened. He remembered names much better that way. For example, if someone told him her name was Carol, he'd imagine her amidst a group of people singing Christmas carols. If someone told him his name was John, he'd imagine he was a walking talking loo. I think John's a slang word for toilet. Someone had a baby daughter they called Elizabeth, and he imagined her as the Queen. And so on.

"In the end he got so good at making up pictures to represent things that he made a game of it, and challenged other people in the hospital to see if they could think up an image to represent a name or phrase.

288

"Imagining pictures helped him easily remember where he'd parked his car too. He'd make a picture in his mind of the car park as if he was seeing it from above, and the picture would include his own car, in the position where he'd parked it.

"He didn't rely on pictures for everything; he started carrying a notebook around with him everywhere he went, and he wrote down any information he needed to remember in it. To remember to look in his notebook to remind himself of what he'd put in it, the psychiatrist set his watch to beep every half an hour. At first he couldn't remember why it was beeping, but after a bit of practice he started remembering."

The Friends Have a Laugh Trying to Help Each Other Not to Forget the Jokes They've Decided to Tell at the Jokeathon

Mandy said, "That's interesting. Hey Becky! Tell us what jokes you're thinking of telling at the jokeathon, and let's help you think of pictures to help you remember them."

The others grinned and enthusiastically said things like, "Yeah!"

Becky agreed, and said, "Alright. The first joke I found that I decided to use goes:

"At an eye clinic, a patient said to a doctor, 'Doctor! I'm really worried! I keep seeing pink striped crocodiles every time I drift off to sleep.'

"The doctor asked him, 'Have you seen a psychiatrist?' and he said, 'No, only pink striped crocodiles.' "

Sharon grinned and said, "How about imagining a psychiatrist rushing around a hospital nervously with a pink striped crocodile on his back, running faster and faster, as if he thinks if he runs fast enough, it won't be able to keep up with him so he'll shake it off?"

Luke grinned and said, "If she makes the picture too complicated, she might still forget the joke, and then try to work out what it was from the picture; and who knows what kind of joke she might eventually come up with!"

They all laughed.

Then Mandy said, "How about imagining a psychiatrist with a pink striped crocodile on a couch opposite him, telling him about his crocodile problems?"

"What kind of problems might talking crocodiles have?" asked Gary, smiling.

"Oh I don't know," said Mandy. "Maybe all the other crocodiles would get scared and try to get away from him when he talked . . . or maybe he'd just be really frustrated because he'd been trying and trying to teach the others to talk but they wouldn't, or couldn't. Maybe that's why he went pink and stripy; maybe he can explain that that's what talking crocodiles do when they're stressed.

"But it doesn't matter what his problems are. Becky can just imagine him talking in this funny croaky voice . . . Well, I don't know if crocodiles would really have croaky voices; maybe she can imagine it sounding like the prime minister or something."

They all giggled, and Becky said she'd think about what picture to try and remember.

Then Mandy asked her what her second joke was, and she said:

"Two boys were talking, and one asked the other one, 'Do you know anyone who can jump higher than the Eiffel Tower?'

"The other boy said, 'Don't be daft! No one can jump that high!'

"The first boy said, 'Actually we all can. The Eiffel Tower can't jump!' "

The others chuckled, and Luke said, "How about imagining you'd been to France and brought back about ten little models of the Eiffel Tower to give to people as souvenirs, and one day they all come to life and start jumping around your room?"

Becky said, "That's a good one! Or maybe I could imagine the real Eiffel Tower jumping right off its foundations one day and leaping across France, bounding across the mountains into Spain and lying on a beach by the Mediterranean Sea to sunbathe."

They all giggled. Then Gary said, "Or maybe it could lie across a river and become a new bridge!"

Becky grinned and said, "Actually, the idea of the Eiffel Tower sunbathing reminds me of my next joke. A tourist said to one of the locals here, 'I've been here a whole week and it hasn't stopped raining! When do you have summer here?'

"The local said, 'Well, that's hard to say. Last year it was on a Wednesday.' "

Gary said, "Maybe you could imagine a tourist wearing swimming trunks with the rain pouring down, sitting in a deckchair that's floating along a street towards the beach because there's been so much rain, and then he can't be bothered to wait till he gets there to have fun, so he jumps off and goes swimming in a big puddle instead of in the sea."

Amid more giggling, Sharon said, "Or maybe you could imagine someone watching a weather forecast on television, and the person giving it says, 'Now here's a very important announcement: Tomorrow the summer will come. It's expected to start at around rush hour tomorrow morning, and last till early evening. Then Autumn will come in from the west. So make the most of the summer while you can. I'd advise everyone in the country to call in sick for work, unless you do a really important job like nursing, in which case I suppose you'll just have to miss the summer, and book a holiday to somewhere sunnier to make up for it, or just hope it arrives on your day off next year.' "

Becky grinned and said, "That sounds like a good idea in theory, but what if I remembered all those words, but forgot what the joke was supposed to be?"

They chuckled again, and Sharon said, "Well, then your joke could be that you heard a weather forecast last summer where it actually said that."

Becky smiled broadly and said, "Now there's a good idea! That could be fun.

"OK, here's my next joke:

"A man visited a psychiatric hospital and asked the person in charge how they decided whether someone ought to be admitted to it. The person in charge said, 'Well, we fill a bath, and then we give the person a teaspoon, a teacup and a bucket, and ask them to empty the bath.'

"The visitor said, 'Oh I understand. A normal person would use the bucket, because it's bigger than the teaspoon or the teacup.'

"The person in charge said, 'No, a normal person would pull the plug out. Now do you want a bed by the window?' "

Mandy grinned and said, "How about imagining someone trying to empty a bath with a teaspoon, tipping the water on the floor in front of him, and some of it goes all over his shoes, and a lot goes on a bath mat he's standing on, till he's squelching around on a really soggy bath mat?"

Luke chuckled and said, "Yeah, or imagine he tips each teaspoonful over the trousers and shoes of the hospital supervisor he's talking to."

They all giggled again, and then Mandy said, "Or how about imagining a man with an upside-down little bucket on his head with water trickling out of it, running down his face and over his clothes, walking around a hospital ward, looking bewildered as to how he just got there?"

Becky sniggered and said, "Maybe. I can just imagine forgetting the joke and remembering those images though!

"OK, another joke is about a boy who comes home from school and tells his mum he's got a tummy ache. The mum says, 'I expect that's just because it's empty; you'll feel better when you've got something in it.'

"Later his dad comes home, sits down and says he's got a headache. The boy says, 'I expect that's just because it's empty; you'd feel better if you had something in it.'"

The others laughed, and Sharon said, "How about an image of an angry man with a boy standing near him, and the man puts his hand up to his head and makes as if to tear some of his hair out in despair at the kind of child he seems to be bringing up, and when he pulls his hair, his head creeks open on hinges, and it turns out that it's completely hollow – there's nothing at all in it?"

Becky grinned and said, "I like that idea!"

The group discussed Becky's other jokes too, and she said she'd think about what they'd suggested.

Then Luke said, "How about helping me think up pictures to help me remember my jokes now?"

They said they would, and Luke told them the first one he was planning to tell, saying:

"Little Jimmy signed up to join the army. His friends warned him that he'd need to act tough if he wanted to be treated with any respect, so the first day he was there, he swaggered around the camp, boasting. He shouted, 'Show me a sergeant and I'll show you a dope!'

"Just then a brawny, battle-hardened sergeant appeared and bawled, 'I am a sergeant!'

"Jimmy whispered, 'I am a dope.' "

The others chuckled, and then Gary said, "Hey, how about having an image of hundreds of soldiers all sprawling around on some grass smoking cannabis, and a sergeant in front of them bawling, 'Get up you lazy worthless brutes! It's time you did some training!' And one of the soldiers drawls in a stereotypical hippy voice, 'Hey, mellow out man! There's no hurry. Come here and have some dope! Then you'll feel more relaxed.' "

They laughed, and Luke said he thought that was a good idea.

Then Gary said he had a joke of his own they could help him with. He said it went, "A GP was speeding to a house call when she was stopped by the police. She knew what she'd been stopped for, and planned to tell the policeman why she'd been going fast. Hoping to get away with it, she appeared shocked when he came up to talk to her, and she said, 'I have never been stopped like this in all my thirty years of driving!'

"The policeman said, 'What do they normally do then, shoot the tyres out?' "

Becky grinned and said, "How about having an image of a desperate police chase with sirens blaring, and then the boot flies open in the car in front of the police car, and a stethoscope starts dangling out so you can tell it belongs to a doctor?"

Sharon grinned and said, "Or maybe you could have a picture in your mind of a doctor walking into a garage and saying, 'All my tyres have suddenly gone flat for some reason; I don't know why, but I suppose it might have something to do with that vandalising bunch of policemen in the police car that was behind me that shot at my tyres. Please can you give me new ones?' "

The others thought that was amusing. Then Mandy said, "OK, how about this joke? A boy had been talking on the phone for about half an hour before he finished. His dad said, 'Wow! That was short. You usually talk for an hour. What happened?'

"The boy said, 'It was a wrong number.' "

Gary smiled and said, "How about having an image of a boy chatting and chatting away on the phone, and then someone else on the other end looking thoroughly confused, as if they're thinking, 'Who is this? Am I supposed to know you?' "

Mandy said, "I actually know someone who said that when she was about thirteen, she used to phone people up at random just as a practical joke, pretending to know them; and she asked them questions about how their kids were and what they were doing and things, just because she thought it would be a laugh to imagine them wondering who on earth she was, trying and trying to remember her, feeling too embarrassed to admit they couldn't. But her mum found out and made her phone them all up again and apologise, admitting to them that she'd just rung them up for fun."

Sharon laughed and said, "Serves her right!"

Gary said, "It might be easy for you to remember the idea of someone chatting and chatting to someone they've phoned up by mistake then, Mandy, if you know someone who chatted to people who really must have been confused about who they were talking to!"

Mandy smiled and replied, "Maybe."

Then Sharon said, "How about this joke? A jolly customer asked for a return ticket at the airport. The person at the desk asked where to, and the customer said, 'Back here please.'"

Becky said, "How about an image of a man at an airport with a massive long piece of strong elastic tied to him, hundreds of miles long, with the other end tied to something out of sight, and he gets somehow flung up into the air with so much force he flies really fast behind an aeroplane, till the elastic suddenly goes taut, and then it rebounds powerfully so it makes him whizz back to the airport again, as if it's a horizontal bungee jump? Or at least, one that's horizontal at first, and then gets vertical when the man's back at the airport."

Luke chuckled and joked, "Yeah, and then you could imagine him being flung up into the air again when he gets near the ground at the airport and the elastic goes taut again, and flying behind another plane, and then whizzing back again when the elastic goes taut and pulls him back, and that could happen on and on all day."

Mandy sniggered and joked, "Hang on, if you were imagining it going on all day, you'd probably forget All your other jokes; you'd just be sitting there while everyone else told theirs, just imagining someone being whizzed around on a really long piece of elastic all day. You might not even notice when the others finished and went away; you might just be sat there day-dreaming about this huge piece of elastic with a man on it pinging and flying back and forth all day!"

Becky grinned and said, "Imagine if you were so engrossed in your day-dream that you sat there imagining it till it was the middle of the night, and then a policeman came along and asked you if you were alright, and you suddenly realised you'd been there for hours and hours, and you said, 'Oh yes, I'm fine; I've just been spending all day imagining someone being whizzed across the sea and back to an airport on a massive long piece of elastic over and over again.'"

They laughed.

Then Luke said, "Alright, help me think of an image for another one of My jokes: A boy comes home from his first day at school and his mum asks him, 'What did you learn today?'

"The kid says, 'Not enough; I have to go back tomorrow!'"

Mandy smiled and said, "How about imagining a boy tramping into school looking disgusted, or coming out of school at the end of the day in a bad mood?"

Luke grinned and said, "No, that would be depressing; it would be too much like reality; I think most of the kids at my school did that."

Becky smiled and said, "Alright then, how about imagining the boy on his last day at school, gleefully ripping up all his course notes, dancing around the room singing to music?"

Luke grinned and said, "I think a lot of us did that at school too, but I'm happy to remember That kind of reality!"

They all giggled.

Then Mandy said, "Actually, I had a bit of a problem finding as many jokes as I wanted to tell, because a lot of the websites I looked on turned out to just have spiteful or dirty ones on them. I didn't think they were funny . . . and that's apart from them being inappropriate to tell in the park."

Luke grinned mischievously and said, "If they were that bad, just imagine you telling some for the jokeathon, and a group of parents getting angry about their kids hearing them, and chasing you out of the park!"

Sharon joked, "Yes, maybe they'd be running towards you as fast as they could, angrily yelling things like, 'You corrupter of youth! You degenerate swine! Get out of our town and never come back!' "

They all giggled. Then Becky asked, "What kind of jokes were on those websites that you didn't like then?"

Mandy made a face and then grinned and said, "As if I'm going to tell You them! Actually I don't think I read to the end of any, but you know, they were things like, 'A blonde walks into a bar and orders half a pint of shandy and a packet of peanuts, saying, "I need this! I'm hoping to get raving drunk tonight!" And the barman says, "You won't get drunk on shandy . . . well, not unless you glug down a whole lot more of it than just half a pint!" And the blonde says, "I know that! Do you think I'm stupid? I'm not planning to get drunk on the shandy! I'm hoping to get drunk on the peanuts!" ' "

The others sniggered, and Luke said, "Actually, that isn't all That unfunny! . . . But hang on! If you didn't read to the end of any of the jokes, how do you know the end of that one?"

Mandy replied, "That wasn't really one of the jokes on one of the websites. They were just similar to that. Maybe it was better than the ones on there."

Luke grinned and said, "But hang on again! This is still as confusing as it was before, because, if you didn't actually read to the end of any of the jokes, how do you even know you didn't like them?"

Becky, Gary and Sharon giggled. Mandy said, "Well, I suppose you've got a point. They just seemed to be the kind of jokes I knew I wouldn't like, you know, jokes that belittle groups of people by making fun of members of them unfairly, like portraying blondes as stupid and so on. Anyway, I found some good websites with some nice jokes on in the end, so that was alright."

Gary said, "You could have made up your own jokes. You don't normally have a problem doing that."

Sharon grinned and said, "Yes, or we could have helped you make some up. That might have been fun. Or you could have decided to tell a few funny stories instead of jokes. We could have told you some of those as well. Like about something that happened to me once. A memory of it came back to me the other day:

"I went to a carol concert with my family at Christmas last year, and some of the carols were sung by a choir; and there was a phrase in one of them that was repeated a few times during the song that went, 'Most highly favoured lady'. It was referring to Mary, the mother of Jesus. Well, one of the people singing it had once told us that he'd been in a choir at school, and they'd sometimes sung that carol, and some of the boys would sing, 'Most highly flavoured gravy' instead. I don't know if they did that in concerts in front of parents and other people, and whether any of the parents noticed if they did."

The friends chuckled, and Sharon carried on, "Anyway, I lost my concentration on what was going on during that song because it reminded me of that, and thoughts drifted into my mind that made me wonder what would happen if all the carol books with the words in had weird misprints in them, so people were singing away, and suddenly the words were all wrong; so if they were singing the carol *Away in a Manger*, it said, 'Away in a Manager', and then it said, 'No bib for a bed' instead of 'no crib for a bed'. I wondered if they'd sing the wrong words, or whether they'd get confused and falter over what they were singing, or start laughing, or whether they'd know the carols so well they'd just ignore the misprints and sing the proper words.

"Just imagine if in the carol *Oh Come All Ye Faithful*, instead of saying, 'joyful and triumphant', it said, 'joyful and tree infant'. I wonder if people would actually sing those things without thinking, or if they'd look at other people to see if they looked as if they were thinking they had strange misprints in their books too, since they might wonder if everyone had them or just them.

"Someone was playing a tambourine, and I wondered what would happen if they called it a tangerine, not seeming to realise they were calling it something that wasn't its real name. Imagine if someone at the front had a tambourine they were bashing out the rhythm to at a concert, and someone else was playing the piano, and at the beginning of the concert, someone announced what song they were about to play, but instead of saying they were going to play the piano and tambourine, they said, with a completely serious face, 'Elsie's going to sway the marshmallow, while Mavis beats time on the tangerine.'

"I wonder if a lot of people would think they'd heard it wrong and that they must be going nuts, thinking they must be hearing things, or just drifting off to sleep and beginning to dream! Maybe they'd look at everyone else to see what their reactions were."

The others grinned.

The group laughed and joked and carried on trying to help each other by coming up with amusing ideas for ways they could try to remember jokes they wanted to tell for the next couple of hours. Then they all went away happily.

At the Jokeathon

The day of the jokeathon was a lovely warm sunny day. The participants all met up in the park as planned, and quite a few people came to listen, while others who hadn't known about it till they saw them in the park that day hung around too, deciding there and then that they wanted to hear the jokes and donate to the charity they were raising money for.

Besides students, the group telling jokes included a couple of nurses, a couple of teachers, a few retired people, and a delivery driver for a supermarket with his teenage son and daughter.

Since there was no microphone, when any of them told a joke, they would raise their voice a bit.

Becky's friends Jane and Shirley, as well as a few people from the local community, were there to take people's money and tell newcomers to the group of spectators what was going on.

No one forgot their jokes in the end, and everything went well.

The first person to tell a joke was a retired lady. Unexpectedly, she gave a little speech before her joke. That wasn't supposed to happen, but no one thought about stopping her. After all, they were all sure she would get to the joke soon. By a strange coincidence, her speech and joke were about having a bad memory.

She said, "I'm going to tell you a joke someone sent me by email. It's kind of appropriate for me. It's all about someone losing their memory a bit. It's funny . . . I mean strange: New research says the brains of teenagers aren't fully developed, so teenagers are more likely to do silly irresponsible things, because the emotional parts of their brains that make them feel like drinking and doing other risky things develop before the thinking reasoning parts that help them decide whether it's really a good idea to do things like that."

The teenagers in the group blushed and grimaced.

But the woman carried on, "Well, I think I must have had a teenage brain till I was nearly 50, because I carried on doing stupid things till I was way into my forties.

"I haven't done anything hugely stupid since then; but not that many years after I stopped, I realised I was starting to get forgetful; I don't know why. But I started doing things and then immediately forgetting whether I'd done them or not, such as putting sugar in a cup of coffee I was making and then forgetting whether I'd done it or not by the time I'd put the coffee in; so I'd sometimes put some sugar in afterwards just in case I hadn't done it before – although thankfully, I never ended up with a really over-sweetened cup!

"And I started forgetting to put bottle tops on, and snacking on things from time to time and then forgetting how often I'd done it, and then some time later I kept being surprised there wasn't as much of the food left as I thought there should have been – although it's quite possible my kids had a lot to do with that happening too when they visited me, although it happened a bit when they hadn't been in the house for a while as well, so I knew it wasn't just them.

"I was a bit worried about why my memory lapses might be happening at first, but they haven't got worse. But I think they're one of the typical characteristics of getting old; so it seems I might be the only person who went almost straight from having a teenage brain to having an old person's brain! Or maybe there are more of us around like it.

"Anyway, here's the first joke I've come here to tell, that I got from an email someone sent me. I'm hoping I've remembered that alright:

"They've finally found a diagnosis for my condition! Hooray! I've been diagnosed with AAADD (age activated attention deficit disorder). This is how it affects me:

"I decide to tidy up the garden a bit, so I head towards the front door. Then I notice the post on the floor where it was put through the letterbox. OK, I'm going to tidy up the garden, but first I'll look at the post.

"I go and put my door keys down on the kitchen table, start looking at the post, but then as I throw away a bit of junk mail, I notice the rubbish bin's full.

"OK, I'll look at the post properly in a minute, but first I'll empty the bin. But then if I'm going outdoors to do that, I may as well nip to the post box to pay the few bills I've noticed I've got in the post.

"So I'll just sit down and write cheques for them. Now, where's my cheque book? Oh here it is. Oh bother, I notice I've only got one cheque left. I know I've got a new cheque book in my desk. I'll go and find it.

"Oh, there's the coffee I was drinking earlier, still half full on my desk. OK, I'll look for my new cheque book in a minute, but first I'll move my coffee further away from my computer for safety. I know, I'll go to the kitchen and put it in the fridge to save it for later.

"I head towards the kitchen and notice my plants. They need watering. I put the coffee down on the kitchen worktop and then . . . Hey! There are my glasses! I've been looking for them all morning! I'd better put them away where they belong quickly, before I forget where they are again.

"But first, I fill a watering can with water to go on the plants, and I'm heading towards them when I suddenly notice someone's left the television remote control box in the kitchen.

We'll never think to look for it there later when we want it. I'd better put it back in the sitting-room where it belongs.

"I splash some water over the plants and onto the floor, throw the remote control box onto a soft cushion in the sitting-room, and then walk back into the hall trying to work out what it is I was about to do.

"At the end of the day, the garden hasn't been tidied up, the bills haven't been paid, the coffee's still sitting on the kitchen worktop, I still haven't found my new cheque book, the bin's still full, the plants are only half watered, and I seem to have lost my front door key!

"When I try to work out how it is that nothing got done for the whole day, I'm baffled, because I know I was busy all day! I know this is a serious condition, and I'll get help, but first I'll just go and look at my email . . .

"Please repeat this to everyone you know, because I can't remember who I've already told!"

The woman's memory must have still been good for something, because she remembered to say all that without looking at notes. Perhaps she'd been using some of the techniques Becky and her friends had been talking about, such as inventing images in her mind to help her remember things, after finding out about the method from somewhere else, or just thinking the idea up herself. Or maybe she'd just rehearsed the joke quite a bit. Alternatively, maybe she found it so true-to-life that it didn't take much remembering!

Becky and her friends went over to her after the jokeathon and told her they'd recently been discussing the problems some people have with going into another room and forgetting what they went in there for, and things like that. They told her about the possible solutions they'd learned about.

She thanked them and said she'd think about trying them.

Everyone else got their jokes from the Internet.

One of the nurses told one that went: "Adam, an elderly man, was seated in the doctor's waiting room. When he was called in to see the doctor, he slowly got up, and grasping his cane and hunching over, slowly made his way into the examining room.

"After only a few minutes, Adam emerged from the room, walking completely upright. Paul, another patient who had watched him hobble into the room all hunched over, stared in amazement. 'That must be a miracle doctor in there,' he exclaimed. 'What treatment did he give you? What's his secret?'

"Adam stared at Paul and said, 'Well, the doctor looked me up and down, analysed the situation, and gave me a cane that was four inches longer than the one I had been using.'"

The other nurse there said when it was her first turn to tell a joke: "Here are some alleged misprints from newspapers I found on the Internet. What I read said:

"The Sunday Times explanation for the extinction of the dinosaurs: The extinction may well have occurred when a steroid hit the Earth.

"Another newspaper misprint: The Welsh international had to withdraw when the cut turned sceptic.

"From a Sunday newspaper: The surgeon said he'd removed my momentum – the funny apron of fat that covers the intestines. [The omentum is the medical name for the sheet of fat that covers abdominal organs.]

"From an article on stomach troubl: Doctors are beginning to accept that stomach ulcers are infectious. They are caused by a bug called Helicopter. [Real name Helicobacter pylori.]

"The Worksop Bugle recently carried a news report about a chap who'd happily 'recovered from a tuna of the kidney'. [Seems those tuna fish don't know their place.]

"An excerpt from 'Pulse' magazine: If we are over-diagnosing asthma, then we must be under-diagnosing the other causes of nocturnal cough, such as post-natal drip. [That should be post-nasal drip.]

"A transplant surgeon has called for a ban on 'kidneys-for-ale' operations.

"From the South Wales Evening Post: Cash plea to aid dyslexic cildren."

The delivery driver's first joke went: "A business owner decides to take a tour around his business and see how things are going. He goes down to the shipping docks and sees a young man leaning against the wall doing nothing. The owner walks up to the young man and says, 'Son, how much do you make a day?'

"The guy replies, '150 dollars.'

"The owner pulls out his wallet, gives him $150, and tells him to get out and never come back.

"A few minutes later, the shipping clerk asks the owner, 'Have you seen the UPS driver? I asked him to wait here for me!' "

The delivery driver's son's first joke went: "George knocked on the door of his friend's house. When his friend's mother answered he asked, 'can Albert come out to play?'

" 'No,' said the mother, 'it's too cold.'

" 'Well then,' said George, 'can his football come out to play?' "

The delivery driver's daughter told a joke she'd found that went, "A young man agreed to babysit one night so a single mother could have an evening out. At bedtime he sent the youngsters upstairs to bed, and settled down to watch football.

"One child kept creeping down the stairs, but the young man kept sending him back to bed.

"At 9 PM the doorbell rang; it was the next-door neighbour, Mrs. Brown, asking whether her son was there. The young man brusquely replied, 'No.'

"Just then, a little head appeared over the banister and shouted, 'I'm here, Mum, but he won't let me go home!'"

One of the teachers told a joke, or possibly a true story, that went: "A high school had a policy that the parents must call the school if a student was to be absent for the day.

"Kelly (name changed to protect the guilty), deciding to skip school and go to the mall with her friends, waited until her parents had left for work, and called the school herself.

"This is the actual conversation of the telephone call:

"Kelly: 'Hi, I'm calling to report that Kelly so-and-so is unable to make it to school today because she is ill.'

"Secretary at high school: 'Oh, I'm sorry to hear that. I'll note her absence. Who is this calling?'

"Kelly: 'This is my mother.'

"Needless to say, she didn't pull it off!"

The other teacher's first joke went: "A little girl came home from school and said to her mother, 'Mummy, today in school I was punished for something I didn't do.'

"The mother exclaimed, 'That's terrible! I'm going to have a talk with your teacher about this . . . by the way, what was it that you didn't do?'

"The little girl replied, 'My homework.'"

The jokeathon went on for hours, and they all had fun. The sun shone for the entire time.

They raised several hundred pounds for the charity they'd decided to raise money for, and they all went away feeling pleased.

Chapter 10

Becky and Her Friends Play a Funny Card Game They Invent For Charity in Front of an Audience of Students

One evening, Becky had another of the wacky conversations she enjoyed with a friend of hers. This time it was Gary. She said, "Imagine if people could cast spells on other people like they do in Harry Potter, so we could turn people into chocolate bars and things."

Gary replied, smiling, "Oh imagine if you did that to someone who was sitting in a chair. Imagine if someone came in and sat on the chair without realising there was a chocolate bar there! It might squash and melt all over them. Ugh!"

Becky said, "Imagine if the chocolate bar that used to be a person could still talk. They'd yell out when the person sat on them. They might say, 'Oy, get off, heffalump! That hurts!'"

Gary replied with a laugh, "That would give the person sitting there a fright, suddenly hearing a yell of protest from under their bottom! If they didn't know people could be turned into chocolate bars, they'd probably think they must be sitting on a ghost. They might jump up and run away."

Becky said, "Hey, those spells could be a great weapon in war! All our side would have to do would be to turn all the soldiers on the other side into cream cakes or something. Then our soldiers could all rush across the lines and eat them!"

Gary replied, "But what if the enemy turned our soldiers into something first! They might turn them into something really useful to them, like computers or washing machines or printers, or knives and forks or bowls. Then they might take them all home and sell them."

Becky said, "I don't know if many people would want them if they talked. Imagine turning a washing machine on and hearing a voice from inside it saying, 'Oh, you're not asking me to wash your clothes again! I've done that a few times for you without complaining; but I'm fed up of doing it; and it seems I'm condemned to wash them for the rest of my life, you scumbag! I could always go wrong one day, you know.'"

Gary responded, "If the people who'd bought them from the soldiers who'd captured them didn't know they used to be people, they might not dare use them again! They might think there were ghosts inside them and get a priest to exorcise them, or sell them off cheaply to others, hoping they didn't talk during the sale and put people off buying them!"

Becky said, "Imagine if ordinary body parts talked, like legs. If you put a tight sock on, your leg might say in a high-pitched voice, 'Ouch! That sock's too tight! Put a more comfortable one on me!'"

Gary replied, "Wow, it might criticise you in public! Imagine if you tripped over something and it shouted, 'Oy, clumsy, watch where you're going!'"

Becky said, "Imagine if all your legs and arms could talk, and they had a conversation while you were talking to someone else, and you could hardly hear the person you were talking to over the sound of your arms and legs talking."

Gary replied, "Imagine if theirs could talk too, and they were all having a conversation with yours while you were trying to talk, so you had to shout over them to be heard. Imagine if they had little eyes on them, and they recognised other arms and legs in the street when they saw them and shouted hello to them."

Becky said, "You'd end up shouting, 'Shut up leg!' and things like that all the time. And then if you met people who didn't know some people's legs could talk, they'd think someone else must have just spoken and that you were going mad for thinking it was your leg, especially if you whacked your leg to punish it."

Gary said, "Imagine if you were in an important lecture and your legs and arms kept criticising what the lecturer was saying, or asking the time, or saying they were bored and wanted to go. Or imagine if, say, a history lecturer made a mistake and said something happened in 1814 when it really happened in 1815, and you decided to keep quiet about it, but your leg chirped, 'You got it wrong! It was 1815!'"

Becky replied, "If it was that clever, I'd take my shoe and sock off, hold my foot above my computer keyboard and tell my leg to write my essays for me!"

Gary said, "It would probably complain that you were holding it in an awkward position."

Becky said, "Imagine if your legs started complaining about you all the time, saying things like, 'It's a bit much to have to carry someone as heavy as you around! Why don't you lose a bit of weight? I think it's time we at least got to sit down for a rest!' And imagine if they had conversations where one complained about you and the other agreed."

Gary responded, "And imagine if our stomachs joined in, talking in deep voices, saying things like, 'I wish I didn't have so much fat around me, but he will keep feeding me burgers and fries!'"

Becky said, "Imagine if you were trying to impress a girlfriend on a first date and yours said that, or she took you home to her parents for the first time and you wanted to impress them, but it kept complaining like that!"

Gary replied, "It would be funny if their stomachs were talking too, and they all started agreeing that we all fed them too much fatty food."

Becky said, "Imagine if arms and legs cried loudly if you hurt them. If you fractured your wrist, the doctors would put a plaster on it, and you'd all hear sobbing from underneath it. It might cry every day for weeks, and you might have to spend a long time trying to comfort it, or quieten it down in important meetings and things."

Gary said, "Or sometimes arms and legs might feel playful. People might sometimes have to argue with them if they kept talking when they were trying to go to sleep and things."

Becky replied, "Oh, I should think your legs and arms would let you at least go to sleep in meetings, at least if they're the kind of meetings I've heard some people have to go to, where some people just waffle on for ages about things most people there don't need to know! After all, they'd probably want the best for you."

Gary laughed. That hadn't been quite what he meant – he'd meant going to sleep at the times people are supposed to, not in meetings. Becky probably knew that really.

They often had a good time making up zany jokes with each other like that.

One day, after Becky and her friends had been larking around and making each other laugh by coming up with amusing ideas, they came up with a plan to do a big charity event in the university, where they could joke around and get people to pay to watch.

They decided to publicise it by walking to lectures and around campus doing funny things that would intrigue people, telling them about the event if they looked curious or puzzled or asked what they were doing.

For instance, one of the group decided to go around for hours with a raw runner bean dangling from the corner of his mouth as if it was a cigarette. Another taped a pin to a piece of cardboard so she could pin it to her clothes, and stuck lots of fresh peas in a pattern on the cardboard instead of beads to make a big brooch. Then she decided to make another one and wear two.

One of the friends stuck a post-it note on each of their cheeks advertising the event. Another one made a pointy hat out of paper and stuck a little twig on top, so it was as if they had a spire sticking up several inches on top of their head. They stuck leaves and little flowers on the hat.

The friends who walked around campus doing funny things asked people beforehand to donate money to sponsor them to be daring enough to do them. They publicised what they were going to do on Facebook and Twitter and elsewhere, and got quite a lot of money in sponsorship.

When they walked around the university campus wearing the funny things, each of them held a sign up that said that one of the funniest charity events people might ever see was going to happen in the sociology lecture theatre the following evening. They said the entry fee was three pounds, which would go to some charities. If anyone wanted to pay more to get in, they'd be very welcome, but it would be up to them.

If anyone stopped them and asked them why they were doing strange things, they would explain that they were a publicity stunt to help them advertise the charity event, and ask the people if they'd like to come along. A lot of them said they would, and the following night, the lecture theatre was quite full.

The friends also advertised the event by putting funny posters all around the university, that they'd made by playing around with images on the computer. They had pictures on them, and underneath, there was writing saying, "This is an attention-attracting device to advertise a fun charity event in the sociology lecture theatre." Then the time and date were written.

Some of those pictures were made by playing around with some countries' national flags, mixing other pictures with them or putting them next to them on the posters. They ended up with an American flag that looked as if it was being eaten by a horse, a French flag, part of which looked as if it was growing a beard, A Canadian flag that looked as if carrots were growing out of it, and a German flag with a big daisy in the middle, that looked as if a woman was about to throw a bucket of water over it to water it. They also asked permission from a couple of lecturers and put photos of them up on some posters, one looking as if he was eating a big flower, and one looking as if cabbages were growing out of his ears.

Other posters had surreal images on them, such as a kettle with legs chasing a schoolboy, a daffodil with hands holding a little stick of rock and bending its head to suck it, a car almost suspended in the air above a driveway with just two of its wheels perched on ice creams for support, and other things.

They got a lot of money from all the donations made by people sponsoring them to walk around campus looking strange, and the charity event itself made a lot of money too. Almost everyone who went there had a lot of fun watching what went on.

Early on the evening of the charity event, Becky and her friends went to the lecture theatre where they were holding it. One stood at the door taking the entry fee.

The charity event itself was to be a special funny card game they'd had a laugh inventing themselves, where all those playing had to put on amusing little acts for the audience. What they would have to do would depend on which card came up.

The idea was that as many of the cards would be dealt out as would mean everyone had an equal number. Becky and four of her friends were playing the game, so they would have ten cards each. The rules were a bit complicated, so they had them in front of them to remind themselves what they were, even though they'd made them up themselves. That was because there was a different funny act for each card number, and they would have to have remembered what they all were if they hadn't been written down.

For example, someone who was told to do the funny act that the rules said had to be done when a 5 came up would have to pretend they loved eating some non-edible thing they chose, such as a hairbrush, and rave about how yummy it was to eat, trying their best to be convincing . . . without actually attempting to eat one of course.

The funny act wouldn't be done by the person who picked out the card from their share of them, but by the person to their left. Sometimes they would join them, but the main act would most of the time be done by the person on their left.

The rules said that if anyone on the team couldn't think of something to do when it was their turn, they had to cry like a baby, and that would be a signal for the others to help them. Or an audience member could pay a pound for the charities the money was being raised for, and then they could go to the front and do the funny act instead that the rule said had to be done.

The people playing the game were Becky, and her friends Luke, Sharon, Mandy and Gary.

Becky dealt out the cards. The rules said the person to the left of the dealer started the game. That was Gary. First of all he picked out a 2. He put it in the middle and told everyone what it was, as the rules said had to be done, and read out to the audience what the person who got the 2 was going to have to do.

The person on his left was Sharon, so she had to do the funny act, which was to pretend to be a radio DJ trying to introduce a song by saying a little bit about the artist or the song itself, but suddenly forgetting all the facts about them that they'd known before, ending up making something up, the more absurd the better. Or she could pretend to be a talk radio host introducing a famous guest, but getting the details about them ridiculously wrong.

Sharon said, putting on a deep voice, "Here's an old song by Kate Bush, 'Wuthering Heights', a song first written in 1546 about the ghost of Anne Boleyn in the Tower of London, who'd perhaps forgotten her name by then in the song and thought she was Catherine Howard who was also executed, which is why she keeps calling herself Cathy. The song's about her trying to escape from the tower where she's been held as a ghost for years. It was written to commemorate the anniversary of her execution by the evil Sheriff of Nottingham."

"Ugh, that's a bit gruesome! Are you always like that?" shouted one audience member.

"Sorry. Only on weekdays," joked Sharon, blushing a bit.

Then it was Sharon's turn to pick a card. She picked a 4, put it in the middle, and told the audience what it was and what the person to the left of the one with the 4 would have to do. She read:

"The one with the card says two words, as random as they like, and the one to the left has to make up a little story that connects the two."

She said, "Scooter, television."

Mandy was to her left. She was silent for several seconds while she thought. Then her little story went:

"Once when I was little, I drove my little scooter right through a television! It just somehow opened to let me in. When I was inside it, I found myself in a set of studios where people were making all the films and programmes people see on their televisions. In the one at the end on the left there was a man doing a weather forecast for BBC1, and in the next one there were people talking about politics for BBC2, and then there were people acting out adverts for ITV, and then there was someone reading the news for Channel four, and then there were people making a film for Channel five, and then loads of other people on other channels, all talking at once.

"They were all so close together I couldn't understand a word any of them were saying. I thought that maybe you'd have to press the button to select an individual channel to just hear and see one thing at once and understand it. But I couldn't reach them, since I was on the inside of the television and the buttons were on the outside.

"No one noticed me as I drove my scooter through the tiny studios. Then I went out the back of the television and ended up back in my parents' house."

Some of the audience laughed, while a few said things like, "You twit!" But they said it good-naturedly.

Then it was Mandy's turn to pick a card. She picked a 7. She put it down in the middle of the table, told everyone in the audience what number it was, and read out the rule for 7 that said:

"The person with the card has to pick a famous historical figure, and whatever the person to their left thinks of them, they have to pretend they were one of the best people who ever lived, and explain why they were such a hero. Making up things about them is permissible."

Then Mandy chose Vlad the Impaler.

None of them knew much at all about Vlad the Impaler, apart from that he was a monarch who lived in what's now Romania in the middle ages, and loved impaling his dinner guests and other people on spikes for some reason.

Luke was to Mandy's left, so it was his turn to do an act. He cringed, making a funny pained face; but then he smiled, saying, "That's cruel!" He thought for a few seconds, and then said,

"OK. Not many people know it, but Vlad the Impaler stopped Europe from being blown up by a massive nuclear bomb in the middle ages. He was a wonderful caring man, and we wouldn't be here today if it wasn't for him. None of us would be. You see, for years there had been a network of evil people working on technology way in advance of its time. They ate burgers and fries that they invented centuries before anyone

318

else did; they had modern washing machines and radios, and most importantly, they were making a gigantic nuclear bomb to blow everyone in the known world up.

"They'd turned against the world after they offered their burgers to a village of people but they all said they tasted horrid; and they told them about their radios, but they laughed and sneered and said it was impossible to make things that would pick up signals being broadcast hundreds or thousands of miles away; and the villagers rejected their washing machines, saying they couldn't possibly do what the men claimed they could. That was true at the time, since electricity hadn't been invented, but the men were working on that. But they turned into evil sociopaths when their inventions were rejected and laughed at, and they decided everyone in the world was brainless and stupid and ought to die. So they started making their nuclear bomb.

"But Vlad the Impaler found out. He wanted to save the world, so he impaled all the men involved in the evil scheme on spikes till they died, and destroyed their nuclear device. He really is one of the biggest heroes of all time!

"Although we had to wait several hundred years for other people to come up with the idea of washing machines, radios, electricity and junk food, it was a price worth paying for the survival of the planet. We owe it all to that wonderful, wonderful man, Vlad."

Then Luke gave a sigh of relief as it was his turn to pick one of his own cards and sit back while someone else had a turn. He picked a 10. Becky was the one who had to put on an act that time.

Luke put down the 10, and told the audience what the rule was for that:

"The one with the card makes up a few nonsense words, and the one to the left pretends to interpret them.

"OK: Quithy quothy quothering stet!"

Becky pretended to be lost in admiration for a few seconds while she thought of something, and then said:

"Luke is using ingenious short-hand to express one of the most profound mathematical equations ever written! I wouldn't want to explain the complex algebraic formula it represents, because it would take too long and no one would understand it. But it's a far more exciting and important equation than the one Einstein came up with when he discovered his theory of relativity. This will shake the world! It will change everything! It will improve the world more than we could ever imagine, leading to a cure for cancer, new passenger aircraft that can fly at 3000 miles an hour, without even creating a sonic boom, and new drought-resistant plants that'll grow in all the countries where there are food shortages because there isn't enough rain, which will even absorb all the pollution from the air and spit it out powerfully from the bottom of their roots so it goes deep down into the earth and never comes back again; and they might even talk, so they can tell their owners when they need watering."

Luke interrupted and said with a laugh, "Come on, there are at least a Few limits to my equation!"

Becky decided to stop there, since she was running out of things to say anyway.

Gary was the only one who hadn't done an act then. It was time for Becky to pick a card from the ones she had. She picked an ace.

Gary was lucky – the rule for what someone had to do when the ace came up was the easiest one. Becky read:

"Make a couple of animal noises in combination, as if you're a cross between two animals."

Gary said, "Woof quack! Quack Woof! Quook waf! Quoof whack!"

Then he did the best imitation he could of a bark a few times, and then his best imitation of a duck quacking, and then he tried to alternate them, going faster and faster till he got muddled up and started saying nonsense syllables the way he might if he was saying a tongue twister very fast.

Then he said, "That was a duckdog. If you've never seen one of those . . . just be grateful!"

The people playing the card game with him grinned, and the audience seemed happy.

That was the end of the first round.

Since each person playing had started with ten cards, they now had nine more funny acts to do each.

It was Gary's turn to pick a card out of the ones he had again. He picked a 5, and read the rule about what funny act the one to the left of the person with the 5 had to do:

"Think of something non-edible, and pretend you love eating it. Rave enthusiastically about how good it is to eat and what you do with it."

Sharon had to do that, and she started:

"I just adore my old school dinners! Most kids called them names like 'dustbin dregs' or 'pest controllers' poison'; but I'd eat them every day for the rest of my life if I could! We weren't given a choice of what to eat at my old school, because the staff firmly believed that if we didn't like the food, it was a sure sign it was healthy, and we needed to eat healthy things, so that meant eating things none of us liked, apart from the fact that I secretly did like them, but I didn't dare say in case they made me eat something different that I wasn't keen on."

The others laughed, but protested, "Hey, that's cheating! Some school dinners might not be nice, but at least you're supposed to be able to eat them! You're supposed to choose something people genuinely can't eat!"

Sharon smiled and protested in return, "You didn't taste them! I'm sure there were lots of days when I heard people say in disgust, 'I can't eat that!' "

They chuckled, and she continued, "Besides, I'm talking about eating my old ones now, say if some leftovers were still around, and someone dug them out of the bin or a landfill site. Yum yum! I'd be so happy to have them, I'd not only gobble most of them up, but I'd keep some under my clothes for later when I was hungry again."

"Oh yuck!" the others said, grinning.

Then it was Sharon's turn to put a card on the table. She put down a queen. She told the audience what it was, and read them the rule about the funny act that had to be done when someone put down a queen:

"The person with the card asks up to five general knowledge questions, and the one to their left gives nonsense answers to each one."

Mandy was to Sharon's left, so she'd have to make up the answers. But Sharon would have to think too, since she had to make up the questions.

First she asked, "Who invented the computer?"

Mandy replied, "A Roman soldier who was bored while he was standing around with nothing to do at Hadrian's Wall. If his wife and family had been there, we'd never have computers today, because he'd have spent his time touring around the wall with them, or chatting and entertaining them and things; but his family were in Rome, so he had nothing to help him wile away the lonely days; and between bouts of running around to keep warm, he sat down and had a go at inventing something, coming up with the computer."

Sharon said, "You're correct. Now what are the ingredients of lemonade?"

Mandy thought for a few seconds and then said, "I know it's a quarter peanut butter. In the best lemonades, they use crunchy peanut butter, and chop the nuts really really fine by hand. Then they use cheese, tomato sauce, Plasticine, chicken, ivy and grass, Brussels sprouts, a touch of brandy, and lots and lots of cold tea."

Everyone else on her team made disgusted faces, and then grinned.

Sharon said, "You're right again. Well done. Now what was the first radio programme ever broadcast?"

Mandy twisted a lock of her hair round her finger as she thought for several seconds, and then she said:

"It was called, 'What do you think of radio then?' and it was broadcast from London to the whole of Britain to coincide with the coronation of Queen Victoria. While she was taking part in the solemn coronation ceremony in church, the radio programme presenters wanted to test out all the sound effects, records and microphones to make sure everything worked. So they had people telling jokes and blowing raspberries, snippets of funny records by artists like George Formby, funny noises, whistles and hooters at unexpected times, cheerful little jingles that must have been made for other programmes, trailers for comedy programmes that would be on later, and a telephone conversation between the DJ and a famous comedian in America.

"Queen Victoria wanted to secretly listen to the programme, so she took a little radio in to her coronation ceremony hidden in her clothes, and listened to it with a small earpiece she hoped wouldn't be seen. But she couldn't keep from laughing all throughout the service, even when the archbishop asked her to solemnly promise to serve her people faithfully.

"The officials thought something was a bit strange, and in private afterwards, they sternly asked her why she'd laughed so much. She didn't want to confess what she'd done, so she lied and said she thought someone must have spiked her dressing room with laughing gas. But she got worried when they said they'd phone the police who'd do a criminal investigation. She told them not to worry, saying there couldn't have been much laughing gas – it had all gone by the time she went back after the service; she said she knew that because she hadn't laughed at all then. She really hadn't; the radio programme had just finished, and she felt ashamed for having laughed all through the service – too ashamed to laugh any more. Still, she was glad she'd listened to the programme, and was a great fan of radio from that time on.

"They decided not to make a fuss about her laughing during her coronation after all, in case lots more people heard about it so it became an embarrassment for the country; so she got away with it. That encouraged her to hide secret little radios in her clothes a lot from then on, especially if she was going somewhere to do something she thought would be boring."

Sharon said, "You're impressively knowledgeable about these things!"

Her next question was, "What would happen to you if you got too close to a wormhole? You know, those things that some scientists believe exist in space that they think can transport things quickly to different dimensions."

324

Mandy was silent for a few seconds, staring into space while she thought of an answer, and then said:

"If you get too close to a wormhole, it sucks you in, and then flings you out the other side with such force you can fly for miles, or even thousands or millions of miles before you land. They travel around the universe sucking things in and flinging them out again. They even come here! Sometimes they bounce at a leisurely pace along the street, seeming to be blowing gently in the wind; but anyone who gets too close to them gets sucked in really quickly.

"I got sucked into one once. It had stopped right outside my house. It was huge! I wondered what it was, so I went right up to it, and it sucked me in and hurled me out somewhere I'd never been. Luckily for me I landed in a huge vat of ice cream in the garden of some really obese people who were having a barbecue. I was really relieved to land on something soft! If I hadn't, that wormhole could have been dangerous! I apologised to the people for ruining their pudding though. They said it was OK and I could eat the ice cream I'd landed in if I liked, so I did. I needed a good meal after my long journey; it turned out that I was in America! It had only taken a few minutes or so to get there!

"It was nice exploring America for a little while after that; but I didn't know how to get back. The wormhole was nowhere in sight, so I couldn't go back in that, and it might have sent me somewhere completely different from home anyway. But I managed to raise the money for my plane fare back easily in the end, because the family whose garden I landed in told the media what had happened, and then lots of television channels and newspapers wanted to interview me about it, and they paid me.

"When I got back, I started investigating wormholes, and found a secret diary of Christopher Columbus. It said he discovered America by being flung there by a wormhole all of a sudden. He realised he was on a different continent, made a boat and came back again, after exploring. But he felt sure no one would believe him if he told them he'd got there in a single minute after a wormhole had loomed up in front of him and sucked him through it, so he made up a story about going there by ship.

"Wormholes can even hurl people into space! If we ever find intelligent life on another planet, we'll probably think it's alien life; but really the people there will probably have lived here once, but will have been flung there by wormholes; they'll have been the lucky ones who landed on a planet with an atmosphere and set to work making it a decent place to live in, instead of just landing somewhere in the middle of space."

Sharon said, "Scary! But it's nice to hear your personal experience, as well as getting a correct answer to the question."

Her last question was, "What's the surface of the moon made of?"

Mandy said, "Tulips. Not living ones. Once the moon had a great atmosphere, and weather conditions were fantastic, and the soil was really fertile, and tulips grew so densely together they all got squashed up really really tight and died. But they were squashed up so tightly together it's possible to walk on them and run and jump around, and even build houses, without them collapsing. Astronauts brought what they thought was moon rock back to earth with them, but really it's squashed-up tulips, packed so close together they just look and feel hard like rock, although anyone who examines them closely will discover they're all fossils of bunches of tulips.

If someone tried to pull a bit apart, they'd find it was quite easy; and if they carried on, they'd be able to peel off individual ancient fossilised tulip petals, and be able to tell what they were."

Sharon said, "Good. You got all the questions right."

Everyone was still enjoying themselves as those playing the game played on and on. Even students who liked nothing better to do than to spend their evenings in the bar stayed that evening to listen. They were having fun.

It was Mandy's turn to put one of her cards on the table. She put down a 3. She said what number it was, and read out the rule about what had to be done when a 3 came up to the audience:

"The one with the card says a few words of nonsense, which the person to their left has to use as the first line of a nonsense poem, and make up three more lines."

A jelly and a belly had a talk about the weather.

Luke had to make up the other lines, since he was to her left. He had a think, and then said:

They piled up the raindrops till there were almost
  twenty-three
Some were made of metal, and some were made
  of leather
And some were like little kittens they could cuddle
  on their knee.

Then it was time for Luke to put down one of his cards; it was Becky's go again, as she was the person on his left. Luke put down a 6. He said what number it was, and read out the rule about what Becky would have to do:

"Pretend you're an animal or insect walking or flying around the home of someone here, or somewhere else, such as somewhere famous like a treasured old library, or the House of Commons, or a banqueting hall the Queen's due to sit down to eat in soon with a lot of guests. Imagine how you might think about what's there, and tell us what you're thinking."

Becky smiled and said: "I'm a magpie flying around the Queen's bedroom. Wow, there's so much lovely jewellery here! I think I'll nick lots of little bits and take them back to my nest! I might even make a bigger nest to put it all in! Actually, there's a lovely big bed here I could use as a ready-made nest! I'll just settle down on it. Oh yes, it's far more comfortable than my old nest! I'm going to put all the bits of jewellery in it and make my home here! Then I'm going to go and tell all my friends and relatives, and they can all fly through this nice open window and come and live in this big bed nest too!"

They all smiled. Then it was Becky's turn to put down a card. She put down a 9. She read out the rule for what happened when someone got a 9:

"The person with the card has to pick a subject, and the one to their left tells a funny story about it, true or one they make up on the spur of the moment."

Gary was the one who had to tell the story. Becky said, "Curtains."

After a few seconds' thought, Gary said:

"There was a time when I thought about getting a job straightaway when I left school instead of coming to university. I had a job interview I was looking forward to one day. But with only hours to go before it, I suddenly realised all my decent clothes were in the wash. I had other clothes, but they looked a bit tatty or had holes in them, so I didn't want to wear those, or get my best ones out the wash and go in dirty smelly ones. So I unhooked a curtain from off my bedroom window, and wrapped it round me to wear that. I cut a couple of holes in it so my arms could go through, hoping my mum wouldn't mind too much. But apart from that, I just left it how it was and went to the interview in that.

"The interviewer stared at me, but resisted asking about it till halfway through the interview. Then he said, 'That curtain's a bit short, isn't it! It doesn't even reach to your knees! You look cold, man! Why didn't you wrap two curtains around you to come here?'

"I said as my teeth chattered that I'd felt embarrassed enough wearing one. He said, 'Nonsense boy! Have another!' It happened that there were curtains at the windows of the room the interviews were being held in. He spent a while unhooking one and draped it over my knees. He told me he wanted it back at the end of the interview.

"He didn't comment again about the curtains. He just asked me the other interview questions, although he was looking at me strangely, as if he thought I was a twit. At the end of the interview, I gave him back the curtain he'd lent me, thanked him and walked out.

"I didn't get the job. To this day I wonder whether it was because I went in wearing a curtain, or maybe because he thought I was rude because I didn't help him hook the one he gave me back up at the window again after the interview; I was on the bus home when I realised it would have been more polite if I'd helped him."

The others laughed and said things like, "I can't believe that really happened!"

Gary said they were right; he'd just made it up.

Then it was his turn to put a card on the table. He put down a king. Then he read the rule about what the person on his left would have to do:

"Pretend you've written what you somehow imagine is a great book or scientific paper, but it's really rubbish, and you're trying to persuade a publisher to publish it by telling them what it's all about. Or you're going for a job interview, and there's some very obvious reason why you couldn't possibly do the job, but you're convinced you should have it. The person whose card was put down pretends to be the publisher or interviewer, and they act as if they're very impressed with your idea, or they take it very seriously and ask questions very solemnly about it."

So it was going to be a double act between him and Sharon.

Sharon started off: "Mr publisher, I'm so glad you've given me this interview after you got my book in the post. As you can tell, it's about life and times in the army, written from the point of view of a muesli bar in an army ration pack. It starts off as it's about to be eaten. Then it dies as the first mouthful's taken. The description of its life before then takes up the first half page, and the rest of the 300 pages are written as if by the ghost of the muesli bar, and they're a massive tirade against the cruelty of eating muesli bars, since they have just as much right to life, liberty and the pursuit of happiness as anyone on earth. The protest against eating them's very repetitive – if it wasn't it would only take up three pages – but it needs to be repetitive so people will take it in, and so it will fill up the whole book."

Gary, pretending to be the publisher, said, "It sounds like a very interesting book indeed! I shall enjoy reading it all."

Sharon said, "Good. I intend to write a whole series of these books. My next book's going to be about the life and times of a sausage in an army ration pack. It's going to be exactly the same as the one about the muesli bar, only the words muesli bar will be changed to the word sausage, since it's about how the poor sausage deserves as much right to life, liberty and the pursuit of happiness as everyone on earth."

Gary replied, in as serious a voice as he could, "I think your compassion is admirable. Do you feel this way about all food?"

Sharon said, "Not all food; not the food I eat personally. It's the food in a rectangular or cylindrical shape that needs to be saved from death by the greedy heartless masses. It's that food I'm pleading for, because food in that shape could be said to be in the image of human beings, because it vaguely resembles the shape of one, although naturally it hasn't got arms and legs and doesn't contain any human parts – or at least I hope it doesn't.

"When I carve meat I always make sure I don't carve any of it in a rectangular shape; if I do by accident, I can't eat it, and I have to consider it worthy of life, liberty and the pursuit of happiness just as much as I'm worthy of it. I set it free in the garden and wish it well, blessing it with a farewell poem I make up. My books don't contain information about that; they're just written as if the ghosts of the foods I write about are protesting about the unfairness of their fate."

Gary said, "Well I'm very pleased to have made your acquaintance. I'll be very glad to have your book published, and I'm sure it'll be very successful. Goodbye now."

Every three quarters of an hour or so, the team stopped the game for several minutes and told the audience they had time to phone friends if they wanted and recommend they come to watch too. Quite a few did, and the lecture hall was soon full of audience members who all paid something as they came in, so they raised more money for charity. Some audience members left, not sharing the sense of humour of the people playing the game but thinking they were just nuts, but others took their places and enjoyed themselves.

It was Sharon's turn to put down a card. She put a jack on the table. The rule for what was supposed to happen then was the most difficult to remember in the game, because the instructions were the longest. Sharon read it out to the audience, after looking at it and saying,

"Blimey the rule for this is complicated! Or at least long . . . I suppose I shouldn't really be surprised by that, since I helped to make it up.

"OK: The one with the card insults the one to their left, and they have to insult them back, with silly insults that don't really make sense as insults. They can exchange up to about a dozen each.

"Note: There's a special rule for this one to stop it getting out of hand: If someone insults someone else with an insult that sounds too much like something genuinely insulting to them, the one being insulted or someone else playing has the right to appeal, and if a majority of game players agree, the person who said the insulting thing has to do a forfeit. There are several possible options for forfeits, and they can choose one:

A. They make a noise that sounds like a train going through a level crossing, starting with the level crossing siren, and then doing the gates going down, the train coming towards it out of the distance, bibbing its hooter, and then going away into the distance again.

B. They sing a nursery rhyme in the highest-pitched voice they can.

C. They sing as much of their favourite pop song as they can remember at double the speed it's supposed to go at.

D. They spend several seconds imitating the sound and actions of a really noisy eater who's thoroughly enjoying a bowl of soup.

E. They imitate the sound of a young child having a tantrum in a toy shop who's getting worked up because their parents won't give them a toy.

F. They pretend they're in a radio play, so without moving, they act out the sound effects of someone who's really unfit, who's on their way to something important that's going to start soon so they have to get there quickly, and they've just run for a bus and they're really out of breath; and then they lurch onto the bus, only to find it full, and they're desperate to sit down, so they ask a person for a seat, but the person in it doesn't feel like getting up, so they beg and plead and then the person does get up; but then they feel desperate for refreshment and get out a bottle of drink, but spill some of it down themselves.

G. They pretend to be a politician who's just made an unpopular speech, who's pleading for silence and respect from a crowd who've begun to throw rotten eggs.

Mandy and Sharon would have to insult each other. Mandy started off. They put on loud angry voices. The conversation went:

MANDY: So I have to put up with having to talk to You, do I, you dishwasher full of cups with faded dog pictures on and dirty cutlery?

SHARON: Oh be quiet, you monstrous barrel of broccoli, dog hair and mustard seeds!

MANDY: Be quiet yourself, you whose grandad was a pot of potatoes and whose mum was just a big cup of tea!

SHARON: Well that's better than your mum! She's just a little cup, without the tea!

MANDY: Well it's better to be little than giant-sized like yours; your mum's so big she could reach up and snatch aeroplanes out of the sky! That's plain dangerous!

SHARON: Your mum's so lazy, she employs a servant even to just come and turn the radio on for her!

MANDY: Oh shut up you lemon-scented great vat of soaking tomato peelings and custard!

SHARON: That's better than you, you nibbled-on rose bush covered in seaweed and old dead sardines!

MANDY: You giant fried gooseberry, covered in the sauces of a thousand used old dinner plates!

SHARON: You can talk, you monstrous Brussels sprout, covered in the remains of fossilised breakfast cereals dug up from inside the skeletons of ancient people in the ground!"

MANDY: You're nothing but a great unnatural growth of cat fur and a pile of old dried leaves!

SHARON: Well you're just a nothing; you're such a big nothing, you tried to make friends with a vacuum and it chased you out of town, saying you must be an inferior alien species of nothing, not fit to associate with! You had to beg on your nothing-knees and plead with your nothing-voice before it even recognised you as a nothing worth saying nothing to!

MANDY: I won't let you get away with this, you upside-down mixing bowl poised to pour your contents over the head of anyone who goes near you, full of the sweat of a thousand old Victorian shoes and a mixture of gravy and ancient Roman public bath water that's been used by a thousand dirty Romans!

SHARON: You cracked old chimney full of soot and grime and squashed Eckles cakes!

MANDY: I'll sue you for that, you muddy pile of stone-age tools, all of them broken!

SHARON: You toad skin full of mushy peas and mouldy raisins!

MANDY: You're like a rat's tail wound around a pile of pond weed in a puddle full of watered-down cheese spread! Anyone who goes near you without being prepared by receiving a toxicity warning first will run away in horror and get to another continent before they dare stop!

SHARON: Well that's better than you, you wooden box of all that is evil, come specially to earth to haunt poor little children! I can hear their screams from my room at night as you go round the country

blowing rotten egg-breath on them at
night and cackling to scare them!

MANDY: You wretched loaf of stale old bread,
covered in cold mashed-up pasta! You're
too yucky even for a school to cook you to
give to the kids for dinner!

SHARON: You fungus-ridden turnip bed full of
broken glass and dead squirrels!

MANDY: Well that's better than eating dead
squirrels and broken glass for breakfast
every morning like you do! I see you every
day snatching the squirrels out of the
trees and chomping them up raw right
there and then!

SHARON: Well at least I don't eat wasps, and smell
of old socks and sound just like a dentist's
drill when I sing like you do!

Becky thought that sounded just a little bit too much like
a real insult – or at least a bit of it did; and she shouted,
"Hey! Forfeit!"

The others agreed that it was time for punishment,
looking forward to it. Becky started banging her fist on the
table in rhythm as she shouted, "Forfeit! Forfeit! Forfeit!
Forfeit!"

Soon the whole audience was joining in, shouting in
delight while stamping their feet or clapping their hands

in rhythm, "Forfeit! Forfeit! Forfeit! Forfeit! Forfeit! Forfeit! Forfeit! Forfeit!"

Sharon shouted, "OK OK, I'll do a forfeit!"

Becky stood up and rang a bell she'd brought with her to get the audience's attention. They quietened down. Then the forfeit choices were read out again, and Sharon was asked to choose one.

She chose to do the first one, and made the sound of a level crossing and a train going through it. Some of the audience protested that they couldn't hear it well, possibly just saying that for a laugh; so the others playing the game told Sharon to go round to both sides of the lecture theatre and then to the back, and make the noise again in all those places till everyone heard it loud and clear.

The audience laughed as she made the noise in one place after another, and applauded her in the end.

After that it was Mandy's turn to put a card on the table. She put down an 8, and read out the rule:

"The person to the left of the one who puts down the card has to tell a story about an event in their childhood. It can be true or false. The others have to guess if it's true or false."

Luke had to do that. He said:

"When I was little, my dad bought a second-hand car. When he got home, he opened one of the back doors, and heard something little clang to the ground. He wondered if it was a screw or something; but when he looked, he discovered it was a pretty gold ring! It was woven together from very thin strands. He thought it must be valuable. He assumed it must have belonged to the man who owned the car before us, so he contacted him and asked him if he'd lost it. The man said it might have been his, but that he wouldn't want it any more, because he'd decided to renounce worldly wealth and luxury and go and live in a little caravan in the woods to be close to nature. He suggested we keep it.

"Well neither my dad nor me felt like wearing it, so we decided it might be good to sell it and make lots of money. We took it to a valuer to find out how much it was worth. He examined it, and we noticed he had a kind of suspicious look on his face. Then he told us to go and sit in a little room he pointed to while he checked.

"We were sitting there, when all of a sudden the police came in and arrested my dad! They accused him of having stolen the ring, saying it belonged to a rich woman who'd been burgled a while ago. It turned out that the valuer had somehow recognised it and phoned the police while we were waiting. My dad protested that he'd just found the ring in his car and had phoned its previous owners, thinking it was theirs, trying to give it back to them, but they'd said they hadn't wanted it, because they'd renounced worldly wealth and luxury and were about to go to live in a cold caravan in a dark wood to be closer to nature.

"The police said they could check that story, and asked for the phone number of the previous car owner. They escorted me and my dad home, and he found the number and gave it to them. They rang the man up, and he said it was true. Then they said my dad was free to go, but went to arrest the other man.

"But the man said he hadn't even known about the ring when he'd sold the car, and that he thought it could perhaps have been somehow pushed into it by someone who'd knocked on his door and offered to look at his roof and fix it if it was damaged for a supposedly 'bargain price' of only several hundred pounds a few months earlier, who'd stood by the car for a while looking as if he was fiddling with something, for some reason. The man reflected that it was perhaps because he thought police might have been after him and he wanted to get rid of the ring. He told the police they could tell he wouldn't have stolen it himself, because they could come and see the little caravan in the cold dark woods he was about to start living in because he wanted to go back to nature and live like the animals.

"The police went to investigate the little caravan, and decided he probably hadn't stolen the ring after all. I think they kept it after that, just in case they found out who had, or in case any of them wanted to wear it sometimes or something."

That was the end of the story. The others on the team laughed, and said things like, "Come on, that can't possibly be true!"

Luke said they were right; he'd made it up.

It was back to being Becky's turn to do a funny act again. The group still hadn't run out of ideas, so they carried on playing as it got later. Becky spotted her mum in the audience – she'd just come in to watch the rest of the game after work before taking Becky home at the end of the evening. They waved to each other.

Luke put down another 8, so Becky had to make up a story too, and the others had to decide whether it was true or false.

Becky said, "Once when I was at school, our science teacher came in and said, 'Scientists have now discovered that sand is really finely crushed-up bits of carpet. They've found that there used to be really really thick-pile carpet under all the oceans, to make them a nice home for creatures that lived right at the bottom of the sea; but the constant movement of the sea and the constant pressure of all the water on top of it squashed and eroded it all so badly it was ruined and became billions of smithereens of ex-carpet, crushed up really really small. So when people make sandcastles on the beach, they're really making squashed carpet castles.'

"Then the teacher told us that scientists have decided to rename the oceans, giving them more technical-sounding names. He said there's a dispute among scientists about what to call them at the moment, but they're sure they'll clear it up soon.

"So he said that from the beginning of next year, the oceans will either be named after body parts, foods, or people's names. So they could be called things like Susan, Peter, John and Jane; or they could be called things like Marshmallow, Peanut, Chocolate and Popcorn; or they could be called things like Toenail, Finger, Nose and Stomach.

"That's what he told us."

Mandy grinned and said, "I can't believe a science teacher would say that! . . . Well, not if he wanted to keep his job for long! . . . Unless he was joking. I think the story's false."

Becky said she was right.

The game went on just as entertainingly, till after some time, the group of friends began to find it more difficult to think of ideas.

That wasn't before a few more rounds of story-telling and other amusing things though.

In one round, Luke put down a 4, and read out the rule for what the person on his left had to do when the 4 came up:

"The one with the card says two words, as random as they like, and the one to the left has to make up a little story that connects the two.

"OK: Car, cobwebs."

Becky had to tell a story that connected those two words! She came up with this:

"Once I saw a car drive right through a cobweb that a spider had made over a very quiet road. Then I saw a whole crowd of spiders jump onto it and crawl in through the gaps between the doors and the frame of the car. Soon the driver stopped the car and leapt out, yelling about how his car was full of spiders, and that they'd started crawling on him!

"He wasn't far from home, and someone was watching who knew him, and they invited him in for a quick cup of tea to recover. He accepted the offer, and was about to walk in when the car door shut. He couldn't understand why, but then the car started and drove off. It looked as if there was no one in it! He couldn't understand it. But it drove out of sight. He wondered if there might be a scary fault with the car, or a ghost in it or something. His friend suggested he call the police and ask them if they could stop it somehow. He was too embarrassed to for a while, since he thought they wouldn't believe him if he told them his car had driven off by itself. He tried looking on the Internet to see if his make of car had a bizarre fault that made it shut the door and drive by itself sometimes. But he couldn't find anything about such a thing.

"Eventually he did call the police. They found the car abandoned 80 miles down the motorway. There was a note in it written in spidery writing that said, 'That's what you get for messing with cobwebs!' The police found the car after lots of reports had come in to them about a car driving by on the motorway that didn't seem to have anyone in it, but the steering wheel was covered in spiders, and they were all over the rest of the car too.

"It seems that when the driver had driven through the cobweb, the spider who'd made it had quickly gathered all his friends together, big and small, and they'd all got in the car. It seems incredible that spiders could drive a car. But it seems that with a combined effort, they'd managed to shut the door, turn the key in the ignition, press down on the pedals, and steer the car down the road and along the motorway for miles.

"They'd also stolen the car radio and some things that had been in the glove compartment. They weren't found for months, but one day, a boy came across a car radio in a wood, with lots of spiders all over the knobs, changing the station. He'd heard about what had happened to the car, and didn't want the spiders to come after him next, so he let them keep it."

Some of the audience thought that was a spooky story! Quite a few enjoyed it though. Then it was time for Becky to put a card down, and for Gary to have another go.

She put down a 9, not for the first time that evening. She read out the rule again:

"The person with the card has to pick a subject, and the one to the left tells a funny story about it, true or one they make up on the spur of the moment.

"OK: Apples."

Gary was getting a bit tired, so he couldn't think as quickly as he had at first. But he said:

"Once when I was ten years old, I lay under an apple tree all day, waiting to see if an apple would fall on my head and I'd suddenly have discovered some great scientific truth, like Isaac Newton did when an apple fell on his head. But nothing happened."

The others chuckled, but then said, smiling, "Is that it? Come on, think of something else!"

Everything went quiet as Gary thought. His mind was a bit blank and he thought for over ten seconds. One or two of the audience started showing signs of impatience. Then suddenly he drew in his breath, and made a loud high-pitched screeching noise in imitation of a baby screaming. Half the audience jumped! They'd forgotten the rule that said that anyone who couldn't think of a funny act to do could cry like a baby, and then the others would help them. Becky jumped too! She was right next to him.

The group playing decided to ask the audience if any one of them would like to tell a funny story about apples in place of Gary, which they could do if they paid a pound, which would go to the charities they were raising money for.

Lots of people put their hands up. The team could only choose one person, so they decided that they'd give lots of the audience the opportunity to tell funny stories related to them when they'd finished playing themselves.

They also decided that when their cards ran out, or when more of them ran out of ideas, they'd shuffle the cards again, and then they'd pass them round the table several times, with each person picking one each time, and then reading the rule that was connected to it, and asking audience members if they'd like to come up and do the funny act the rule said had to be done when a card with that number came up. Then as many audience members as wanted to could do a funny act in turn, even though it might be late when they finished. It would mean they raised more money.

But just then they had to choose one audience member to tell a funny story about apples. Becky's mum had put her hand up, and shouted, "Me! Me!" So they let her come to the front and tell a story.

Becky said to her, "Pay us for the privilege of telling your story first, and then you can tell it."

Her mum paid, and then said, "Well I can't remember saying this myself, but my sister Diana says I did. When we were little, we lived in a house with a couple of apple trees in the garden. We used to enjoy collecting the apples in the autumn when they fell off the trees. One day our mum asked us to go and bring lots of them in, and she said, 'For every five apples you pick up, I'll give you 1p.' I was only about five at the time. But I made a joke – at least, Diana says it sounded like one, although neither of us are quite sure if it was really a joke or just a misunderstanding. Diana thinks I said it with a straight face. I said, 'I don't like peas!' "

Several audience members smiled, and the group playing the game all chuckled. Becky asked her mum if the story was true, and she said it was.

Then the team carried on playing.

When they ran out of cards, and some of the audience had come up and told funny stories involving apples, they put the cards in a pile again, shuffled them, and then took turns picking one out, reading the rule that corresponded to it, and asking the audience if anyone would like to come up, pay a pound and do the funny act the rule said should be done. Quite a lot of them did. Some of them weren't as good at the game as Becky and her friends, but still they all had fun. It was late when they all finished!

They all enjoyed the evening, and the next day the group of friends counted all the money they'd made from the event for charity. They'd made nearly two thousand pounds!

Becky's second year continued as successfully as her first year had. She coped well with the work, and had more interesting and amusing discussions with her friends.

Acknowledgements

Here are some books that have provided some of the psychological information and true stories Becky and others pass on in this book:

Chapter 3

The stories Becky tells about the people who found ways to make their boring jobs more tolerable: *How to Stop Worrying and Start Living* by Dale Carnegie.

The story Bonnie tells about the man who found a way to feel more content to get down to work: *One Small Step: Beyond Trauma and Therapy to a Life of Joy* by Yvonne Dolan.

Chapter 6

Coping with anxiety and panic attacks: *How to Master Anxiety* by Joe Griffin & Ivan Tyrrell with Denise Winn.

Coping with flashbacks: *One Small Step* by Yvonne Dolan.

Chapter 9

Improving the ability to remember things: *Your Memory: How It Works and How to Improve It* by Kenneth L. Higbee, Ph.D.

The story of the brain-damaged man learning to find ways around his memory problems: *I Am Not Sick I Don't Need Help* by Xavier Amador.

About the Author

Diana Holbourn has written self-help articles and is the author of *The Early Life of Becky Bexley the Child Genius* and other books about the same character. Taking short psychology courses, working on a helpline and reading psychology books has prepared her for writing the self-help information that appears as part of the story in the Becky Bexley series. Diana lives and works on the south coast of England, where the sun shines ... sometimes.

For more about the author and her books, visit:

www.DianaHolbourn.com

Other Books in this Series
Becky Bexley, Book One

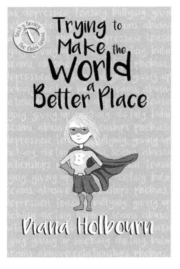

Even from the moment she was born, it was clear that Becky Bexley was not like other children. Her family were shocked by her behaviour!

Just a few years later, and she's in secondary school, often seeming wiser than her teachers. She does her best to help people, whether they like it or not. She has advice for her teachers when they want to give up smoking, gives a boy advice he uses to stop himself being teased, and even gives the headmaster some advice on improving the school's anti-bullying strategy.

She helps people outside school too, including rescuing her mum from a con artist. She even gets to go to the White House, where she ends up giving the president advice about his behaviour!

He invites her to help some politicians with the depression they have. But will a few tactless remarks she makes and their own fierce disagreements unwittingly stirred up by some of the insights she tries to pass on ruin her efforts?

Becky's advice is based on genuine therapy techniques and psychological research, and the books in this series combine humour with handy information.

350

Becky Bexley, Book Two

Becky Bexley the child genius goes to university at a much younger age than most people do. She copes with the coursework, but has a few unexpected difficulties.

Things begin well, as she makes friends she has fun with, and finds herself giving one of her psychology tutors some psychological help.

She has a laugh working on a local community radio station with other students, and interviews the brother of a founder member of the pop group Fleetwood Mac.

The paranormal comes up for skeptical and sometimes amusing discussion after a student tells the others about scary night-time experiences he's been having that seem to be supernatural.

However, at a Christmas party in the psychology department, a succession of stressful events begins involving tutors behaving badly that makes Becky worry she risks being thrown out of university.

Becky's advice is based on genuine therapy techniques and psychological research, and the books in this series combine humour with handy information.

Becky Bexley, Book Three

Child genius Becky Bexley entices a group of her fellow university students to play a rowdy game in class for fun one day that has worried tutors coming to investigate what's going on.

On another day, she and a group of other students have a long long discussion where they talk about such things as world leaders taking foolish risks, false rumours, and interviews with transsexuals, and they tell stories about scams and broken friendships.

The discussion often becomes humorous though, as they tell each other funny news stories, make up jokes, and think up wacky ideas for fun.

Printed in Great Britain
by Amazon

27434600R00202